CHICKEN OF THE SEA

Book II

CHICKEN TOO

NEIL BARRY

Summary

The first book of the *Chicken of the Sea* trilogy concluded with Victor Joshua Walker's family safely reunited in the Marquesas Islands of French Polynesia after Barkov nearly murdered him. Barkov worked for Zagarovsky (a Russian drug dealer), who wanted vengeance by killing the eldest son.

Chicken Too begins two weeks later. The sun is a fireball on the horizon when Victor's grandmother sees a ship steaming towards them. A near collision leaves the *Spray* without an engine and drenched from bow to stern. They divert to Tahiti to make repairs, only to discover Victor is still in great danger, this time from Faro, another of Zagarovsky's thugs. His father relocates to nearby Moorea, rebuilding the *Spray's* engine while the rest of the family stays at a luxurious tropical resort hotel. What should have been very enjoyable, turns tragic.

With a $100,000 reward on Victor's head, each new port is a step closer to disaster. Despite murderous Russians and Filipino pirates, the Walker family, like the truth, remains just out of reach. Despite losing almost everything, Victor is never closer to his father than when they arrive in Australia. A breathtaking conclusion leaves Victor more confident, wiser, and with a family he never expected. With the mystery seemingly revealed, except for one question, and Zagarovsky now taking a personal interest in Victor's demise, the family continues the journey into the final book, *Free Range Chicken*.

ISBN 978-0-9962926-2-7

First Edition, Published in November, 2015

In Appreciation

The author extends his heartfelt appreciation to those people who assisted and supported him in writing the *Chicken of the Sea* trilogy and bringing it to public attention. In particular, the author offers his sincere gratitude to Kathryn, who inspired him to finish the trilogy, who reported discrepancies and errors in Book II, and who made helpful suggestions.

To readers,

If you enjoy this book, the author would be very grateful if you encourage your friends and others to read it. Please visit the author's website, neilbarrybooks.com for more information and background about *Chicken of the Sea*, *Chicken Too*, and *Free Range Chicken*.

Contents

Please visit neilbarrybooks.com for background information for many of the places and things in this story.

What Happened in Book I, Chicken of the Sea

Readers are strongly encouraged to read the first book in the trilogy before proceeding. For those who want to be reminded of what has already transpired, the following review may be helpful.

Chicken of the Sea is the story of Victor Joshua Walker, seen through his eyes. For most of his life he lived in a trailer on the outskirts of Norfolk, Virginia, believing his mother to be an emergency room nurse at the local hospital. His father was an assistant manager of a nearby supermarket, obsessed with Russian composers and Captain Joshua Slocum, the first man to sail alone around the world 100 years earlier. Not only are his kids named after Slocum's children, much to the family's dismay, John Walker planned a similar journey, and built a boat in the barn next door.

After a neighbor's trailer burned to the ground, he launched his boat, a replica of Slocum's *Spray*, and the family moved aboard, just in time for Christmas. After nine years, his *Spray* still wasn't finished; it was the dead of winter; the marina was deserted; the boat was the size of a school bus, heads (toilets) didn't work; and no heat! His father remedied the situation by bringing aboard a kerosene heater. Josh, (he is Victor only to his father) would not go near it—his parents told him he fell on a heater when he was three. He has unsightly scars on both arms to prove it.

Josh's family slowly adapted to living aboard. His father continued to work on the boat while providing nautical lessons, a long list of rules, and a rigid routine, which began every morning with Mom homeschooling Josh (now 13), his ten-year-old brother, Ben, and his seven-year-old sister, Jessie.

Three days of rain ended February. After being cooped up in the leaky *Spray*, Josh willingly took the trash to the dumpster. In the parking lot, a stranger told him he was interested in buying the family minivan, even though he was driving a new black Cadillac. Within hours, Josh's father was ready to depart the marina. It didn't matter that the boat wasn't finished, that Josh had an important swim meet in a few days, or that his kids had no time to say goodbye to their friends. Despite telling everyone they would follow Slocum's route across the northern Atlantic, for seemingly no reason at all, his father suddenly decided to head south.

Their journey proceeded along the Intracoastal Waterway, through the rivers, canals, and sounds of North and South Carolina. Josh helped his father sail the boat. For most of the trip, Ben's head was stuck in his *Encyclopedia Britannica*. As the weeks passed, Josh's resentment diminished. Despite a few unpleasant incidents with his father, living on a boat wasn't as awful as he expected. However, there were also disquieting revelations: his grandparents died in a house fire when he was three, and his aunt and uncle were missing. Rare Russian Christmas ornaments, valuable first-edition books, and a guitar once played by Segovia are just some of the clues to Josh's mysterious past.

They were looking for a place to anchor, with Josh at the steering wheel, when the *Spray* became entangled with a submerged buoy attached to a plastic drum full of house bricks, smelly water, and a small unidentified nut. Two days later, in Beaufort, South Carolina, the family narrowly escaped being hit by a black Cadillac when they crossed the street. In St. Augustine, Florida, the kids were playing hide and seek on the docks when Jessie overheard someone on a big power boat threaten murder. Josh had seen the boat earlier, when it came too close to the *Spray*, and in Charleston, where the argument was about losing a 'bucket of esnortiar.' It was not the only boat that kept cropping up as the

Spray headed south; there was also a mock-trawler tagging along when they left West Palm Beach in Florida.

By the time the Walkers arrived in the Bahamas, things definitely weren't what they seemed. Josh's outwardly paranoid father not only went out of his way to avoid other people, but he changed his mind erratically. On a desolate Acklins Island in the southern Bahamas, an old man arrived just in time to save Josh and Ben when they encountered a Hammerhead shark while diving for conch. Within days, Josh and Sal were good friends, sharing a love of fishing and ice cream aboard Sal's luxury ship, the *Marionette*. Josh (now nicknamed Sharkbait) reminded Sal of his dead son, Dante, aiding the unlikely relationship. Not surprisingly, Josh's father distrusted the elderly diamond trader from New York and demanded Josh stay away from him. However, like the men who had followed the Walkers from Norfolk, Virginia, Sal was always nearby. Only later will he reveal that he recognized Josh's father from when he lived in New York.

In the Dominican Republic, on the way back from a rafting trip, Josh witnessed the exchange of drums from a farmer's truck to a pickup, with Sal and two henchmen standing by. The next day, Josh is kidnapped after discovering the drums are full of drugs, hidden under a layer of macadamia nuts. There are also suitcases full of cash on the *Marionette*—Sal laundered money for a Colombian cartel. Josh escaped being fed to the sharks when his father arrived just in time; however, their relationship hit a new low. Using long-range SSB radio, his father reported Sal to the US Coastguard. Within days, the *Marionette* was scuttled hundreds of miles away. Despite being on the run, Sal soon reappeared to make good the damage he had caused.

Six months later, the *Spray* was sailing off the desolate coast of Brazil. It was still being followed. After a terrible storm that seemed to confirm Josh's father was, in fact, crazy, the Walkers headed to Rio de Janeiro, only to encounter three men who had been following them since departing Norfolk, Virginia. Josh confronted his fear of fire to enable the family's escape, yet a thousand miles later, the mock-trawler was just around the corner. According to his father, the man aboard was an insurance investigator, who was following him because of the fire in Norfolk.

After passing through the Magellan Strait, the family sailed up the west coast of South America. In a storm, Josh suffered severe stomach pains. His mother diagnosed a burst appendix, and performed an emergency operation in a remote cove in Patagonia, not something even a highly trained emergency room nurse could do.

The next leg of their journey took them across the southeastern Pacific with a stop at Easter Island. On the way to the Polynesian islands, they listened to a garbled radio message from their grandmother. What little they heard suggested bad things had happened. Upon arriving in the Marquesas Islands, Josh's father caught a flight to Tahiti and returned to the US to find out what happened to Grandma. The rest of the family sailed the *Spray* to a remote island and anchored in a small bay to await his return.

After a few days of catching up on schoolwork and exploring the bay, they trekked to a nearby village to see the remains of an ancient cannibal culture. Upon their return to the *Spray*, Grandma came on the radio once again. This time she sounded cheerful, yet there was a voice in the background. Josh's mother decided the risk was too great to talk to her. Shortly after, there was a cryptic message from their father, ending with, 'I'm on it, going a new way.'

The following afternoon, the last thing they expected to find was Grandma reclining in the *Spray's* cockpit when they returned from spearfishing. Sal's sailing yacht, the *Maid Marion*, was anchored nearby. With Sal, his wife, Marion, and his gorgeous granddaughter, Dani, on the *Spray* for dinner, no one worried when another boat entered the anchorage.

In the middle of the night, Josh awoke to the smell of gasoline, and a man (Dmitri Barkov) creeping through the cabin. Barkov was one of the men who'd followed them since West Palm Beach. After firing the spear gun at him and missing, Josh was moments from being choked to death, when his brother slammed a volume of the *Encyclopedia Britannica* on his assailant's head, knocking him unconscious. With the *Spray* awash with gasoline and the imminent risk of explosion, the family hastened to shore. The man followed, pursuing them through the jungle.

Just as the man closed in to finish off Josh, his father appeared. His puzzling 'I'm on it, going a new way,' actually meant, 'I'm on it, going Aranui.' He sent the message already aboard the *Aranui*, a tramp steamer going from Tahiti to the Marquesas. The men grappled on the beach until Sal's bodyguard arrived. Barkov was 'ex-KGB, the Bratva's top man.' He worked for Zagarovsky, a Russian drug dealer. Josh had heard 'Zagarovsky' before, when he met an elderly man in a sculpture garden in South Carolina. He claimed Zagarovsky ruined his life.

As the sun slowly set over the lagoon... an infatuated Josh played *Dani's Song* on his guitar. By nightfall, he knew his real name was Alexander, named after his Russian grandfather, a composer and musician, and an even more famous great grandfather. His father was one of two brothers, one a musician, the other an undercover FBI agent. His mother had been in the final stage of internship, prior to becoming a doctor, when the family had to change their identity to escape Zagarovsky's vengeance. Zagarovsky gets to the father by killing the eldest son—he had murdered Sal's son, Dante, years earlier. Josh's long repressed memories slowly returned, remembering when he stayed at his grandparents' house on Long Island. Barkov had started the fire that killed Josh's grandparents, and burned him so badly he spent one month in hospital.

Chicken Too picks up the story, beginning two weeks later.

The *Spray* is modeled on Bruce Roberts-Goodson's Centennial Spray 38 ©, which is based on Slocum's *Spray*. Reproduced with permission.

CHICKEN TOO

Chapter 1

I was fourteen when my father shaved off his beard. Since I was four, he'd had a mustache and a goatee, a bristly tuft on his chin dyed to look like the rest of his hair. A beard never belonged on his face, yet after two weeks of shaving, I still wasn't used to seeing him with soap and a safety razor, instead of trimming stray hairs with his manicure scissors.

"What are you looking at?" he demanded, foamy shaving brush in hand.

"What a nice day it is," I fixed my gaze on the peaceful Pacific Ocean behind him and tried not to smile. He looked ridiculous with a blob of foam on the tip of his nose.

When I looked again, he scowled at me, lather covering one cheek and streaks on the other. He made a few more strokes, put aside his razor, and wiped soap from his face. I quickly glanced down at my book. I was a heartbeat too slow.

"It won't be long before I'll have to teach you how to shave," he said, turning my head to the side.

I jerked away and dabbed foam from my chin. "It's not so difficult I'll need instruction."

"All it takes is a steady hand, right?"

He hummed with Modest Mussorgsky's *Night on Bald Mountain,* normally one of my favorites until he joined in. My little sister was less annoying.

He leaned over to check our speed. "We're making good time. We'll be there in no time if this wind keeps up."

Under my breath, I said, "Good luck on that."

No sailor ever complained about trade winds. Sailing with the trade winds from behind was mind-numbing, yet vastly better than battling storms, or being becalmed.

My father built our 38-foot yacht from scratch the old-fashioned way. The *Spray* was far too small for six people and a cat, yet he was always quick to point out that small had advantages when it came time to put up the sails. The *Spray* was also slow, to which he countered his boat had an agreeable motion. It didn't. It wallowed through the long ocean swell, up and down, rolling from side to side. It was like living inside a washing machine day after day. I was lucky; I seldom got sea sick. My little sister and grandmother were constantly puking.

I turned back pages of Joshua Slocum's *Sailing Alone Around the World*, glimpses into the Captain's journey until I found what I wanted. "This part took him 29 days."

A month without setting foot on land!

"We'll do it in two weeks," he replied airily. "The wind hasn't changed in three days."

"Slocum arrived in Apia on July 16th. It's the same time of year."

He dispatched my point and the possibility of fluky winds with a shrug. He was brushing his teeth when the wind veered south. Shortly, it expired. With feeble puffs, the *Spray* slowed to a crawl. I hated the thought of being cooped up a day longer than necessary.

"A temporary lull, right?"

He missed my sarcasm. "The wind will be back. A couple of hours, give or take."

Doubtless, our captain was right—astern, puffy clouds loomed on the horizon. However, prognostications of weather conditions based on cloud formations were as fraught with uncertainty as such ancient mariner sayings as 'Red sky at night, sailor's delight. Red sky in morning, sailor's warning.' Magnificent sunsets preceded some of our worst storms at night.

"Two weeks to Apia," he said, back to humming.

Apia, Samoa, where we were headed, was 1,250 miles west, only two or three days on American expressways, rest stops and fast-food restaurants included. It didn't seem to bother my father that reefs dotted the course he'd mapped out. All around us, the sea was deep dark blue; however, atolls could appear without warning when the tips of volcanoes reached up from the depths. Usually, they didn't break the surface before coral took over. Captain Slocum wrote of the same stretch of ocean: 'coral reefs kept me company, or gave me no time to feel lonely.'

However, I was lonely. The gap between my father and me was as far as Apia. I had more in common with my brother, three years younger. Ben spent every spare moment reading his *Encyclopedia Britannica*, insisting it held the answers to all of life's questions. My sister and grandmother talked endlessly, making up for lost time. Whenever we went ashore, my mother collected postcards and travel brochures. At sea, she shunned the technology of the 21st century and documented our journey in scrapbooks with floral cloth covers. And me? I read novels from my father's collection of classics when I wasn't playing my guitar or doing school work by long distance.

Daniela, my closest friend, was 590 nautical miles astern in the Marquesas Islands. I'd known Dani for only twelve days, yet we'd become inseparable. She gave me a journal as a going away present. I missed her even more than I missed her grandfather's stories.

"Sal must think Zagarovsky's in Tahiti," I said, hoping to steer the conversation in that direction.

Dani, her grandfather, Sal, and his wife, Marion, were headed to the Society Islands: Tahiti, Bora Bora, and Huahine. Sal hadn't said why they were going to Tahiti; however, everyone knew it was because of Zagarovsky.

"More likely he's back in New York selling crack. You'd think after twelve years, Sal would get over it."

"If someone killed my son…"

"Revenge is self-destructive." He always interrupted me.

He was about to lecture me on life's lessons when my brother came up from the cabin, lugging a *Britannica* volume. Ben occupied the opposite seat, choosing shade from the mainsail over sunburn and peace and quiet.

"Zagarovsky tried to kill me and you don't seem to care," I said, choosing persistence over common sense.

My father inclined his head as if he hadn't heard properly. After a few moments, he said, "You think it's only luck you're still alive?"

I considered saying other than being the eldest son, none it was my fault. Zagarovsky wanted vengeance for something my father did.

"I didn't mean it like that. You always say running away from your problems doesn't help."

He made me wait. It was never a good idea to confront him directly. "What makes you think we're running away?"

"Aren't we?" I looked around. The sea, like the sky, was as empty and endless as I'd ever seen it.

"I've always wanted to sail the seven seas," Ben muttered from behind his hand.

It was my father's dream, not shared by the rest of his family, to sail around the world. He said we'd be gone as long as Joshua Slocum—it took him three years, two months, and two days to travel 46,000 miles. After one year and four months and 13,549 miles, we were still a long way short of the halfway point.

"We've seen the last of Zagarovsky's goons," my father declared. He hadn't heard Ben.

"What about Faro? Sal said…"

He cut me off again. "I know what Sal said."

"What if we report what happened to the police?"

"We'll be cooling our heels for six months. We're getting as far away as possible. We should've left right away."

"He said Faro was even more dangerous…"

He glared at me so I skipped the rest of what Sal said about the need to be very careful. He also said running wasn't the solution. Zagarovsky would catch up eventually.

When I looked up again, he was watching me. "What?" I heard my voice break.

"Your eyes are just like your mom's."

"Mom's eyes are green."

"I meant my mother. You're a lot like her."

"She had blue eyes, huh?"

"Ben looks more like my father," he said.

Ben put aside Volume XI. "What color were his eyes?"

"The same color as yours and mine. Brown."

Ben muttered what might have been 'no way,' his usual response when something aroused his interest and he couldn't explain it.' He picked up the pencil we used to record the *Spray*'s position, frowning as he scribbled on the scrap of paper serving as his bookmark.

"What color eyes did Grandma's husband have?" he inquired.

My father pulled on his chin as if he expected to find a goatee. "The last time I saw Thom was before you were born. Ask your grandmother."

Ben went to find her, lugging his encyclopedia with him.

I took advantage. "Did I get anything else from your side of the family?"

"Your grandfather's love of music." He checked his watch. "You're on duty, Victor."

He used 'Victor' to annoy me, his way of letting me know he'd heard me earlier.

"We left him in the Marquesas, remember?"

He tapped the wheel. "Good luck on that, Mister. You've got the wheel until eight. No shipping channels to worry about until this evening. Keep an eye out for Caroline Atoll. Give me a call when we're closer."

He recorded our position, cast his gaze over the sails and rigging, and scanned the horizon. He always followed routine as if getting a step out of order would result in catastrophe.

"Aye, Captain."

"Pay attention. Just a mile off course could be a disaster in these waters."

I blocked my ears to the rest of his lecture and returned to my book. He knew I hated 'Victor.' He never called me 'Josh' like everyone else. After he'd gone to his cabin to nap, I occasionally looked up—no sign of civilization, no ships, no vapor trails all the way to the horizon. There were a few wispy clouds far astern, a reminder of where we'd come from.

+ + +

Unlike the rugged volcanic islands of the Marquesas, Caroline Atoll was flat and deserted, a skinny necklace of dozens of tiny sand islets and coral heads defining a half-a-mile-wide lagoon. Scattered coconut trees burst through thick clumps of vegetation on the three largest islands. Everyone trooped on deck when I called them, even my father, rubbing sleep from his eyes. It was the first atoll we'd seen. For an hour, we sailed beside it, staying clear of reefs extending far into the sea.

Still unused to the *Spray's* constant up and down, my grandmother preferred to sit in the rear of the cockpit. She braced herself, tilted down the brim of her sunhat, and folded her arms.

"Your boat rocks a lot, John." She grimaced, her expression rapidly approaching what my mother called 'squeamish.'

"Watching the horizon usually helps, Sarah."

She was already staring at the horizon. She gave a dissatisfied sigh. "It doesn't help."

"You're taking it remarkably well," my mother said. She meant my grandmother's house, burned to the ground, everything gone.

My grandmother coughed, the usual prelude to retching. "It could have been worse." She shifted her gaze from the horizon to my eight-year-old sister to my eleven-year-old brother. "After all these years, I still have some things in storage."

Her gloominess struck a chord with me. I could think of nothing worse than losing my home.

"I was awfully sad when you left last year," she added, now looking at me.

"We didn't have a choice," my father said. "You should've left with us."

"I'm here now." She didn't sound happy about it.

My grandmother's queasy face and frequent cough all but guaranteed another bout of seasickness. It didn't stop her from helping Jessie arrange feathers on a square of plywood, scrounged from a dumpster in Hiva Oa, our first port of call in the Marquesas. They ranged from delicate colorful feathers from small tropical birds to straggly, long feathers from sea birds. My sister even had a huge albatross wing feather someone had given her.

Jessie was quick to draw our attention to a Great Frigatebird, black as night with a seven-foot wingspan, and a long, forked tail. There was a splash of crimson under its long hooked beak. It soared close to the waves, veering away at the last moment. Ben barely glanced up; we'd seen so many since departing South America.

"*Fregata minor*." With my grandmother's help, he'd mastered Latin pronunciation in two weeks. Now, she was teaching him Greek for good measure. "It's a male," he added, as if we cared.

"They eat flying fish right out of the air." Jessie had my brother's enthusiasm for science.

"Because they can't land in water." Ben was the voice of authority on anything natural.

My grandmother turned to watch the bird swoop down over swirling water. All of a sudden, she gulped air and swallowed, making a wry face. I hated the taste of bile even more than the actual throwing up.

"Try some of Jessie's ginger," my mother suggested, although it seldom worked for my sister.

"I'm fine, really. Just a little bit nauseous." My grandmother coughed with each passing wave. She handed me the pin jar, her face green, like an olive. "Be a dear and help Jessie with her feathers. I'm going to lie down for a while."

My mother and Ben went below too. My father watched Caroline Atoll disappear behind the waves. "About 30 miles to the shipping channel," he reminded me. "It shouldn't be a problem. It runs north-south, and not very busy."

"You have to pin both ends so they don't fall off," Jessie said as soon as he left. "I want the pins straight," she added after I bent the first pin.

"You want to do it?" I pulled out the pin and inserted another. There wasn't much room left on the board.

"It's loose." She wobbled the pin from side to side.

"The wood's too tough." I tried again, pushing until the head of the pin hurt my thumb.

"Stop doing that," Jesse complained.

"Doing what?"

"You're doing it like your thumbs are broken."

"You want the pins pushed in or not?" I snapped.

"Mine don't do it." Jessie pressed her thumb pads together. Hers were straight. My thumbs bent back.

"Josh's got hitch-hiker thumbs," Ben called from the cabin. "Double jointed is recessive." He was studying eighth-grade science, two years ahead for his age. "No one else in this family has them. It proves he's adopted."

"Ben!" my mother barked from the galley.

I'd finished pushing in the rest of the pins, mostly the way she wanted, and returned to my book before my grandmother popped her head through the companionway.

"It's so stuffy in the front room." She inhaled deeply, savoring salty air. "I opened the skylight, but it's much nicer up here."

The 'skylight' was the forward hatch—she'd opened it all the way. I should've told her my father's seventh rule for safety at sea:

'all hatches and ports closed and locked.' The sea was so calm it wasn't worth worrying about.

"I think the sea air agrees with me." She handed me my history book. "I hear you have a big test tomorrow. "If you tell me what to do, I'll be lookout and you can study, Alex."

Except for my grandmother, my real name was never used; and then it was quietly. It was as if my early years didn't exist.

I grinned back at her and gave my version of my father's ten-points on keeping watch. "Just stay on this heading and don't touch his sails."

"What if I see something?"

"If it flies or swims, call Ben. We're 22 miles from the shipping lane, but if you see a ship, take a bearing on it."

"What on earth is a bearing?"

"The compass direction." I showed her how to sight over the compass. "If the bearing changes, we're not going to collide." As seafaring rules went, constant bearing-decreasing range (CBDR) was spot on, which was why my father said not paying attention always preceded collision.

"You're the same as your father and uncle. More information does not make it easier to understand," she teased.

While my grandmother kept watch, I studied Russian history, a long march through wars, tyrants with impossible names, court intrigue, and social turmoil. The late afternoon sun grew steadily stronger, heating up the air under the awning until my clothes prickled. The wind was a hot humid breath sucking out my energy. By 1905, I was ready to revolt too.

With no ships on the horizon and nothing else to do, I took off my T-shirt and stretched out on the cockpit seat with my arm blocking the sun. My grandmother went below to see about dinner.

11

It seemed like only a minute later when she shook me awake. She pointed into the sunset and said quite calmly. "I'm not sure, but I think a ship is coming towards us."

Chapter 2

Orange and red streaked the sky, the sun hazy and huge, so close to the horizon it would soon be gone. Nebulous clouds approached from astern, though still too far away to worry about. My grandmother pointed ahead, into the sun. I squinted and cupped my hand on my forehead to block out the worst of the glare. Blinking, I put on my sunglasses. The sun was so bright everything else turned dark.

"How long has it been there?" I was sure she was mistaken. She wasn't used to being at sea.

"I don't know. I've been cooking."

Dinner smells, chicken sautéed with pineapple, papaya, and plantain banana, wafted from the galley. Unlike my mother, whose culinary skill peaked at tuna casserole, salad, and macaroni and cheese, my grandmother's meals were an adventure. She called her latest creation, 'Chicken Marquesas.' It belonged in an exotic cookbook.

"There shouldn't be any ships headed east near here." The longer I looked, the less certain I was.

My father plotted our course to avoid shipping channels. The Great North East Channel was hundreds of miles north, running east-west across the Pacific Ocean to the Panama Canal. Ships used it to take goods from Asia to America. However, we'd cross the less-traveled north-south Honolulu-Papeete Channel in an hour or so.

I looked into the sun until my eyes burned, worrying the watery blur I saw might be a ship, more likely my retinas burning up. After I closed my eyes for a while, it turned into a shimmering square in a blinding gold halo already dipping below the horizon. The ship was a few miles away, headed straight towards us.

She hurried below to fetch our captain. I'd untied the steering wheel and disconnected the self-steering system before he arrived on deck. By then, the sun was a golden glow, and the squat outline of a ship was dead ahead, and bearing down quickly.

"Not a problem. They'll have seen us by now," he said, his hair unkempt and blinking like a sleepy mole dragged from its hole.

He sounded confident; however he was always quick to point out modern cargo ships had undersized crews, just a handful of men to run the entire ship and keep watch. Ships had radar, yet small sailing boats were easy to miss in sea clutter. We had a special reflector on the mast to bounce back radar signals.

"We'll leave it to port," he said. It was standard procedure to turn to starboard to avoid a collision.

I steered while he hauled in the sails. The *Spray* wallowed like a whale as she turned broadside to the waves, booms and gaffs creaking as we rocked from side to side. For a minute, we stared at the ship until it was so close I could see its bow slicing through the darkening sea.

"Ought to be able to see its side by now," he said to no one in particular.

"Don't sailing boats have the right of way?" my grandmother asked brightly.

"When a ship's doing 20 knots you get out of its way." He grunted, "A bloody idiot must be steering it! Go more to starboard so he gets the message."

I changed course again, both of us watching the ship. "Start the engine?"

"Give it a minute." Our sails began to flap. Unflustered, he winched in the jibs. "A ship that big turns very slowly."

"I don't think they see us."

He nodded vaguely. It was a container ship, with containers stacked six high. They blocked the view from the bridge.

My grandmother clambered onto the cockpit seat to get a better view. "Can't your boat go faster, John?"

"Better start the engine, just in case."

The key wasn't in the ignition. He kept it on a hook next to his chart table when we were at sea. He scrambled down the stairs. "No need to panic. Everyone in life jackets, and on deck, now! Ben, put down the damned encyclopedia! Move it!"

He tossed the key into the cockpit and I started the engine. It was supposed to warm up for a minute, but I shoved it into gear and opened the throttle all the way. The *Spray* shuddered and began to pick up speed.

My grandmother stared at the onrushing ship. "They don't look that big when they're docked."

I heard my father on the VHF radio over the roar of the engine.

"Sécurité! Sécurité! Sécurité!" It wasn't a full-blown emergency yet. It took 'may-day' to do that. Sécurité was a warning. "Sailing vessel *Spray* calling container ship between Caroline Atoll and Vostok Island. You are on a collision course. I am turning to pass port to port! Please confirm your turn to starboard. Over." He was always polite on the radio.

Lacking a response, he rushed on deck again. The container ship was now less than a mile away. It pushed up a huge bow wave. Two enormous anchors protruded from its flared bow, streaking the sides with red rust stains.

"I'll take the wheel." He pushed me out of the way. "Get your lifejacket on, Victor."

15

"We ought to turn the other way," Ben muttered, fumbling to insert the plastic clips of his lifejacket.

My father heard him and scowled. Ben bravely stared him down.

"He's right!" I pointed. "Constant heading means it's turning with us."

"Damn!" He spun the steering wheel and the *Spray* turned hard to port. "Gybe ho!" he called as the wind switched sides. Suddenly, the booms swung across, flinging the *Spray* about. The jibs flapped violently. My grandmother screamed.

"Get the jibs across!" he bellowed over her.

I leaped to release the sheets from the winches; however, Ben was already there. We hauled in the sails on the other side, slowly picking up speed.

"It's going to hit us," my grandmother said. She muttered something else. She'd never used profanity in front of us.

"John knows what he's doing."

She regarded my mother as if she'd said 'pigs can fly.'

"Going to be close. Everyone hang on." My father gripped the wheel.

"Sweet baby Jesus," Ben said, kneeling on the seat beside me.

I barely heard him over the roar, offering my own silent prayer of 'God help us' as the *Spray* surged through the sea. My sister closed her eyes tight.

The ship blocked out the sun. Its starboard side appeared, a vast red wall looming up. In seconds, the ship's bow passed us, so close I could have thrown a ball against it. The *Spray* staggered in a blast of wind. A vast wave raced towards us like a breaker on a beach. My mother clutched Jessie. The *Spray* plowed into it, tilting so much I thought it would turn over.

The *Spray* pitched up and down as the ship thundered on. With each wave, sea water cascaded over the bow and poured through the open hatch. The engine screamed each time the propeller came out of the water, barely heard over the rumble from the ship. I could see squares in the faded paint where steel plates had been welded, ugly scuff marks where the ship had scraped against docks. When I looked up, the top of our mast wasn't as high as its deck.

My father steered with the waves, keeping them so they pushed the *Spray* away from the ship. Suddenly, there was a change in the sound of our engine. The *Spray* slowed down as if dragging something astern. He pushed the throttle lever down to make sure it was all the way open. The engine didn't run any faster. Instead, it stalled.

He cussed the diesel god out loud. Ben gaped back at him, though he'd heard it before. With a shrug came a curt, "Take a look below."

Ben leaped down the stairs. Immediately, he shouted up, "Dad, there's smoke coming from the engine room."

My father bolted from the cockpit, leaving the wheel unattended. With a grim glance at me, my mother took command. Immediately, the *Spray* began shaking, an awful pounding noise coming from below. The oil pressure warning light came on and the engine alarm went off.

"Now what?" she shouted over the deafening screech.

"Shut it off," he bellowed.

Before she could stop the engine, it banged and died. A cloud of smoke billowed from the stern. Smoke poured from the cabin. I could hear Ben coughing, my father cursing. The diesel god paled in comparison.

"Wave!" my mother screamed.

Ahead was a churning white wall. It lifted the *Spray* and thrust it sideways through the sea. I clung to my sister. My grandmother slammed into her, knocking her onto the seat. The smoke alarm wailed in the galley, drowning out my father's shouts from below.

My mother jerked me close. "Release the life raft, just in case!"

We'd practiced 'abandon ship' at the start of our journey. Like fire drills at school, my father required an orderly procedure. He assigned responsibilities for assessing damage, gathering survival essentials, getting everyone on deck, and releasing the straps securing the life raft. 'Abandon ship' took on new meaning after a glancing blow from a log off the coast of Puerto Rico. In the dark, we freaked out. Things weren't in their proper places, and straps that were supposed to be quick-release didn't release. Before heaving the life raft over the side, my father went below to check for damage. According to him, we went down with the ship, though his ship wasn't actually sinking. We practiced four times during the night before we got it down to his three-minute goal.

Before I could get to the life raft, the ship's stern rushed past us. The *Spray* barged into a maelstrom of breaking waves.

"Hang on, Josh!" my mother shouted.

The ocean, ripped apart by enormous propellers, took its revenge on us. One wave heaved the *Spray* sideways, spinning us around while another wave crashed onto the fore deck, submerging it completely. Water cascaded over the cabin and poured through the companionway, knocking Ben off the stairs. I jumped into the cockpit to catch my sister as the *Spray* plunged into the next wave. Another wave hit from the opposite direction with a tremendous thump. The *Spray* tilted more than ever before, the starboard rail completely underwater. My sister was ripped from my grasp and flung to the opposite side of the cockpit. Somehow, she grabbed a winch before she went over the side. I tried to stop my grandmother when she slid off the seat. Both of us fell into the cockpit, with her wedged under the steering wheel. Only my mother remained standing in the cockpit, half-filled with swirling seawater. She hauled me off my grandmother.

"Life raft!" she screamed at me.

Before I could move, the next wave thrust the *Spray* upright again. It skidded into a trough, the mainsail flinging across with a cannon-crack. The jibs flailed wildly, shaking the boat. However, the worst was over, just a Niagara torrent rushing past us.

My grandmother clambered up, soaked through, her hair dripping. Already, the rusty red stern was so far away I couldn't make out the name.

"I haven't done that before," she remarked, unruffled and wiping salt from her eyes.

Ben scrambled up the stairs. "It's a mess down there. Everything's soaked." He looked around before going back to make his report to the Captain.

We'd taken water before when freak waves came over the side, never more than a couple of buckets down the companionway. It quickly escaped into the bilge. This time, ankle-deep water sloshed through the cabins along with bits of Chicken Marquesas, Jessie's feathers, and postcards supposed to go in my mother's scrapbook.

Single-handedly, I lowered the mainsail and furled the inner jib. With one jib and the mizzen sail, the *Spray* sailed at a snail's pace through the tranquil waters of the south Pacific, while two bilge pumps spurted out thousands of gallons an hour.

When my father reappeared, I could tell he was pissed. Grease streaked his face, his hands smeared black.

"Oil seal burst on the filter. No big deal," he said.

"You fixed it already?" My grandmother had assigned herself the task of tidying the cockpit. With every line coiled, she spread the chart out to dry on the cabin roof, holding it down so it wouldn't blow off.

With a grunt, he turned the key to start the motor. Usually, a quick cough preceded a steady vibrating hum. Instead, the engine clanged.

"Maybe the engine needs oil?"

He greeted her suggestion with a frown. "I refilled it." He turned the key again. The clang sounded worse.

My mother finished tying a handkerchief on Jessie's sprained wrist. "That doesn't sound good."

"It sounds bloody awful!" He turned the key one more time. Something banged in the engine room. "Crap! It must be worse than I thought."

I was so used to his confidence; his tone took me by surprise.

"It's bad?" my mother said.

"It is if it's seized. It couldn't be any worse." He wiped grease from his hands on the first thing at hand.

"Hey, that's mine."

He tossed my sodden 'I love New York' T-shirt on the seat. "Get over it!"

He splashed back to the engine room. When he came on deck again, he brought our cat with him. He handed Jag to my sister and retrieved his chart from the cabin roof. He spread it out on the cockpit table.

"Frigging navigation hazards non-stop. I don't want to risk going to Samoa without a motor. We'll head to Tahiti and make repairs there."

"What about Zagarovsky?"

"He's back in New York, Victor." He plotted a course and went below.

Chapter 3

The container ship was a dot on the northern horizon before the *Spray* turned to head in the opposite direction. It wallowed through the waves, water swilling in her bilges until the pumps did their job. Jessie cradled a bedraggled cat; Ben was an artist's study in glum; my mother and grandmother talked quietly about how difficult it might be to find mechanics in Tahiti. I steered and kept my thoughts to myself.

My father ended the mechanic discussion when he joined us in the cockpit. "Not a problem. It's finding spare parts I'm worried about." Even he couldn't misinterpret the prevailing mood. "Slocum had his share of problems too. No need to be upset."

We had every reason to be upset after almost being rammed by a container ship. That the Captain ran aground and nearly lost his vessel in South America didn't compare in my opinion.

"We can learn a lot from situations like this," he went on.

I kept my mouth shut while he reviewed the things we could from, like making sure we'd closed the hatches. There was audible relief when he went below to unclog the bilge pumps for the second time.

"We'll eat first, and then clean up." With grimy hands, he passed up an open carton of crackers, two tins of tuna, and a papaya.

My grandmother gave a rueful shrug. "I'll cook a proper dinner tomorrow."

We'd purchased the crackers in Chile. They were stale, and the papaya was squishy; but no one complained.

As soon as he finished eating, he returned to reviewing our situation. "Four hundred and thirty miles with the wind against us. With luck, it'll take a week." He paused as if waiting for someone to disagree. "I'm not going to assign blame."

My sister was first to defend me, needed or not. "It's not Josh's fault."

"I didn't say it was."

However, I could feel him looking at me, silence like a wet blanket. I loaded a cracker with tuna and gave it to Jessie to feed Jag before I met his eyes. "It happened on my watch."

My grandmother plunged in. "If anyone's to blame, it's me. I told him I'd be lookout while he studied for his test."

"I was going to say, we're in this together. The important thing is we worked as team." He sounded sincere. "Victor, take my watch while the rest of us clean up."

Assigning me back-to-back watches was unfair, but better than being below. They stripped the sodden berths in the forward cabin, removed the covers from the seats in the main cabin, lifted every floorboard, and emptied every locker to dry out the boat. Ben tossed soggy sheets and pillowcases into the cockpit before he climbed the stairs. He draped them over the cockpit, the rails, and cabin roof.

"You're lucky your guitar was in its case."

"What's wrong with you?"

"The *Britannica's* ruined." He wiped his eyes. He hadn't cried since we left our trailer in Norfolk.

"I'm sorry."

He lowered his voice—all the hatches were open to help dry out the cabin. "Not your fault. Dad said I have to throw it away. He

23

didn't want it on board in the first place. He wouldn't dump his books if they got wet."

Worse than his sniffle was watching his eyes, red and wet, and constantly blinking.

"Bring up the worst one and I'll try to dry it."

He lugged Volume XI up the stairs. "It fell off the table."

Water dripped from the split spine. I lifted the cover; inside, a thousand pages clumped together like wet toilet paper. I peeled back the first page, illegible because the type showed from the other side.

"Ben, get down here and wipe out the lockers," my father shouted from below.

"I hate him!" Ben whispered and left.

I turned each flimsy page, carefully holding it up so the wind blew against it. It took five minutes before a page didn't stick to my fingers. Below, my father issued a constant stream of demands. Ben bordered on insubordination, answering back when muteness made more sense.

Finally, my mother intervened. She took my father into the aft cabin. "There'll be mutiny if you don't lighten up, and it won't just be your son."

"I'm doing the best I can." He didn't even try to whisper like she had. "If it wasn't for him…"

"This isn't the time, John! Like it or not, we're seeing this through."

"Maybe we made the wrong decision." He paused. "We're lucky we're still alive.."

"It was the only thing we could do, John." She'd never sounded so determined.

"I need to get back to work."

'So much for peace and harmony in the Pacific,' I thought to myself.

Drying Ben's book went much faster after I figured out how to use the wind to dry dozens of pages at a time. I'd dried hundreds of pages before I found a piece of notepaper stuck to one page. I used the light from the compass to see he'd drawn a crude family tree, and scribbled 'Brn,' 'Grn', and 'Blue' under our names. There was only one 'Blue' on the tree. Beside 'Josh' he had added a question mark, as if disputing the color of my eyes. I rolled Ben's bookmark into a ball and flipped it over the side.

I finished the first volume at midnight, too tired to care that most pages were wrinkled and damp and didn't lay flat. Mussorgsky's *Pictures at an Exhibition* blared when my father came on deck to begin the next watch.

He gave me a curt nod, watching me trying to flatten Volume XI by sitting on it. "You're wasting your time."

"It's almost done." I was tired of his moods, his sarcasm, and his music, which he always played too loudly. "You made Ben cry."

He adjusted the volume. "Before you go to bed, bring up another one, Victor."

"It's Alex! I also answer to Josh." I was exhausted.

"It's Victor. You might not like it; but it isn't your choice."

"Victor's the name on my passport. I don't have to use it."

"It's your name."

"It's not my real name."

No one in my family had their real name. My father changed our surname to Walker within a month of the fire that killed his parents. My mother was Virginia Walker, the same name as Joshua Slocum's first wife. His kids took their first and second names from Joshua Slocum's children. I thought it was creepy until he told us it was to conceal our identity from Zagarovsky.

"You were christened 'Alexander Victor.'" He relished my surprise.

"You mean there's a Russian composer named Victor?"

"Kalinnikov wrote choral music. Appropriate as it might've been, you're not named after him." He inclined his head, listening to Mussorgsky. "Sheer genius... How about Modest for a name?" he inquired. Mussorgsky's *Night on Bald Mountain* was a favorite.

"It beats Victor for awful."

"Blame my brother. It was his idea."

"Tell me about him."

"You'd like him. Not bad-tempered like me," he chuckled.

I returned a halfhearted smile and went below to fetch another volume of my brother's encyclopedia. There were 32 volumes. It took my family five days and nights to dry them out. Hundreds of pages came loose. It was like having a Persian cat onboard, constantly shedding fur; however, you put up with it because the cat was family.

+ + +

Like clockwork, my grandmother scanned the horizon with binoculars every 15 minutes, making two complete turns to be sure there were no ships headed towards us; no reefs waiting to sink us. Far more likely was a collision with a container that had fallen off a ship. They floated right at the surface, often for months before they sank. I didn't tell her; she was already worried about a whale surfacing under us. By then, I'd seen hundreds of whales, usually far away and spouting water. Only one came close enough to see barnacles on the back of its head. I hadn't seen any floating containers; I figured we'd passed them at night.

Satisfied we were safe for 15 minutes, she stretched out on the seat. "I have lost my cell phone. Have you seen it?"

"He perdido mi teléfono celular. Usted lo ha visto?" I said. It was my last test before taking the exam for Spanish AP. "Sounds like the wind is shifting again."

While she checked the answer in the back of the book, I got up to adjust the sails, hauling in sheets until the fluttering stopped.

"I knew you'd be good at this," she said.

"I ought to be after sailing halfway around the world."

"I was thinking of something else. I left my cell phone on the table."

"Dejé mi teléfono celular en la mesa. Quizás cayó en el piso."

"What else did you say?"

"Perhaps it fell on the floor. What were you thinking?"

She laughed. "You're so good with languages; it's like listening to Kate. She'd switch between languages, just like you do. You ought to take French next year. She'd like that."

Kate was my other grandmother.

"I don't remember much about her. He won't talk about them."

My grandmother put down my Spanish book. "We were all at the same university. Kate taught French and German. Thom and I were in the Department of Classics. Your Grandpa Alex had the Lansing Chair in Piano in the College of Music. We played bridge every Saturday, after a gourmet dinner, of course. Our kids came for the food."

"That's how they met, huh?"

"Actually, your mom and dad met before dinner." She smiled oddly, as if there was more to the story. "How much do you remember about staying at their house on Long Island?"

I dodged the question. "Other than she had different words for everything?"

"You were speaking German before you turned three."

"He played the piano nonstop. I used to sit on his lap."

"They adored you. From the moment you were born, you were destined…" She hesitated. "John said you remember the fire."

"Some of it. It scared me so badly part of my brain shut down."

"You didn't speak for two months, and when you finally did start talking again, you'd forgotten everything. All things considered, you were very lucky."

I looked at my arms, burn scars from my elbows to my wrists like a wrinkled old man. "I don't think I am."

The sails fluttered until the self-steering adjusted the course. I made a note of the new compass heading, taking us farther away from Tahiti. My father wouldn't be happy.

"Barkov made the fire look like an accident, so the police didn't investigate properly. However, your father wasn't taking any chances. He stayed by your bed day and night. Of course, after Zagarovsky tried again, you had to disappear."

"What's Zagarovsky like?"

"Cruel and as cunning as a wolf; only you wouldn't know it from looking at him. When I saw him at the trial…" She pushed a lock of gray hair behind her ear. "It was very unsettling, watching him after what he'd done. He seemed quite gentle."

"Because of how he looks?"

"He's not what you'd call manly. He's thin and pale, especially his face. It makes him look harmless. When he smiles, it's like there's something wrong with his mouth."

"I might have met him. Does he wear oblong glasses like yours?"

She nodded and waited for me to continue.

"We were still at the marina in Portsmouth. Some wimpy guy in the parking lot asked me about our van. He stared at me the whole time."

"You told John, right?"

"It wasn't like the guy was interested in buying it. He found out from the dock manager. You think it was why we had to leave so quickly?"

"You'll have to ask him."

"Not going to happen. When we were leaving Anaho Bay, I asked him what he'd done to Zagarovsky for him to want to kill me. He said it wasn't something I needed to know right then."

"I expect he'll tell you when the time is right."

"It's never right, not for him! Did you ever find your cell phone?"

"You only score points if you say it in Spanish," she laughed.

+ + +

We were a day away from Tahiti when the wind shifted southeast. We faced a slow slog through six-foot waves, the sails winched in, drum-tight, heeled over. It was back to living on a steeply sloped hill, always hanging on. Jessie stayed in her berth with Jag, my grandmother, and a bucket nearby. When I wasn't on watch or asleep, I listened to the same ancient Greek stories I'd heard as a child: Ulysses, Alexander the Great, and the Gods of Olympus.

In a lull between gusts, Ben bolted down the stairs. He wedged himself in the seat before the *Spray* returned to an angle. "Dad says we'll be there in six hours."

I grimaced at my mother from across the table—we had the next watch. "Ready to go up and battle Neptune?"

She stopped perusing her oldest scrapbook and held it up. "I bet you don't remember this?"

She'd taken the photo with a flash on the front porch of our trailer at Arcadia Park after she'd dressed me as a vampire for Halloween, a cheap black cape, plastic pointed ears, and blood-sucking fangs. I should've been happy with a bag full of candy; however, I was so sickly I looked like a vampire's victim. My wrists were pink and scaly, my arms still bandaged at the elbows. Next to me, in a carry-cradle, my six-week-old brother had a moustache drawn under his nose. Both of us had shocking red eyes.

"Aw, he was so cute when he was chubby." I pinched Ben's cheek.

"Do you have photos of him when he was a baby?" Ben's smirk was evil.

"I didn't start keeping scrapbooks until after the fire." My mother closed her scrapbook. "Josh, start our watch, will you? I'll make some sandwiches." She got up to put her scrapbook on the shelf. "Does anyone else want one?"

"Me." Imminent puking was a minor inconvenience to Jessie when her mouth was full of crystallized ginger.

"What happened to please? And masticate with your mouth closed. Your manners are worse than Ben's."

Ben shrugged it off. "You must have photos of Josh somewhere. Everyone takes photos of their first baby."

"Everything was at your grandmother's house."

"It's sad, not having anything left." Jessie outshone all of us at commiserating.

My grandmother looked up from peeling yams for dinner; curried fish and sweet potato pie. "I have a photo of Josh in my handbag. Grampa Alex took it a few weeks before..." She stopped when my mother coughed abruptly.

My grinning brother was already on the move. He retrieved her handbag from her locker and carried it to her. He plopped onto Jessie's berth—he'd swapped berths with her when our grandmother arrived. I got the berth behind the dining table, a coffin with a canvas curtain--no space to move and no privacy.

She wiped her hands on a towel and opened her handbag to poke around inside. All of a sudden, she brightened. "I forgot I had this with the fire and all." She pulled out a small foil-wrapped package. "Better late than never. Happy birthday, Ben. You'll get a real present when we get to Australia."

He beamed when he discovered a deck of cards for a budding marine biologist. After an appreciative hug, he started sorting cards by genus, his interest in family photos sidetracked.

Jessie wasn't so easily diverted. "Can I see the photo, Grandma?"

"Don't bother her when she's busy," my mother intervened.

"I may have lost it. I haven't seen it in a while."

"You have photos in the back of your purse." Jessie craned her neck to look inside the handbag.

My grandmother pulled out her purse, worn brown leather with a gold clasp. I could tell it had been expensive a long time ago.

I crowded into the tiny cabin as well. She shuffled through photographs of us, including one of the *Spray* being launched, my mother whacking a bottle of fake champagne against the bow.

"I thought he'd never get it finished." She smiled at the last photo, the one I'd sent of Ben and me catching blue crabs in South Carolina. "Seems I've lost it."

"Is that the photo?" Jessie pointed at a dog-eared edge of paper.

It was easily overlooked, or carefully preserved, inside a silk flap in the last compartment of the purse. My grandmother glanced at my mother.

"Show us!" Ben's malevolent smile was back.

She took it out. There were three people, one of them a boy about three years old. It was taken before I was burned. I was grinning. I had a toy fishing rod.

"Aw, he's so cute he needed two babysitters." Ben scooted out of reach.

"The babysitters are your uncle and aunt," my mother said from the main cabin.

A dozen years ago, my father and his brother could've been twins.

Jessie pointed at our aunt, a woman in her early 20s. "Is she going to have a baby?"

"It's just her T-shirt. The wind is blowing it out," my mother said.

"She's really pretty."

Something about her made me look long and hard. She was fair-haired and slender as a sapling except for her billowing T-shirt.

Her hands were on my shoulders, holding me still for the camera as she looked down at me with an enigmatic smile.

"She's got Josh's hair," Jessie said, glancing up at me. "Only his is lighter."

"He looks bald," Ben teased.

"We were in South Carolina. He got a marine-style buzz for the summer," my mother explained.

"I don't remember being in South Carolina."

The long spiky grass and murky inlet in the background could be anywhere from Chesapeake Bay to Florida. You could tell it was hot.

"We were on a holiday at Beaufort. The whole family," my father said from behind me. I hadn't heard him.

"Where are you guys?" Ben asked.

"Your mom had morning sickness because of you, so she stayed at the hotel."

"And you stayed with her?"

"Who do you think took the photo, Ben?" my father said.

Jessie frowned. "But Grandma just said…"

"It doesn't matter who took the photo. The important thing is we still have it." My father pointed up—it was my turn on watch.

I went gladly. Already, a few puffy clouds painted the horizon over Tahiti and the neighboring island of Moorea.

Chapter 4

Inside the reef was the busy harbor of Papeete, a vast cargo pier with cranes loading and unloading freighters stacked with containers. A luxury clipper ship and four small cruise ships occupied finger piers on the other side of the harbor. Sheltered by the town and Mt. Faiere, the breeze faded to wavering puffs. The *Spray* drifted closer, finally stopping near the main quay, wallowing in greasy green slop.

"Will someone tow us to shore?" my grandmother asked brightly after we lowered the sails.

"The cheapest tugboat is $800." My father hadn't been in a good mood since he'd radioed the Papeete harbor master for instructions. "Ben, Josh, help me get *Squirt* in the water."

"Your little dinghy has enough power?" My grandmother was skeptical.

"We'll find out, won't we?" He climbed into the dinghy and started the motor.

He used *Squirt* to align his boat after my mother dropped the anchor to hold the bow. Shouting instructions, he pushed the *Spray* backwards towards the quay. A friendly sailor caught our line and looped it over the nearest bollard. Then, my grandmother, Ben, and I hauled the stern up to the quay.

"Stop looking for Sal's boat and put out a second stern line, Victor," my father called.

Already coiling a second line, I snapped a salute and shouted back, "Aye aye, Captain."

After a good-natured wave, he headed up the channel. He soon returned, looking pleased with himself. The dinghy was close to capsizing with two burly Tahitian mechanics from the local boatyard. He escorted them to his engine room. We could hear the starter motor trying to turn the engine, a loud clunk accompanied by metallic grating. Then, they conversed in French. I knew 'moteur', and guessed at 'ruiné', enough to know it wasn't good.

"We'll go shopping." My mother wanted to get us off the *Spray* as quickly as possible.

The first and last thing we did in every port was replenish our supplies at the local market. At the top of the shopping list was fresh milk—we hadn't had any since South America. Cat food came next, followed by a proper litter box to replace a cardboard box and beach sand, which smelled like a sewer and was impossible to keep clean. All told, there were 53 items on the list, most marked with urgent asterisks.

The Papeete market was a big, open-air shed in the center of town. Farmers and merchants sold their wares from trestle tables. There were hundreds of tables, half of them loaded up with brightly colored clothes printed with tropical flowers. The aisles were jammed with local people and curious tourists, squeezing between crates of produce and jostling to be served. We trooped behind my mother, single-file, staying close together, each lugging two canvas shopping bags acquired during our travels. My grandmother trailed behind, appraising the stands in wide-eyed wonder, whether tropical fruit, spices, pastries, straw bags and hats, shells on strings, hand-carved furniture, or fish so fresh they still had their heads on.

"This is more fun than shopping at Wal-Mart." She stopped in the middle of a busy aisle to watch two Tahitian women haggle over the price of a toothbrush.

"No one pays the asking price." My mother steered her out of the current. "I need to buy postcards. Josh, keep an eye out like we talked about."

"Even here?" I said airily, looking around at the bustling shoppers.

"You heard Sal say nowhere is safe."

Nearly every face was Polynesian, friendly and full of life. Not one was menacing. Instead, I said, "I'll be careful."

"I want Ben and Jessie in sight at all times. Stay in this aisle and I'll catch up." She headed off, skirting a burly worker wheeling a dolly loaded with three crates of yams.

"How much should I offer?" my grandmother asked, picking out a bag with six bars of mauve hotel soap.

"One hundred francs, Madame," the merchant called out. He was Chinese, a wizened little man with a straggly gray beard. Tattoos covered his arms.

"Dad always starts at half." Ben headed to the chicken store, wings, drumsticks, gizzards, necks, and yellow-clawed, scaly feet.

"You have to assert yourself," Jessie sounded like my father. She followed Ben.

My grandmother pointed to the bag of soap. "Fifty francs, Monsieur."

Immediately, the storekeeper began a long winded explanation of why 95 francs was cheap for his made-by-hand soap—he used perfume imported from Paris. He opened the bag to prove his point. It smelled of lilac, like cheap hand lotion.

They went back and forth in five franc increments until they settled on 75 francs—one dollar. My grandmother handed him the money and the soap went into her handbag.

"Where's Jessie?" she asked, looking around.

Suddenly, in the throng of shoppers, a gap opened. Two stands away, Ben pored over used library books. I hurried over to him.

"How hard can it be to watch your sister?"

"Mom told you to, not me." This time it was Polynesian birds and plants that enthralled him.

I snatched the book from his hands and put it back on the rack. "Go to the end of this aisle. If you don't see her, go find Mom. And tell Gran to stay where she is in case she comes back."

I stalked through the crowd. No local children—they were in school in July; however, every tourist on Tahiti had picked Tuesday to bring their kids to the market. From behind, all little girls looked like my sister. I accosted two of them before I moved to the next aisle. I was close to panic, with no sign of Jessie, until I passed a table heaped with a dozen varieties of tropical fruit. I spotted my mother in the next aisle. Jessie was beside her.

I was still flustered when I caught up. "You were supposed to stay with Ben!"

Jessie had three loaves of bread and a red plastic litter box in her canvas tote-bag. She looked very pleased with herself.

"Guess what I caught?" She held up a rubber mouse by the tail. "Sal bought it for Jag. He said hi."

I expected to run into Sal in Papeete, but not within an hour of arriving. I looked to my mother. "Where is he?"

She dumped her shopping bags, both bulging with cans. "He had to leave. He has an appointment with someone at the bank."

"Was Dani with him?"

Jessie giggled. "She's horse riding with Marion."

"I didn't see the *Maid Marion* at the dock."

"It's on the other side of the island in Port Phaeton Bay. Sal said the bus goes right past them. You can't miss it from the road."

"That's good to know."

My mother looked amused. "You can visit them tomorrow when we go to the Gauguin Museum. Right now, I want you and Ben to find…" She examined her shopping list. "Three gallons of milk, only if it's fresh and not too expensive."

"Cheap milk, right from the udder. Got it!"

"I want it pasteurized, Josh. If it's more than three bucks a liter, get powdered milk instead. Two big boxes of spaghetti, the thick kind. Better get rigatoni too, anything with a hole will do. With Grandma doing the cooking, bow-tie and lasagna, if they have it here."

She handed over Polynesia-themed banknotes. "Oh, and you need new swim shorts for when you go swimming with Dani." She peeled off more 1000 franc notes. "If you'd prefer a French-style Speedo, I saw some on a table in aisle three."

Jessie smirked. Under my suntan, I was beetroot red.

+ + +

My father waited for us in the cabin, too dirty and too tired to help with our bags, not too tired and dirty to help himself to a slice of crusty French bread.

"Forty-three thousand dollars, and they won't start until it's paid in full."

Realizing where the conversation was headed, my grandmother scooped up the bag of clothes she'd purchased and ushered my sister to their cabin. Ben took to the head with a secondhand book on Tahiti's flora and fauna he'd acquired at the market, which left my mother and me to put away the butter, fruit, vegetables, chicken, and bread covering the galley counter.

"So pay it." My mother was upset; however, he didn't notice.

38

"Just the motor is $24,000. Freight, taxes, and installation make the rest..."

"John!"

"It'd be cheaper to rebuild it. They have a few parts in stock, the rest I can get from a tractor company on the other side of the island..."

"I'm sure a man was watching us at the market today," she interrupted.

"What?"

I stared at her too, my hands full of greasy chicken breasts. My job was to rip off yellow skin pocked with pimples and missed soggy feathers. "No way!"

"You walked past him before I realized. He followed us to the dock."

My father climbed two stairs and poked his head above the companionway. "Where?"

"The end of the quay. He was wearing a suit. I didn't get a good look at his face." She hesitated. "I think I've seen him before."

"Hand me the binoculars, Victor. You're not certain?"

"The only thing I'm sure of is the walking stick."

"Walking stick?" my father repeated, shaking his head.

"It's how he uses it, John; as if he's got it for show. I might be mistaken," she added.

I handed him the binoculars. "He was in Rio, right?"

She gave me a cautious nod. "In George Town too, I think."

"I didn't see him."

"I expect you were busy thinking about Dani. He looked right at you; it's what gave him away."

"No sign of anyone with a cane now." My father handed back the binoculars and stepped down. He leaned over his navigation table to examine a chart. My mother looked over his shoulder.

"We're leaving already?" Ben dried his hands on his shorts. He had sunglasses on with blue Tahitian Lories stuck on the frame.

We gaped at him.

"Don't you look cool." It took all my willpower not to laugh.

"Maybe we should leave." My mother shook her head in disbelief.

"It's the new me, Mom," Ben grinned. "I got another pair with mahi-mahi. Five bucks including the book."

"You see a skinny guy in a suit when we were leaving the market?" I asked him. At the time, he'd been dragging behind, his head in his book. "He had a cane."

"Sure. He pointed it at your back, Dude."

It was the last straw for my father. "We're out of here. Too noisy, too crowded, and too friggin' dangerous."

Papeete was noisy, crowded, and dangerous—cars, trucks, and buses raced along Pomare Boulevard, not a ball's throw away from the *Spray*. If that wasn't enough, sidewalk merchants hawked their wares along the quay, and cruise ships were coming and going. As an exotic destination, I rated it C-.

My grandmother came out of her cabin wrapped in floral-print cloth, a Tahitian pareu. "What about your engine?"

"I'll fix it myself," he declared, not looking up from the chart.

"You're not a mechanic, John," she said, turning around with a flourish. Twenty dollars made her look 20 years younger. The rest of us beamed approval; however, his head stayed down. "If it's a matter of money, I have some."

"I appreciate the offer, Sarah. I rebuilt the engine once; and I can rebuild it again. I just need a few days of peace and quiet, and a place to do it."

"Even I know an engine has hundreds of moving parts."

"I think I can handle it." He continued to study the chart. "There's nowhere to anchor and not be seen from the road. Moorea's our best choice," he decided. "I can take the ferry back here to buy what I need."

He rolled up his chart, now smeared with grease, and stalked back to the engine room. He emerged an hour later, engine manual in one hand and pages of notes in the other.

"I'm going to get parts for the engine. Leave at seven sharp, whether I'm back or not," he said before he climbed into *Squirt*.

He motored away, not going towards the boatyard, the opposite way, so close to the quay he had to dodge around yachts.

+ + +

My mother checked her watch every ten minutes. She was washing dirt from a ragged romaine lettuce when the ship's clock chimed seven pm.

"I knew he'd be late." She struck back at the lettuce, ripping it apart.

My grandmother took charge of the salad bowl before she could inflict more damage. "Jessie can help me get dinner while you and the boys get everything shipshape."

Ben and I left our chess match on the table. We followed our mother up the stairs. Still no sign of my father.

"Where's Captain Bligh when you need him?"

41

My joke fell flat. She shrugged.

"What if he's not back in time?" Ben's blue-tinted sunglasses with green mahi-mahi were even more ridiculous than Tahitian Lories.

"He'll find us at Moorea. We're leaving on schedule," she said. "Take those off before you have an accident."

Her sharp tone surprised me. Ben knew better than to argue when she was worried.

Tourists streamed back and forth along the quay, enjoying an evening stroll before dinner. None of them paid any attention to us, although three people stopped to photograph the *Spray* against the ruddy sunset and Moorea's craggy mountains silhouetted in the distance.

As soon as I'd untied the stern lines and jumped onboard, Ben unfurled the jibs. Together, we cranked sheets onto winches while my mother raised the anchor, hauling the *Spray* back from the quay. The fluttering sails filled, yet there wasn't enough wind to stop the *Spray* from drifting sideways. I rushed from the cockpit, ready to fend off the fancy French yacht beside us. We came within inches of scraping before a feeble gust pushed us away. The *Spray* crept forward, the anchor clanking as it hung over the bow roller.

With so little wind, the *Spray* was a lumbering hulk. Three hundred yards away, the crew of a cruise ship cast off lines, its upper decks lined with raucous passengers on their way to an adventure in paradise. A plume of smoke rose from its raked funnel and a flurry of water churned at the stern. It backed away from the dock and turned towards us. My mother tried to steer away from it. The *Spray* obstinately veered closer.

"Mainsail up. Be quick!" She gave orders like he did.

We leaped into action. Ben unfastened the straps keeping the sail folded on the boom. I hauled on the halyard. The sail rattled up the mast and the *Spray* began to move faster, though still meandering down the channel.

My grandmother came up to see what the fuss was about. "Aren't we getting close to that ship?"

"No need to panic." My mother's confidence was wasted.

"I think you need to steer the other way."

"Mom, please. Will you be quiet, just once?"

She looked back at the quay, not at the looming freighter now on the other side of harbor. She touched my arm and pointed. I saw only tourists.

"Why do we have to leave as soon as we get somewhere interesting?" Ben's timing was awful.

"Tighten the jib sheets! Now!"

My grandmother said calmly, "John's doing what he thinks is best. We need to support him."

A faint breath freshened the air until the sails bulged like plump aprons. The *Spray* picked up speed, now perfectly content to sail out of the harbor.

"There's *Squirt*!" Ben pointed behind the cruise ship.

Soon, my father was alongside. He tossed up the painter, heaved up three heavy cardboard boxes, and climbed over the rail before he awarded a cursory nod to my mother. "Couldn't have done better myself."

It wasn't often he complimented his crew.

We hoisted *Squirt* and tied it down before he took the wheel. Moorea's blue-gray peaks beckoned west; we headed south.

He smiled when Ben asked. "Just in case someone is watching."

"You haven't changed," my grandmother said.

"Planning for the worst has worked for eleven years." He nodded at me. "I'll need you in five hours. As soon as you've finished dinner, go to bed."

+ + +

I woke up at midnight and stumbled upstairs. A three-quarter moon lit up the sea, six-foot-high waves far apart.

"This ought to be far enough if they're watching us on radar." He yawned. "Lucky for you, the wind eased over the last hour."

Before I could ask, he pointed a flashlight at the radar reflector attached near the top of the mizzen mast. Reluctantly, I got into his bosun's chair. He tightened the straps, tied a wrench to the canvas seat, and issued instructions. While my mother steered, he manned the winch, hauling me up the mast. I'd gone up the mast five times before. At anchor during daytime was bad enough; at night and underway, it was daunting. Every wave swayed the mast. On the way up, I banged against it twice. My grandmother held the flashlight, a beam of light wavering back and forth between me and the radar reflector. It was impossible for me to stay in position long enough to undo the bolts. Finally, I clamped my legs around the mast and held on to a shroud. With only one hand, everything took longer.

I was halfway back to the deck when a large wave struck the *Spray*, shoving her over. I swung over the sea, dangling like shark bait as the *Spray* plunged into the trough. A moment later, she rolled back and I grabbed for a halyard. Momentum wrenched me away. My shoulder struck the mast and I dropped the radar reflector. In slow motion, it clattered on the deck and bounced over the side with barely a splash, more like a 'plop'.

"Not my fault," I called down.

44

There was no reprimand. Instead, he frowned, likely saving his anger for later on, when no one would hear him. I completed my descent in halting slow steps. When I stood on deck, he unfastened the straps and helped me out of the seat.

"Sorry about the radar thing."

"Should've tied a rope to it. How's the shoulder?"

"He could've been killed!" My grandmother thrust the flashlight at him and went below. He changed course 100 degrees to head west of Moorea.

+ + +

We sailed through the night, circling Moorea. It was dawn when we drifted through an opening in the reef into Vaiare's small harbor, cradled between very steep hills. When there was no more wind, I towed a line behind *Squirt,* attaching it to the dock of a small marina opposite the terminal for ferries from Papeete. With my father hauling on the line, my brother and mother fending off, and *Squirt* pushing at the bow, we finally got the *Spray* tied to a pier. Then, we hoisted *Squirt*, positioned to conceal *Spray* on the stern. From a distance, it looked like any of the two dozen other yachts in the marina.

Chapter 5

We'd barely finished breakfast before he began stripping the motor. Having appropriated our dining table as his workbench, my mother scheduled my Spanish AP exam in the cockpit. I kept my headphones on, trying to concentrate as he banged and cussed in the engine room. Three hours later, I breathed a sigh of relief and went downstairs. Sheets of newspaper spread out under an assortment of oily cloths, engine parts, and three lines of greasy bolts of various sizes.

My grandmother emerged from her cabin, shook her head and muttered, "Men maketh mess."

Before I could stop her, she scooped up his bolts and dumped them into a plastic shopping bag. With terrible timing, my father emerged from his engine room.

"What are you doing?" He smelled like burned rubber.

"I'm making a place for Jessie to do her research project. Your bolts were all over the table. Everything is in here." She handed him the bag. "I'll put them back when we're finished."

"They're cylinder head bolts, Sarah. They have to go back in the right order."

"Why would it matter when they're all the same?"

"They are NOT all the same!"

"Then, you should be able to figure it out."

He was moments from exploding when my mother intervened. "How about some coffee and a fresh croissant, John?"

He scowled at her as if it was her fault his engine seized. I'd had enough. I scowled back at him on her behalf. My brother discreetly closed the curtain in front of his berth.

46

"Jessie and I are going for a walk." It was clear my grandmother had had enough too.

My father gave an indifferent shrug. My mother gave a reassuring smile. She waited until she heard their footsteps clatter down the dock.

"She's just trying to help. There's no need to be rude, John."

"I wasn't rude!"

"You shouted at her." I'd planned to stay out of his way as much as possible.

He turned on me. "This is difficult enough as it is. I don't need you against me." He stormed back to the engine room, clutching the bag of bolts.

"Can I help?" she called after him.

+ + +

By the time my grandmother and sister returned, engine parts littered the cabin. Valves, springs, camshaft, and assorted metal rods covered the table. Other parts wrapped in plastic bags occupied the seats. Pistons soaked in plastic buckets. Shiny bearings littered the galley counter. The cylinder head lay on towels spread on the floor. We had to step over it to get to the stairs.

"You'll never guess what we did. We walked all the way to a hotel," my sister shouted from the cockpit. "Grandma rented the Sunset Suite for us."

My mother stopped scrubbing a piston. She pulled off rubber gloves as they came down the stairs. "Mom, there's no need for this. He's calmed down already."

"It's my treat. We can check in any time this afternoon."

My father poked his head out the engine room. Grease streaked his face and covered his arms. "I'm sorry, Sarah. I

47

shouldn't have flown off the handle. The bolts have a number stamped on top of them."

If he sounded sheepish, it was because Ben had shown him the section in his engine manual describing how to identify bolts and reassemble the cylinder head.

"And I shouldn't have touched them. I apologize." She winked at me.

"About the hotel…" He wiped off his hands.

"A couple of days, John, until you get the motor put back together. It's not expensive if we stay for three nights."

He shook his head. "It's not safe, Sarah."

"Your brother once told me the best place to hide is where you won't be noticed, and where you're least expected. You thought a trailer park qualified."

"It worked for ten years."

"Maybe so. Here, it would be a tourist resort," she said, looking back at him.

"The kids deserve a vacation. It'll be easier without them in the way," my mother added, looking around—he'd turned the main cabin into a grease-smeared workshop.

"I'll clean it up by tonight."

"Why bother! It won't hurt them to sleep in real beds for three nights, John." Her message was clear.

"The smell's pretty bad," I said.

Every hatch was open and the cabin still stank. It was as bad as when my father had used a kerosene heater to keep us warm in Norfolk, Virginia.

He dispatched my point with, "It'll be gone in an hour."

Ben jerked his curtain open. With a berth surrounded by engine parts, he had the most to gain. "It's not safe for us kids to be here, Dad." He faked a spluttering cough. "Kerosene fumes can cause neurological and kidney damage."

My mother managed not to smile. "He's got a point, John. Plus there's a chance of blood clots damaging the brain and heart."

"Please say yes, Daddy," Jessie begged. "You'll be able to fix the motor much faster if we're in a hotel."

I could tell he was thinking about it as he picked up the piston my mother had been cleaning, rotating it to find imperfections. There was a blackened crack on the bottom. He put it aside. "What about Victor?"

My mother gave me a knowing look. "He can stay if you need him to help. If he gets dizzy, he can sit in the cockpit."

"I'll be in your way if I get sick," I added, trying not to sound hopeful.

He shrugged. "I suppose. You should be safe at a resort."

+ + +

Within an hour, we'd packed our bags. My father walked us to the ferry terminal. After hurried good-byes and promises to meet for dinner, we climbed on Le Truck. Le Truck was the Polynesian version of mass transportation—privately owned trucks converted to open-air buses. You got on using steps at the rear and sat on wooden slat seats along the sides, leaving the middle of the bus for cargo, from farm produce to furniture. Our Le Truck was painted blue and green and decorated with idyllic scenes of Moorea. It went from the Vaiare wharf to Cook's Bay. It was already packed with local people who'd finished shopping at the market, and adventure-seeking tourists who'd arrived on the ferry from Papeete.

49

Finding two vacant seats together, my mother and grandmother sat down with Jessie squashed between them, our bags piled at their feet. At the end of the row, a chubby man bounced and hummed to music blaring from the speakers. The seat next to him was unoccupied until a nun in a pristine white robe plopped into it. A gaggle of Polynesian schoolgirls squeezed past me so they could stand beside her. Ben and I clung to the overhead handrail as the bus surged into the traffic, swerving past a truck loaded with bananas.

Every house we passed had a garden, peppered with trees with glossy green leaves, most laden with tropical fruit. Scrawny chickens, orange brown with flowing black tails, pecked at the ground. On the right side of the bus was a serene, coral-reefed lagoon, often only a few steps away. On the left side was a crazy quilt of coconut palms, rainforest trees with tangled vines, and plots of spiky pineapple plants. The farms ended when the hills became steep, angled ridges, turning into jagged black pinnacles, the remnants of a vast volcano.

After a bumpy ride, the bus jerked to a stop, letting off an elderly French couple. There was room to sit down at the front of the bus; however, the next stop, a tin-roofed shed, was already in sight. Across the road was a resort hidden behind a dense thicket of hibiscus and palm trees, glimpses of a lagoon, little grass-roofed huts, and distant Mount Orohena dominating the island of Tahiti. Chubby and four noisy Germans got off. Three of the schoolgirls grabbed their seats. The nun shifted sideways and gestured for Ben and me to sit on her other side. The four still-standing schoolgirls whispered among themselves, stealing peeks at us.

"They like your sunglasses, Nature Boy," I said under my breath, squeezing against the rear of the bus to make space for him next to the nun.

Ben beamed as if I'd complimented him. "Cute, huh?"

50

"No. Just totally out of character, dude."

He pulled his sunglasses to the tip of his nose, even more ridiculous. "You do zany stuff all the time. Why can't I?"

I was thinking of a put-down when the bus stopped again, another tin-roofed shed across the road from an even bigger resort. An American family got off, the kids whining about how hot it was—'an oven' compared to their home in Columbus, Ohio.

"It's much nicer where we're staying." My grandmother's excitement was contagious.

Suddenly, a man shoved past the schoolgirls, knocking my leg with his cane. He barely got off before the bus pulled away. He glared at the rear of the bus, fanning his gray cotton suit for the tropical oven. With icy blue eyes and sunken cheeks, he looked like my old science teacher, Mr. Metwager. I got detention on my last day at school when he demanded the chemical symbol of potassium oxide. I said 'KO'. The entire class laughed, not because I left out the '2' in the middle—it sounded like I told him to 'kiss off.'

The bus took off again, protesting loudly as it began to climb a hill. Between breaks in the trees were little thatched–roof houses stretched out along a white sand beach, and bungalows on piles over water. All of a sudden, my grandmother jumped up and pressed the stop button.

"That's where we're staying! We'll have to walk back."

A minute later, the bus stopped on a bend and we quickly got off. From the side of the road, we gazed down on the resort, tropical gardens, traditional square huts, sparkling swimming pools, people sunbathing, a couple of catamarans sitting on the beach. The lagoon seemed to go on forever, its sweeping reef separating a turquoise playground from the deep-blue Pacific Ocean.

"It looks very expensive," my mother scolded.

We lived on a strict budget aboard the *Spray*. Even when we traveled inland, we stayed at cut-rate hotels and ate at the local market, or snacked in our room.

"We're in the money; we're in the money," Ben sang, skipping around like a chorus girl.

"Ben! Act your age!" she barked.

"I'm eleven, Mom."

"Then, behave like you have half a brain."

"I do. This is the creative half."

"After being cooped up in a boat all this time, I think he should let off steam." My grandmother took Jessie's hand and started to walk.

It was mostly downhill; however, we lugged bags with a three-day-supply of our best clothes, school books and games, snacks, and bottles of fruit drink. Mauve bougainvillea draped the arbor greeting us at the front of the hotel. Romantic Polynesian music wafted from discreet speakers. Fountains splashed. Out of the sun, my mother and grandmother paused to admire bright yellow hibiscus blossoms, while Jessie dawdled over goldfish in fishponds carved into the black stone floor.

Ben and I went on, eager to see the resort. The man from the bus was at the front desk when we entered the foyer. He turned to leave, staring right at us as he skirted a blue-porcelain vase festooned with lilies, orchids, and what my grandmother called Heliconia. There was something about him that made me uneasy. He disappeared behind a bamboo screen, making a staccato click as he walked.

A plump, pretty Tahitian woman manned the front desk, her head buried in a fashion magazine. Exotic frangipani flowers patterned her dress, red hibiscus flowers behind each ear. Her name tag said 'Shala.' She looked up to find my brother before her.

"Bonjour, monsieur. Puis-je vous aider? How may I assist you today?"

"We're staying here." Ben managed to keep a straight face.

Shala viewed the world with exotic dark eyes. Her hair was long and straight, glossy black against her honey-hued skin. No wonder the crew of the *Bounty* mutinied after leaving Tahiti.

"You have a reservation, oui? Perhaps the Blue Moon Villa for your honeymoon?"

It was enough to make an eleven-year-old boy blush. Instead, Ben looked perplexed.

I took over. "My grandmother said she reserved the Sunset Suite. Sarah Daniels, or maybe Walker."

"Oui. I remember. A garden villa. It was available. Unfortunately it is taken, just minutes ago." Finally, she noticed my grandmother. "I am sorry, Madam."

My grandmother deflated. "Oh. That's that! I should've paid a deposit, only I wasn't sure we'd be back."

"It's not a problem, Mom." My mother stepped up to the desk. "Do you have another villa available?"

Shala consulted the reservation book. "There are no garden villas until next month. I have a beach villa for tomorrow night only."

"There's nothing else?" my mother persisted.

"The Blue Moon Villa is open. It's paid for the week, but they haven't arrived. You could have it for the same price as the garden villa."

"We'll take it," my grandmother interrupted.

"There's only one bed, Madame."

"The boys can sleep on the floor." My grandmother took out her credit card.

Our bags went onto a trolley, pushed by an unsociable bellboy. We expected to stay in one of three dozen villas lining the beach; however, he led us to the end of a long dock, past fancy lagoon villas set on piles. We peeked into windows on the way, each villa seeming more luxurious than the last, passing scantily clad sunbathers, some darkly tanned, others disturbingly ruddy.

From outside, the Blue Moon Villa resembled a traditional Tahitian hut. It had woven reed walls and a roof thatched with yellowing palm fronds. On the inside, they'd spared no expense with vibrant Polynesian fabrics, polished native woods, and a king-sized bed with a muslin mosquito net going all the way up to the ceiling.

My grandmother popped her head into the bathroom. "We'll be spoiled after this. It's the latest in Euro-fashion."

Apparently, Euro-fashion required copious snowy marble and a Jacuzzi bathtub with glistening gold fittings. Black glass panels enclosed a shower the size of our bow cabin. The vanity was similarly vast, and the biggest mirror I'd ever seen covered the wall. While the rest of my family enthused over a bathroom smelling like a lemon orchard, I checked out the kitchenette, no more than a tiny refrigerator packed with overpriced drinks, a bar sink, a weird-looking coffee maker, and a built-in ice-maker. The microwave was big enough for one bag of popcorn. The room service menu was in French, with prices in francs, and US dollars in small print underneath. A cup of coffee cost twice what I had in my pocket. Buying school lunches for a week was less than a single croissant.

"Better tell him to bring breakfast," I said to no one in particular.

My grandmother looked over my shoulder. "Escargot! I know what I'm having for dinner." An appetizer of snails cooked in garlic and parsley butter cost $42, and bread was extra! However, the price didn't faze her. "Everyone come pick out what they want for dinner."

My brother and sister abandoned the bathroom and took over the menu, demanding translations for every item. Undaunted by French sophistication, they chose lobster—we stuffed ourselves with it whenever we were lucky enough to catch it. Homard au beurre de corail was on the menu under Les Spécialités du Chef; $84. The 'beurre de corail' was a sauce made from tomalley, the green goo inside the lobster's body, cooked in butter.

"Mom, it's really nice here, but we can't afford it." My mother hadn't put down her handbag.

"It's my treat." She looked at Jessie, then Ben, then me. "I might as well tell you now. I've decided to fly home at the end of the week."

"You can't leave," Jessie murmured.

"You only just arrived," Ben added.

I came right to the point. "Because of him?"

She shook her head. "No, Josh. It's time to go home."

"There's nothing for you to go home to. They burned your house to the ground."

"I need to get my life back together."

My mother sat on the bed, smoothing the cover where it wrinkled beside her. "Mom..." Words failed her.

"It's not safe for you to go back."

My grandmother didn't answer, yet I could tell she agreed.

"Why can't Grandma live with us?" Jessie's voice wavered.

55

"I can't." My grandmother dabbed at her eyes. "I have things I need to do at home."

"We want you to stay." Ben, without wacky sunglasses, blinked tears from his eyes.

Jessie trembled. "You have to stay."

"Grandma's only doing what she thinks is right." My mother was unhappy too.

"She's wrong! We have to stick together no matter what."

My grandmother patted my shoulder. "Oh Josh, you remind me so much of your father."

"Meaning I'm stubborn?"

"Even when you're wrong, but it's only because you have good intentions."

"There's a lot more to him than meets the eye," my mother said.

"After what he's been through…" She hugged me and kept the rest to herself. "The important thing is to have fun while we're together so we have good memories." She was trying to be cheerful.

"You sound exactly like Dad." My mother sniffled too.

My grandmother unzipped her snack bag. "I think we should have lunch. Afterwards, Josh and Ben can take me snorkeling again."

+ + +

My father arrived at six pm sharp, having walked the whole way. He said he needed the exercise. Instead of 'Les Spécialités du Chef' all-round, he insisted on a 'prix fixe' dinner. 'Prix fixe' was the nightly special, three courses with early-bird seatings for 3,000 francs ($35) per person. My grandmother called it 'tropical haute cuisine on a budget.' The tropical part was fresh island fruit and vegetables and tasty grouper caught off the reef; the 'haute' part was exotic sauces and tiny portions; and 'cuisine' because it was deliciously French.

Before dessert, I thought my grandmother had never been out of the U.S. until she visited us. She was a junior in college when she won a three-month fellowship to the Sorbonne in Paris. It was the Harvard of Europe. She met my grandfather there, a recently arrived visiting classics professor who was as lonely as she was.

"What was Grandpa like?" Jessie asked, eager to know more.

"He was a middle-aged Prince Charming, and very good looking. I'd just turned 21. I was completely infatuated," she reminisced fondly. "It was spring time, so we went to see the gardens at Versailles. It was beautiful. We identified hundreds of statues before lunch. We had Brie cheese and chardonnay at a restaurant overlooking the lake. Truly unforgettable."

"You miss him a lot," my mother said.

She smiled at my brother. "Ben always reminds me of him."

"I'm sorry, Sarah." Until then, my father had been uncharacteristically quiet. I was sure it was because of the prices on the menu. We could've purchased food for a month at the local market for the cost of one night at the hotel restaurant.

"It was his choice, John. He could've come with us," my grandmother said.

"Dad was never an adventurer like you," my mother added. "He much preferred reading."

"That explains the resemblance to Ben." I scratched my wrists. They itched when I spent too much time in the sun.

"At least I inherited something from him," Ben shot back.

"Did Grandpa have style too?" Jessie beat me to it.

For our fancy dinner, Ben had ditched his customary beach-bum attire for Madras shorts in three shades of blue and a button-down short-sleeve shirt. His silly sunglasses perched in a pocket better suited to calculators.

My grandmother stifled a laugh. "Fashion wasn't his forte. He used to say it was thoughts that maketh the man, not his clothes."

"What about the Prince Charming part?" Ben looked smug.

"After seeing Dani chase after Josh, I think he inherited that."

"Mom, really."

"Nothing wrong with chasing. I chased Thom in Paris for three months before we started to date."

"Dani didn't chase me!"

Jessie erupted in giggles. "Yes, she did."

Everyone laughed, except me. My face was hot.

"Genetically speaking, Josh has to get more than Prince Charming from him," Ben said, deep in thought.

"A love of Ancient Greece is all I can think of," my grandmother said.

"Having an interest in something is not inherited, Grandma."

"There might be a gene for it, Ben. Your great grandfather taught Greek at Yale."

My mother looked up abruptly. She swiveled around, knocking over her wine glass.

My father grabbed a handful of paper napkins and sopped up the worst of it. "What set that off?"

"I just had the oddest feeling of someone watching us." She glanced over her shoulder again.

Two tables away, a waiter took the food orders from the American family we'd seen on Le Truck. No prix fixe menu for them; the kids were demanding hamburgers and fries, their mother trying to convince them to try something more exotic, like homard. Their father, like my father, kept out of it. Spending so much money for a meal surely bothered him too.

A couple of cats sat on a ledge, watching goldfish in the pond below. Across the table, Ben went on about genetics and inheritance as if the rest of us were interested. We finished dessert within a minute of it arriving at the table—my grandmother's crème brûlée was much better, even without the tropical touch of a frangipani on the side of the plate. Afterwards, she and my parents discussed American foreign policy, my father deferring to her opinion quite often.

"Why didn't you tell us before?" Ben was hungry for information. We all were after we'd learned she had traveled extensively throughout Europe and the Mideast when she was a classics professor.

My grandmother glanced at my father. "We thought it best. At the time, it made sense."

"We had to start our lives over again after the accident." My mother always referred to the fire as an accident.

I'd grown up with lies, beginning with my falling on a kerosene heater when I was three. Now, the desire to know everything raged inside me; my brother and sister, too. We peppered our grandmother with questions. After my mother was born, she'd spent the summer on an archaeological dig in Turkey, lugging her baby around on her back. If that wasn't enough of a shock, my mother was the oldest of three sisters. One set of cousins lived in Vermont, another in Connecticut, seven in total. She didn't say she'd given up the rest of her family to stay with me, but I knew.

We talked until my father headed off to spend the night alone on the *Spray*. He was in a good mood—I wondered if he knew my grandmother was leaving at the end of the week.

Chapter 6

My father would not have been happy had he known his children went to bed at midnight after an epic game of Monopoly. We ordered breakfast from Room Service at 9.15 am, and spent the rest of the morning swimming and sunbathing instead of doing schoolwork. After spending so much on breakfast, we settled for lunchtime snacks.

With a handful of crackers, I went back to the swim platform. Through gaps in the planking, I watched fish hide from the sun. Like a ballet seen from above, they drifted in transparent water. Splashes of yellow, white, and black were butterfly fish, hundreds of them in fluttering schools weaving through lacy coral sprays. Black-striped triggerfish were even more inquisitive until bigger fish scared them away.

I dozed, my hair clinging in salty strands, sweat from my forehead beading in my brows. I realized Ben had joined me when he blocked out the sun. He stood over me, wearing recycled swim shorts, a band of faded surfboards loose around his waist. They were too small for me, and too big for him—they came all the way down to his knees.

"Mom said you have to put on sun lotion." He dropped SPF 40 lotion next to me. I left it there. "She said to do it now."

I yawned. "Go away!"

"You can get skin cancer from too much sun."

"Go sit in the shade then."

"I'm supposed to tell you if you don't put it on, you have to put on a shirt, or go inside."

I lifted my head. My mother watched from the door. She nodded once and mouthed 'now.' I flipped the cap, squirted my hand, reached behind, and slathered it over my shoulders before I mouthed 'happy?' back at her. She shook her head and turned to talk to my sister.

"She said to put it on properly or it won't count." Ben and a grade school teacher had a lot in common.

I swiped at my lower back and glared at him. "There!"

"I'll do it." He knelt next to me, dribbled long, cool ribbons over my back, and gleefully slapped his hands in it. "I'm way hairier than you are. No wonder you're so fast in the water."

"Why are you such an ass?" I growled. My greasy hands smelled like coconut.

He kneaded his knuckles down my spine, grinding vertebrae, his thumbs spreading hot, slippery lotion on the sides, until he reached my tailbone. He returned to my neck, chopping and slapping and squeezing. It felt nice, his fingers working in circles, pressing in and skidding from side to side.

"I'm done!" He squatted on his haunches. "Do the rest yourself."

The sleepy, hot sun burned my back. I stretched, exhaled, and closed my eyes. Suddenly, ocean air wafted my face, the first fresh gust of the afternoon breeze coming in. With this much wind, the *Spray* would start heeling.

"Keep massaging and I'll give you one of my keeper shells."

"Two shells and I get to pick." After I nodded, he shifted to his knees and straddled me, smearing areas he'd missed. He erupted into giggles. "I bet you wish Dani was doing this."

I ignored him. His hands followed my spine, his thumbs kneading each vertebra before he began pummeling my shoulders. Before I could say 'stop it,' Ben flopped onto me. I was too old to wrestle. In fact, I couldn't remember the last time; however, it didn't stop him from squirming on top of me. He pummeled my back and dug his fingers into my sides. I skewed my head to tell him to stop. The sun was in my eyes. I elbowed his flank and he sucked in air as if he was going to scream. Instead, he made an awful gagging noise.

"Act your age!" I tossed him off.

He scrunched up his face, clenching his jaws and his eyes. I thought it was a game until I saw the blood. Bright red splatters covered both of us, from our waists to our knees. It came from a hole in his shorts, spurting out in gushes.

Page 62 of *A Practical Guide to Lifeboat Survival* described what to do for serious bleeding. I rammed my fist into Ben's thigh and screamed, 'Help,' again and again. My mother came running, my grandmother and sister close behind her. I heard her gasp before she shoved me aside and replaced my knuckles with hers, jammed next to his groin. She tugged up the leg of Ben's shorts.

"Frigging hell!" Blood oozed through her fingers.

No one else spoke. Jessie hung back, peeking over my grandmother's shoulder, her eyes wide. My mother forced her fist into the blood.

"Still too fast... Three minutes, maybe less..." She looked up. "Josh, get the hell out of here!" With her free hand, she unknotted the cord at the front of his shorts. "Lift him up, Mom." She took away her fist.

Immediately, blood spewed out of Ben's thigh. She dragged his shorts to his knees and poked her finger into the hole before his back hit the deck. The bleeding slowed to a trickle. I didn't think my brother had so much blood inside him. It was all over the sun deck. He gagged and started to shake.

"I'll get help!"

"Josh, for God's sake, just go!" she screamed.

I bounded up the steps. The handrail popped beside me, showering me with splinters of dark-oiled wood.

"Get inside! Stay out of sight!"

I backed away and ran into our hut.

"Phone the front desk. Tell them shark bite," she shouted after me.

The overhead fans circled leisurely, wafting the curtains. Our Monopoly game was still set out on the table, along with the breakfast scraps waiting for Room Service to clean up. The telephone buzzed five times before Shala answered. I told her to call an ambulance and stumbled through a sham shark attack.

I'd wiped off the blood before she bustled along the walkway, carrying a little red first aid kit. From the door, I watched her go down the stairs, warily looking about for a shark, gripping the rail as if it would leap from the water. She knelt a safe distance from my trembling brother. Other hotel guests gathered like moths around a lamp.

"Stingray do this. No shark." Shala kept shaking her head, staying away from the blood.

"Did you call an ambulance?" My mother checked Ben's pulse with her free hand.

Shala muttered something and stared at Ben's thigh.

My mother ripped open the first aid kit, scattering plastic sachets of sanitized wipes and latex gloves. "Aspirin! Antiseptic cream! Insect repellant. Sunburn ointment! Jesus!"

"He'll have to go to Papeete." Shala clambered to her feet. "I'll phone Vaiare to hold the fast ferry."

My mother gave up on the first aid kit. "You call it in!"

"Mommy, is he going to be okay?" Jessie buried her face in her hands. Ben was shaking.

"I think so…" She salvaged the gloves from the side of the landing. "I have to get the bleeding to stop."

With her free hand and teeth, she ripped open the sachet and withdrew a glove. I thought she was going to put it on. Instead, she poked it into the hole where her finger had been. She yanked the cord from Ben's swim shorts and looped it twice around his thigh with the aspirin bottle underneath. She tightened the cord, jamming the bottle into the wound. Ben screamed.

"Bring some ice, Shala. Lots of it. As much as you can find. In plastic bags. Hurry"

Shala walked a little faster. I wanted to shout 'Now, not tomorrow!' Instead, I emptied the ice from the ice-maker into the trash can, tied off the bag, and called my sister from the doorway.

"Josh, stay inside for God's sake!" My mother almost never got flustered. "Phone the marina and leave a message for the *Spray*. Say there's been an accident, nothing more. We'll meet him at the fast ferry terminal."

Five minutes passed without sight or sound of an ambulance. My mother decided not to wait. We rode to the ferry terminal in the hotel taxi, my sister and me in the front, my mother and grandmother in the back with Ben. He was unconscious. In the middle of a Norfolk winter, he was never so pale.

Chapter 7

My mother stayed with the gurney, disappearing behind a 'staff only' door after pushing past an orderly who dared to get in her way. She was gone for 42 minutes by the clock on the waiting room wall. When I saw her again, she looked like a nurse with a green smock instead of her blouse and shorts.

"The artery is sealed off for now." She sagged against the wall.

"Is he going to be okay?" Jessie had asked her the same question nonstop during the ferry trip, and received the same answer, 'I think so.'

"He's asleep, Honey." Dark smears covered her front. A bandage wrapped her arm near the elbow. "Mom, I'd like something to drink. Take Jessie with you. She knows what I like."

My father waited until they were out of sight. "How's he doing?"

"He's still unconscious. The doctor seems to know what he's doing." My father started to say something about Zagarovsky. She stopped him. "Not now."

She cast her gaze over a threadbare couch, battered plastic seats, paper drinking cups lined up on the window sill, a sad potted plant in the corner. There were fly spots on the ceiling; wallpaper peeled from the walls; the air-conditioning unit rattled whenever it started up. The vinyl tile floor was squeaky clean—it gleamed like a school hallway on Monday.

"Ben needs blood. I gave him two pints." She whispered in my father's ear. I heard 'he nearly bled out.'

He murmured something back. "Where do I go?"

"As soon as they've got him set up in the operating theater, someone will come to get you and Mom."

"What about me?" They could take every drop and I wouldn't care.

"You can't." She blinked and rubbed at her eyes.

"Why?"

Her gaze shifted to my father. After a moment, he said, "You're too young."

"I'm 14. I'm nearly as tall as you." I stood tall, as if it made a difference.

"You have the wrong blood type," she said.

"I'm his brother."

"Josh, I know you want to help, but you can't. Ben's type A. So is Grandma. You have to be the same, or type O like him." She nodded at my father.

"What am I?"

"Tell him, John."

My father stepped close enough to rest his hand on my shoulder. "All you need to know right now is..." He stopped when a nurse came to the doorway.

"This is crap!" I shrugged off his hand and glared at him.

"Get over it."

He followed the nurse, his hands clenched by his sides. The door closed behind him. My mother sighed deeply.

"How bad is it?"

"The doctor thinks Ben will lose his leg."

The 'f'-word caught in my throat. "You said once they got the bullet out..."

"It severed the artery, Josh. He still has some feeling, but cells begin to die when they don't have blood. That's why I packed ice around his leg. The doctor I worked with at Norfolk General swore by ice packs," she said. She took my hand. She had dried blood around her fingernails. "It's been one and a half hours. Maybe too long. We'll know if it worked by this evening."

I went over to the window. It was closed to keep out the grime and noise from the street below. Far in the distance, Moorea's ragged peaks impaled a mantle of woolly clouds. It looked like a postcard in the Papeete market.

"You've always been lucky," she said from behind me. "Maybe it'll include Ben this time."

+ + +

When Ben was four, we camped for a week at Spruce Knob Lake in the Monongahela National Forest in West Virginia, a dozen miles from the nearest town. The hospital had the same pungent pine smell. It was worse in the toilets across the hall.

My father was gone long enough for me to skim February's *Tahiti Pacifique* magazine four times. I was tired of looking at pictures and words I didn't understand, unable to turn more than a few dog-eared pages before I had to look at the clock again. It seemed later than 2:45 pm. when he joined us.

"Any word on Ben?" His voice wavered.

"They repaired the artery. Nothing more until he wakes up." She was pale as vampire's prey. He wasn't much better.

"A policeman interviewed me while I was giving blood. The inspector will be here at three o'clock."

"We need to stay calm." She nodded at my grandmother. Her grim face worried me more than my parents. She hurried to the door whenever she heard footsteps in the corridor. This time, it was an orderly pushing a cart.

My father sat next to me. He had tape and a gauze pad just below his shirt sleeve. "He's going to be okay."

"He was looking for shells this time yesterday."

He smiled weakly. "Nature Boy find any keepers?"

For over an hour, Ben waded waist-deep in Moorea's lagoon, his goggles like bug eyes, looking for Cypraea. He kept only perfect examples.

"A couple of cowries. I still have his sunglasses in my swim shorts. He wouldn't want to lose them." I passed them to my father.

He examined Tahitian Lories with a shaky hand. "You think he'll want to be a doctor after this?"

"He'll probably start studying Mom's medical book."

He rubbed his forehead, no sign of a smile. Finally, he shook his head. "There are cobwebs on the frigging window."

"It's not Norfolk General," my mother said evenly. "Waiting rooms are always awful."

Outside the door, a nurse talked with a man who was trying to find a patient. She told him he was on the wrong floor and insisted he leave. He was almost rude to her.

"The inspector will be here any time now," my father said to me, yet watching my sister. She'd finally stopped crying. Now, she stared at the pink-flowered wallpaper, her arms folded across her chest.

"You going to tell him about Zagarovsky?" I asked, my voice low.

69

"No, and neither will you." He licked his lips, dry and cracked since we'd exhausted our supply of lip balm. "As far as we know, it was an accident. Got it?"

I nodded.

+ + +

The inspector's suit belonged in Paris, not Papeete. His moustache was comic, like Chief Inspector Clouseau's, thick and angled down, emphasizing his very straight nose. He studied us between glances at a sheaf of pages. Finally, he shook his head with a flourish and handed the file to the policeman behind him.

"Who would shoot a little boy? A psychopath? A terrorist?" He turned back, clapped his hands and rubbed them together. "Inspector Moreau, Gendarmerie Nationale. You are the family?"

My father stalked over. "We were told you'd be here at three." It was 4:15 pm.

The inspector looked him up and down, stuck out his lower lip, and arched his eyebrows. "Bof," he said, with a hunch of his shoulder.

My father's mouth twisted in frustration. "My son almost died today."

He turned again. "Docteur," he called through the open door.

The doctor motioned to join him in the corridor. We watched them talk while the inspector scrutinized each of us, even my sister.

"Moreau's a moron," my father said under his breath.

"Let it go, John," my mother said just as quietly. My father shrugged.

After four minutes, the inspector strode into the waiting room. "The Docteur removed this from your son's leg."

70

He opened his hand to reveal a gray pellet. It was smaller than I expected, about the size of a bean.

"An accident is unlikely." He looked around the waiting room again, my mother and father, my grandmother, my sister. He stopped on me.

"You Americans bring your drug problems with you."

My father stepped forward. "This has nothing to do with drugs."

"Tell me, Monsieur, do you know Salvadore Saccoccia?"

"We've met a lot of people on our travels."

He raised an eyebrow. "Monsieur Ames said you were in the Marquesas recently."

"I don't know anyone named Ames, but yes; we left last week."

"He said you met this Saccoccia there. Most people call him Sal, I believe."

"We met him in the Caribbean," my mother interrupted.

"Ah! And did you meet him again in the Marquesas?"

"I don't understand how Sal's involved?"

The inspector turned on his heel. "Neither do I, Madam." Again, he extended his hand, his thumb trapping the little bullet in his palm. "A bullet like this is very unusual. 5.45 mm caliber. High velocity rifles use them."

"It would've gone through his thigh."

He stared at my mother. "You are an expert in ballistics, Madam?"

"I used to be an emergency room nurse. I've seen a lot of gunshot victims over the years." My mother sounded tired.

"Ah, my next question is answered. The docteur says you are brilliant; to use a glove as a plug, and the ice. By any chance, did you hear a gunshot? A sound like a car backfiring?"

My mother stared back. "No."

He nodded, frowning and pulling at his earlobe. "It is strange no one heard a gunshot."

"It might have been fired from one of the beach villas."

Inspector Moreau turned to my father. "I think not, Monsieur. You cannot see the swim platform from the beach. I think it came from the hill. Five hundred meters would account for your son's injury. A lucky shot, or a good shot, that is the question?"

"Or an accident?"

"An accident with a silencer; I think not. Monsieur Ames said you were at Nuku Hiva on the 21st."

"We left on the 25th," my father said after a few moments.

"A motor boat departed from Nuku Hiva on the 21st. It has disappeared."

"I don't see what that's got to do with my son being shot."

"A coincidence, perhaps. And Saccoccia, was he with you on the 21st?"

"I don't remember."

Inspector Moreau looked amused. "This Saccoccia, he is American mafia. Monsieur Ames says he is a very dangerous man."

"I wouldn't know. Sal's always been ready to lend a hand."

"Perhaps one of his drug deals went bad?"

"It doesn't explain why someone would shoot my son."

Inspector Moreau clucked and beckoned to me. I didn't move. "Your name is?"

"Josh… Victor Joshua Walker. I go by Josh." He seemed not to hear until I added, "Sir."

He gave another Gallic shrug. "You were beside your brother when he was shot. It must have been very upsetting. What did you do?"

"I called for help."

With a glance, he made me feel like a liar.

"I phoned the reception desk from our villa."

He looked down his nose before he held out his hand. It was a different bullet, same size, squashed with a silver scrape on the side. His eyes bored into me. "I dug this out of the handrail."

"What handrail?" I rubbed my thumb against my finger. The splinter was a bump with a needle point. I stopped when I realized he was watching.

"The one at the top of the stairs. I think this bullet was fired at you, hmm?"

"I wouldn't know, Sir."

He turned to my father. "I'd be worried if they were my sons, Monsieur. The bullets are Russian military issue. For sniper rifles."

"This is ridiculous. They haven't done anything wrong."

"The missing boat, Monsieur; its name is *Orel*. Did you see it at Nuku Hiva?"

My father twitched. "I saw lots of boats at Nuku Hiva."

My heart thumped when I saw him, the same man who'd checked into the resort at Moorea. He walked by the doorway, not stopping, yet his head twitched sideways. My father saw him too. He could've been an off-duty doctor in his gray casual suit. He went down the corridor, swinging a walking stick. My mother was right—it was for effect.

73

"Monsieur Ames said *Orel* looks like a small fishing trawler."

My father hesitated. He crossed to the window. "Our son might lose his leg and you want to talk about a damned fishing boat."

It was cruel how he said it. Far worse, it was loud enough that Jessie heard him. She murmured 'no', defiantly shaking her head. My grandmother tried to comfort her. She squirmed away. She burst into tears as my mother scooped her up and hugged her tightly. She started to cough, her usual run-up to puking. The inspector gave an understanding nod and stepped back. He took the file from the policeman, and flicked through the pages. My father stared down into the street, one hand jangling his key fob.

"Jessie needs a drink," he said suddenly.

The last thing Jessie needed was a drink. He jerked his head sideways before he stepped back from the window. He crossed the room, still jangling his keys. He looked through the doorway and down the corridor before gesturing me over. I thought he was going to hand me the keys. Instead, they went in his pocket. He pulled out his wallet and gave me a blue and orange 5,000 French Polynesian franc note.

"Get her one of those fruit drinks, the same as you bought at Vaiare."

"Tahiti is expensive. Not that expensive," Moreau said.

My father stuffed the money into his wallet and pulled out a 1000 franc note. "Is this too much?"

Moreau dismissed sarcasm with a shrug. "It's enough for a drink at our best restaurant."

When my father gave it to me, he also pressed the key to the *Spray's* cabin into my hand. "Use your best judgment," he said.

I crumpled the note in my fist and started towards the door.

Moreau moved quickly to block my exit. "Don't leave the hospital."

I looked him in the chest. "Yes, Sir." I side-stepped and kept walking.

Behind me, the inspector said something in French to the policeman. The corridor was empty. I headed towards the stairs as someone came out of the toilets.

Moreau called out, "Monsieur Ames?"

The back of my neck prickled; however, I didn't look back. I could hear them talking about *Orel* behind me. I wanted to run. I walked to the stairs, not too fast, not too slow. Out of sight, I took the stairs three at a time, pirouetting on the landings, crashing into the railing when I side-stepped a janitor lugging a bucket and mop up the last flight of stairs. At the bottom, I pivoted on a carved pineapple newel post. Behind me, the policeman cursed the janitor when he didn't get out of his way. Two floors higher, the man with the walking stick glared at me over the railing.

Chapter 8

A gendarme in a blue shirt with oversized epaulettes on his shoulders and a shiny black holster on his hip guarded the hospital entrance. He moved to block the front door. I darted around him, into the Rue du Général de Gaulle and the afternoon exodus.

Papeete squeezed onto a narrow strip of land between a volcanic mountain and the lagoon. Trucks and buses choked the streets, made intolerable by hordes of little French cars like squabbling roosters, pushing in when the slightest gap opened. I stepped off the curb, staring down a taxi driver before I dashed across the road, only just evading a motorcycle. When I reached the sidewalk on the other side, I glanced back. The policeman was pinned in the middle of the street, unable to move as vehicles swerved around him.

"Hey kid, is there a shop near here that sells black pearls?" A thin, red-faced man obstructed my way. "Good but cheap."

A woman stepped between us. She was as pale under her orange sun-hat as he was sunburned. "For heaven's sake, Gordy. Don't pester the boy. He's probably staying at our resort."

"Look at his tan. If anyone knows this joint, he ought to."

"Arrêtez ce garçon," the policeman shouted.

On the other side of the street, Ames brandished his walking stick and shouted too; however, honking horns drowned him out.

I snapped, "Try the market," and stepped into the street to get past them.

The man grabbed my arm and yanked me out of the way as a Le Truck roared past, missing me by inches. It stopped a dozen yards down the road.

"Heaven's sake, boy, didn't your parents tell you to look both ways."

I jerked free and backed away from him.

The policeman stuck out his hand to arrest an onrushing truck. It squealed to a halt. Across the street, Ames strode down the sidewalk, swinging his stick. People got out of his way. I bolted down the sidewalk, dodging another group of tourists who'd wandered from the center of town. Someone grabbed my shirt. I twisted away, slamming into the side of Le Truck. It was camouflaged, painted lime green with dark green palm fronds. Two grinning Tahitian kids hung out the windows, their teeth white like their shirts. Suddenly, the bus pulled away from the sidewalk, into the rush of vehicles. A few yards away, the policeman was breathing hard. He seemed as surprised to see me as I was to see him. I ran after the bus.

The Tahitian kids spurred me on. I leaped for the rear stairs and grabbed the door frame. I almost fell down before I hauled myself onboard. Feeling smug, I waved to the policeman and flopped into the nearest vacant seat.

People stared at me: an elderly Tahitian man, women with bulging plastic bags from Carrefour, the big supermarket on the outskirts of town, a mom and dad and three boys, all with clothes out of *Vogue* magazine. No wonder they stared; blood trickled down my leg; I didn't have shoes; there were dark streaks on my shorts, and I'd ripped the front of my T-shirt.

The Tahitian kids, a boy and girl both about Jessie's age, jabbered at me in Tahitian and French before the girl said, "You American?"

Someone tapped my shoulder. The bus conductor had his hand out. He snapped his fingers impatiently.

"How much?" I searched my pockets for my father's money.

"Where you go to?" he demanded.

"Where do you go?" I wasn't trying to be funny.

"Taravao, two hundred francs."

I had no idea where Taravao was. I planned to stay on the bus until it was safe to get off. I handed over my 1,000 franc bill.

"Any stops?" With three brassy coins and a grubby 500 franc note in my fist, I hoped for a refund.

The conductor was on his way back to the front of the bus; however, the boy rattled off, "Punaauia, Paea, Papao, Papara, and Papeari," rolling his tongue around vowels like a word game.

"Where's Port Phaeton Bay?"

"Taravao."

Diesel fumes poured through windows. It made me nauseous until the bus picked up speed on the only freeway in Tahiti. It ended at Punaauia. The road narrowed, a boring strip of houses, garden plots, work sheds, and shops until Papeete's suburbs ended. Between villages, we passed dozens of creeks, one in each of the tortured gorges reaching up to the summits of Mt. Orohena and Mt Aorai. By Paea, where the Tahitian kids got off, boiling gray clouds hid the mountains, wisps coiling among tree-covered ridges.

Everyone got off at Taravao, a busy little town stretched across the narrow isthmus joining Tahiti-iti, the little island, to the big island, Tahiti Nui. Rain arrived in a thundering deluge. I sheltered under the post office awning, drenched and thirsty—I couldn't risk spending his money.

The downpour ended as abruptly as it started. I trekked down a long straight road, splashing through deep puddles to reach Port Phaeton Bay.

Port Phaeton Bay was peaceful, with glassy water mirroring patches of blue as the clouds disintegrated. Steamy hills surrounded the bay, covered with so many trees it was difficult to see any houses. Except for a few anchored boats, it might have been deserted.

I easily recognized Sal's *Maid Marion*, a ketch with a green stripe at the waterline. It was twice the length of the *Spray,* far bigger than most sailors could afford. No one was on deck, and no dinghy floated off the stern, which suggested no one was aboard. It was too far to shout. I sat on the trunk of a fallen coconut tree, watching land-crabs scuttling about. The sun reappeared, casting long shadows over the bay. With sunset fast approaching, I had to do something. I waded into the water. When it reached my hips, I started to swim.

Sal spared no expense in outfitting the *Maid Marion.* Metal gleamed, teak trim glowed with a golden luster, every line carefully coiled. The deck was silky smooth under my feet. There were winches, blocks, or cleats wherever I looked. The coach-house had windows all around, while the wood inside was varnished as bright as a grand piano. The mainmast towered overhead, so much taller than the *Spray*'s mainmast that the thought of climbing it made me glad I wasn't one of the crew.

"You're supposed to be on your way to Samoa, Sharkbait, not trying to pirate my ship." Sal's voice was like a wood-carver's rasp grating against wood.

I hadn't heard him come up the stairs. Water dripped from my shorts and shirt, making puddles on his sun-bleached deck.

He beamed back at me. "I don't know who'll be more pleased to see you, me or Dani, though if I had to guess..."

"Someone shot Ben."

His smile vanished. He sat down heavily. "Is he okay?"

"He lost a lot of blood."

He gestured for me to sit in the shade of the coach house, across from him. "He's okay though?"

I nodded, unable to say he might lose his leg.

"When?"

"A few hours ago. We were staying at a resort on Moorea while Dad worked on the *Spray*. Ben and I were messing around on the sundeck."

Sal's eyes narrowed. "A man with a cane, did you see him at the resort?"

"When we checked in."

He almost smiled. "I knew Faro would be here."

"The police inspector said his name was Ames."

"He'll be someone else tomorrow. He works for Zagarovsky."

"The policeman said the bullets came from a Russian sniper rifle."

"Definitely Faro." Sal let out a sigh, his eyes focused behind me. "You're lucky to be alive. What I don't understand is why he shot Ben?"

"He was leaning over me."

"Shouldn't matter. Faro doesn't miss. "

I told him what happened, about our near collision and diverting to Papeete, about my father deciding to repair the engine himself, what happened at the resort, the hospital, my escape on the bus.

Sal scanned the beach with binoculars. "One thing's certain; he didn't follow you here."

"How can you be sure?"

"You're still alive. Faro was a sniper in Afghanistan before they kicked out the Russians," he said, back to eyeing the shoreline. "There must have been wind right as he fired."

"There was a gust just before."

"When Virginia says you're lucky, she doesn't know the half of it. You'd better get below, just in case. They'll be back from the Gauguin Museum soon."

Chapter 9

Curved stairs, ornately carved from creamy curly-maple, olive leather lounge seats, a dining table with a decorative compass rose in different wood species, thick Persian rugs on a floor so polished I saw my reflection —the *Maid Marion* was more like a luxury cruise ship than an ocean-going yacht. While Sal scavenged for snacks in the galley, I looked at sepia photos of a yacht race from a bygone era, grand schooners with vast canvas sails, men hauling lines through big wooden blocks.

"You can change out of those wet clothes in my cabin. I'll find a robe to fit you," Sal said.

For five days at Nuku Hiva, I'd spent every afternoon on the *Maid Marion*; however, I hadn't explored beyond the vast air-conditioned salon. I wandered past the chart table, panels packed with navigation and radio equipment, and shelves of maritime books. Sal's boat was so wide there were cabins on either side, along with stacks of lockers and drawers—no shortage of storage space on Sal's yacht. His cabin was in the stern. It was bigger than our main cabin; his bed larger than the entire forward cabin I used to share with Ben.

A portrait beside the bed stole my attention. His children were dressed in white, a little boy who seemed very serious, and a college-aged girl with a smile that said it was going to be a good day. She had an uncanny likeness to Dani, the same coiling brown hair, sparsely freckled nose, and deep dark eyes.

"Dante and Donatella," Sal said from behind me.

"She's Dani's mom, right? She's beautiful."

He nodded. "Mom and daughter are nearly identical."

"Same with Jessie. Ben looks like her too."

Sal looked at me oddly. "You don't."

"I'm not like Dad either. Ben says I got mixed up with another baby in the hospital."

"You never know." Sal chuckled at his joke. "Dante was seven when the painting was done. If he looks scared it's because I threatened to whack him to make him sit still."

"Did you?"

"No!" he chuckled. "There were times I should have. I spoiled him rotten instead." He opened a louvered door and took out a robe with 'Maid Marion' embroidered on the breast.

+++

Sal and I were playing five-card stud in the salon when Marion and Dani returned with the rest of Sal's crew. Dani beamed when she saw me. Her smile vanished after Sal told them what happened.

"John did the right thing by getting him out of the hospital," he finished.

Marion gave me a hug. "He'll be safe here, won't he?"

"If he doesn't go on deck." Tony was blunt at the best of times.

"Faro's that good?" Rick said.

Rick was Tony's younger brother. Between them, they took care of the boat and guarded Sal.

"The best." Tony hesitated. "His specialty is head shots at 500 yards."

No one spoke. I was lucky, no doubt about it.

"The police know it has to do with what happened in the Marquesas," Sal said.

"We need to hide him before the cops come looking, Sal."

Sal turned to me. "Tony's right. They'll be here tomorrow; you can bet on it. The *Spray*; is she ready to go, Josh?"

"The engine's in pieces."

Sal nodded at Rick. "Good job for you. Take the dinghy across to Moorea tonight. You've got till tomorrow evening."

"No problem if I've got all the parts."

"Josh goes with you."

"Faro will have someone watching the *Spray*," Tony said.

"I'm counting on it. It's the last place they'll expect. Have a look around before you sneak him onboard. Any trouble, get him out of there fast," Sal said to Rick. "Tony, find out where Zagarovsky's holed up." He turned to his wife. "First thing tomorrow morning, I need you to go to the hospital to tell them Josh's safe. Also, I have to know when Ben will be okay to travel." Then, he turned to Dani and me "Why don't you see if your clothes are dry?"

+++

Sal had put my swim shorts and shirt in the clothes dryer. Dani checked them while I sat in the cockpit, doing my best to stay out of sight. My shorts were still damp so I remained in the robe while Dani and I watched the shadows on Mount Ronui grow longer, painting Tahiti-iti's valleys with concentrated colors before turning black.

"Ben will be alright, won't he?" Dani asked after a while.

My throat was dry. I nodded.

"I thought I'd never see you again."

"When I first met Sal, he said you always run into people you know when you least expect it. I didn't believe him, but it turned out to be true."

Her eyes darted away when I looked at her. "Nonno told me the same thing after you left Nuku Hiva. I thought he was just saying it so I wouldn't be sad."

She was so close our knees touched. Neither of us moved. Her eyes were dark, intense yet spellbinding, like the girl in the portrait.

+ + +

It took a catamaran ferry 30 minutes to go from Papeete to Moorea in good weather. It was farther from Port Phaeton Bay, five long, cold hours to go 37 miles. I huddled in the bottom of Sal's big inflatable dinghy, wind-driven spray whipping my face as we bucked up and down. Rick hunched low in the pilot's seat, peering into the gloom, trying to avoid the largest waves. For the first time in three months, my stomach grew restless. I was glad we'd left before dinner. Throwing up Marion's ham and cheese sandwich was never farther away than the next wave. I passed the time by staring at Moorea's jagged outline, spreading out to gather pinpricks of light like feeding fireflies.

It was after midnight when a few yacht masts rose through the yellow glow around the Vaiare ferry terminal. Soon, we passed through the reef and puttered towards the beach where I'd swum with Ben on our first morning in Vaiare, three days earlier.

"SEALs couldn't do it better." Rick grinned, yet I could tell he was worried.

"You think they're watching our boat?" I asked.

He rubbed salt from his eyes. "It's likely. You're waiting here. I'll flash your masthead light if it's safe."

85

He hopped over the side. He turned the dinghy around and pushed it into deeper water before he waded into darkness. I stared at the masts in the marina and waited. I woke up shivering, wavelets slapping the side of the dinghy, rocking it up and down. Every cycle, the outboard scraped loudly. The dinghy had drifted over the reef. I rowed back into the lagoon. I was halfway to the beach when a light flickered among the masts, six times before it stopped. I started the motor with a push of a button and proceeded into the harbor.

Rick hauled me over the *Spray's* bow. "I figured you fell asleep."

I gave a sheepish nod. "Anyone waiting?"

"It didn't go quite as Sal planned. One was in your cockpit, listening to his iPod. I found his friend snoozing in the storage shed. Local hoods. More tattoos than brains."

"Did you..."

"Only in Hollywood and parts of Chicago," he chuckled. "If your dad asks what happened to his duct tape, it's in the shed. Marvelous stuff, duct tape. All kinds of uses."

I followed Rick down the stairs. The *Spray* was just as we'd left her except fewer bits of my father's engine cluttered the cabin, and our cat looked thinner than ever.

"Your dad got most of it back together," Rick said. "The good news is I ought to be done by morning. Get some sleep."

+++

It was just before dawn when Rick woke me. Grease covered his hands and arms.

"I just radioed Sal. He wants you out of Vaiare."

"How's the motor?"

86

"Good as when it came out of the crate." He looked so pleased with himself I wasn't about to tell him my father recycled it from a 1985 Ford tractor.

Vaiare's scattered lights disappeared one by one as we hoisted *Squirt* onto the foredeck. Then, Rick tried to start the engine.

"Takes a while for fuel to get through."

He pushed the button again. The motor whirred without firing up, just as it had done when my father first launched his boat. He cranked the motor six times before it came back to life, coughing unevenly.

"Take your time, baby," he coaxed. "Like taking your first steps, always a few stumbles."

Two yachts away, a man poked his grizzled head out of a companionway. Bare arms dragged a towel from the boom. He wrapped it around his waist before he climbed into his cockpit, standing among plastic buckets, tomato plants, and rust-stained sail bags. Bruce McKenzie was the last person I expected to see.

"Keep it down, mate. People are trying to bloody sleep."

"Sober up more like," Rick called back. He adjusted the throttle, the engine settling down to reassuring gurgling throb.

Bruce saw me and rubbed his eyes to be sure. "Yo! Where are you off to, mate?"

Bruce had a habit of popping up unexpectedly. The last time I'd seen him was at Hiva Oa, when we first arrived in the Marquesas Islands. Our problems got worse after that.

I jumped to the dock. "My brother's in the hospital in Papeete."

He looked so stunned he might've been hit on the head by his boom. He asked why.

"He had an accident."

He asked what happened; however, I had more important things to do than talk to him. I unfastened the dock lines, climbed aboard, and the *Spray* pulled away from the dock.

Instead of heading back to Tahiti, Rick turned to port, staying close to the reef. I kept a nervous eye on the depth sounder as we reentered the reef at Pointe Aroa, a narrow entrance to the lagoon, just a few yards between waves churning over coral heads. I pointed out the resort where we'd stayed.

"Where are we going?" I said, wondering if our stuff was still in the Blue Moon Villa.

"You're going to Opunohu Bay. Find somewhere safe to anchor. I'm going back to Vaiare. Faro will know something's wrong when his men don't report in. Guaranteed he'll be on the morning ferry."

It didn't sound like a plan Sal would approve of. I was about to say so when Rick moved away for me to take the wheel. "What if something happens?"

"Stay out of sight." He untied Sal's dinghy, hauled it close to the *Spray*, and climbed down. "Listen to your SSB radio, Pacific Net. It'll be *Maiden* calling for *Squirt*. If you don't hear from Sal before midnight, he said head for Huahine."

"Huahine?" Huahine was 90 miles northwest.

"You can do it, Josh," Rick said. "Sal can tell spaghetti from spaghettini."

+ + +

Opunohu Bay was beautiful with jagged pinnacles enclosing a deep lagoon and pristine sandy beaches lined with coconut palms. There were a dozen yachts docked at a marina, clusters of two or three boats anchored near the beaches, and a couple of loners scattered in remote parts of the harbor. I anchored in a small, deserted cove. A few minutes after 10:00 am, I went below, hungry and worried. After eating half a stale croissant, and feeding the rest to Jag, I cleaned the *Spray* from bow to stern. Hour after hour, I scoured and polished, removing every trace of grease and grunge, listening to sailors chatting on the radio. There was nothing from Sal or my father.

I was thinking about an early dinner, vaguely tuned into a discussion about equatorial weather patterns when a British-accented voice said, "They just pulled a body out of the lagoon opposite the Vaiare marina. The cops aren't saying anything except he's American."

"A sailor?" Her name was Marta, from *Sea Horse*. She'd been a regular contributor on the radio since I turned it on, no different to the busy bodies at Acadia Park.

"All I know is someone shot him in the head."

"I wonder if it's got something to do with the *Spray* boy." Marta asked.

"How's he doing?" someone else asked.

"I heard he was in pretty bad shape yesterday," came a voice from the ether.

"His name is Ben and he's doing okay," Bruce interrupted. He hadn't spoken until then. "The hospital's like a bloody prison. No visitors allowed, but a nurse told me he's awake and talking. I took the ferry over to see him after they moved the *Spray* to Papeete this morning."

"Not bloody likely," another Australian voice interrupted. "I'm looking right at her, mate. Old-fashioned ketch with *Spray* on the stern. She's moored at Opunohu Bay, up the beach from me."

"Gaff rigged right?" Bruce asked.

"Yep. A teenage boy brought her in by himself a couple of hours ago."

"No one else onboard?"

"Dunno. I only saw him, mate."

"Keep an eye on it, will you? I'll be on the first bus tomorrow."

My father didn't trust Bruce—not enough money and too many coincidences. Also, he'd told everyone within range where I was. No matter what Sal said about waiting until midnight, my father would leave as soon as it was dark. I unrolled his chart for the Society Islands. The course from Moorea to Huahine was out of the shipping channels with no reefs to get in the way. With considerable relief, I switched the radio to check the weather report, just as I'd seen my father do every day since we left Portsmouth, Virginia. My confidence grew when I heard there were no cold fronts, low pressure zones, or storms expected in the Central Pacific. With a fair breeze, I'd be in Huahine by mid-afternoon. The worst part would be staying awake during the night.

I cooked dinner; macaroni and cheese with chopped up tuna fish out of the can, and washed it down with one of my father's beers. For the next four hours, I read and listened for a radio call from *Maiden*.

Chapter 10

With a sliver of moon and few lights on the shore, Opunohu Bay was surreal, fantastic peaks chiseled against a star-studded sky. I donned my life jacket and safety harness, started the engine, and motored slowly while the electric windlass hauled in the anchor. Every clunk of the chain bounced back at me until the anchor pulled free of the bottom. I skirted the masthead lights of shadowy yachts and turned towards the sea. With my heart thumping, I constantly checked the chart plotter and depth sounder until I passed through the reef. A safe mile farther, I headed into the wind, raised the mainsail and unfurled one of the jibs, and engaged the self-steering. Only then, I turned off the engine, immediately missing its reassuring chug.

After a lonely hour on a menacing black sea, I went below to find some music, not my Guns and Roses, my father's Borodin. When his *Polovtsian Dances* started, I succumbed to wagging my finger. *Prince Igor* was still playing when I woke up. Choppy waves slapped the bow as the *Spray* surged through the long ocean swell, a loose halyard clanging against the mast. I settled into the lee side of the cockpit, drawing my jacket over me. Not even ten miles and I was already exhausted. It was going to be a long trip. At 11:00 pm, I got a handful of cookies and struggled to stay awake while I ate them.

I woke up again when spray splashed my face. I yawned and wiped salt from my eyes. It was 12:25 am. I hurried below and switched on the radio.

"*Squirt* calling *Maiden*." You were supposed to use proper call signs on the SSB radio. Ours was on a card taped next to the microphone. I might as well broadcast my real name.

"*Maiden* here." It was Sal's voice. "You okay?" He sounded relieved.

"I'm fine. How's Einstein?"

"He's still got all his parts. You're on the go?"

"Eighteen in the bag." I had 72 miles to go.

"Keep your transmissions short. Next call is eight sharp unless there's a problem. *Maiden* out."

I wanted to talk; however, I switched off the radio. I yawned, pulled the blanket from my berth, and went to keep watch.

+ + +

A flying fish woke me up when it crash-landed in the cockpit. It didn't happen very often. Usually, flying fish whacked the side of the cabin and we found them dead on the deck. It bounced about until I skewered it with a knife. Twelve inches long, black and silver, with oversized fins like shiny wings. I scaled it, sliced out its guts, and went below to fry breakfast.

I switched on the SSB radio at 7:50 am. Exactly ten minutes later, Sal said, "*Maiden* calling *Squirt*."

"*Squirt* here. Everything's cool. How about you guys?"

"We're good. Einstein said hi. I'll call you at noon. Out!"

I fed Jag leftover flying fish and cleaned his litter box before I returned to the cockpit to look for other vessels, just a fleck of a sail on the horizon. I checked the *Spray's* position, well past the halfway point, though three miles farther north than I'd planned. I put it down to current, corrected the course, and dozed for a while. By midday, when Sal radioed again to tell me 'Einstein' was eating bread pudding, the hazy outline of Huahine was on the horizon. Cloud halos identified other Leeward Islands: Raiātea, Tahaa, and Bora Bora.

The *Spray* romped through the waves, pushed by a stiff breeze towards a mountain rising out of the sea. The miles rushed past as seagulls wheeled above the masts. With my father's chart spread before me, I planned my arrival. It was the latest edition, 1988, grubby, and covered with pencil marks from its previous owners. Most sailors stayed in the easily accessible and large Baie de Maroe. I chose the other side of the island, where my father would have anchored.

At 3:15 pm, with the entrance to the lagoon in sight, I dropped the sails, started the engine, and motored through Ara'ara Pass. Ahead was a channel deep enough for cruise ships. I turned the other way. With the motor running just enough to keep the *Spray* moving, I crept through straggling remnants of the reef into a turquoise lagoon with crystal water, a maze of undulating sandbars, colorful coral heads, and black volcanic rocks.

I was watching a fisherman cast his net from an outrigger canoe when the *Spray* scrapped the bottom. Quickly, I threw the gearbox into reverse and backed off before letting the *Spray* drift until the current carried her back into the channel. I motored on, seven long miles of dodging coral heads before I reached a small island guarding Bourayne Bay. A salt water creek joined it to the main bay on the other side of the island. But for a sand spit at low tide and a bridge for the road, the island had been cleaved in half.

I found a remote cove, uninhabited except for a handful of tiny huts with canoes pulled up on the beach, and dropped the anchor. My father couldn't have done better. I munched on tuna fish sandwiches and played my guitar, listening to birds in the jungle. At dusk, the birds became quiet and I could hear the distant surf crashing onto the reef. At 8:00 pm, I radioed *Maiden*. No one answered. I tried again at midnight, at 4:00 am, and again the next morning.

+ + +

In the evening, increasingly desperate for news of my family, I turned on the radio again and began, "*Maiden...*"

"*Maiden* here," Sal replied immediately.

"How's Einstein?"

"You can talk to him, but keep it short."

Seconds later, Ben squeaked, "Hi." I stared at the microphone. "You there?"

"I'm here. You okay?"

"Mom says... I'm... fine..." He croaked out a laugh. "Lucky like you ... I can still kick your butt."

We played soccer on the beach at Nuku Hiva; Dani and Ben thrashing Jessie and me.

My father interrupted. "Enough for now! Where are you? Over."

"Under the road." Maybe I was too obscure. Before I could elaborate, he said, '*Maiden* out.'

+++

It was late in the afternoon when my father and Sal came to fetch me in Sal's dinghy. Even before I climbed in, I could tell something was wrong. Sal just nodded. My father seemed colder than usual. Not even 'hi', or a slap on the back.

Instead, he muttered, "You found a good place to anchor."

I was uneasy after they glanced at each other. "Is Ben okay?"

He's going to be good as new." My father sounded grim.

"What's wrong?"

"Rick's dead." Sal started the outboard and cast off.

I murmured, "I'm sorry, Sal."

94

"Faro, more than likely!" Sal spit over the side.

The dinghy rose onto a plane, zipping over a turquoise mirror. On either side, volcanic peaks loomed over lush green hills, while tall palms clumped along the shore.

"How's Tony doing?"

"He's in New York for the funeral. Marion and Dani are with him." Crows' feet pulled at Sal's eyes, bloodshot in the bright morning sun. "Hindsight's always 20-20. I should've had Tony go with you and Rick. Got you out of harm's way before we worried about Ben."

"Leaving Vaiare when you did probably saved your life," my father said.

Sal was gloomy as I'd ever seen him. "Your 'under the road' comment had us confused for a while."

Ahead was a small bridge on piles. It belonged at a French chateau with its old-fashioned balustrade. It carried the road from Huahine Nui to Huahine Iti.

+ + +

They'd converted the *Maid Marion's* salon into a hospital ward. Ben slept on the couch. He looked like a skinny Tahitian kid under a plain white sheet. A tube ran from a bottle overhead into his forearm; a catheter emptied his bladder into another bottle on the floor.

On the opposite couch, my sister played doctor with a roll of gauze and a doll, one of Dani's from when she was younger. "All he does is sleep," she whispered.

My grandmother hugged me. "He asks about you every time he wakes up."

"Worried about his *Britannica*, I expect."

95

She stepped back, looking me up and down as if expecting to see cuts and bruises. "He was worried about you. We all were. I can't believe you sailed here by yourself."

"Jessie could've done it. What happened after I left you guys?"

My father sat on the couch, his hand on Ben's foot. "Moreau knew something was up as soon as you went out the door."

Jessie snickered. "Mommy told him you were crazy."

"That's not what I said," my mother interjected. "I told him you couldn't deal with stress, so you ran away."

"The running part's true. They chased me until I got on a bus," I said with a smile.

"We watched from the window. You're lucky you weren't hit by a car," my grandmother said.

My sister made a bandage like a tourniquet. "The policeman wouldn't let us leave the room except to go to the toilet."

"Luckily, Marion arrived before Moreau put guards at the door. No one allowed in or out, just like a prison," my father grouched.

"Bruce said the same thing."

"What about Bruce?" he demanded.

"He was at Moorea." I told him what happened at the Vairare marina and the radio call.

He mulled it over. "Might be a fluke. You did the right thing by leaving."

"How did you get Ben out of the hospital?"

"They had to evacuate after a dumpster caught on fire," he chuckled. "We wheeled Ben out on a gurney. Sal had the *Maid Marion* waiting at the dock."

"The only problem is it won't take Zagarovsky's people long to figure out where we went," my mother said.

My father agreed with a guarded nod. "The good news is Faro probably doesn't know this is Sal's boat; and unless he rents a boat, he won't find the *Spray*."

I slept on the *Maid Marion*, in Tony's cabin. I stretched out in a berth twice the size of mine, surrounded by photos in black frames, most of pinup girls posed beside Tony, one of him and his brother, all taken on exotic beaches in the Caribbean islands.

+ + +

Ben was awake the next morning. My mother was changing his bandage when I came in. His upper thigh was the color of raw tuna. I looked at her to confirm he was okay. She gave me an encouraging nod and I hurried into the bathroom. By the time I returned, she'd covered him with the sheet.

We said 'hi' together.

"The bullet came within a half-inch of the femoral nerve." Ben hadn't changed.

"You're lucky it missed the important stuff." I sat on the corner of the couch and watched her massage his leg.

He grimaced when she pushed on his knee. "I wish I had my *Britannica*. It has loads on anatomy."

"If you tell me what volumes, I'll bring them back when I go to feed Jag."

"You're staying here," my mother said. "Maybe you can get him to exercise so his leg doesn't atrophy."

It took all of Ben's strength to lift his leg and move his foot from side to side. He lasted a few seconds before he whimpered. "It beepin' hurts."

"You'll have to do better if you're going to beat me at soccer."

He made a face. "Can you rub my leg for a while?"

I rubbed from mid-thigh down to his foot like she did. "Now, kick the ball."

He gave it his best shot. I kept score of make-believe goals. We stopped when my grandmother brought him breakfast in bed— milk, toast, and a scrambled egg, the first real food he'd eaten in four days.

My father and Sal were discussing what to do when I joined them at the table.

"If it's okay with you, we'll stay till Ben's better," my father said.

"Of course, it's okay. Now Faro knows I'm involved, he'll steer clear for a while," Sal added.

My father rubbed where his goatee had been. "We still need to be careful. I want you to stay out of sight," he said to me. "It's a good opportunity to get ahead on your schoolwork." I was about to tell him even home-schooled kids had summer vacation when he added, "Don't waste your breath, Victor."

Chapter 11

Two days passed before Ben got out of bed and tottered to the bathroom, my arm around his shoulder. After lunch, my father carried him up the stairs. He sat in the cockpit, flexing his leg as he kicked imaginary soccer balls. Another four days went by before Ben hobbled from the bow to the stern with me close behind.

"You're doing great," I said after he did it again.

My mother was pleased with his progress. "He needs more space to move."

"A walk would be good for all of us," Sal agreed.

My father thought it was too risky. He changed his mind later in the afternoon when Tony returned from New York. The next morning, I held my breath as Ben straddled the rail and climbed into Sal's dinghy.

The road skirted Maroe Bay, never more than a few yards from the shore. Ben limped along happily, my mother and grandmother on either side. We walked slowly and stopped often, once to buy fruit from a beautiful Polynesian woman. She wore a pareu and had hibiscus flowers in her glossy black hair. Five kids, from a grubby toddler to a boy Jessie's age played in the dirt or ran into a hut built of palm fronds and woven grass mats to bring out toys to show us. None of them spoke English. The boy discussed the prices of papaya and pamplemousse in French with my father, and translated for his mother. Ben was on his knees, studying long-legged insects crawling over red, spiky flowers.

"Nature boy is back to normal," I said to my father.

He smiled. "A lot of it is due to you." Helping Ben recover had brought us closer.

"Did your mom teach you to speak French?"

"Plus German and Russian. I was fluent by the time I was your age."

A little farther, we stopped again, this time to gaze at a waterfall, a silver ribbon spouting from a crevice in a high basalt cliff. Clouds of mist swirled among vivid orchids sprouting through the steamy green foliage, tangled vines encircling the rotting trunks of palm trees, tropical birds in piercing profusion. Overhead, trees blotted out the sky.

I flapped my shirt to waft air up my chest. "How about Spanish?"

"I picked up enough to get by when we went there for holidays, Italian too."

I gaped at him, beads of perspiration dripping from his nose. Speaking six languages was hard to believe when I'd grown up thinking he was an assistant store manager.

We'd gone only a dozen yards before he peered through a gap in the trees. "About time he turned up."

A small yacht motored across Maroe Bay, looking for a good place to anchor. It listed to starboard, trailing a small rubber dinghy covered in repair patches. Boxes, gas cans, and plants growing in buckets always cluttered the deck of Bruce's yacht. There was even more junk than the last time I'd seen it at Moorea. It looked like it was ready to sink.

"Might be a fluke, but it's not worth the risk. We'll leave right away."

+ + +

We departed after lunch, my father and me on the *Spray*. The rest of my family sailed on the *Maid Marion,* leaving from the far side of the island. Our destination was 24 miles from Huahine, four hours with the trade winds behind us; however, they had to sail 50 percent farther. My father bet Sal a case of beer we'd beat him into the lagoon. It didn't seem fair.

As soon as we cleared Huahine's reef, we raised every sail, making constant adjustments to keep the *Spray* at maximum speed. Two hours later we saw the twin islands of Ra'iātea and Taha'a. Ra'iātea meant 'bright sky' in Tahitian—only a few wisps of clouds ever crowned its mountains. We were a quarter of a mile from the lagoon when the *Maid Marion* passed, its enormous sails bulging, heaving out sheets of spray as it surfed into Teavapiti Pass. The reef was partially submerged, angry surf breaking on either side. In a storm, it would be as dangerous as sailing around Cape Horn.

I put down my guitar to watch Sal's crew lower the immense green spinnaker. Sal gave a 'victory salute,' chatting to my grandmother while he steered. They would dock at the marina, pick up supplies at the Uturoa supermarket, and join us the next morning. With the race over, my father changed course, heading up the reef to Taha'a. It was smaller than Ra'iātea, without its dramatic mountains, and proportionately fewer tourists.

"Tighten the jib, Victor." Apparently, the race wasn't over for him.

"Victor? He's not still with us, is he?" I pushed Jag along the seat so I could sit next to the winch. If he needed his sails adjusted, I would do it the easy way.

My sarcasm brought forth a response I didn't expect. "It's probably time we changed our names."

I had a better idea. "We ought to find somewhere out of the way and stay there."

He glanced over his shoulder as if expecting someone behind us. "We will. Now Zagarovsky knows who we are, he won't give up."

"So why call me Victor? You know I don't like it."

"When I told you 'Victor' was my brother's idea, I left out his wife's nickname was Victoria."

"What happened to her?"

"She's dead."

"Tell me about her?"

I didn't think he was going to answer.

"The first time I met her, your grandfather was working on a composition for a Broadway play; piano and two violins. She was one of the violins, a virtuoso compared to my brother."

"What instrument did you play?"

"Piano, of course; plus the cello, but it was by paternal command. Your grandfather thought you weren't a musician unless you played String."

I couldn't help thinking it was why he was so mean to me.

"Her real interest was the organ," he went on.

"Weird."

"What is?"

"Nothing." Sometimes, I dreamed about being in a church, reverberating with a crescendo of organ chords. Perhaps it came from living on a boat, listening to the wind howl through the shrouds. "Any good?"

"She won a fellowship to Juilliard because of it. Every Sunday she would play at a church near Times Square. It was like being in a cathedral. She used to come to our house afterwards. We'd play for hours, as long as it took to perfect his latest composition, and then she'd stay for dinner. My brother didn't stand a chance," he said wistfully.

"She was beautiful, huh?"

"Inside and out. She was from Melbourne, Australia. She always talked about growing up in Victoria, hence the nickname."

"Did she die in the fire?"

His head snapped around—he'd been watching Sal's yacht on a course parallel to ours, now motoring inside the lagoon. "Some other time."

He went back to scanning the reef with binoculars. He was always cautious, even though the pass he was looking for was five miles away, specks of palm-tree-covered islands marking the entrance. A whale spouted between us and the reef, a plume and a tail splash before submerging again.

"You don't see a Humpback very often. Kind of makes this day special," he said.

Idle conversation, or was he trying to build bridges? "I wonder if Ben saw it."

"He was walking a lot better this morning, thanks to you." He focused his binoculars where the whale had been. "There's another whale closer to the reef. I think she's got a calf."

"I'm sorry about what happened to him."

He cleared his throat. I hoped he was going to say something in the vein of 'it wasn't your fault.' Instead, he took off his sunglasses and pinched at his eyes, squinting to avoid the glare from the late afternoon sun.

"Sailing to Huahine by yourself was very grown up," he began. "Taking my beer wasn't."

Jag stretched out, expecting a back rub. I avoided his eyes and petted the cat. "I had one can, that's all."

"Don't do it again." He wasn't angry like I expected.

I went back to playing my guitar, the composition I'd worked on while I was by myself in Huahine. After a couple of bars, my father nodded approvingly; however, my heart wasn't in it. I stopped.

"Take care of the guitar. It's worth a lot of money."

"How much?"

"The Probate Court appraised it for $25,000. Nowadays? I don't know; twice that."

Given what I'd seen in Norfolk's music shops, I thought $1,000 would be generous for an acoustic guitar, even if it was made in Spain. I fingered the frets. Tiny mother-of-pearl flowers decorated the spaces along the ebony fingerboard. I carefully plucked strings, making chords. It had beautiful tones, better than anything I'd ever heard. Maybe he wasn't making it up.

"Because Segovia played it?"

He smiled. "Because of the label inside. Ignacio Fleta made it."

"How did it get the crack?" There was a small, barely visible split in the rosewood side.

"You were jumping on the couch and fell on it. It was being repaired the night of the fire."

+ + +

The sun was setting when we anchored in the lagoon behind a little island guarding Toahotu Pass. The next morning, my father and I snorkeled along a waist-deep channel in the reef, close enough to the ocean that the sound of waves breaking was a constant roar. Like a tropical underwater jungle, colorful coral sprouted fronds and branches, sheltering swirling schools of fish.

Conch shells littered patches of sand, and spiny lobsters scurried from one shadowy crevice to another.

We returned to the *Spray* when we saw the *Maid Marion* arrive. I left my father to prepare the grouper he'd speared and went below to shower. He allowed a half-gallon of water to get wet before soaping, a damp sponge to wipe it off, and another half-gallon of water to rinse. I was trying to get the shampoo out of my hair with the last of the water when the door opened. My sister stuck her head in, took one look, and slammed the door shut again.

She giggled, "Oops!"

"Next time, knock!" I yelled.

"Sorry!"

I put on clothes and went on deck to complain about the broken door lock. He was in the cockpit, making short tie-down lines from rope on a spool.

"I'll repair it when I find parts. Make yourself useful and put these on the boom." He handed over the replacement lines.

It was such a nice day, I did it without protesting.

Sal stood in his inflatable dinghy, drifting closer with the current, leisurely casting flies over the turquoise lagoon. My mother and father sat in the cockpit, talking and drinking coffee. My sister sat on the cabin roof, cradling Jag while she waited for the inevitable lecture about knocking before entering. A blue skiff zipped over the lagoon, on a beeline to us. It stopped a few yards away. Fruit and vegetables in cane baskets, and stacks of yellow and green bananas weighed down the bow. A Polynesian man sat in the stern next to a tiny outboard. Unlike most boat-boys, who boasted of their skills as guides or shouted the superior quality of their wares, he strummed a ukulele painted with hibiscus flowers and palm trees.

"Ia Orana. Bonjour," he called out between chords. "Welcome to Taha'a."

Jessie hopped onto the cabin roof to wave back. "His name is Norbert. We met him at Uturoa."

"Everything cheap. You buy five dollar banana, get papaya free," Norbert said, polishing his ukulele.

"How many bananas?" My father was always ready for a bargain.

"How many you want?" He strummed light-hearted chords, grinning at Jessie, who was now standing beside me. "Dis love song for beautiful girl. You tell handsome boy-fren, 'Ua here vau ia oe.' 'I love you.'"

Jessie gushed giggles. "He's my brother."

"He your boy-fren'!"

"My brother!" Jessie said indignantly.

"He got hair like Madonna, you like coconut," Norbert pointed out. "He no brother!" He looked at my father, raised an eyebrow, and then smirked at my mother.

"Blond hair means nothing of the sort." My mother was trying hard not to laugh.

"Maybe he should use my hair dye," my father joked.

Still smirking, Norbert plucked a few notes. "Maybe I sing love song for beautiful mother who like to have fun." He added an exaggerated wink.

"I'm adopted," I shouted back to preserve her honor.

My father glanced at me. I grinned at him.

"I'd tell him," Sal called out, his dinghy drifting closer.

My father was thinking about something else as he leaned over the side with a generous handful of Tahitian money. "We'll take two dozen bananas and three pineapples."

With pineapples tossed and caught by my father, Norbert scrambled over boxes and seats to get bananas from the bow. "You want cabbage too. Very cheap mango? Ripe tomato? All pick this morning."

"Tell me what?" I asked.

"Not today," my father said.

I wasn't sure if he was talking to me or Norbert.

"It's a good time to..." my mother began.

He cut her off, clearly not amused. "Now is not a good time."

Norbert handed up bananas and a papaya. He shoved my father's money into his pocket. "I come back tomorrow. Sing love song to mother," he laughed, brandishing his ukulele in one hand and steering with other. "Nana. Bye-bye."

After everything we'd been through, I deserved more. "When is a good time?"

My father's hands were full of bananas, and a complimentary cabbage. "Finished those ropes yet, Victor?"

I glared back at him.

Sal's inflatable bumped against the *Spray*. "John?"

"I'd appreciate it if you kept out of things that are none of your business."

Sal hesitated. "If he was my son, I'd want him to know."

My father's face darkened. He dumped the bananas on the cockpit seat. The papaya rolled off before he could stop it. It split open, disgorging orange flesh and black seeds over the floor. Jag jumped down to investigate.

My sister jumped into it. "What should Josh know?"

"Nothing!" he snapped.

"He deserves to know," Sal said.

"It doesn't concern you."

My mother touched his shoulder. "After all Sal's done for us..."

"What he's done, he's done for himself," my father said.

He scooped up pieces of shattered papaya and tossed it over the side. Jag sniffed at his fingers until he shoved him away.

Sal wasn't about to let it end there. "I agree it's none of my business, but you're not helping matters."

"I appreciate everything you've done for us; however, it's time we went our own ways," my father said, just as grimly.

I looked from my father to Sal, to my mother. I could tell she was as surprised as I was. Only two nights before they'd stayed up past midnight, drinking beer and talking about sailing.

I thought Sal was going to say something. He didn't. He directed a forgiving gesture to my mother, more like a sympathetic salute. My father busied himself picking seeds out of the floor grate, flicking them into the water.

My mother was the voice of reason. "John, you need to cool down."

He looked up, his hands covered with orange mush. "Revenge got us into this mess. I've had enough! I need a frigging towel." He went below.

Sal reeled in his line before he met my eyes. "Watch out for sharks, Alex."

It was hard to believe he was saying goodbye. Before I could say anything, he started his outboard motor and headed into the same channel where I'd been snorkeling with my father. My sister resumed stroking Jag. No one spoke until my father returned, still wiping his hands with the soiled gray towel he used to clean the engine. He tossed it on the seat and climbed into our dinghy.

"I'll fetch Ben and Sarah. Virginia, I'll need your help loading our stuff. Jessie, clean up this mess. Victor, get the *Spray* ready to leave."

I couldn't remember seeing him in such a foul mood.

Chapter 12

We were back to following Captain Slocum's route across the Pacific, a course tracking the Pago Pago-Papeete shipping channel to Apia, Samoa. We saw no ships at all. There wasn't as much as a reef in the way after passing Maupihaa, the last tiny atoll of French Polynesia. Under normal conditions, the trip should have taken about ten days; however, the trade wind lasted until we were out of sight of land. We wallowed in an occasional stingy gust, and an endless, gut-churning swell. After three days and 190 miles, my father started the motor and changed course a few degrees.

"Palmerston Island," he said after I asked where we were headed. "You said we should find somewhere out of the way."

I strained my eyes to find Palmerston Island on his chart. It was a straggler in the string of fifteen islands and reefs known as the Cook Islands. "It's a dot in the middle of nowhere!"

He wiped sweat from his brow. "Even Bruce won't go there. You're on watch. Keep off the radio and go easy on the motor. We need to make the fuel last until Tonga."

He assisted Ben up the stairs before going to his berth to sleep. Ben winced when he sat down. He was getting stronger after doing my 'kick-the-ball' exercises for an hour every day. After a while, he stopped and massaged his thigh, avoiding purple-brown bruises and a small red scar. He winced again when he stood up.

"You want me to get a *Britannica*?"

Ben grinned. "Stop trying to suck up. It wasn't your fault, despite what he says."

"He said it was my fault?"

He made sure the aft cabin's hatches were closed before he confided, "He told Sal none of this would've happened except for you. Sal got really angry at him."

"While I was by myself?"

"He didn't mean it, Josh. He was worried."

"He's always worried." I almost said I hated him.

Pitiful waves rocked the *Spray* as Ben shuffled from bow to stern, again and again.

+ + +

We arrived at Palmerston Island in the middle of the night, in a rain squall with waves flinging buckets of water into the cockpit. We furled all the sails except a small jib and sailed back and forth, a mile off the leeward side. Eventually, a faint glow on the horizon revealed an atoll, the remnants of an extinct volcano. It rose a few yards above the sea, six scattered outcroppings of windswept coconut trees, and waves pummeling the coral reef. Each tiny island had a name; the largest was the home of the original settlers.

At 7:00 am my father turned on the radio and hailed for directions. Ed of 'Alpha-sierra Palmerston' was eager to talk. Shortly, with my mother in the bow and me hanging off the end of the bowsprit, he cautiously motored up to the reef.

"I'd rather not anchor in deep water. If the anchor drags we'll never get her back. Ed said there's a narrow passage." My father checked his position before pointing the bow at an area of foamy water more turbulent than the rest. "We'll go slowly. Everyone stay alert."

"Twelve feet." My job was to drop a lead weight into the water and call out depths by counting knots on a string.

"It shallow ahead," my mother warned. He'd assigned her lookout.

"There's six feet at high tide," he shouted back.

The *Spray* needed five feet to float. The tide had been going out for an hour. He increased the throttle, charging into a gap between two rock outcroppings. Only inches showed above the surface, pink slabs crusted with brown and orange, and speckled with black shells. Twelve feet deep became eight and a rush of water. The *Spray* slowed to a crawl even though the engine was near maximum power. I leaned out, trying to see when the lead hit the bottom. The current was so strong the depths I called out were just a guess.

"Six feet!" I shouted, hoping he'd turn around before it was too late.

Blue-green water swirled below, chunks of broken coral and shells littered the bottom of the channel, and seaweed streamed flat as a wall of water buffeted the *Spray*.

"This is crazy," my mother muttered. Like me, she held the rail with a death grip.

The *Spray* vibrated as he applied full power. Directly ahead, a dark green shadow grew larger. It might have been seaweed, yet it was causing a wave. I pointed it out to her. She signaled with her left arm, directing him to port to avoid it, just in case. There was no rush; the *Spray* was moving slowly, straining against the current. I dropped the lead weight again. Suddenly, amongst a flurry of bubbles I saw patches of brown.

"Rock!" I shouted, waving to starboard.

"Port. Starboard. Which is it?" he shouted.

There wasn't time to converse. "Go right!" I screamed back at him.

My grandmother scurried up the stairs and looked over the side. "You do realize I can see the bottom, John?"

My father spun the wheel. The onrushing water thrust the *Spray* sideways, closer to the reef. My mother raised both arms, the signal to stop. A few yards away, patches of brown turned into a jagged rock.

"Back up!" I screamed.

He flung the gearbox into reverse, and raced the engine. The *Spray* shuddered under the load. A second or two sooner and he might've avoided the rock. The *Spray's* keel slammed against it with a sickening thud.

"That didn't sound good," she said. "Is there anything I can do?"

"Not at the moment, Sarah!"

"Why don't we park like that boat?" she asked, drawing his attention to a yacht anchored on the sea side of the reef.

"Because we'll be here for a while." He spun the wheel to avoid hitting a rock ledge as the swirling current shoved his boat back.

"How much room at the bow?" he bellowed. My mother was looking the other way. "Wake up!"

"None!" I bellowed back. If I stepped off the bowsprit, I'd be on land. "Go to starboard!"

He spun the wheel the opposite way. Still in reverse, the *Spray* jerked away from the ledge. When the bow pointed into the channel, he applied full throttle forward. Bit by bit, his boat forged through the surging water.

"Rock ahead," my mother shrieked, flailing her right arm. I'd missed one.

The rock passed under the bowsprit before the *Spray* veered away, again scraping the keel. Then, the rock outcroppings ended and the channel divided. My mother and I exchanged a frustrated glance.

"I don't think it matters." She waved and called, "Port."

It took 20 minutes to traverse a narrow, winding passage, often with only a few inches under the keel. The passage ended in a placid lagoon, bright turquoise water with clumps of flowery seaweed and vast schools of fish. My sister and brother hung over the side, spotting species so rare we'd seen them only in books. I stayed in the bow, pointing out coral heads in case he missed them.

Soon, a battered aluminum skiff raced towards us. It came alongside and my father heaved out a line. A burly dark-skinned man flung himself onto the *Spray,* his arms as thick as my thighs, his head all but shaved. He greeted my father with a knuckle-breaking handshake.

"I told my wife you'd try the channel," Ed said after we'd introduced ourselves. "Ain't many with the skill not to run aground."

My father returned a grizzly grin, not mentioning he'd scraped a few times.

"You'll want to anchor over there." Ed pointed past a line of coral heads. "It's close to the beach so your kids can swim ashore. My brood will keep 'em busy." He handed over a sheaf of immigration, customs, and health clearance forms.

Before he left to go fishing, he invited us to lunch, part of his responsibility of being our 'host family.'

+ + +

My father backed away from where he'd dropped the bow anchor. I waited for his signal to drop the stern anchor, thinking I'd

114

never seen so many coral heads. The *Spray* was right in the middle of them after he took up the slack on both anchors. It wasn't a place to be in a storm; however, the beach was only 100 yards away. Beyond a narrow strip of sand, spindly coconut palms angled away from the wind, tall mahogany trees sprouting behind.

He handed me flippers and goggles. "Check the anchors and have a look at the keel." Ben promptly stood up and took off his shirt. "Where do you think you're going?"

"To help Josh," Ben said brightly.

My mother winked at him. "Good idea! You need a bath."

I jumped in. He used the ladder, placing each foot carefully. He sculled away from the *Spray* before he stopped, beaming and treading water. Suddenly, his shorts sailed over my head, landing with a wet thump on the cabin roof.

"They're too tight. It's not like anyone's will see me," he added, waving at the beach. The only sign anyone lived on the island was a wonky wooden shack.

"You're crazy!"

Jessie leaned over the side, giggling. "You're chicken!"

"Am not."

"Chicken too!" Ben grinned.

He splashed water at me before he rolled over and dove, again and again like a playful dolphin. I waited until Jessie went below before I heaved my swim shorts on the deck and swam after him to check the anchor. We were spearfishing when my mother came on deck with breakfast: coffee, fruit, and bread my grandmother had baked using gooey bananas. My father tossed down our shorts and we climbed onboard.

"I'll look at it later," he said after I told him about the missing paint on the side of the keel.

115

After a bite of papaya, Jessie asked, "Why are boys different?"

My mother stopped cutting slices of banana bread. "Different how?"

"She means Josh and me, because we're different down there." For once, Ben didn't use anatomical terms.

She glanced at my father, as startled as she was. My face got red. My grandmother covered her mouth, pretending to wipe her lips.

"Josh is older so he's more grown up." It took a lot to fluster my mother.

"Not the hair. Their things are different."

"Why did you circumcise me and not him?" Ben wasn't embarrassed. I was mortified.

"Medical reasons," my father said.

"What's circumcise?"

My grandmother choked as she tried not to laugh. "I'm sure your mom will explain it after breakfast, Jessie."

"What medical reasons?" Ben asked; however, my mother was already on her way to the galley to refill her coffee cup. He turned to my father. "What medical reasons?"

He forked into a buttered slab of banana bread. "The doctor recommended it."

Lie or excuse, I couldn't decide.

+ + +

At lunchtime, we paddled ashore, dragged *Squirt* up the beach, and followed a sandy track to the village. Palmerston's original house was still standing, a simple cottage made of heavy slabs of wood salvaged from a wrecked ship. Four settlers eventually became 70, their houses made of boards with rusty metal roofs. A few houses were painted, the others bleached gray under the tropical sun. Every house had a metal tank on the side to store rainwater. There was no shop; however, there was a two-room school, a church, and a 'clubhouse'. A diesel generator provided electricity from 6:00 am to midnight, while solar panels powered a public telephone. My mother thought it best not to ask about sewage treatment.

Every family on the island came to lunch under the trees, bringing dishes of food. We shared a tropical cornucopia of curried parrotfish, baked birds, fried coconut patties, mangoes, bananas, papaya, and rice, washed down with coconut milk. Twenty eight children swarmed among the tables, flowing back and forth like a school of fish. Not one was shy. They were polite and, like their parents, eager to make friends.

After months without the company of other girls, Jessie eagerly played on the beach, wove baskets from palm leaves, and made jewelry from shells. Ben found three boys near his age and learned how to play cricket. There was no one my age; once the children reached high school age they went to school on one of the other Cook Islands.

My mother and grandmother took charge of distributing the gifts we'd brought—we'd emptied the *Spray* of clothes we'd grown out of, toys and games we no longer played with, surplus school materials, and paperback books, some I'd read so often I could quote word for word. I wandered over to where my father chatted with Ed and three other men about our voyage around the world. My father introduced me before he continued.

"Almost no wind until yesterday, so we've used the motor a lot. Now, we're low on fuel. Any chance of buying 100 gallons?"

"Can't help, I'm afraid. We were hoping you'd sell us some," George said. He was the mayor. "The freighter won't be here for a while."

"How long is a while?" my father asked.

"Middle of next month. It usually pays us a visit every five or six months."

"You like to fish, Josh?" Ed was easygoing and likeable. He'd probably never had a bad mood.

"He'd play his guitar all day if he could," my father said jovially. "Just like my brother."

George laughed. "A beach bum, like us, eh? He'll fit right in."

"If you're interested, I could use some help on the boat." Ed said to me,

+ + +

Ed kept me busy, beginning at dawn, every day except Sunday, motoring along the edge of the reef in search of parrotfish. We used thick nylon lines weighed down by lead slugs salvaged from car wheels in New Zealand, with table scraps as bait. Some days, an entire morning would pass without a single bite; however, when a school of fish passed we hauled up a fish every minute until the floor of his runabout was covered with iridescent blue-green fish. After we filled cane baskets and lugged them to the village, his family gutted them and stacked them in freezers to await the next freighter. They sold the fish for enough to live on.

We quickly settled into routine; my mother spent her mornings nursing the locals; my grandmother gave reading lessons at the school Ben and Jessie attended when they were bored with home school; and my father spent his days helping the islanders take care of their generator. We bartered odds and ends from the *Spray* for whatever we needed, which wasn't much with my share of the catch. We'd been on Palmerston Island for four weeks when he decided to leave.

"High tide in an hour. Plenty of time to say goodbye," he announced, getting up from his chart table. He'd been restless since the previous evening when the freighter made radio contact with the islanders to announce impending arrival.

"He hasn't changed," I whispered to Ben.

My father spun around. "It takes one person to recognize us and it's over."

Someone had to tell him he was being paranoid. "We're on a dot in the middle of nowhere."

"Josh has a point, John." It was obvious my mother wanted to stay longer, too.

"The wind is from the wrong direction, Dad," Ben pointed out.

"We're still leaving. We'll motor to Tonga if we have to."

Chapter 13

"We'll refuel at Niue." My father thrust his chart into my hands.

I headed back to the cockpit to plot the new course, holding back 'aye Captain.' With the fuel tank needle hovering a tick above empty, it wasn't good timing.

Niue was a tiny island between Palmerston Island and Tonga. No sooner than it breached the horizon, the wind returned with rain squalls and boisterous waves. They crashed onto cliffs over 70 feet high, a vast limestone plateau, one of the world's largest and strangest atolls. Clouds of spray rolled like fog over stunted trees, exposed roots clutching surreal rock outcroppings. Scrawny sea birds wheeled overhead. Even on the protected side of the island, waves barged against the Alofi town wharf. It was carved out of coral, and impossible to dock at without risking a collision. We turned away, skirted a dozen yachts bouncing up and down at their moorings in the bay, and anchored behind a low headland a mile away.

The next morning the weather improved enough to hoist *Squirt* from the aft deck and dump it into the sea. Passing waves tossed it to and fro as they raced towards the reef. It was too rough to go to Alofi so we motored ashore to explore Niue's shallow limestone pools and wind-eroded coral outcrops. Ben scrambled about chasing boobies, gawky birds with oversized heads and yellow duck feet. Crevasses sheered through cliffs, opening into deep gorges filled with fine sand, palm trees, and scuttling coconut crabs. My grandmother said it was charmingly desolate.

When the waves moderated, my father and I took *Squirt* back to Alofi. Waves still crashed into the dock, the surge so strong it was dangerous to land. He crouched in the center of the dinghy as I motored up to the dock. Between waves, he flung himself onto the stairs. He skidded on slimy green seaweed as I swerved away, barely avoiding the concrete wall. When I turned around, he'd reached the top of dock, soaked through. He gave me a wave and headed off.

I puttered back and forth in front of the dock until he returned. His drum of diesel fuel was so heavy it took four men to roll it down to the dock and lower it into the sea. After securing a rope to the drum, we towed it back to the *Spray*. Waves heaved so hard against *Squirt* I was sure we'd flip over. Once, a wave came over the transom and soaked the outboard. It started again only after my father dried out the spark plugs wires.

While I tried to keep the drum from slamming against the *Spray's* boarding ladder, he hung a block and tackle from the end of the mizzen boom. It was only luck we managed to lift the drum onto the aft deck without someone getting hurt. After we hauled the empty drum back to Alofi, we trudged downstairs to clean up.

My mother saw my grease-smeared face and matted hair and voiced her opinion. "We're not doing that again!"

My grandmother discreetly closed the door to her cabin.

He washed his hands in the galley sink. "Damn right! Too expensive!"

We'd pumped 44 gallons into the fuel tanks, a quarter of what we needed to fill them, just enough to reach Tonga

"I've heard it before, John!" One look at her face was enough to see she was irked.

"No need to be rude about it," he shot back.

She removed warmed-up tuna casserole from the oven. It was pitch dark, and my father and I still hadn't eaten dinner. "I'm not the one who's been complaining all day about the cost."

"Ten bucks a gallon is worth complaining about!"

It was hard not to smile. "It's preposterous!" I'd listened to him say it again and again.

"Stay out of this!"

She took a step, blocking his way with the casserole. "He deserves better than this."

He looked right through her. "We'll get underway immediately. Victor, Ben, on deck now!" He snapped his fingers.

My mother dropped the dish on the table. "You're not ordering a waiter. They're your children."

"I wish!" he snapped.

"Enough, John!" she snapped back. She glared at him until he left, stomping up the stairs and into the cockpit, grumbling to himself.

"Dad's pissed," Ben said under his breath.

"He's just tired. We should've waited until the weather improved and refueled at the dock."

"That would be too easy!" I got her to smile.

"I'll talk to him. I'll tell you when it's safe to come up." She started up the stairs. We were still leaving Niue—the anchor chain clanged as he hauled it onboard.

My parents spent the night in the cockpit, sharing the watches and arguing on and off, their voices kept low. When I emerged from the cabin the next morning, he reviewed our position and future course as if nothing had happened. Tonga's Ha'apai group, Captain James Cook's 'Friendly Islands,' was only 290 miles away.

The *Spray* raced through the waves, her sails bulging full until late afternoon. Then, he started the engine, the sails still up to take advantage of faint breaths of wind, hardly Slocum's steady trade wind.

Jessie picked out a defiant dark ringlet, clicking her craft scissors.

"Not a good idea," I said.

"I wish I had straight hair like yours."

"Curly is cute."

"Only because you think Dani's cute," she giggled.

I shrugged coolly.

"She thinks you're cute."

"You're supposed to be in bed."

The ship's clock on the bulkhead showed 11:13 pm, way past her bedtime, another long night as we chugged westward.

"Do you want to know what else she said about you?"

I knew better than to let Jessie get to me. I buried my irritation in *Society and Culture*.

"I can tell *you're* not interested." She giggled and went back to trimming blue paper into rectangles, adding to her collection of red triangles, yellow trapezoids, and green lopsided circles. When I looked up again, she was staring at me. Instead of asking what else Dani said about me, I put my book aside and pointed to the picture in her upside-down book, her paper shapes a messy mosaic by comparison.

"It's supposed to look like a fish, Jess."

"Why don't you have freckles?"

"No idea."

From the front cabin, my grandmother said, "You get freckles when you spend too much time in the sun."

"Josh is in the sun more than I am," Jessie said. She leaned over the table to peer at my face. "He doesn't have a single freckle."

"Ben has freckles," I said, hoping to divert her before she pointed out the zits on my nose.

"I hate having freckles. It looks like my face is dirty."

Ben stuck his head into the companionway. "Freckles are inherited, Jessie. Skin type is from DNA. I can show you in the *Britannica* if you want."

"Who did I inherit them from?"

"From Mom, duh."

He started to come down the stairs as my grandmother breezed into the main cabin. I hid my smile behind my hand. A long-sleeved blouse and a skirt just didn't cut it on the *Spray*. Even as shore clothes, they weren't appropriate in the tropics.

"When I was your age, I had freckles," she said. "So did your mom. If you stay out of the sun most of them will go away."

"Why doesn't Josh have any?" Jessie asked.

"I guess he has Dad's skin type," Ben said, minus his usual authoritative tone.

Chapter 14

"The first European in Tonga? It would've been Captain Cook's second voyage." Ben pondered the year. "I'm going with 1773!"

He was so convinced he was right, I laughed. "Wrong!"

He went downstairs to check his encyclopedia. My grandmother and I shared a smile. Ben hated to lose at Cruiser Questions, a game she'd invented to pass the time. The first to get 20 correct was the winner. Ben was at 19, one ahead of me.

"It defies logic!" he called out. "The first Europeans to visit Tonga were Dutch, in the 1600s."

He should've argued my question wasn't fair, or with his encyclopedia in hand, turned the question back to me with which island in particular —Tonga had 176 of them stretched over 500 miles. Countless reefs and shoals were scattered among them, mere specks in the sea, yet deadly if we weren't paying attention. We'd stopped at larger islands, anchoring in placid lagoons, the peace and quiet disturbed only when my father ran the engine to recharge the batteries. It was a daily routine lasting up to an hour—even with solar panels we needed more electricity: to make fresh water, run the refrigerator, and power pumps, cabin lights, and radio. After staying a day or two, the urge to wander returned, the next island already in sight.

We approached Vava'u from the south, scudding along under full sail with a brisk breeze. The closer we came, the more sea birds shadowed the *Spray*, Black Noddies rising and swooping with the air currents spilling over white-capped waves. I looked forward to going ashore. Tongan islands lacked the exotic drama of volcanic French Polynesia; however, so far the people were friendlier and the pace of life calmer. I liked Tonga.

"Before you start gloating Victor, my question to you is which Dutchman?" My father oozed coolness. He had 19 points too.

He checked his chart and our GPS position, while he waited for my answer. I wracked my brains, trying to remember the names of Dutch explorers. Trying to remember where I'd read about European explorers in the Pacific didn't help.

"He's stumped!" Mostly for show, he added, "Here's a hint; Dutch East India Company."

He adjusted the heading after scanning for breaking waves with his binoculars. Some reefs hid just below the surface, invisible except for waves washing over them. Rather than give the wrong answer, I conceded defeat, giving the twentieth point to my father. It was his third win in a row. I was glad when the order came to lower the sails.

"Ben, take the wheel. That's your mark." My father pointed to a distinctive headland before he descended the stairs. "We'll be in the dinghy by three o'clock," he said to my mother. "Plenty of time for sightseeing before dinner."

"I'd rather we went to the market."

"Tomorrow morning. Victor, what was the fuel gauge showing yesterday?" he called out.

I looked into the cabin. "It was on the quarter mark when we left Oua."

He tapped the fuel gauge. "Ought to be lower than the quarter mark." He picked up the ship's log, turning pages and muttering as he went. "It was a quarter at Mango Island. Twelve days and we haven't used any fuel according to the gauge." He switched the gauge off and on. "Uh oh."

My grandmother lifted her head from her paperback. "Another problem?"

"Messed up gauge; no big deal."

"Do we have enough gas?"

Calling diesel fuel 'gas' always brought forth a lecture. He began it by differentiating between propane gas used in the stove, and petroleum used in the outboard.

"We've got plenty; between five and ten gallons. We'll fill up at Neiafu. I'm taking a shower. You're in charge, Victor. Find a place close to town; somewhere quiet."

He meant 'anchor away from other yachts.'

Ben steered into Port of Refuge harbor. There were dozens of yachts moored in front of the two-story buildings stretching along a narrow peninsula, so we dropped our anchor on the far side of the main wharf.

+ + +

A sign at the Neiafu wharf advertised diesel fuel, the price in Tongan Pa'angas and New Zealand dollars. It was cheaper than Niue; however, it wasn't cheap enough for my father. He stalked off the wharf, down a busy main street lined with office buildings, banks, shops, a library, and post office. The price was the same at the marina dock. My mother and grandmother were inspecting over-priced wood carvings and intricate woven-grass baskets when he told them. They'd expected as much.

"Locals can't afford it," he declared. "It's got to be cheaper out of town."

We walked all the way to a boat chartering company to find even more expensive diesel fuel. He wheeled on his heel and headed back the way we'd come. He ducked into a hardware store and came out lugging a yellow fuel can in each hand. We followed him past the elaborate St. Joseph's Cathedral, pausing to watch a crowd tossing flower petals on the heels of the bride and groom,

127

parents, grandparents, and four little bridesmaids. They parted for a red Toyota pulling out of the parking lot of the Puataukanave Hotel. The driver looked like a businessman in a hurry, rudely beeping his horn and waving his arm out the window.

"It's a wedding. You'd think he'd cool it," my father grumped.

The passenger was calm by comparison, a tourist with a vivid flowery shirt open in front. He swiveled to take in the local culture before the pink hibiscus trees planted around the hotel blocked my view. The next time I saw the car, it was a hundred yards down Fatafehi Road, horn still beeping.

With buying fuel prevailing over Tongan wedding customs, my father headed into town. We hurried after him, not catching up until he stopped at a metal-covered shed with wide-open doors. Cars and trucks in various stages of repair spilled onto the street. He avoided puddles and dog droppings to reach the main office, a box slapped on the side of the shed, its tiny window filled with a derelict air-conditioner. Inside, a couple of grease-covered Fijians sprawled in recycled car seats, arguing politics and smoking cigarettes. My father opened the negotiations for a rental car. My grandmother took in the smoke haze and pinup posters and took Jessie and Ben outside. My mother and I followed them across the road to a small outdoor market where locals bargained over fresh fruit and vegetables.

We filled a shopping bag with cabbage and bananas before my father emerged from the garage. He'd rented a car for the afternoon, a Jeep Wrangler that might have been left behind after World War II.

"My brother had a Jeep like this."

Before I could ask about my uncle, he switched on the radio, punching buttons until it played the 'island romantic' music he wanted. The rest of us called it 'tropical mush.'

His Jeep only had two doors, so my mother and I had to squeeze behind the front seats. With no room for my legs, I sat with my knees splayed apart, still more comfortable than Ben and Jessie, squashed in the rear with the gas cans. The Jeep protested the overload with a cloud of smoke.

"It sounds like your motor before it seized, John. I hope it's okay," my grandmother ventured from the passenger seat.

"It just needs to warm up."

It only got louder.

After driving through town to get his bearings, he headed inland on the main road. His plan was to find cheap fuel at a village and spend the rest of the afternoon sightseeing. There was a general store in Mataika, but no fuel, so he continued on. Leimatu'a, the next village, also had a small general store, with a gas pump outside. He left the engine spluttering and went into the store to ask about buying diesel fuel. He came out, climbed in, and gave an offhand shrug.

"Same price as the dock." He looked sheepish. "The coast is supposed to be pretty."

He turned the car around and went back to the last intersection. A signpost pointed in six directions. He chose 'Vaiutukakau Bay.' After a hundred yards, the bitumen-covered road ended, no more than two bumpy ruts separated by long spiky grass.

"This is what they made Jeeps for," he proclaimed over the engine roar.

It was the opening I needed. "Did your brother want one because the streets in New York are so bumpy?"

"He was in Texas on an assignment."

129

My mother touched my knee with enough of a headshake to know I shouldn't pursue it.

We passed farms by the dozens, the rich smell of vanilla pods filling the air, little brown kids running after us; scruffy dogs, brown and black pigs, and chickens scattering as the Jeep rattled past.

He slowed to a crawl to negotiate a furrow deeper than the rest. It was temporarily patched with bundles of pandanus palm. The Jeep slewed and slowed, so he gunned the motor. The wheels spun and chewed up the fronds, spitting foul smelling water and clumps of green leaves into the smoke swirling behind. The Jeep sank almost up to its axles.

"Should we get out and push?" My grandmother had to shout to be heard.

"You can if you want, Sarah," he shouted back.

He shoved a lever down and the gearbox grated under the car. He floored the accelerator. All four wheels hurled out slush until the Jeep bounced out of the furrow, almost flinging out Ben and Jessie.

"Still want to get out and push?" He thought it was funny. No one else laughed.

Rainforest replaced pineapple and sugar cane farms when the land became steep, or was too rocky for growing. Soon, the track was no more than a path carved out of the trees—in the middle of the afternoon, no sun reached the ground. My father jammed on the brakes and turned off the motor. Brilliant-hued parrots and dusky pigeons flitted from branch to branch, pecking at rotting logs, squawking, fighting over berries and fruit.

We wallowed in steamy tropical splendor for an hour before he turned the car around. We were off again, grinding gears and hanging on to the grab rails, all the way back to the signpost. If there was a bay at Vaiutukakau we never saw it. This time, he took the road to 'Houma Fakalele.'

It was only a few miles to a narrow headland overlooking rugged cliffs on both sides, several hundred feet straight down to the sea. My father parked the Jeep and went off to find a way down, taking an overgrown path along the cliff. The rest of us walked to the end of the headland, much easier although constantly buffeted by the wind. My sister lagged behind, pausing at every bush to look for green iguanas.

"Who's Dad talking to?"

I barely heard Ben over the thunder of waves on the rocks below.

I looked back the way we'd come, shielding my eyes from the glare. My father confronted a backpacker, one of hundreds who tromped through Tonga. A straw hat kept blowing off his head.

"He's probably telling him where to rent a Jeep." I kept walking.

"Something's bugging him," Ben said.

I turned to see my father wave at us. I waved back. He started back up the cliff. He was nearly at the top when he began shouting; however, it was too far to hear him.

"We better see what he wants." My mother was already on her way, beckoning to Jessie to follow.

My grandmother shook her head. "We should've worn hiking boots if we're climbing all the way down there."

My sister was head first in a bush. "I found an iguana, a big one."

"Jessie, you can look for iguanas some other time." She hauled my sister out, brushed leaf bits from her hair, and hustled back to the Jeep, the rest of us in close pursuit.

My father was breathless, his hair a windswept tangle like Jessie's. "We're leaving."

"See Tonga in an hour." My grandmother was amused. "Where to next, John?"

"Bruce hitchhiked from Neiafu with Faro," he huffed.

He threw open the passenger door and urged me and my mother behind the passenger seat before he rushed to the rear of the Jeep and boosted Jessie over the tailgate. Ben scrambled over by himself. As he got in the driver's seat, he frowned at me.

The Jeep lurched over the grass, plowing through clumps of pandanus palm. He accelerated down the track, the Jeep bucking up and down. It was torture by bump while we waited for him to fill in the gaps.

"Bruce met him last night at a bar on the harbor." He worked the steering wheel and gear stick like he was driving a rally car, not a rickety Jeep. "Faro had to pick up someone from the airport today, so Bruce begged a ride. He got out at the signpost."

Smart would be keeping my mouth shut. "Was Faro in the red car when the wedding went past?"

"You saw him and didn't tell me?" he exploded.

"It was only a glimpse. I didn't think it was him. I was watching the wedding. You saw the car too. You said he should cool it." Judging by the silence, my reminder wasn't appreciated.

My father stomped on the brakes to avoid hitting a pig, obese and hairy, with tiny black eyes. It lumbered into the middle of the track and stopped. He thumped on the horn until the puzzled pig moved on. He kept his foot down until he stopped at the intersection in Leimatu'a. Taxis streamed from the direction of the airport. Among them was a red Toyota. There was no mistaking the driver. Faro had a blond-headed woman beside him. We followed them all the way to Neiafu, four cars behind. My father dropped us off at the wharf with instructions to take *Squirt* back to the *Spray*, wait 30 minutes, and pick him up at the fuel dock.

Chapter 15

From across the bay, the boat looked like a seagoing fishing boat with a high, curved bow to plow through waves. It was one of thousands we'd seen traveling the oceans in search of a catch. Closer, it was too narrow to be stable, so they'd added outriggers on each side, crudely welded metal pipes, hewed-out tree trunks, and bamboo railings lashed together with rusty wires. Three wonky wooden masts held wires to the outriggers, brown canvas awnings to shelter the crew, long strings of fishing hooks tied to pink plastic buoys, and hundreds of withered gray triangles like flags at a car dealership.

"Frigging shark fins!" No save-the-environment banalities for science-boy.

"They make good soup." I relished provoking my brother.

Ben scowled back; he appreciated the importance of predators in balancing species. I hated sharks, though not enough to enjoy seeing their fins strung up to dry.

Two crew were on deck. One man with black shaggy hair sat idly by the steering wheel, watching us pass. The other man's head didn't move, just his eyes. A thick ponytail dangled behind his back. He was bare to the waist, leather brown with black tattoos over his arms and chest. He blew his nose on a yellow rag and went back to sharpening a machete. It was big enough to hack the fins from live sharks before heaving them overboard. The smell of rotting fish drifted over us.

My grandmother popped her head above the companionway. "Mmhmm! I'm glad we came here."

Not amused, my father eased back on the throttle. "We'll refuel and be on our way."

Behind the fishing boat was a catamaran. Its mast was tied down on the cabin roof. Blue tarpaulins covered most of the boat, parted where someone had been working on patches of gray plywood. Its metal fittings were homemade, rusty steel daubed with black paint.

My grandmother looked from fishing boat to catamaran. "Will we fit between them?"

He concentrated on backing up. I climbed over the stern rail, ready to jump. The wharf, a jumbled construction of warped, splintered logs, shuddered as the propeller churned. Brown muck swilled among barnacle-encrusted piles. He pinched every last bit of space until inches remained between the *Spray* and the fishing boat.

I didn't notice her until she called a relaxed 'hola.' Her couch was a tangle of fishing nets in the bow. She was lean like a runner, dark-brown like a surfer, and older than me by a year, if not more. She had long, glistening hair as black as her T-shirt, a handgun and red roses pushed out in front. She looked me over before she resumed tearing at a chicken leg.

"Hola. Parece sabroso?" I said, spluttering to remember 'tastes good' in Spanish.

She flashed me a smile, baring white pointy teeth like a carnivore.

"You going to stand there all day, Victor?" my father shouted.

The top of the wharf was six feet higher than the *Spray*'s deck, thick slabs of lumber prickled with rusty nails poking through years of gull droppings. Used car tires and heaps of green fishing nets lined the side. The stairs were wood, covered with slippery green slime. I missed my footing; however, I grabbed a handful of fishing net and dragged myself up.

With a knowing smirk, Ben tossed me a dock line. "Smooth, dude!"

I glared at him and tied the end to a corroded cleat, stealing peeks at the girl in the bow. She watched me like a wild cat, cunning, with dark brooding eyes.

"Bow!" My father made everything sound urgent.

I made a point of taking my time, dodging stacks of wooden fish traps on the dock, knowing her gaze was locked on my back. Still smirking, Ben tossed the bow line to me.

+ + +

There was a general store at the end of the dock, a converted Quonset hut from the 1940s. Next to it, someone had erected a shelter of palm tree poles dug into the sand, rafters of various lengths, and a dented sheet-metal roof. A crude sign in front read 'Fiji Yacht Club,' even though the main island of Fiji was 220 miles west. Tables and chairs spilled out three sides. A bamboo bar filled the other side. A few yards away, smoke coiled from a barbecue, an oil drum cut in half standing on steel-pipe legs. Ben and I went over to see what was cooking. Three small trussed birds that might have been chickens, but more likely terns, sizzled over glowing red coals. Ben grumbled 'bird murderer' and walked away. I was hungry.

"Welcome to Harry's Bar," a man called out. He wandered over to greet my father.

Harry was an expatriate Australian, a disgruntled merchant sailor who decided to jump ship when he found a port he liked. His New Zealand wife, Ellen, ran the Fulaga general store. He practically dragged us inside to meet her. With only 400 people eking out a living on the island, there wasn't much to buy, mostly beer, a small selection of over-priced canned food, some fishing equipment, and boxes of $3 paperback books and $10 videotapes, all marked with the name of the previous owner, 'Ellen Kincaid.'

"We're attracting a lot more sailors now the word's out, y'know," she announced, dipping into a jar of homemade candy. "Kiwifruit or pineapple?" She handed me a sticky green lump to try. "Everyone likes kiwifruit."

"We had three yachts here last month," Harry went on. He waved his hand at the mostly bare shelves. "We restocked to meet demand."

My father inspected the books and picked out three. "How about diesel fuel?"

"Three hundred bucks a drum, mate."

He hid his displeasure remarkably well. It was the same price in Niue. "I'll take two."

"Not bloody likely. That Filipino fishing boat took my last drum." Harry popped the top on a can of beer. "We're thinking about getting a tank installed."

"Ten gallons would see us through."

"Got every last drop, they did. We're expectin' a ship." Harry gulped a mouthful of beer, walked to the door, gargled, and spit into the sand. "A week or two, I'll have a dozen drums out back."

"Anyone else have diesel they'd be willing to sell?"

"Patrice; he keeps a spare drum for his generator. Bit of a hike." He jerked his thumb inland. "You'll need a tractor to haul it, mate. Only one on the island and it's waiting on parts."

"A week or two otherwise?" My father made sure.

"I doubt it'll be any sooner. You want a beer, mate?" Harry reached into the refrigerator.

+++

He told my mother a freighter was due in a couple of days.

It was scorching hot, yet she looked at him coldly. "Could it get any worse?"

"If the smell bothers you, we can anchor."

The lagoon was a vast turquoise crescent lined with beaches and dotted with mushroom-shaped rock outcrops. Stunted trees clung from the fissures, like bonsai gardens from a distance. Except for the Fulaga wharf, it was deserted. It was the perfect place for my father to anchor.

"I've smelled better," she said, still chilly.

"It's worse than the toilet," my grandmother added for good measure.

We constantly pestered my father about fixing the leaky head—it needed new seals. Rubber seals, like most things, were unavailable until we reached civilization.

He wasn't amused. "We'll stay here tonight. Spend the afternoon cleaning the *Spray*."

I could tell my mother liked the idea, already at work cleaning sticky globs from the galley countertop. Books, school projects, bits of coral, bird feathers, and dirty clothes cluttered the cabin. The head looked like it hadn't been cleaned in a year. He handed me a tin of polish and rags from the cleaning supplies locker.

"Winches, stanchions, anything metal. I want to see my face." He fixed his gaze on Ben, trying not to be noticed in his berth with his encyclopedia propped in front him. "You polish the portholes, mister. Outside first, so you can see the difference when you do the inside."

Ben climbed out of his berth, his Tahitian sunglasses in hand. "What if I scratch them?"

"Don't! Do the hatches as well." He handed Ben a rag and window cleaner before he turned to my sister. She stared back at him, silently daring him to assign her a task. "Jessie, help your grandmother."

He poked around in the locker to find what he needed to clean the engine room. On his way aft, he stopped before his chart desk and searched through his rows of CDs. He pushed Stravinsky into the player and went on his way, humming the opening bars. Safe behind zany sunglasses, Ben snapped a mocking salute to his back.

My grandmother waited until he was out of sight. "Yes Sir, Captain Bligh."

Under my breath, I added, "Mutiny, there's no other way Mr. Christian."

My sense of humor resembled hers, and we shared a love of ancient tales, nothing else. With brown curly hair, Ben and Jessie looked a lot more like her.

Chapter 16

She was back in the bow, peeling yams with a fishing knife, shaving long curling strips which she tossed over the side; the yams she put in a bucket. I kept my head down exploiting my peripheral vision while I polished the winches. It was hard work—there was no easy way to clean off sea crud. When a winch was a mirror, I moved to the next one. Every time I looked at her, she glanced away, only for a moment before her wandering eyes returned. Finally, she stood and looked directly at me. I felt like an idiot, squatting before the starboard jib-sheet winch, cloth in one hand, can of polish in the other, rubbing off grunge.

"Hey, you clean my boat next?" she laughed.

In a flash, my face burned. Ben's whispered 'Do it, dude. She's hot,' didn't help.

He ditched the role of environment warden to wave to her from the aft cabin hatch. She waved back good-naturedly, shaking out long dark hair. Tanned, tight black T-shirt, tatty miniscule red shorts; no wonder Ben was dripping window cleaner on the deck.

She smirked at me as she stepped onto the outrigger. Like a cat on a fence, she walked to the end, sprang to the wharf and strolled away, sashaying her butt like a fashion model. We watched her all the way down to the general store.

When she returned, she stopped opposite Ben. "What your name, Sunglasses?"

"Ben."

"Americano?" She extended a bony foot, red-tipped toes nudging a coil of seaweed off the dock. I gave up polishing.

"Si," he peeped.

She pointed to the stern. "*Spray* is long away?" When Ben didn't answer, she asked, "Cuánto tiempo téngale que viaja?"

Ben's forte was science. He looked to me.

"She wants to know how long we've been away."

"You tell her. You're the one with the diary."

She tilted her head, her eyes locked on mine.

"Diecisiete meses. About 17 months," I added for Ben's benefit. I'd made 433 entries in my diary since we left Portsmouth.

"You Spanish better my English. What your name?"

"Josh. Cuál es su nombre?"

She teased with a smile. "Maleah." She pointed to a man with black bushy hair. "Manila, he my brother; he say your family work like Filipinos."

"Who's working? This is fun." I rubbed extra hard.

"Walk on beach is fun. Come with me?"

"When I've finished, okay?"

She smiled mischievously. I went to work on the winch, buffing briskly as she ambled down the wharf.

+ + +

Four hours later, the *Spray* gleamed, never as clean since we left Norfolk, Virginia. No mold, no fingerprints on mirrors, no salt-encrusted portholes, brilliant metal fittings, even the floors were bright with wax. My grease-covered father was taking a shower when I announced I was going for a walk on the beach.

Maleah waited at the end of the wharf. We walked beside the lagoon, miniature crabs scuttling in every direction, skirting canoes carved from trees, eventually kicking off our sandals and splashing

141

though lukewarm water. When we stopped, a giant necklace of mushroom-shaped rocks surrounded us. The water was shallow and crystal clear. Waves had rippled the sand into endless furrows. Pacific Reef Herons stepped on greenish legs, pecking on a bottom littered with shells.

"How long have you been living on board?" She didn't understand so I asked again in Spanish.

"Always. Fifteen years." She scooped up a handful of shells, flipping them one at a time into the water. "Shell no good. How old you?"

"Fourteen. I couldn't live on a boat all my life…"

"What is family name?" she interrupted.

"Walker."

She leaned closer, brushing my front. Unhurriedly, she drew her finger down my cheek, to my chin. Her fingernails were bright red like her toenails. Her dark eyes bored into me.

"Victor Walker from *Spray*…" she mused. One finger held my head still. "Even more handsome."

Sunlight shimmered in her hair like electrical charges. Suddenly, she laughed and stepped away. We waded into waist-deep water, picking up shells. One was an Imperial volute as big as my fist. She rinsed off sand and bits of coral and held up the shell for me to see.

"In Suva, this sell five dollar. Too bad it chipped." She tossed it away.

"Where's there's one, there are usually others."

"Deeper is better. We swim, yes?"

She raised her arms over her head, pulling up her clinging-wet T-shirt. I got more than a glimpse of bare brown skin.

After a dinner of grilled 'chicken' and greasy yam fries that Harry called 'chips', my family went for a walk on the beach. My father, intent on exercise, strode ahead with my mother. The rest of us lagged behind, stopping frequently to pick through twisted driftwood, palm fronds, and broken shells; scallops, turbans, cowries, and helmet shells. Only one shell was worth keeping, an unusual nautilus resembling folded paper. I'd seen them at the Papeete market, as big as cereal bowls, selling for $200.

My grandmother was still enthusing over the shell, when something caught her eye. She knelt down, scraped away debris, and carefully dug something out of the sand.

Expecting she found a second nautilus, I said, "Lucky you."

She looked at me the same way throughout our walk on the beach, like I'd done something wrong. "Is this valuable?" She carefully handed it to Ben.

"Wow! You almost never find them on Pacific islands."

He grinned and tossed a small yellow rubber ball to Jessie. She tossed it to me. We played catch all the way back to the wharf, when my father decided it was time for family photographs. He posed my mother and grandmother at the water's edge, gazing out to sea, a spectacular red sky behind them.

Ben made a face. "Our turn next."

Not if I could prevent it. I threw the ball to Jessie. She threw it to Ben. The next time it sailed over her head. She ran after it. Ben and I took off after her. At the end of the wharf, Maleah and her lanky long-haired brother talked with the man with the tattoos. He sprawled on copra bags, beads of perspiration on his forehead, his eyes bloodshot. He picked up our ball.

Jessie halted in front of him. "Could I have my ball please?" She held out her hand.

The man kept squeezing his eyes shut. He had an ugly pimpled rash on his neck.

Maleah smiled in my direction. "He good fisherman, but coconut is smarter."

My mother came over. She had a frown under her sunhat.

"This is Maleah and her brother, Manila. They're from the fishing boat," I explained.

She pulled Jessie back as the man coughed, again and again. He tossed the ball to Jessie before he slumped back.

"He needs to see a doctor," she said to Maleah.

"Doctor in Suva, Mrs. Walker."

"He has an infection, viral judging by the rash. If it continues, it could be bad."

Before Maleah could ask, her brother said, "Next week okay."

Ben pushed in front of him. "You shouldn't kill sharks."

Manila looked down at him. "Why?"

"They're an important part of the ecosystem."

"Ben!" My mother jerked his arm to get him moving. "I wouldn't waste time getting him to a doctor. He's probably highly contagious."

"Get over it," Manila laughed as we walked down the wharf.

"What do you think of Josh's new girlfriend?" Ben ducked when I tried to shove him into the lagoon.

My mother gave me a disapproving look. "I think Dani is much nicer."

"It's not like that!"

Before we reached the *Spray*, I knew something was wrong. Jag met us on the wharf, hungry, purring, and bumping our legs. However, we'd left him locked in the cabin in accordance with Fiji's rules for visiting pets. Someone had forced the latch and opened the hatch. My father quickly climbed down the ladder and hurried below. He soon reappeared, as angry as I'd ever seen him.

"Both radios gone; hacked out of the frame. Nothing else." He glared at the fishing boat. "It doesn't make sense. They left the kids' laptops on the table."

"It's not worth a fight, John." My mother always sided with caution.

+++

Fulanga was too small to have a full-time policeman; however, a man in his sixties came by the next morning. He was also the mayor. He asked a few questions about the radios, examined the damage, and scratched his head. With his official investigation concluded, he assured my father he'd contact us if the radios turned up.

As soon as he left, my grandmother addressed me. "Josh, I don't butt into something that's none of my business…"

"What?"

"Maleah disturbs me."

"How?" My father put aside his pen and closed the Ship's Log. Recording the robbery only added to his bad mood.

She let out a deep sigh. "It's her manner."

He pounced. "Meaning what, exactly?"

"I'm sorry, Josh… She's very…" She settled on, 'forward;' however, she meant more than 'forward' because she looked right

145

at me. "I went for a walk on the beach after we cleaned the boat yesterday. It wasn't my intention to spy... What I saw really bothers me."

"What happened, Victor?"

At my father's tone, Ben peeked over his encyclopedia. In the bow cabin, my sister stopped a one-sided conversation with the cat.

I glanced at my grandmother. "We went for a walk on the beach."

"What happened?"

"He doesn't need an inquisition," my mother interrupted. "I'll talk with him upstairs."

She followed me up the stairs, directing me to the bow, as far away as we could get and still be on board.

"You didn't say you were going for a walk with her," she began.

"I didn't think it was important."

"Maleah reminds me of some of the girls I went to high school with. They flirted with every boy they met. They never achieved much."

I wanted to say that Maleah wasn't a flirt, but she was. We were a world apart, like our boats. Her boat was chaotic, yet exotic, with a high prow of intricate carved wood. It reminded me of a beak, its scrawny outriggers like wings. Our *Spray*, like Joshua Slocum, was solidly New England, practical and puritanical.

"What happened?"

"Why'd she have to bring it up in front of him?"

"She's worried about you. Josh?" She watched me, waiting.

"Maleah wanted to dive for shells, so she took her shirt off. She didn't have anything on underneath."

"Oh?" My mother smiled a little.

"She doesn't have our hang ups about being seen."

"I guess not. Nothing else happened?" she asked. I shook my head. "You're at the age when everything starts changing."

"I've had the talk already. Twice."

"There's a big difference between theory and practice." She smiled and shook her head.

"You're not upset?"

"After four years in medical school, they're just mammary glands." She smiled at my relief. "It's normal for a teenage boy to be interested in boobs."

I grinned back.

"However, your grandmother's right to be worried. You need to be careful with girls like her."

"She's only a year older."

"I'm afraid you're out of your league with her," she teased, yet she meant it.

My father appeared in the companionway. "We're leaving. Right now."

"What happened to refueling?"

"We've got enough. Victor, I need you on the wharf. Bow lines last."

Chapter 17

"John! Get up here! Now!" My mother was worried.

Just out of the shower, my father bolted through the cabin, still wet as he pulled on a shirt. I scrambled from my berth and followed him up the stairs. Astern, a bank of menacing gray clouds raced towards us; however that wasn't the reason.

Ben knelt on the cockpit seat, peering through binoculars. "It's the fishing boat, Dad."

My father stepped over his legs and jerked the binoculars away. He focused on a speck on the ocean. "Why am I not surprised?"

Soon, the boat was close enough to see dense black smoke churning behind it.

He handed the binoculars to my mother. "It looks like they've got issues. We'll see what they want."

"Should I start the engine?"

"Not enough fuel, even if we could outrun them. Pity you didn't see them earlier."

"Mom was reading and I was asleep," Ben whispered to me.

"Right now, the squall's a bigger problem."

Silence ruled while I helped him lower the mizzen sail, the breeze already getting stronger. Cloud plumes curled under the approaching storm. It was a bad sign, enough to furl the outer jib and tie down *Squirt*. He was still debating whether to reef the mainsail when we heard Maleah shout 'help'.

"Is that Victor's girlfriend waving from the bow?" He didn't intend it to be funny.

"Accidente! Accidente!"

"Accident, bull shit! Then again, you never know... Kids below!" He pulled me aside. "Sorry about the girlfriend comment. It was uncalled for."

I followed Ben down the stairs, glad my grandmother wasn't into recriminations. She was dressed for a faculty dinner party, a white blouse and floral print skirt she'd stitched by hand. Her latest creation, fresh Pacific Bonito and bananas sautéed in coconut waited for us on the stove, and the smell of baking bread filled the cabin. Ben flopped on the couch, my sister beside him. She had Jag in a death grip. We could hear every word through the companionway.

"My brother hurt," Maleah shouted.

Another man bellowed 'stop' in Spanish. My father bellowed 'no' back.

"Oil fire burn his eyes. Please help him," Maleah begged.

"What's the plan?" My mother sounded worried too.

"I'll ram them if I have too. Take out one of those flimsy outriggers. It'll put an end to this nonsense."

Through the porthole, I watched the fishing boat come alongside, belching black fumes. One man slouched in the stern with a towel wrapped over his face. He might've been Maleah's brother.

"He dying. Help us please," Maleah cried.

"We can't. Someone stole our radios," my father shouted back.

"John, what if it's true?"

The boat's outrigger was only a few yards away from the *Spray* before he steered away from it.

"Manila need doctor, Mister Walker. He hurt bad!"

149

Maleah ran to the stern as the fishing boat swerved in again. My father changed course until the sails flapped. The fishing boat turned with us, a foul-smelling black cloud spewing from a cargo hatch.

"Keep off," my father yelled.

Maleah peeled up the side of the towel. The skin underneath was black as diesel soot. "You help. I don't want him die."

"Maybe I should take a look at him," my mother said.

The fishing boat veered towards us again. My father boldly jerked the steering wheel towards it. The *Spray* came within inches of its outrigger before he chickened out. Every sailor we met had a tale of international injustice involving collisions at sea.

"Victor, get the flare gun. We'll scare them off."

He stored his flare gun and a plastic box of shells in the 'emergency' locker.

"What about the other gun?"

He had a real gun hidden under his chart table. It was a pain to get out—the sliding panel was so tight it jammed.

"Flare gun!"

I carried his flare gun and shells upstairs. Thirty feet away, the crew lined the rail, one picking at the wood with his knife, three smoking cigarettes, all of them staring at us. Suddenly, one of the men tossed his cigarette in the sea. He clambered over the rail and onto the outrigger frame, gripping the ropes when waves sloshed over his feet.

"Throw rope!"

"Go to hell!" my father shouted.

While I tried to open his clunky Cold-War-era flare gun, my mother ripped the seal from the box. Inside, were twelve flares bigger than shotgun shells.

"Stop playing with the frigging gun and load it!" my father growled.

"It's friggin' jammed!" The release latch needed a hammer to free it.

He adjusted the wheel lock so the self-steering could do its job. By the time he opened the latch and inserted a flare, Manila stood in the stern of the fishing boat, his long hair tied in a dangling pigtail. He wiped soot from his face with the towel.

My father leveled the flare gun. "Back the hell off!"

With a laugh, Manila pointed a rifle at him, a black military carbine. "You lose, Mister Walker."

Our flare gun clunked on the seat.

Maleah and three men swarmed across, jumping from the outrigger to the *Spray*. One of the men took control of the wheel. He tried to steer, shaking his head when the *Spray* changed direction with the wind. Manila crossed last, handed his rifle to the still-puzzled man behind the wheel, picked up the flare gun, and stuck his head in the companionway.

"Get up here!"

My mother got in his face. "Leave my children alone."

He pointed the flare gun at her head. He grinned and pushed her down on the cockpit seat. "Too pretty to shoot." He turned to me and smirked. "Maleah tease, yes?"

"Pig!" Maleah slapped at him.

"I think she likes you." Manila laughed and thrust me towards her.

She stepped aside and I banged into the binnacle. I clambered up, my fists clenched. From behind, my father held my shoulder. "Cool it, Victor."

"Feed you to shark, boy," Manila sneered as Ben followed my sister up the stairs. "Save ecosystem. Ha!"

My grandmother stood behind Ben, her floral dress billowing in the wind. "What are you going to do with us?"

"What you hide, boy?" Manila reached for Ben's arm.

Ben backed away, squirming past my grandmother, something clutched in his hand. He scrambled over the cockpit seat and onto the roof of the aft cabin.

Manila saw a stubby antenna and laughed. "No one hear toy radio."

Ben inched towards the stern, keeping his surprise where Manila couldn't see it. "We passed an atoll an hour ago."

"No water. No one live there." Manila curled his lip and held out his hand.

Maleah tried to grab Ben's leg. He jumped behind the mizzen mast, ducking under its boom. He pressed the waterproof switch on the side of our lime-yellow EPIRB and tossed it over the side. It bobbed to the surface, LED light blinking, transmitting a distress signal to satellites as it swirled away. The man with the rifle rushed to the stern and fired four times before the EPIRB disappeared behind a wave. On the way back, he seized Ben by the wrist and dragged him into the cockpit.

Manila shoved Ben against Jessie, knocking her against the steering wheel. A spoke struck just above her eye. My father leaped up, fists clenched.

My mother lifted my bawling sister into her lap. "It won't help if you're dead."

"Do what she say or this one feed shark." Manila poked Ben in the chest.

"What a charming young man," my grandmother said quietly.

"Old cow!" He elbowed Ben into her arms and scratched at a long razor cut on the back of his hand. "Where pussy cat?"

Jessie launched herself into the companion way. Manila grabbed her arm and dragged her back. She flailed and kicked at his shins. He hoisted her higher. She went for his knees.

"Kitten with claws fight dirty like you, Maleah." Laughing, he yanked on Jessie's hair, bringing her face close. He licked his lips. "I think we keep this one."

His grimy fingernails dug into Jessie's arm until she squealed. His crew laughed loudly.

"You said you'd let us go."

Manila pushed my mother onto the seat with his free hand. He turned to face me. "How you know Faro?"

"Faro? He plays for the Red Sox, right?"

He tilted his head. "What Red Sox?"

"A baseball team in Boston," I smirked at his frown. "You never heard of the Major Leagues?"

It just made him worse. He dumped my sister on the cockpit seat and jerked his thumb at our dinghy, strapped to the cabin roof behind the mast. "Put in water."

His men were untying it when a blistering gust struck from behind. The next gust switched direction by 90 degrees. The self-steering tried to follow it, though not fast enough. The *Spray* pitched from side to side, plowing through the waves. After things settled down, Manila hurried into the cabin.

"Here pussy! Pretty pussy; come here, pussy. Where you hide cat? Hey, is nice boat," he called to his crew. "Two hundred grand easy."

My father waited until Manila reappeared. "I can give you money."

"How much?"

"Twenty thousand."

Manila's head came to his chin. "Faro pay more."

My father didn't hesitate. "Forty thousand."

Manila shook his head; however, he was thinking about it. He was still undecided when his crew heaved *Squirt* over the rail. It banged against the *Spray*, dragging through the waves. A gust howled past, shoving the *Spray* away from the fishing boat. Huge rain drops slapped the sails. Overhead, black clouds turned the sea much darker than it had been only a minute earlier.

My grandmother tried again. "I have money too."

Manila turned on her. "Get in dinghy, Grandma."

She stared back. "How much did Faro offer you?"

He got in her face. "Now!" She didn't flinch. "NOW COW!"

He roared with laughter and thrust her away with the heel of his hand. His crew shoved her into the bouncing dinghy, followed by Ben. When they grabbed Jessie and pushed her towards the cabin, my father leaped from the cockpit seat. The long-haired man pointed the rifle at my father's head, a tobacco-stained finger hooked on the trigger. My mother screamed.

"Fifty thousand for all of us." My father's voice was unwavering.

"Shut up!" Manila glared at me. His eyes were bloodshot and mucus crusted. "Faro pay hundred grand for him, dead or alive."

"All I have is fifty. Twenty now, the rest when we're safe."

Manila laughed at my father. "Go, before I shoot you."

No sooner than my mother had climbed down to the dinghy, another gust slammed the *Spray* onto her side, the end of the boom dragging through the sea.

My father gave it his best shot. "For God's sake, man! Fifty thousand is all we've got."

"Not enough. Too bad. You make wheel work or I shoot Grandma."

My exasperated father released the self-steering in time to stop the *Spray* from colliding with the fishing boat. With the wind from behind, she raced through the waves. He stared at the chart plotter, flicked his head at me, and jiggled the wheel back and forth.

"She's all yours, Manila; however, I'd let Victor steer if I were you."

Instead, Manila took the wheel. My father timed the roll and swung himself over the rail, kicking waves before he let go. He dropped into *Squirt*, almost turning it over. It bucked in the waves, my family clinging to the ropes along the sides. No one had a life jacket.

Maleah smiled. "Bye-bye, Mr. Walker."

She untied the dinghy line and threw it into the water. *Squirt* quickly dropped back as the *Spray* rolled with the next gust, turning away from the fishing boat. Her mainsail strained, ready to fling across, the remaining jib flapping wildly.

"Do it," Manila barked.

The man with the rifle stepped onto the cockpit seat, his feet wide apart, waiting for a clear shot. Maleah looked amused. I turned away; I hated her. Another gust shoved the *Spray* into a huge rolling wave, submerging the rail and the side deck. Maleah shrieked. I lunged for the steering wheel and spun it in the opposite direction. The rifle banged. A moment later, the wind flung the mainsail across as the *Spray* gybed. The boom, a thick white aluminum tube, hit the man's head, a resounding crack as loud as the gunshot. He soared over the side, arms and legs spread wide. His rifle clattered on the floor of the cockpit.

The *Spray* charged the fishing boat, accelerating with the new wind direction. She slammed into the outrigger, crushing handrails, struts, and fishing poles.

"I kill you myself," Manila screamed in my face.

I dodged his fist, keeping the steering wheel between us. Maleah thrust me towards him. I jerked back. I didn't intend to elbow her in the mouth. Spitting a tooth and blood, she clawed my arm.

All around was a hopeless tangle of sails, rigging, nets, and strings of dried shark fins. Manila grabbed at me as I leaped from the cockpit. I felt fingernails like talons, slicing my arm as I went over the side.

Chapter 18

I clawed my way to the surface, bursting into foam and wailing wind, the *Spray's* flapping sails louder than thunder. Waves surged around me, trying to drag me down, rain droplets stinging like slingshot pellets.

"Josh! Over here!" my grandmother shouted.

I couldn't see *Squirt* for the waves smashing into my face. Choking on seawater made swimming next to impossible. I turned onto my back, kicking hard to stay on the surface. Amazingly, the *Spray's* bowsprit had punched a hole through the side of the fishing boat, skewering them together. Her sails were full of wind, forcing the fishing boat to turn too.

I was ready to give up and swim back to the *Spray* when I spotted my family two waves away. My mother and father used the oars as paddles; Ben bailed water with a cutoff milk jug; my grandmother and Jessie crouched in the bow, searching for me. I shouted until a wave smacked my mouth. I coughed it up. After I caught my breath, I swam towards where I'd seen them.

A wave boosted me high enough for a glimpse of gray rubber and my family huddled down to avoid tipping over. I thought I would catch up; however, at the next crest, *Squirt* was three waves away. I screamed 'help' until I coughed so much I couldn't breathe. A lifeguard would've made me get out of the pool.

When I looked back, the *Spray's* bowsprit had snapped off, yet she was still stuck fast, tangled in the outrigger. Men with axes hacked at ropes and wires. One brutal gust threatened to tip her right over. Then, something broke with a bang and the *Spray* went sideways. Seconds later, it rammed the fishing boat's stern. Slowly, the boats turned, side by side but in opposite directions. The *Spray's* jib flogged in tatters, her mainsail ripped down a seam.

Manila bellowed orders to his crew in Spanish and what might have been Chinese or Malay. They rushed about, throwing truck tires tied to ropes between the boats and then lashing them together.

"Josh!" Ben shouted from behind me.

With no waves between us, my mother and father paddled as hard as they could, and I swam. Suddenly, my father towered over Ben. He caught my hands and dragged me up the side of the dinghy. I was too exhausted to climb in. All around me, thunder boomed and lightening lit up the sea, ferocious gusts driving rain into the waves, roaring in my ears.

He grabbed the back of my shorts and heaved me in. It was terrible timing; a wave boosted *Squirt*, tilting it near vertical. Jessie screamed and clung to my grandmother. My mother leaped to the other side of the dinghy, pulling Ben with her. Somehow, they managed to stop it flipping over. He pushed me onto the floor, picked up his oar, and went back to paddling. *Squirt* slewed sideways before my mother resumed paddling on the other side.

Squirt slammed into the next wave. I felt a sickening gush and vomited lunch. Buckets of ocean poured over the side and washed it away. Ben went back to bailing, flinging water over the side.

Jessie touched my cheek with little icy fingers. "It's going to be alright, Josh." She sniffled; rain drenched her hair, matted with blood from a cut over her eye.

My grandmother was so cold she was shaking. "Oh my god! A man just fell in."

My father grunted approval. "Serves the blighter right!"

Another wave rushed the bow. After it passed, six inches of water sloshed in the dinghy. I got some of it out by cupping my hands together. It was like emptying a bathtub one leaky cup at time.

"Stay down, Victor! You've done your share."

My mother paddled until her hands were raw. I took over her oar. By then, the rain came straight down, so much rain it was difficult to see farther than a few waves ahead.

My grandmother's face was gray. "We'll be okay, won't we?"

I thought he hadn't heard over the rain. Eventually, he said, "The current is half a knot and the wind is behind us. If we paddle north, we'll see Moala tomorrow evening."

"Don't we need a compass?"

"There are other islands if we miss it." He nudged me. "Probably a good time to take a breather."

He retrieved the storage canister from under the seat, unscrewed the lid, and emptied the contents on his lap. He opened a waterproof flashlight and pried out batteries wrapped in five $20 bills—'emergency money'. There were two plastic water bottles—empty, a tube of sunscreen—half-full, a moldy nylon jacket Ben thought he'd lost in the Marquesas, six pieces of candy we'd purchased months ago in Chile, and the knife he'd given to me for Christmas in Rio de Janeiro. It was made in China, rusty with a thick blade and a marlinspike for undoing knots. He pocketed my knife and the flashlight.

We spread out Ben's jacket to form a valley emptying into the bucket. We filled the bottles and the canister before the rain ended in the middle of the night.

+ + +

By the next morning, the sky had cleared and a steady breeze pushed us towards a bank of fluffy clouds over an island, probably Moala. Our clothes soon dried in the sun, beating down so strong my mother worried about sunburn and sunstroke. We slathered on sunscreen and took frequent sips from the bucket; and we rowed.

Jessie slumped against my mother, sucking the last piece of candy. "What about Jag?"

My mother brushed tangled curls from Jessie's forehead. "He'll be okay, Honey."

It was my grandmother's turn in the bow, the only place where there was room to sit with any semblance of comfort. "I bet he's hiding in your bed. When he gets hungry, he'll sneak out and steal their food."

"What if they catch him?"

"Jag's been lucky ever since he was a kitten." My mother felt Jessie's forehead again.

He noticed immediately. Jessie was getting sick and everyone knew it except her. "He was Josh's third birthday present. His luck must've rubbed off."

Jessie pushed her hand away. "He's my cat now!"

The name came out of nowhere, like peeling off bedroom wallpaper and finding another layer, familiar yet foreign.

"I used to call him Tiger," I said. "He's everyone's cat now."

My father acknowledged me with a nod. "He was always with you. He slept in your bed every night."

A shiver ran through me. When Barkov started the fire that killed my grandparents, I'd been downstairs looking for my furry little bed companion.

"He got away from you when they carried you out of the house," he added quietly. "I found him the next day, hiding in the garage."

+ + +

Moala was a dusky smudge on the horizon by midday. My father was convinced we could reach it by nightfall until the wind ended. We rowed across a glassy sea, my shoulders and arms aching, my hands so blistered it was agony to hold the oars. Water sloshed over my feet until they were bleached and wrinkled. Sunburn, sea lice, and salt rash made me itch all over. When it was my turn to rest, I sprawled in the bow, my hands clamped over my ears to block the endless slap of waves.

I awoke after sunset. Moala was close enough to see a cluster of lights, a beacon directly ahead. My grandmother dozed between my brother and sister. My father and mother bickered and took turns rowing, slowly moving *Squirt* closer to the island. After an hour, we could hear the distant roar of waves crashing over the reef.

"You think we'll make it?" My mother was exhausted.

He licked and blew on his hands. They were swollen, his blisters far worse than mine. "Just pray the current slows behind the island."

Squirt drifted into the night. Every few minutes, he pointed the flashlight at a few tiny pinpricks of light and pressed the button three times. I'd almost given up on Moala when my father nudged me.

"Your turn to row."

With the widest part of the island behind us, the current swept back to fill in the sea. It carried us along at walking speed. We came close enough to see palm trees silhouetted on the shore. Up close, the reef was impenetrable, eddies of foam swirling over ragged coral heads just inches below the surface. I pointed out a reef shark fin a dozen yards away. In the dark, even small sharks were lethal.

"Now what?"

"Now we paddle!" My father unscrewed the oars, took one for himself, and passed the other to me. "Got to be an opening eventually." He jerked back his paddle, spinning *Squirt* around. "Paddle, damn it!"

I was about to say 'stick it' when my grandmother said, "Over there!"

In a patch of dark, rippled water was a buoy with a stick through the center, leaning at an angle in the fast moving current. My father headed towards it. My hands burned; I made one stroke for his two until my mother took my place.

'Tabas' had painted his name on his fish-trap float. So much for marking a channel. Before my parents could paddle away, the current swept *Squirt* into churning foam.

"Dad, there's a rock!"

Ben's warning came too late. *Squirt* slammed into a rock a few inches above the surface. Waves appeared out of nowhere, lifting one side and shoving everyone sideways, pushing down the other side. Our water containers tumbled out and swirled away. I was sure we'd tip over, until with a terrifying rip, *Squirt* tore free. My father thrust his paddle at me, the inflated tube on his side of the dinghy already sagging. I beat at the water as he leaned over the side, feeling under the tube with his hands. He found the tear and plugged it with his T-shirt, jamming it in until the hissing stopped. Immediately, *Squirt* bumped on another rock. I shoved us off with the paddle.

The shore was still a half mile away, a painful hour of paddling a partially deflated *Squirt,* followed by dragging it through knee-deep water to reach a tiny patch of beach surrounded by palm trees. We staggered onto gritty dry sand and flopped down. Only my father remained standing.

"Thirty minutes rest and we'll head off."

"We'll stay here till morning." My mother stretched out next to Jessie. Without the breeze, it was stifling hot, yet Jessie shivered nonstop.

"The sooner we report it, the better the chance of catching them." He'd talked of nothing else all day.

"Then go report it!"

He looked at her, shook his head, and stumbled off into the darkness. She didn't comment beyond a tired sigh. My grandmother hugged Ben until he fell asleep. My blistered hands hurt too much to sleep properly. I dozed against *Squirt*, listening to wind whisper through palm fronds, waves lapping on the beach, the chirp of giant cockroaches.

Chapter 19

I woke up to the shrill calls of seagulls harassing tiny birds pecking for seeds. The mosquitoes had been hungry during the night—I scratched red lumps on my arms and legs and worried about Dengue Fever and Elephantiasis. Farther down the beach, a storm had knocked a coconut palm sideways. It hung over the lagoon, a mirror for a perfect blue sky. Ben straddled the trunk, creeping towards large green pods tucked among its festooning fronds. With his legs clamped tightly, he leaned out and knocked off three coconuts before he wriggled back.

After we smashed off the pithy husk, we tried to make a hole by chipping with a shard of black stone. I spent ten frustrating minutes chiseling before I gave up. Ben kept on gouging. His persistence paid off when he brushed off bits of shell and took a swig. He carried the coconut over to my grandmother. She looked awful, her hair in knots, her face burned and peeling. Like Jessie, she'd vomited over the side of the dinghy a couple of times. She'd taken only a few sips of rainwater, barely enough to wet her lips. She took a small drink from Ben's coconut and handed it back.

"Drink it Mom." My mother used her stern nurse voice.

"I can't. I'm going to be sick any moment."

Ben held out the battered coconut. "You'll be a lot sicker if you get dehydrated, Grandma."

My grandmother smiled weakly. "Thank you, Doctor Kildare."

Science boy was up to the challenge. "Coconut water's got sugar, vitamins, proteins, antioxidants, and minerals; plus it balances your electrolytes. It's better than water."

There was no escaping my determined brother. We chipped holes in six more coconuts before my father returned with two young Polynesian men and a two-wheel hand cart. Mick and Mack Tabas were lean and wiry with frizzy black hair, identical twins with matching hole-infested T-shirts, baggy shorts, and machetes, which hung from rope belts.

My father handed out plastic bottles of water. I dropped mine when I tried to unscrew the cap.

"How are your hands?"

I held them out, palm up. I couldn't straighten my blistered fingers. He dug in his pocket, pulled out a tube of sunburn ointment, and handed it to me.

"We'll be lucky if we don't get malaria." Mosquitoes had dined on my mother's face.

He barely glanced at her. "How's Jessie?"

"She's still got a fever."

"I got through to the police. Fiji's sending a patrol boat in case they're still in the area."

"They'll pick us up?" she said.

"Not their job. It'd be different if we were injured."

"Two days adrift in a dinghy; we're in great shape."

Chagrined, he looked to Mick and Mack. They were busy loading our damaged dinghy on their rickety cart. "We need to keep a low profile. There's a ship in a week. We can wait at their village. It's rather rough going; a couple of hours." He was almost apologetic.

My mother got to her feet. "We might as well get started."

+ + +

For a week, the islanders gave us mangos, bananas, and homemade bread. For $2, my father purchased a hand-line, hooks,

165

and sinkers, and caught yellow-spotted trevally fish. For another $2, my mother bought a battered frying pan to cook it in. Ben and I foraged for conch and coconuts, and scrounged a small axe to bust them open. My father steadfastly refused offers to let us sleep in a hut. Instead of dealing with the mangy flea-ridden dogs roaming the village, we slept on the beach, under a borrowed mosquito net propped up on palm fronds. My sister shivered while the rest of us sweltered. When it rained, we huddled under *Squirt*. It was horrid.

At sunrise of the seventh day, my father strapped *Squirt* on the cart he'd borrowed from Mick and Mack. We crossed the island to Naroi, the main village. Hidden by hills and trees, metal-roofed huts half the size of a single-wide trailer, clustered along the shore. The biggest building was the school. Children ran out of the classrooms to greet us, waving and chattering as if we were the first white people they'd seen. The stench of rotting fish arrived in the breeze. It grew stronger until we passed the trash pile, scattering seagulls and rats by the score.

We walked down to the sea, every step lifting our moods. Palm trees lined the shore, fronds fluttering in the afternoon breeze. Crystal water lapped the shore. Women in traditional dresses waved woven fans and sang farewell songs to passengers who lugged rolled-up bedding and bulging bags to the waiting area. Men bustled about unloading carts of bananas and bags of coconuts. Other men dragged motorboats down a ramp and readied them for the trip out to a small cargo ship. The *Tunatuki* had been a Russian fishing boat until the Fijian government confiscated it. Its current owner added a shed for passengers to sleep in and painted the ship green with vivid yellow and red trim. It carried everything, from cows to cement.

The local travel agent had a beach umbrella, a table, and chair. He chatted with every passer-by while he sold bottled drinks and sandwiches, cigarettes, and tickets to Suva priced in Fiji and US dollars—forty dollars per person, children under 14 half price.

Hoping for a family discount, my father went over to find out. Four minutes later, he returned.

"The family package is eighty bucks."

Ben grinned and saluted the heavens. "Yes!"

So far we'd spent $5.65 of the money stash. There were still four $20 notes rolled up in the flashlight, and $14.35 in his pocket.

"A 'family' is two adults and two kids. One-twenty is the best he'll do for all of us."

My grandmother had ripped the arms from her blouse and six inches of hem from her dress and turned the remnants into a sunhat. She looked like a feisty rooster.

"You told him about our dire situation, John?"

"Why do you think he reduced the rate?"

Miffed, she thought for a moment. "I'm sure the embassy has funds for situations like ours."

"We have to get there first. Plus we don't have passports, Sarah."

I took over the role of feisty rooster. "So what? We lost them."

My mother had been quiet until then. "As far as the embassy's concerned, we don't exist."

"Our passports are fake?" The look on Ben's face was worth a week on Moala.

"Your passport is okay; so is Jessie's."

"Grandma's?" Ben was still stunned.

"Forged years ago. I expect she can use her real name." She looked at my father.

He shrugged, now standing apart after delivering the bad news. Mick and Mack had offered him $50 for *Squirt*. He'd turned it down, and carted the dinghy across the island. I felt sorry for him.

"What's Grandma's real name?" Jessie's eyes were inflamed.

My father regarded her fondly. "Marjorie Ryder, Ph.D."

"She's famous. She wrote five books, two of them novels. They were best sellers." My mother was proud.

My grandmother began to laugh. "I also gave the keynote address at the National Society of Historians, and now I'm sitting on an island in the middle of the Pacific Ocean without a penny to my name. C'est la vie!"

My father cleared his throat. "I bought the 'family' package."

"We're sticking together, John." My mother's voice was as sharp as a nail.

"Victor and I will stay here."

"And live on what? Fourteen bucks?"

"He can fish. I'll do odd jobs. It won't be more than a few days. I figure the embassy will be more willing to assist two women with kids, stranded after their ship went down."

My mother dabbed sweat from Jessie's forehead. "For God's sake, be serious."

"I'd prefer we stay together. There isn't a choice...."

My sister sneezed green mucus and smeared it away with the back of her hand. She had difficulty breathing and it seemed to be getting worse.

He looked at me. "It's safe enough here."

I hoped I wouldn't make him angry. "I think we should contact Sal and let him know what happened."

"Already done, hopefully." My father helped Jessie stand up. "I should've mentioned it earlier. I asked the police to broadcast a message on the Pacific Net: 'Shark bait is available in Suva.'"

My mother looked like a beach bum, no shoes, tattered shorts and T-shirt, hair like tumbleweed. "Cryptic; but he'll figure it out."

"Assuming he gets it. I thought we'd be there together." He handed her four tickets and a package of sandwiches. "Be careful when you go to the embassy. If you see our friend with the cane, leave immediately. We'll meet up later."

"When and where?" she asked abruptly.

"He said the Opera House steps at 10 pm on my father's birthday. I'm sure it won't be a problem."

My grandmother brushed out her dress. "I've heard it before."

"It's been a week since the storm. I'm sure Zagarovsky's people think we're dead."

"Assuming they don't listen to the radio."

"Even if they do, they won't understand my message. Trust me; in three days you'll be back with someone from the embassy."

I wondered whether my father believed what he said as we exchanged hugs and goodbyes. He waited until they were aboard one of the motorboats, chugging across the lagoon to the freighter before he spoke, and then it was to say we should find the man who was supposed to take the cart back to the village.

When the freighter tooted imminent departure, he hoisted *Squirt* onto his shoulder. "No point in waiting around, Victor."

Tired to my core, I picked up the sack containing our few belongings and followed him. We hiked around the lagoon, about a mile until we found a place to camp. Few islanders ventured so far from town. The only footprints were ours and birds, a crazy pattern of wandering toes. We draped *Squirt* over a fallen tree and used driftwood to secure the sides. Dinner was wild mangoes and conch, which we sautéed in coconut water over an open fire.

"A few days like this and I'll be fat as a Tongan pig," my father joked, licking juice from his fingers.

Unable to come up with a witty comeback, I gazed at the darkening sea. The rest of my family had four sandwiches to see them through until morning. No cabin; they travelled on deck. My father worried about them even more than I did.

+ + +

Five days later, I sat on the beach, my arms wrapped around my legs, my chin propped on my knees, staring out to sea. Every nine seconds, a wave crashed on the reef, throwing up a plume of spray. With the sun already behind the trees, the day was cooling down, still too hot to move.

My father loomed over me, a can of beer in one hand, and a plastic shopping bag in the other. "Thinking about the meaning of life, I see."

He was too tired to be funny. His clothes were dirty and spotted with tar. There was paint smeared on his face. His current job, assisting the islanders to rebuild the church roof, paid $3 an hour. He said he had to sweat for every cent of it.

I squeezed my eyes shut. "Anything new?"

"I got through to the embassy."

The last time the phone in the store worked was three days ago; however he lost the connection before he got past the embassy receptionist.

"And?"

"No one knows a damn thing about them." I barely heard him over the constant roar rumbling across the lagoon. "Six friggin' dollars wasted."

"They didn't go to the embassy?" My head ached. If I clenched my jaw; the ringing in my ears stopped.

"Apparently not!" He squatted. "You catch any fish?"

"No."

He let out a sigh. "I didn't buy dinner." He emptied the bag on the sand, two misshapen yams he'd probably mooched from a farmer, four cans from a six-pack of Fijian beer, a bottle of lemonade, and a small bar of chocolate. "You spent the whole day on your butt?"

"I don't feel well."

"Neither do I, Victor. I worked all day. At least you could've cleaned up. The place is a pigsty." He tossed his empty can on our pile of garbage, pulled the top from another can, and gulped it down.

"Maybe they went to a hotel?" When I swallowed, my throat hurt.

"They don't have money."

"Maybe they met Sal and…"

He spilled his beer as he stood. It trickled down his shirt.

"It's a possibility, isn't it?"

"I'll go buy a chicken."

"Not my fault the fish weren't biting."

"It's never your fault," he said.

171

"This whole thing is your fault. You forced us to leave. No one wanted to go on your stupid boat. Not me! Not Ben, and definitely not Jessie! You made us go!"

"It was the only way!"

"We lost everything because of you," I shouted back. My face was red hot.

"You lost your computer and a few lousy clothes. It's not the end of the world."

"I lost my guitar!" I struggled up; it felt like my knees were broken. The horizon swayed, everything blurred. I squeezed my eyes shut, anything to stop the throbbing.

"Get over it, Victor!"

"I hate you!"

He stalked off, down to the shore, kicking sand and shells and muttering obscenities, stopping every few paces to swig beer.

"I shouldn't have shouted at you. I'm sure they're okay," he called over his shoulder.

I crawled under *Squirt*, sipped tepid water from a milk carton, and wished we'd never left Portsmouth.

Chapter 20

A yacht arrived the next day. It was old with a varnished-wood coach house and a tall white mast. It was a classic racing yacht, long and low, with the bow and stern extending over the water. There were two crew, a man and a woman, old enough to be retired for years. It was obvious they knew what they were doing when they set the anchor. With no sign of a local boat-boy rushing to offer his services, I waded into the lagoon, hoping they'd pay me to wash the deck, or polish the hull, or lug freshwater from the village.

When I reached the ladder, she beamed down at me. "Sharkbait?"

I was breathless after swimming 50 yards; I thought I hadn't heard correctly.

She brushed back wisps of gray hair and offered me a wiry suntanned hand. "Up you come, dear."

The yacht was impeccable; everything gleamed, each halyard and sheet coiled neatly, elegant and efficient the way yachts were supposed to be. There were flowery cushions on the cockpit seats, a glistening teak steering wheel, and an array of little brass plaques listing the major races it had won half a century earlier.

Her husband, a stocky, gray-haired man emerged from the cabin to greet me. "Didn't expect we'd find you right away, did we Leah?" he said. He pumped my hand formally. "Welcome aboard, Josh."

Before I could ask how they knew, she laughed. "Everyone's looking for you, from Tahiti to New Zealand. My Angus was sure you'd be on Moala."

I dripped water on the deck while she gave me a hug.

"The current was a wee bit confusing," His brogue was as Scottish as a plaid kilt and bagpipes. "Sal thought ye'd be farther north."

"You know Sal?"

Suddenly, steely straps wrapped my chest, getting tighter until it hurt to breath.

"Everyone knows Sal." Leah stepped back. Her blouse was damp. She smiled from deep inside, like my grandmother.

"Yer here by yerself, laddie?" Angus had a frown.

"My father's working... the church... We ran out of money. We're camping, kind of..." I waved towards the shimmering beach. The sand was so bright it made my eyes water.

Leah looked me over. "The poor boy looks half-starved."

"One of your sausage sandwiches will fix him right up."

Before I could back away, she took my hand. "You're running a fever. No wonder you're shaking. Angus, why don't you take the dinghy and see if you can find his father?"

She guided me down the stairs, still holding my hand like a kid until I was safely seated. She bustled about the galley, cutting slices of homemade bread, slicing a greasy fried sausage, slathering mustardy sauce she'd made herself. I gnawed, chewed, and gulped. No sandwich ever tasted so good, though I could only eat half of it. Between bites, I looked around the cabin. The yacht seemed bigger below; lots of stained wood, more plaques, brass oil lamps hanging from the bulkheads, striped canvas upholstery and matching curtains over the portholes. Like the *Spray*, there were books crammed into every nook. She brought a glass of cold pineapple juice to the table and sat down before me.

I held the glass against my forehead.

"You okay, Josh?" she asked quietly.

She was blurred, like looking through thick glasses. It hurt below my right ear. I rubbed at it. One moment I was hot, then shivering cold.

She reached over and touched my forehead. "You're on fire."

"My sister was sick... when they left... on the..." I couldn't remember the name of the freighter.

She said something. It made my head throb. I tried to brush hair from my forehead. It was like I had dreadlocks. In a rush, my stomach turned queasy.

"I need to go up... up..."

I bolted up the stairs. I made it to the rail with a second to spare. She was sitting at the radio when I came back. She helped me crawl into a quarter berth, a narrow tunnel under the cockpit lockers. It was supposed to be the most comfortable place to sleep on a yacht at sea. At anchor, it was claustrophobic and hot, yet I soon sank into sleep.

When I woke up again, it was night, the cabin lights casting a yellow glow through the cabin. Voices droned a few feet away, my father's among them.

"... rammed right into it, he did."

"Best thing he could've done, mate."

I would've recognized Bruce's accent anywhere.

"Perfect timing. He takes after my brother like that. He probably saved our lives. One of them had his rifle on us when he gybed. The boom probably killed him." My father coughed loudly.

"Anything new?" I asked.

"He's delirious again, John." Leah sounded nearby.

"You can't imagine the mess he made of the fishing boat. Punched a whopping great hole through the side..."

I was almost asleep before he stopped.

"With luck, he sunk it," Angus said. "What about your boat?"

"Sal heard a ketch limped into Suva last week," Bruce said. "Bowsprit broken, railings mangled, paint off the side. She was listing pretty badly."

"Bad enough to haul her out?" my father asked.

"Let's hope so, mate. If they need a hoist, it cuts the number of places we need to look."

"You need to go to Suva, John. Not tomorrow; right away," Angus declared.

"I don't know. I'm worried about him."

Bruce cut him off. "He's over the worst of it. All you need to do is find her, mate. Sal's mates will do the rest..."

I sank back to sleep. It seemed only minutes before my father woke me up. He wiped my face with a damp cloth and wrapped a blanket around me. With Angus' and Leah's help, he lifted me up the stairs. It took all of them to get me onto Bruce's yacht, tied alongside. *Down Under* looked as shabby as the last time I saw it, a dozen plastic cans of fuel and water strapped to the rails, tomato and passion fruit plants stacked in the stern, big fish scales stuck to a slab of wood bolted to the deck. *Squirt* was rolled into a bundle and tied down behind the mast.

Inside, Bruce's boat was jam-packed with clothing, fishing gear, pieces of carved wood, rolls of charts, and paperback books. His galley was my grandmother's worst nightmare; unwashed plates filled the sink; scraps of food stuck to the counter; empty beer cans filled plastic shopping bags. Mess aside, his cabin smelled like her dessert pudding; both forward berths were full of cartons of stringy dried vanilla beans he'd purchased in Vava'u.

He tossed books and clothes into lockers to clear a space for me to lie down. I was so exhausted, I was barely aware of my father covering me with a moldy wool blanket.

"A-a-anyth-th-thing n-n-new?" I heard myself stutter.

"He's trembling again." He might've been talking through a pipe.

Bruce shoved newspapers from the seat. "He'll be fine, mate. Make yourself comfy while I cast off."

"You need help?"

"Not bloody likely." He grinned. "Sorry about the clutter. I ain't into housework."

My father waited until Bruce went upstairs. He looked down at me. "You'll be okay."

"A-a-anyth-th-thing n-n-new?"

He sat down beside me, pulling the blanket over my shoulder. "I don't know how Bruce survived this long."

"A-a-anth-th-thing n-n-new?"

"Go back to sleep. Everything's okay."

A minute later, the engine cranked futilely. Bruce tried again. Curses followed threats with a few obscenities for good measure. When his engine finally fired up, everything in the cabin vibrated. A locker jolted open and books spilled onto the floor. He stomped overhead, shouting goodbye to Angus and Leah as he cast off. Back in the cockpit, he engaged forward gear. After a disturbing clang from down near the keel, the boat shuddered and began to move.

"A-a-an-an-th-think n-n-new?" I tried again.

"It'll take two days to reach Suva. Get you to a hospital. You'll be fine."

The noise from the engine room was so loud I didn't hear the rest of what he said.

He shifted Bruce's clothes from the remaining spare berth to the settee and clambered over bags of sails to lie down. I listened to waves slap the bow, getting louder until the engine spluttered and stopped. The mainsail rattled up the mast. *Down Under* heeled, thumping into the bigger waves outside the reef.

+ + +

I awoke to the creaking sound of a boat pitching through a long ocean swell. It was either early morning or evening, a dull glow through the portholes, inside the cabin still eerily dark. Water dripped on my head. My feet were wet. I buried my face in the musty pillow and tried to block the smell of wet wool, a leaky head, and vanilla beans. My father huddled in the far corner of the settee, his shoulders hunched. He was wrapped in a blanket, studying a chart under the scant light of an ancient kerosene lamp.

He snorted before he sipped from a cup. "Good morning."

I blinked through crust on my eyes. "We're on Bruce's boat?"

"Can't you tell? You want milk? It's powdered."

I made a face. "Coffee?"

"He's only got instant. You're better off with tea."

He gestured at the companionway, where Bruce's bare feet protruded from under a blanket. He snored in bursts, synchronized with the waves.

"Great sailor, god-awful house keeper," he whispered.

"Anything new?"

"I spoke with Sal at midnight. They're heading to Sydney. Apparently, he's got passports arranged. We'll meet them there."

"How's Jessie?"

"She's up and about. You look better."

"I feel like crap."

"You've been asleep for two days."

"Yeah, right." I sat up, hitting my head on the lockers overhead. "Crap!"

"If you want a cuppa, you'll have to make it. That's a cup of tea down under."

I crawled from my berth. Every joint ached. I had to force myself to stand up. "We near halfway yet?"

"Forty-eight miles to go. I wasn't kidding about the two days." He yawned, forgetting to cover his gaping maw.

"You think we'll find the *Spray*?"

His forehead was sweaty. "Even if we do, there's no guarantee Sal can find someone to help us." His hand shook so much he spilled tea from his cup.

"You okay?"

"I'm not feeling too good." He leaned his head on his wrists and breathed deeply. "Sorry for ripping into you on the beach. I had no idea. I can barely move."

He crawled into his berth after he told me how to make tea using a strainer to remove the leaves. When I went upstairs, Bruce gave a sleepy nod and took the cup I'd brought him.

"How's your dad doing?"

"Sick as a dog."

"Figures. He was sweating worse than a coolie earlier." Bruce took a long drink. "I needed a pick-me-up. He said you've been sick for four days."

179

Four days with mosquito bites all over me, frenzied visits to the edge of the jungle, squatting over holes I scooped in the dirt, throwing up even more than when I was seasick.

"It was gross."

"You and he had a fight, huh? You got upset about losing your stuff."

"My guitar mostly; it was my grandmother's before she died."

Below, my father stumbled from his berth. A door slammed. As disagreeable as diarrhoea was, using Bruce's antiquated head made it far worse. I drank some tea. Coffee was better.

"No worries, mate. We'll find it when we find your boat." After a moment, he looked up from his cup. "What I don't understand is why Sal said you're to stay on my boat until his people arrive. Three bloody times he said to keep you out of sight."

"He's worried about someone recognizing me."

He regarded me oddly. "Y'know, it's funny how something takes you back. The first time I met your dad, he looked familiar, dead ringer for a bloke I know back home. They both sound posh, like Brits."

"He grew up in Boston."

He emptied his cup and handed it back. It was stained brown inside, tiny tea leaves sticking to one side for a lopsided future.

"The thing is, you remind me of him; maybe even more than your dad. He played lead guitar in a pub band."

"How did you meet him?"

"It was a few years back, when I lived in Gympie, before I took up sailing. Saved my arse, Ron did." He hunched his shoulders and wriggled his head. "Still got a stiff neck from it."

"What happened?"

"A couple of local goons picked a fight with me. Lucky for me, Ron knew karate."

"Where is he now?"

"He moved to the coast; bought a restaurant at a tourist resort. It's a bit out of the way; you have to drive through a national park to get there." Bruce blinked into the pale glow of dawn. "We'll be in Suva for lunch. Keep an eye on things so I can snooze for a while. Course is 280 magnetic, mate."

I peered down at an old brass compass, the glass so filthy it was almost unreadable. His self-steering wobbled. Even the smallest waves knocked his boat off course. I settled in the lee of the cockpit, one hand on his steering wheel, spray dousing my face.

A ruddy dawn revealed land, larger than anything I'd seen since leaving South America. Wind dragged streaks of cloud tinged with gold and orange across the sky. Gray, cold sea became a deep dark blue. Another hour revealed buildings, ships in the harbor, and TV towers. Bruce came up with a chart, two cups of tea, and a plastic bag of chewy ginger cookies to share.

"She's there, I'm sure of it, mate." Bruce picked at his teeth. "The question is where."

He spread out the chart on the cockpit seat. Bays and secluded coves serrated Fiji's main island.

"The best place to hide something is where it belongs, but not expected."

Bruce smiled as if he'd heard it before. "That'd be the Royal Suva Yacht Club; except given how badly you mangled her, they're probably still fixing her in one of the boatyards."

Chapter 21

Suva, the steamy capital of Fiji, covered a peninsula between Laucala Bay and Suva Harbour. It was a sprawling metropolis with communications towers, modern hotels and office buildings, white-painted colonial buildings, and a busy waterfront lined with warehouses and workshops. Large freighters cluttered the harbor, while small island traders and yachts crowded close to the shore. Bruce steered among them, dodging ferries and fishing boats. My father and I searched for the *Spray*'s old-fashioned rig.

"Could be anywhere, Bruce." The humidity made his cough worse.

"No worries, mate. Nadi's next, if we don't find her here."

Nadi was a resort town on the other side of the island.

I pointed to Kings Wharf. "How about over there?"

A dozen small piers extended into the harbor. Some were docks for deep-sea fishing boats, or for unloading freighters, others for carrying out repairs. Those piers flanked ramps with cradles on train tracks, or had travelling hoists to carry vessels.

"Looks promising." Bruce steered closer.

"The *Spray* could be in one of those sheds." Some of the piers had huge metal sheds nearby. Yacht masts poked between them.

Bruce considered it. "Not worth pulling the masts for a few dings. Recognize any of those masts, John."

"Too far away."

When my father breathed, I could see his chest shudder. He shivered even though his face was red hot.

We were at the last of the piers when Bruce turned to starboard. *Down Under* crept into a canal, squeezing into the gap between a barge and a small freighter spouting a steady stream of black water. The work crew was a cauldron of the Pacific, Fijians, dark Solomon Islanders, Chinese, Filipinos, and Tongans. One of them, a man with arms as thick as thighs, was in charge of hammering off rust and brushing on brown paint.

Bruce waved. "G'day mate."

He jerked his bald head in our direction. "What you want?"

"I need someone to work on a diesel," Bruce replied. "Cuts out when she's cold. Smokes like a chimney till she's warmed up."

The man leaned over the rail. "Saul in office." He indicated which building with a stump of a thumb.

"Hey, maybe you can help. I'm looking for a mate of mine. Old-style yacht with two masts, called the '*Spray.*' Arrived about a week ago?"

The man shrugged and went back to eating a banana.

"Drongo!" Bruce nudged my father. "How about them?"

My father squinted at a dozen masts poking above the nearest shed. Even more masts protruded over the adjacent warehouse.

"No gaff-rigs that I can see."

"We'll go ashore and look around." Bruce headed back to the harbor.

+ + +

Suva had an area designated for arriving yachts. Bruce switched off the engine, drifting in the ebb tide as we waited for Fiji Immigration. Within five minutes of the launch arriving, it departed, a pompous official waving jovially from the stern.

Bruce burst into laughter. "I'd say Sal greased his palm while he was here. No fees. No quarantine. No drug search. No questions about your missing passports."

While he motored into the crowded Royal Suva Yacht Club marina, I guided my father down the stairs. With the sun beating down, the cabin was unbearable. He crawled into his berth, his skin clammy, shivering even with a blanket over him.

"Not much use, am I?"

"The worst part is being so tired you can hardly move."

And the constant pressure in the ears, the nagging pain in the jaws, constant snot, not wanting to eat, waiting for the next bout of diarrhea, and a hacking cough.

He managed a nod, blinking tears. He hadn't said so, but it was clear we had to look for the *Spray* without him.

"Zagarovsky's people may still be here…"

"I'll be careful."

I pumped a mug of lukewarm water, put it beside him, and hurried back to help Bruce dock *Down Under*. After setting the bow anchor, he backed up to the shore. I jumped onto dry land and looped his line around a stump.

"We'll get some lunch at the yacht club." Bruce handed me a shirt and sneakers, scuffed on the sides with frayed laces. "Probably cost an arm and a leg, but Sal's paying the freight."

We dined on the terrace, watching people come and go from their luxury boats. An American-style hamburger restored my appetite, the first I'd eaten since leaving Rio de Janeiro the day after Christmas.

Bruce pushed back his chair. "Now, we look for your boat, mate."

I followed him through the clubhouse and onto a busy street. It was full of trucks, buses, and cars leaving town after the markets closed down for the day. The first boatyard we came to was closed for lunch. Behind a high chain-link fence, a handful of small yachts rested on stands; more masts poked above the roof of a two-story shed, all too skinny for our old-fashioned *Spray*.

Next door was another boatyard. It looked more promising. Masts soared over a stone wall, most tall enough to be the *Spray's*. Before we reached the gate, a workman closed it and looped a thick chain around the rail. We turned down a side street, past a fish-processing factory and rows of warehouses with boatyards and parking lots filling the gaps. There were dozens of masts poking above the roofs, some belonging to ketches. Only one was gaff-rigged like the *Spray*.

"How about it, mate?"

"Our masts aren't black."

Bruce wiped perspiration from his face. "Sorry I got yer hopes up. We'll look more when it cools down."

We walked on the shady side of Rodwell Road, over Walu Bay Bridge, and into downtown Suva. It was a bizarre mix of garishly painted buildings from colonial days, modern four-story hotels, offices and apartment buildings, and buildings under construction. There were duty-free stores wherever I looked. We didn't stop walking until Bruce spotted a secondhand bookstore among the vendors' stands and tents along the side of a creek.

While I sweated, swatting flies and ready to return to searching the wharves, Bruce rambled on about the golden age of detective novels, poring over battered books like a glutton in gourmet food store.

"Something for you to read on the trip to Sydney." He handed me two paperbacks. "Miss Marple and Hercule Poirot." He handed me another. "And Lord Peter Wimsey." He jabbed his finger at Miss Marple. "The classic whodunit, this one. Nothing like a good mystery."

"How about where's the *Spray*?"

Bruce started to laugh. "We already found her, mate."

I gaped at Bruce for several embarrassing seconds. "They painted the masts?"

"Your dad will spit the dummy for sure."

"Dummy?"

"Pacifier, mate. I better tell him. He won't hit me."

I was still laughing as he went over to pay for the eight books he'd picked out. The vendor was an old Fijian man, his face riddled with tiny cracks from drinking too much Kava juice.

We detoured through a park on the way back, taking a break on a bench overlooking the harbor. We looked like a couple of weary tourists. Directly opposite, was a freighter so long its stern protruded into the harbor. At the freighter's bow, two buildings backed up to the canal, each with a roller door in the rear and a miniature wharf. There was an alley between them; and at the end of the alley, was a gaff-rigged ketch with black masts.

Bruce stood up. "Stop gawking, mate. Let's find a way in."

We crossed the bridge and wandered through nearly empty streets before turning into a narrow lane. One side was a smelly fish factory. On the other side was a sheet-metal fence with barbed wire on top.

Bruce stopped at a gate in the fence. "Value privacy, don't they?"

A sleepy caretaker watched us consider a list of yachts for sale pinned to a notice board. When he returned to his lunch, we peeked through the gate. Eight yachts away, in the far corner of the storage yard, was the *Spray*, propped on stands, tarpaulins draped from bow to stern.

"I think I know how we get her out, mate."

Next to a two-story workshop was a travelling hoist, a huge steel frame on four wheels.

"We wait till dark, climb over the fence, find the keys to the hoist, and put her back in the water. Shouldn't be too difficult."

"Why don't we wait until Sal's men arrive?"

He ran his finger down the list of yachts, stopping next to: '12 meter classic ketch, beautiful wood, as new condition. Must sell, owner returning home. US $259,000.' Someone had scrawled 'sold' in red next to it.

"Ten to one it's your *Spray*. It might not be here tomorrow."

"So we go to the police right away."

"And say what?"

"It's stolen."

"They'll have a fake bill of sale from the previous owner, plus whatever else it takes to sell a yacht in Fiji. You've got nothing except your word. You don't even have passports."

"What can we do?"

He pulled me away from the fence "We steal it back, mate. I drove a hoist a couple of years ago. It's easy; just like driving a tractor."

+ + +

My father didn't believe we'd found the *Spray* after less than an hour of searching. "A gaff-rigged ketch doesn't mean it's ours." He gasped for each breath.

187

"The masts are the right size." I left out his white masts were now black.

"Coincidence."

"It has a new bowsprit," I added, leaving out the bowsprit was shorter.

"What's the name?"

"We couldn't see the stern. The hull looks sort of the same."

"You just said it was covered with tarps!" My father sipped some water and wiped his face. "You reckon it's her, Bruce?"

"Darn good bet, mate. There's only one way to find out for sure. If it is her, I wouldn't waste any time. It's already sold."

My father struggled to his feet, grasping the bulkhead to steady himself. He was so pale I was sure he was going to puke.

Bruce moved out of his way. "Yeah, you're looking much better."

He rushed for the head.

Bruce thought it was funny. "Maybe he'll perk up by tonight."

I stretched out on the settee, where I slept for seven hours after reading Miss Marple and eating a box of ginger cookies.

Chapter 22

Bruce shoved my shoulder at 10:00 pm, handed me a black T-shirt, and went over to wake my father. He broke into a coughing fit as soon as he sat up, bleary eyed and perspiring profusely. When he tried to get out of bed, he lurched against the bulkhead and almost fell down. He stumbled again as he made his way to the table. He looked like he'd been seasick for a month. He grunted when he breathed.

Bruce tossed my father's T-shirt on the table, now even more cluttered with six plastic bags of pineapples.

"Camouflage, mate."

My father held it up. "We're advertising pineapples?"

His T-shirt, like mine, had 'Fiji Pineapple Company' in gold on the back.

"I got 'em while you were snoring. Buy two bags of pineapples, get a free T-shirt." Bruce looked as happy as my grandmother when she got a good deal in the market. "I checked out the boatyard. It's her alright. They had ten men working flat out to get her finished."

My father took each breath slowly. "Any word from Sal?"

"I radioed him when I got back. I told him they were probably moving her tomorrow. Two days is the best he can do. He has to call in favors."

"So it has to be tonight."

"Looks that way, mate." Bruce shuffled through books and papers until he found his flashlight, a long black metal tube. He switched it on and off. "You ought to be in bed."

My father lifted his head slowly, blinking red eyes. "I can do this."

189

He might've been drunk as he pulled on his T-shirt and slowly got up. He held onto the table until he stopped swaying. I got out of his way as he climbed the stairs and flopped onto the cockpit seat.

"How far, Bruce?"

"Maybe a mile, mate."

He nodded and dragged himself up again. He looked at me through bloodshot eyes. "Help me off, Josh."

I jumped ashore and hauled on the stern line to get *Down Under* as close as possible. The shore was still too far away when he stepped over the rail. He flung himself forward, missed his footing when he slipped on seaweed, and crashed into me. We both fell down. He crawled away, nursing a bloody elbow.

I sat up. "Nice jump."

"Awful catch," he grouched.

Bruce and I pulled him up. He tottered a few paces, turned, and motioned to me. With his arm around my shoulders, we headed off to the boatyard. The front gate was chained and padlocked. Bruce kept going. At the next building, he stopped, tapping a finger on his lips. He turned into a narrow passageway separating two long walls of corrugated metal sheets. A cat screeched when one of us stepped on him. It fled into the shadows. We followed, avoiding trash, pieces of steel pipe, and rolls of fencing wire. My father paused to catch his breath, sniffling and mopping his brow.

"Take a breather, mate. Josh and I will have a gander. A look around."

My father nodded weakly. We left him resting on a stack of concrete blocks near the end of the alley.

The storage yard glowed yellow from lights at either end. The *Spray* was the first yacht in the line of boats against the back wall of the workshop. They'd painted out the name and home port on the stern, and changed the stripe on the side from blue to crimson, yet she was still our *Spray*. Her keel was touched up to cover the scrape from hitting the reef at Palmerston Island. Bruce tugged on my arm and pointed to the second story of the adjacent shed. Light flickered from a television.

"Reckon I'd better have a chat with him first. Wait here, mate."

He crept down the line of boats, keeping in the shadows. After a man's silhouette passed the window, Bruce ran across the yard and entered through a door directly below. The man returned, stopping in front of the window. He plucked notes on a guitar, its tone mellow like mine. The telephone rang and he stalked out of sight.

Almost five minutes passed before Bruce emerged from the doorway and strolled across the yard. I hurried over to join him.

He rubbed at his eye. "He got a punch in before he bounced off my flashlight. Get your dad. Then, take off the rest of the tarps. I'll find the hoist." He disappeared into the darkness.

I found my father at the end of the alleyway. He was slumped against the wall, holding his arms close to his chest and muttering to himself.

"Look who I found." He lifted his hand. Jag raised his head, purring and sniffing at me. Both of them smelled like rotting garbage. "Your luck's definitely rubbed off on him," he added with a smile.

+ + +

My father untied the ropes securing the bottoms of the tarpaulins, while I climbed up a ladder propped against the *Spray*. I dropped Jag through the bow hatch and began to untie the tops of the tarpaulins. I was still working on the starboard side when the travelling hoist crawled into the yard. By the time it reached the *Spray*, three tarpaulins lay in heaps on the ground.

"You need to be closer to the building." My father waved like he was directing traffic at a major intersection.

Bruce backed up and realigned the hoist. He came within a half inch of scraping the hull before my father yelled 'stop.'

"Keep it down, mate. All bloody Suva heard you." Bruce signaled for me to come down.

The hoist used straps at the bow and stern, connected to cables by huge steel shackles. It took ten minutes to attach the first strap, the second even longer because the shackle was rusted. Then, Bruce took up the slack, the straps creaking as the *Spray* lurched off the ground. The engine roared and the hoist began to move.

My father rode in the *Spray's* cockpit; I walked behind. The hoist rumbled through the wide-open gate and onto the road. Bruce didn't stop. He negotiated a mostly empty parking lot, managing to leave long scrapes on two cars before he knocked down a chain-link fence to get into another storage yard. After squeezing through a narrow chasm between two warehouses, we reached the harbor. Bruce lined up the wheels on the sides of the hoist with the guides on either side before inching forward onto the wharf. When the hoist straddled the water, he stopped. Cables squealed over rusty metal rollers and the *Spray* gradually descended.

Bruce jumped from the driver's seat. "If I didn't get caught, I could make a good living stealing boats."

While he unfastened the shackles, I climbed down before the *Spray* floated away. I tossed a stern line to Bruce and started down the companionway.

My father grabbed my arm. "I need you up here."

"You want the batteries switched on?" Before he could stop me, I looked into the cabin. It wasn't our boat.

Behind me, he said, "They stripped her. All our stuff's gone."

I bolted down the stairs.

Chapter 23

The *Spray's* cabin had never been so tidy; not even before we moved onboard. There were no clothes tossed on the bunks, no books or half-finished school projects on the table, no encyclopedias lying in Ben's berth. I checked the locker where we kept toys and books, and the drawer where Jessie stored her collection of sea shells. Both empty. There was no box of snack crackers on the galley counter, no laptop computers, no sign of my mother's painstakingly compiled scrapbooks. All that remained were the carefully organized essentials of a cruising yacht: fishing gear, first aid kit, spare parts for the boat, charts, my father's computer, and his library of sailing books. Except for Jag curled up on my sister's berth and Slocum's photo on the bulkhead, it was as if my family had never lived on the *Spray*.

"They took my guitar," I shouted.

He stood in the companionway. "Most of it we can replace."

"Not my guitar!" I pushed past him.

"Where are you going?"

"Where do you think? Our stuff's back at the shed; you know it is!"

"You're staying right here, Mister."

I leaped onto the wharf, paying no heed to his order. Bruce said something to me. I ran past him.

"It's not worth it," my father called after me.

I kept running, back the way we'd come. I didn't stop running until I was below the window where I'd heard someone playing my guitar. I went in the same doorway Bruce had gone into an hour earlier. There was a glazed partition separating the front office and the workshop, a couple of doors opening into storage rooms and a toilet, and a stair to the second floor. I climbed the stairs two at a time, smelling curry that belonged in a Chinese take-out. I almost slipped on someone's dinner. It covered the floor, gobs of yellow paste, chunks of fish, and sliced carrots.

Cardboard cartons were stacked along the landing overlooking the workshop. They'd taped down the lids. My 'I love New York' T-shirt lay on top of one box as if someone had been trying it on. I ripped off tape and opened the flaps. The clothes inside were Ben's. I ripped the tape off the next box to find cans of cat food, Jessie's shells, Science Boy's playing cards, and my grandmother's handbag on top of some of my father's old books. Ben's encyclopedia filled the three biggest boxes. Another carton contained my father's CDs and Jessie's stuffed cat. I was fuming after I opened the next box. They'd shoved my mother's scrapbooks in with plates, cups, and cutlery.

I smelled him moments before I heard him.

"I weren't drinkin', boss. Come out of nowhere, didn't he?" A man stepped from behind the door, rubbing his head with his knuckles. His other hand held a cell phone to his ear.

"… Don't know what he wanted… No, I ain't looked outside."

He stared at me through one eye, the other swollen shut. He wasn't expecting visitors; he hadn't shaved in a week.

"Who the blazes are you?"

I backed away, squeezing along the wall, boxes of encyclopedias scraping my legs. Before he could accuse me, I pointed at the boxes, festooned with strips of ripped-off tape.

"This is my family's stuff."

His mouth twisted from disbelief to a smirk. "You're him! Zagarovsky's got people looking all over the south Pacific, and you turn up here." He spoke into his phone. "Tell Manila what he's looking for is standing right in front of me."

195

He snapped his cell phone closed and slipped it into his jeans' pocket. His eyes never left me as I backed down the landing. He followed as if he had all the time in the world, casually brushing dirty black hair from his forehead. When I reached the top of the stairs, I thought I heard footsteps on the floor below. I risked a glance over the rail. He lunged for my arm. I jumped back, shoving the box of Ben's clothes in front of him. It blocked the narrow passageway; however, he kicked it so hard the box caved in, wedging it even tighter. When he tried to step over it, I turned and bolted down the stairs.

He charged after me. I missed a stair and smashed into the railing. It saved me from falling the rest of the way down. He grabbed my shoulder and spun me around. My right foot twisted under me and I shrieked.

"Let me help you up, kid." His breath smelled like curried fish.

He dragged me to my feet by my T-shirt, tearing it from the neck to the sleeve, slammed me into the handrail, and slapped my head for good measure. With a hand tangled in the remains of my shirt, he tried to force me back up the stairs. I clung to the railing and flailed with my other arm. He kicked at my right ankle and I screamed. All of a sudden, a light flared in my face before it swung away. I ducked.

"Bloody hell; you again!"

He toppled back, still holding my shirt, dragging me with him until he ripped my shirt off. He slid all the way down the stairs before he stopped. Bruce shone his flashlight. The man got to his knees, grunting loudly.

"You won't stay down, will you mate?" Bruce chuckled. He went down the stairs two at a time. After a dull thud, he came back, adjusting the bulb to a wider beam. "Looks like a flashlight, but it's really a billy club."

"Thanks Bruce." I started up the stairs, wincing if I put any weight on my foot.

"No way, mate. We need to go."

"My guitar's up there! I'm not leaving without it."

"Wait here. I'll bring it down.

"All of our stuff's on the landing."

Bruce followed me up the stairs. He groaned when he saw the boxes. "We'll need a bloody forklift, and the rest of the night." He glanced at my face. "Okay, two boxes. Make it quick."

While he ripped off tape and opened lids, I emptied Ben's encyclopedias out of two boxes. We shoved my father's old books and as many of his CDs as we could find into one of them. We filled the second box with my mother's scrapbooks, a shoebox of family photos, and my grandmother's handbag. While Bruce lugged the boxes downstairs, I searched through the rest of the boxes.

On the top of the last box was my father's document case where he kept the *Spray*'s papers and our passports. Below it was the Ship's Log and a silk-covered box full of heirlooms, tissue-wrapped ornaments my mother brought out every Christmas, and a lace tablecloth. Under a sheaf of newspaper clippings were three silver-framed sepia photographs I had never seen, and an old blue and green fountain pen in a leather-covered tube.

"Hurry up, mate," Bruce called from downstairs.

"Another minute, okay?"

At the very bottom of the box was a suede bag with pockets, each holding a hefty dinner knife with a crest incised on the gold handle—a sword and shield with flowery letters, 'K','A' and 'T'. They were old, definitely keeper material. I tossed in Jessie's stuffed cat and Ben's playing cards, along with an old leather-bound book. It looked interesting, if not important.

Bruce said two boxes; however, I dragged the box to the top of the stairs. The rest of our belongings we could replace or do without.

"Move it, mate! A truck just came through the gate."

"There's another box ready to go up here. I'm getting my guitar."

I hobbled across the landing and into the room overlooking the storage yard. My guitar lay on a desk, its battered case beside it. Through the window, I watched four men skulk among yachts. One of them looked up at the window. I ducked back and peeked around the frame. Two men crept towards the workshop, staying in the shadows; the others headed to the gate.

"Hurry up!" Bruce filled the doorway, carrying the last box.

I placed the guitar inside the case, closed the lid, and tottered after him, grabbing my 'New York' T shirt and Ben's mahi-mahi sunglasses on the way.

He waited at the bottom of the stairs, all three boxes stacked on a dolly. He turned abruptly as I started down, pointing his flashlight at the night guard. He crawled towards Bruce.

"You must be stupid, mate."

He strode over, thumping his flashlight into his other hand. The guard cowered, both hands covering his head. Bruce whacked him on the back of the neck. Someone hammered on the front door as he wheeled the dolly past the office and into the workshop.

I stuffed Ben's sunglasses in my pocket and limped after him. "We should be going to the *Spray*. Two men went to find her."

"No big deal," he said over his shoulder.

"We can't get out this way. There's only the wharf, remember?"

He picked up speed as we passed shelves of paint cans, spare parts, and recycling bins. The dolly banged into a garbage can and nearly tipped over. He righted it again and kept going. I picked up the leather-covered book that had fallen from the box. It was a music book with parchment pages and tiny ink notes.

A door slammed in the front office.

"Be quiet, and keep low," Bruce whispered.

We passed long wooden benches covered with engines in pieces, swerving around grinders, saws, and drill presses, almost invisible in the dim light from the skylights. He stopped once to tell me to move a trolley of tools, buckets full of nuts and bolts so it blocked the path behind us. I caught up when he reached the roller door at the rear of the workshop. He hauled on the chain and the door rattled up. Moonlight spilled through the opening. At the other end of the workshop, someone shouted, 'They're in here.'

Beyond the door was a narrow wharf cluttered with anchors, diesel motors, and filthy oil drums. Bruce left the dolly beside the drums.

"I told you there's no way out." I jammed the music book under Jessie's stuffed cat. I thought my guitar would be safer on top of the drums.

He grinned back. "Bloody know it all, aren't you?"

I followed him back into the workshop.

"Hey Walker, fifty grand; I let you and boy go." The voice came from the far side of the workshop.

Being called 'boy' was the last straw. "How's your sister's mouth, Manila?" I shouted back.

199

Bruce touched my shoulder, one finger to his lips, staring into the gloom. Something crashed to the floor. Ball bearings bounced across concrete. He gestured outside and nudged me to go.

"There's your dad." He pointed to a boat turning into the canal. "Guide him in. I'll fix the door so they can't get out."

He handed me the flashlight and dashed inside. I pointed it at the *Spray* and flicked the switch on and off. The *Spray* plowed through the water, too fast for the narrow channel. Inside the workshop, the chain clattered over its pulleys.

"Forty thousand, Walker," Manila shouted.

The steel door rolled down much faster than it went up. At the last moment, Bruce ran out, ducking low. Manila followed him. The bottom of the door struck his shoulder, and knocked him flat on his back, pinning him underneath. He tried to lift the door by himself. I pointed the flashlight at his face. The veins in his neck swelled from the effort. Without warning, he grabbed Bruce's foot.

"Help your dad dock!" Bruce shouted. He tried to shake Manila loose, kicking wildly.

The *Spray's* engine roared, churning waves into the stern until it stopped several yards out. My father tossed a dock line to me. It slapped on a coil of rotting rope and slid back into the water. It was only luck that I grabbed the last few inches. I wrapped it around a huge rusted cleat, and took the strain as my father shifted into forward gear. The rope creaked and the *Spray* drew closer.

When I looked away, another man was under the roller door, trying to shove it up. Bruce kicked at Manila's arm until the other man caught his foot. With his leg wedged against the bottom of the door, Bruce screamed. I ran to help. I kicked Manila's shoulder as hard as I could. He screamed Filipino obscenities and punched at my legs until I got out of the way.

"Put the boot in, mate," Bruce shouted.

I kicked again, aiming at Manila's head; however, swimming was my sport, not football. Bruce snatched the flashlight from me, gripping it at the end for maximum leverage. He slammed it down on Manila's head, twice, hard.

"I reckon I need a bigger flashlight. You want a go, mate?"

Before I could answer, Manila let go of his leg and grabbed mine. I toppled sideways, crunching Ben's sunglasses. Bruce did what I should've done; he jumped on the edge of the door, crushing Manila's chest on the concrete sill.

Bruce dragged me after him. Between us, we heaved the boxes on board. With my guitar case in one hand and his flashlight in the other, Bruce jumped as my father reversed away from the wharf. I released the line. The *Spray* was moving too quickly. I flung myself into the gap. I missed the railing, clinging to the gunwale, my feet thrashing, screaming until Bruce hoisted me over the rail. He shoved a box aside so I could sit in the cockpit.

My father reversed all the way to the harbor before he turned towards the marina. "I don't know how I can ever repay you, Bruce."

"No problem, mate. I'll send you a bill." Bruce winked. He stepped into the companionway. "I'll radio Sal and let him know you're okay before he has a stroke."

My father glanced in my direction after Bruce disappeared below. "Happy now?" He nodded at my guitar case.

"We should've left his books there," I called to Bruce.

My father cocked his head. "Books?"

"They're in a box with your CDs. I might not have found all of them," I said as he leaned to open the box, his eyes bright with hope. "There were boxes and boxes of stuff."

I took over steering as he shoveled through his CDs, pawing at his books like old friends. "You didn't happen to find…" He started to cough.

Bruce switched off the radio and clomped up the stairs. He looked at me curiously. "Dunno what's got Sal so flustered. He's sure as heck worried about you. Insists we leave right away. I was hoping we'd have a few hours of sleep before we head off."

Suddenly, my father gagged. He shoved his precious box aside and pushed past Bruce.

"He won't be much use for a while."

Pain burst in my ankle when I squatted to pick up a CD. It had fallen out of the box in my father's excitement.

"You okay, mate?"

Through clenched teeth, I said, "Just great!"

He made me sit down so he could look at my ankle. It was as big and hard as a baseball.

"No worries, mate. You'll be on your bum most of next week."

We were headed into the Suva Yacht Club when he handed me a sheet of paper. "Sal expects you here." He'd written GPS coordinates and underlined '23' twice. "After you drop me off, head for Beqa. It's 25 miles. I'll catch up in an hour or two."

I brought the *Spray* within a few yards of the marina breakwater. Bruce climbed over the bow pulpit and dropped into the water. He clambered up the rocks and gave me a thumbs-up sign. I waved and backed away.

Chapter 24

Suva's glow faded with each passing mile. Ahead, was Beqa, a pinprick on the chart. It was an island surrounded by a large lagoon, which joined to the coast of Viti Levu, Fiji's main island, a dark shadow four miles north. There were a few miniscule lights on the northeast side of Beqa, either from farms or villages, nothing marking a passage through the reef.

With no sign of a boat in pursuit, and no obstacles immediately ahead, I went below to check on my father and get something to eat. He'd fallen asleep on the settee. He woke up when I placed a blanket over him.

"Bruce should've caught up 20 minutes ago." I told him the plan.

"After seeing his engine, I'm not surprised." He pulled the blanket around him. "How's the fuel?"

I wasted no time finding out. The fuel gauge hovered on empty. I stopped the engine, and unfurled the sails. Just the inner jib and mizzen sail remained, about a third of the *Spray's* sail area. It was barely enough to push her through the waves, and the self-steering didn't work like it was supposed to. It needed constant adjustments.

With dawn, my father poked his head out the companionway, unshaven, his hair clinging in greasy strands, his eyes red and crusted.

"How are we doing?" He seemed more interested in wisps of cloud over Beqa.

"No worries, mate!" I was dead-tired; my ankle was on fire; there was no sign of Bruce's boat; and my stomach rumbled.

"When you're up to it, check the hiding place I showed you in Luperón."

Five minutes later, he was asleep in his berth. I checked his hiding place under the chart table after I used a screwdriver to wedge out a plywood panel. Everything was in its place, one Smith and Wesson handgun, a box of bullets, and five plastic-wrapped packages. On the bottom of each package was a bank sticker. Someone had written $10,000 on them. Wondering where he'd gotten the money, I put everything back. Then, I searched the *Spray* for something to eat, every locker, drawer, and storage compartment. Two compartments in the bilge had been overlooked. We were still in Norfolk when Ben and I had filled them with cans of chicken noodle and tomato soup, peas, green beans, and tuna. Only 35 rusted cans remained, either tuna or beans. I took a can of tuna and a fork upstairs, sharing breakfast with Jag when I wasn't adjusting the self-steering.

+ + +

Despite waves churning over Nanaku Reef a few hundred yards away, I kept the sails up. I aimed at the largest passage, crossed my fingers, and watched the depth sounder. Only when the *Spray* was safely inside the lagoon did I relax. Sheltered behind Beqa's hills, I furled the jib and lowered the mizzen. The *Spray* drifted in sparkling water, so calm I didn't put out an anchor. Beqa was a diver's paradise. I watched deadly bull sharks flirt with slow-moving turtles in a gorge lined with spectacular soft coral formations. Some coral was like lace fans, others like dripping candelabra; it was a slow, swirling ballet.

While I waited for Bruce, I dragged out the spare jib. It was yellowed, patched in six different places, and had wrinkles all over after I hoisted it. It wasn't much to look at; however, as my father would say, it was better than no sail at all.

Down Under arrived at noon while I sat in the cockpit, digging out chunks of tuna from my third can of the day. Bruce eased his sails and glided alongside the *Spray*.

"Some hour?" Was I glad to see him!

"The cops paid me a visit. They kept me at the station for four flamin' hours, mostly asking questions about you. All very strange. Not a word about your boat."

He tossed me a line to secure. Together, we manhandled a rolled-up *Squirt* from his foredeck onto our aft cabin roof.

He sat in the cockpit and helped himself to a tuna chunk. "Nice jib, mate."

I grinned. "Dad got it cheap on eBay."

"Free, I'd say." He cast his gaze up our mast. "You need a mainsail?"

He disappeared into his boat. A minute later, he dragged a sail bag across to the *Spray*. We spread his spare mainsail out across the cabin and cockpit.

The sail was chafed and covered with patches, yet it fit on our boom as if it'd been made for it. However, the rest of the sail was a problem—it was made for a sloop. The top of the sail hung over the gaff.

"We could sew it, Bruce."

"You got a sewing machine on board, mate?"

"We could do it by hand."

"Not bloody likely. I repaired it myself in Jamaica after the hurricane." Bruce pointed. "See those seams; I did 'em by hand. I'm never sewing again."

It was Bruce's idea to roll the sail around the gaff. The sail was baggy with a big crease down the middle; however, it wouldn't matter if we were sailing downwind.

"What about food?" I was still hungry. "We've only got enough for a week."

"Same here. There's plenty of fish, and Norfolk Island is halfway. Let's just hope we don't run into any bad weather. Cyclone season starts this time of year."

I swapped seven cans of beans for four pineapples, a can of chicken noodle soup, a loaf of week-old bread, and most of a jar of instant coffee. Bruce tossed in a bag of powdered milk, which he'd acquired in Florida two years earlier. He wanted to get rid of it.

"Pacific net, 9:00 pm," Bruce said as he stepped across to *Down Under*.

I yawned. "If there's no answer, I'm snoozing."

I unfurled the inner jib and hoisted the mizzen. Ahead, was 960 miles of lonely ocean and an island barely five miles wide.

+ + +

By mid-afternoon we'd passed through Frigate Pass, where a few surfers rode the 'Fiji Pipeline,' oblivious to a tiger shark dorsal fin slicing through the water. With a steady breeze over the stern and the self-steering working properly, the *Spray* plowed an unwavering course. Down below, I restored our things to their rightful places, CDs in their slots above the chart table, books in their racks, scrapbooks in a locker behind the dining table. Finally, I carried our family heirlooms to the aft cabin.

"What's missing?" my father demanded.

"*Moby Dick.*" I waited. He seemed not to care. "Five or six CDs."

206

"Which ones?"

"The Stravinsky's."

He sat up, rubbing his forehead. It sounded as if he said 'Zagarovsky.' "All of them?"

"They left you one."

It was a compilation of Igor Stravinsky's lesser known works, which only he enjoyed. I put it on for him, and took Agatha Christie to read in the cockpit.

By dusk, we were midway between Vatu Lele and Kandavu, the last land until Norfolk Island. I heated chicken noodle soup for my father. I opened a can of tuna for myself, mashed it up, and spread it on a slice of bread. I was just sitting down to eat when Bruce called 'Sharkbait' on the VHF radio.

"G'day mate!" He was always in good spirits. "Howza he doin'?"

"He slept all afternoon. Right now, he's puking up soup." Jag jumped onto the table, stalking my sandwich. I tossed a pillow at him. "What's dinner for you?"

"I've got shish kabobs on the barbie, fresh mahi and pineapple. I'd invite you over, only there's no room at the table."

We laughed. The latest weather report was trade winds from astern. I switched off the radio and went back to the table. In a flash, Jag pounced, pawing at my arm. I pulled off a corner of my sandwich and put it in front of him. He licked off the tuna, and then he stuck his nose in the empty can. I relented and opened another can. He wolfed it down and wanted more.

+++

Two days later, *Down Under* was a tiny white triangle four miles ahead when I stumbled on deck. It was a gloomy morning,

207

the sky overcast, the wind puffy and changing direction. My father looked exhausted, bristly, bleary eyed, and a nose like Rudolph's. He handed me his scrawled notes on position and course, bundled his blanket around him, and went below.

"Thanks for breakfast," he called on his way back to bed. The previous evening he'd turned down the bean and tuna sandwich I'd prepared for him.

It was an hour later when the fishing reel screamed. I scrambled for the rod, the frenzied fish nearly jerking the rod from my hands. I adjusted the drag, pushed the butt of the fishing rod into my thigh, and levered it back, winding as fast as I could before the fish ripped off more line. With a loud splash and a streak of silver and blue, a tuna broke the surface. Fifteen minutes later, I gaffed it and dragged it over the rail. It flipped across the deck until I stood on its tail—it was as big as my sister.

"You look like my brother," my father said from behind me. "He always fished while your grandfather and I sailed."

"I'd like to meet him."

"You will one day."

"When?"

"Soon enough. I came up to tell you to do your schoolwork."

"No books, no pencils, no laptop."

"Use my computer. I've rigged the radio so you can download what you need."

He stayed to watch me slice thick red fillets.

+ + +

My father used his computer to download weather conditions, research ports we visited, and store his digital charts. I'd never used it—he didn't want his children deleting his files.

"We pay by the minute," he shouted from his berth.

"I could skip Math," I shouted back.

"By the way, I signed you up for Intermediate French."

Each page crawled onto his monitor. Ten minutes later, I started downloading three weeks of language arts assignments. After an hour, only science and history remained. While I waited, I went to his cabin to see if he needed anything. He lay on his back, snoring lightly. I went back to his computer. Science still hadn't finished downloading so I browsed through his files, one folder for each month with weather reports and photos of places we'd visited. I was looking at photos of the Magellan Straits of Cape Horn when History started.

History came in workbooks with reading, assignments, and quizzes bundled into 'themes.' I started downloading 'Capitalism and War' and clicked on his 'email' icon to pass the time. There were two accounts, 'Spray' and 'Borrowedin.' 'Spray' collected email from people we'd met on our travels, friends from school and Arcadia Park, and my grandmother before she joined us. I was hungry for news, yet I chose 'Borrowedin'—I'd never seen it before.

'Password' and a box appeared on the screen. I wasted time with 'Spray', 'Jessie,' 'Ben,' 'Victor,' 'Jag', and 'Jenny,' which was what he called my mother. By the time the first workbook finished downloading, I'd tried 'Walker', 'Slocum,' 'Tchaikovsky,' 'Rimsky,' 'Korsakov,' 'Borodin,' and their first names: 'Virginia,' 'John,' 'Joshua,' 'Pyotr,' 'Ilyich,' 'Peter,' and 'Nicholai.' Then, I typed 'Alexander.'

A new page slowly appeared. 'Borrowedin' had three emails in the Inbox. There were eleven emails in Outbox, one each year, dated in the middle of February.

I clicked midway down the list, sent on February 17th 1999, the same day as my birthday. It was sent by 'Slocum,' no subject, just 'Re: News,' the same as the others.

'I can't believe it's another year already. He's in his bedroom, playing Mum's guitar. Last week, I told him I'd heard Segovia play it. He didn't believe me. He practices every night, just like you did. He's already reading music on the fly; not bad for seven and no music teacher except me. Dad would be thrilled. Like you, he's also taken to swimming. He's made several good friends on the swim team. On the downside, he's having problems at school. His teachers say he's very bright, except he can't stay focused and he doesn't talk very much. The pediatrician wants to treat him for attention deficit. Susan says he doesn't need more drugs. She thinks we should tell him. I don't think it's time. He's made a lot of progress, but it's slow. The bedwetting still happens whenever he has a nightmare. He still doesn't remember anything.'

The next email was dated February 21st. I clicked on another email, sent on my birthday a year before we left Norfolk. It began with few lines about sending a pen.

"Are you still on?" my father demanded, already on his way from the aft cabin.

"I'm waiting for files to download." I closed his email program before I turned.

He stood in the passageway behind me, staring at me. "You don't need to be doing anything except fetching your school work."

"That's what I'm doing," I shot back.

"You're on watch."

Grizzly bears in spring weren't as grumpy.

"I checked for ships a few minutes ago."

"Check again. And wash your T-shirt next time you take a break. It's starting to stink"

He jerked his thumb. As I stood, the last workbook started downloading.

"I saved the files on the desktop," I warned as he moved to take my place.

"I won't touch them. You can do your school work after I've got the weather report."

The next time I ventured below, he'd retired to his cabin, leaving his computer running. He'd taken the cable to the radio modem.

+++

Two days later, I stepped into the cockpit to find my father peering at a mirror propped on the cabin roof, while he scraped his chin with a razor. He gave me a nod.

"You look less like a Grizzly," I said, loud enough to be heard over his music.

"Thanks; I think." He wiped off soap with his towel, his right hand now conducting an imaginary orchestra.

"We're catching up on Bruce." *Down Under* was a speck on the horizon. At the end of my previous watch, it was out of sight.

"Four more days with wind like this and we'll be at Norfolk."

"You want something to eat?" Ten minutes remained before my next watch started.

"I finished the beans." He grinned. "We'll have to eat the cat soon."

"You can tell Jessie. Tchaikovsky's *Orchestral Suite No. 2*?" I ventured.

"My brother sent it to me from Sydney when Ben was born. The fourth movement is superb. Rather disconcerting for a lullaby, though he had good intentions."

"What was he doing in Australia?"

He made me wait until the music ended. "He was taking care of some business."

I wanted to ask what business, but he avoided my eyes. Ben was born on September 17th. The fire that killed my grandparents was July 7th. It was all tied up somehow.

"Is he still in Australia?" I pressed. When he didn't reply, I started down the stairs.

I was slicing pineapple when he called, "After you've eaten, bring up your guitar."

"The guitar you said wasn't worth going back for?"

"I was delirious at the time." He leaned through the companionway, smiling at me. "It's worth a great deal; still not worth getting killed for."

He dozed while I played ballads, slipping in a few songs of my own. When my fingers became tired, I carefully wiped the guitar with a soft handkerchief, polishing away smears. I returned the guitar to its felt-lined case and closed the lid before I realized he was watching me.

"Now what's wrong?"

"My brother took care of his guitar the same way you do."

"He played the guitar?"

"He was your age when he got it; mowed lawns until he had enough money. He got it at a pawn shop in Brooklyn. A custom-made Fender. It drove your grandfather crazy."

"I thought your father liked guitars?"

"He did. It was the electric part he didn't like," he chuckled.

"What happened to it?"

"I expect he still has it. I shouldn't have told you he died," he said before I could ask. "Everything turned to crap after the fire. I tried to forget."

"I'm trying to remember."

"I know." He rubbed his thumb over the face of his watch, scraping off salt and grime, the glass hazy with scratches. He looked up. "He wanted to be in a rock band."

"I bet your dad was happy about that."

"He used to say music was the spirit of the age. Rock expresses today's culture, the same as classical music did in its day. One's not better or worse than the other. Simply, bad music fades away over time."

Unlike his other lectures, it was interesting.

Chapter 25

Norfolk Island emerged from the gloom of early dawn. Australia's penal colony was the hump of an ancient volcano, with precipitous cliffs punctuating the coast, dark green pine trees covering knobby hills, and seagulls wheeling over barren wind-lashed beaches. It was a welcome sight after 12 days at sea. The main harbor was at Kingston; a few scattered stone buildings and a wall of the prison where brutal guards disciplined the worst of Australia's convicts—100 lashes with the cat-o'-nine-tails for singing, another 100 for smiling. There was a short stone pier with a hoist to lift the town's small fishing boats out of the waves, and a few storage sheds. It reminded me of the desolate ports in Patagonia in the southern tip of South America. On the hills, creamy-stone colonial houses greeted the sun.

"I'm going for a long walk after Customs," I announced as we lowered our improvised mainsail.

"Good place for a walk. My brother came here for a holiday; said he hiked every day."

"All the way from New York to stay at a prison."

He tugged on sailcloth, pulling out creases. "It was three years ago. His version of a honeymoon, I expect."

"So he married again?"

He brushed me aside. "I'll tie it down."

Waves swept into the otherwise unprotected harbor, relentlessly buffeting the *Spray*. I sat on the cabin roof and watched spray explode over the pier.

"Does he have kids?" I asked. He tilted his head as if he hadn't heard. "Any kids?"

214

"One boy I've met. They wanted two..." he trailed off. "Get off your butt and check the anchor." He had a unique way of ending a conversation.

It had taken five attempts before the anchor dug in properly, and then my father wasn't confident it would keep the *Spray* off the rocks. We repaired and inflated *Squirt* before Bruce arrived. He dropped his sails and used his engine to keep a safe distance away.

"Not very safe, mate," he bellowed.

"I've been on the radio. There's nowhere else," my father shouted. The wind carried his words to the hills.

"I can wait for a beer, mate. How about you?"

"No choice. We've only got tuna." He held up two fingers and pretended to puke.

"I'll stay," I said—it was either offer or be told.

"We'll take turns going ashore. Better safe than aground."

Bruce had his boat anchored before we heaved *Squirt* over the side. My father headed to shore and I settled in the cockpit with one of his sailing books, *'Self-steering Made Easy'*—I'd read everything else. It was full of complicated diagrams of pulleys, levers, and gears, and rambling discussions of theory. I'd figured out the *Spray's* system before my father returned. He was going full tilt when he diverted to *Down Under*. He tossed up three cartons of beer and climbed onboard. After giving a quick wave to me, they went below.

A minute later, Bruce and my father reappeared. They shook hands before my father swung over the rail and dropped into our dinghy. He jerked on the starter rope, not the measured pull he insisted everyone else use. He raced back to the *Spray*, not even trying to avoid the waves. He zoomed around the *Spray's* stern, cut the motor and threw the line to me, not caring that *Squirt* banged into the side.

215

"Help with the groceries," he shouted.

He hoisted up a carton soaked with seawater and dripping from the bottom. It held cans of tomato soup, corn, and baked beans. Fortunately, he'd filled the next carton with cookies and crackers, bread, four boxes of spaghetti, and eggs.

"Hurry up!" He handed up plastic bags of vegetables and fruit.

I dumped the bags on the cockpit seat. "Why the big rush? The anchor's holding fine."

"Faro's here! He was in the café next to the supermarket."

"Did he see you?"

"I don't know who was more surprised." He passed up a bag of bananas, brown and black. "I was getting in the taxi. There's only one on the entire island, can you believe it?"

Faro always seemed to be a step ahead of us, though it made sense that he would be waiting at Norfolk Island, a logical stopping point on the way to Australia.

"So much for buying fuel tomorrow." He climbed aboard with the last carton, full of beer cans, tuna, and cat food.

He was in such a rush we hoisted up *Squirt* using the mizzen boom, balancing it on the rail until he unfastened the outboard. Bruce motored by, waving wildly. He pointed to the pier. A wave crashed onto it, throwing up a cloud of spray. When it cleared, I could see several people in orange wet weather gear lifting a launch from a trailer. With a heave, my father upended the dinghy, wedging its bow against the mizzen mast. A minute later, we'd tied down *Squirt*, started the engine, and hauled up the mizzen sail.

"Keep the wind over the bow, Victor!" He was already on his way to the bow.

As soon as the anchor pulled free, he scrambled back to the cockpit. He hoisted the mainsail and unfurled the jibs, flapping furiously until he winched in the sheets.

"Kill the engine, Victor." Only then, he looked behind us. "Looks like they're having second thoughts."

The men on the dock contemplated their wildly swinging launch, suspended above waves passing beneath. All of a sudden, a larger wave thundered against the launch. It sent the men running for cover. Another man watched from the end of the pier, swinging his walking stick against his leg.

My father took the wheel. "We'll follow Bruce until dark, then head for Sydney."

I picked up a carton to carry it downstairs. "You want a tuna-fish sandwich?"

"The cookies are homemade, chocolate chip," he called after me.

+++

When my father checked the weather forecast two days later, the announcer reported a fast-moving low pressure zone 300 miles south east. It was headed our way. We veered west to avoid the worst of it. It was pitch dark when I shook him awake. He jerked up his head and scrutinized his watch. He expected the storm to arrive an hour after daybreak, not two hours before.

"The barometer's dropping fast," I said.

"Nothing like waking up to bad news," he grouched.

He got one arm and half of his head into his T-shirt before grabbing an overhead rail for balance as the *Spray* rolled through a wave. He threw on his life vest and harness and we went up on deck. The storm raced towards us, lightening flashing through clouds boiling across the horizon. The wind came in erratic gusts, swinging from side to side, each one stronger than the last.

"We'll run with it." He changed the self-steering course. "I'll get the outer jib furled. You drop the mizzen. Then, we start reefing the main."

I lowered the mizzen sail, lashed it to the boom, and went to help him. He'd clipped the tether of his safety harness onto the rail and climbed onto the cabin roof. He fought with the mainsail, his arms full of cloth, the wind trying to tear it away.

"Take her into the wind!"

Before I could get to the steering wheel, an enormous gust hit the *Spray*, almost turning her over. It was as close as we'd come to capsizing. She slewed through the waves, shuddering as the mainsail and inner jib flogged. The rigging howled. Lightning lit up the sea, and an eerie wall racing towards us.

"Hang on!" my father bellowed.

I clung to the wheel as sheets of water hurtled out of the darkness, rain like shotgun pellets peppering my face. It soaked me to the skin and, in seconds, sloshed ankle-deep in the cockpit. When I cleared my eyes, he wasn't on the cabin roof.

I screamed even as I spotted him behind the cabin, sailcloth thrashing around him, his harness tether stretched tight. He clung to a stanchion with one hand, untangling ropes with the other. The next wave washed him into the sea. Only a thin nylon strap saved him from being swept away until he could grab the stanchion again. It took all of his strength to hold on.

Unable to lift himself over the gunwale, he shouted, "I need you to help me."

I forced the wheel over, spoke by spoke, fighting the sea and the wind until the *Spray* righted herself, bow into the wind. A little farther to port and the jib was on the wrong side. I lashed the wheel to keep it there. Sailors called it being 'heaved to'.

"Make sure you're clipped on!" he shouted.

I didn't need reminding. A sailor never left the cockpit at night, or in bad weather, without his harness tether being attached to a jackline. A thin piece of nylon webbing running along the deck from bow to stern was all that stood between you and being lost at sea.

Even clipped on, I crawled along the deck with a death grip on the handrails along the cabin roof. Waves burst in my face as the *Spray* plunged up and down. In a lull, I reached down and grabbed his harness. The next wave boosted him up, high enough that I could drag him over the gunwale.

He gave me a grim look when he finally slumped onto the cockpit seat, coughing up seawater and rubbing his left elbow.

"Banged it rather hard."

"Is it broken?"

"Don't think so." He tried to lift his arm. He grimaced, shuddering and cussing to himself. "We'll stay heaved to. Ride this one out in the cabin. If you can, get the mainsail in, but be careful." He caught my lifejacket. "Thanks, Josh."

After I strapped the mainsail to the boom to his satisfaction, we went below and played poker with Ben's biology cards. Some waves swamped the bow as it lurched up and down, a thundering roar as water rushed overhead. The squalls eased with the first dim light of dawn. By then, we were exhausted.

The next day, blustery winds and long rolling waves kept us below until late afternoon. Then, we hoisted the sails again, heading southwest for Sydney, Australia.

Chapter 26

Every hour we were five miles closer to Australia. It stretched across the western horizon like someone had drawn a hazy gray line as far as the eye could see. Above, banks of cumulus clouds formed mushrooms in an otherwise perfectly blue sky. By the end of my watch, Australia was so close I could smell it, not the eucalyptus of cough drops, smoke like someone was barbecuing. I stayed on deck, sweltering in summer's dry heat and snacking on crackers.

My father was recording our position and current weather conditions when the first bird appeared. A shaggy silver gull, like the Herring gulls I'd seen at Norfolk, landed on the cabin roof. It was missing one of its bright orange-red legs.

"Been through some difficult times, like us," my father said. His elbow was a lump under a stretchy bandage.

I tossed a piece of salty cracker. The seagull pounced. "I never thought we'd make it to Australia."

He nodded, picked a cracker from the box, and flicked it onto the cabin roof. The seagull gobbled it down. It stopped at the companionway hatch, inspecting us through dark round eyes.

"We've never been as close as these last couple of days," he mused.

I didn't know what to say. He saved me from agreeing with him by going below to radio Customs for arrival instructions.

+ + +

An hour later, the sea had turned from dark blue to green. The cliffs guarding Sydney Harbour loomed like the walls of a fortress, with scalloped beaches on either side. While I steered for the entrance and kept watch for other boats, my father studied the chart and gave directions. We passed between North and South Head, trading the predictable ocean swell for disturbed splashy waves, churned by hundreds of yachts, power boats, and ferries. We passed a red-striped lighthouse and turned sharply to port.

My father pointed out the Customs buoy. "We won't need the motor." He furled the jibs before he hurried to the bow with the boat hook.

I eased the mainsail as we approached. The *Spray* drifted up to the buoy and stopped an arm's-lengths-away. After 20,000 miles, we knew how to sail. Soon, a launch left the wharf, headed towards us. A sailor waited in it while an officer climbed onboard. He was polite, unlike some officials we'd met. He made a cursory inspection of the cabin, examined our passports, and compared them to the Ship's Log.

"What happened to the rest of your family?" he asked my father.

"They're waiting for us here. We got separated after we ran into pirates in the Fiji islands. Lost everything except the clothes we're wearing and a few other things."

"You're lucky. There've been a few cases in recent years. They didn't end nicely." The official flicked through the Log again, perused the latest entries, and reexamined my father's passport. "We had an inquiry about you three days ago. He was sure you'd already arrived. He said you were at Norfolk Island last week."

My father coughed suddenly, a warning for me.

"You stopped there, Captain?"

He hesitated. "We didn't plan to. We ran out of food. Our anchor broke out five times. We were there for an hour at most."

The official looked incredulous. "It's not in your Log."

"The pirates nearly killed us. They stripped our boat. We were lucky to get it back."

"Your point, Captain?"

"It was so stressful he forgot, Sir. It was kind of an emergency."

My father shot me a 'shut up' glare; however the official smiled.

"He said you're feisty." He turned to my father. "You should've reported to Customs at Norfolk Island. However, an emergency is an acceptable excuse. Your friend left his card so we could call him when you turned up. Like we have time for personal messages."

"I'll phone him and let him know we've arrived."

The officer handed back our passports. "No guns, illegal drugs, or illicit materials?"

"None that I know of, but with a teenage boy on board, who knows."

My father's humor earned a chilly stare. "Pets have to be quarantined for a month or remain on board while you're in Australian waters."

Jag was stretched out, sound asleep on the settee.

My father decided in an instant. "On board."

"Not even a cursory look through our stuff," he remarked as we watched the launch return to the wharf.

"We've got nothing left to search," I pointed out.

+ + +

I had the wheel as we headed down the harbor. Summer, Saturday, and sunny brought out every sailboat in Sydney, from 80-

foot-long luxury yachts to tiny dinghies sailed by kids my sister's age. When he returned from the cabin with Bruce's GPS coordinates and a can of beer, a fleet of racing yachts zigzagged towards us.

He looked around. "Blooming with yachts, just like he said."

"Your brother?"

"Slocum, actually. My brother called it 'sailor's heaven.'" He stretched out his legs.

"It's your watch until four pm," I reminded him.

"Do I hear mutiny, or are you just mouthing off?"

Red-roofed houses battled with straggly trees for control of the headlands, becoming increasingly crowded the farther we went. With a whoosh, a racing skiff hurtled past with three husky men in black wetsuits suspended on thin wires from the mast, vast translucent sails straining. A second skiff followed close behind. I gripped the wheel, ready to take evasive action.

"I could do with some help here."

"You're old enough to stop muttering." Another skiff rocketed past within feet of our bow. "Blimey!"

The rest of the fleet whooshed by. By then, I realized they weren't going to hit us. The ferries I wasn't so sure about.

A little less than an hour later, we gazed up at the massive girders of the Sydney Harbor Bridge, its ends flanked by skyscrapers coming right down to the water. It took all my concentration and a great deal of luck to avoid the flurry of ferries and water taxis. I needed another pair of eyes; however, my father was more interested in the Sydney Opera House.

"We'll go at least once." He looked me up and down. "You'll need new clothes."

I owned one pair of filthy shabby shorts. "What's wrong with my Fiji Pineapple Company shirt?"

"His sense of humor too. Head that way." He waved under the bridge.

I turned into Lavender Bay, past an amusement park with a Ferris wheel and arcades. An enormous head with lunatic eyes guarded the entrance, its gaping toothy mouth, great black eyebrows, and orange-spiked hair screamed fun as much as the cries of delighted children on a roller coaster.

With dozens of boats crowding the bay, my father started the engine. It idled roughly, spluttering as it sucked from the bottom of the tank.

He took over the chart plotter, checking our GPS position against Bruce's scrap of paper. "If Sal's right, '23' is over there."

Our sails drooped as McMahon's Point blocked the wind. With the engine idling, I weaved among moored boats towards 33°50'44.88" south, 151°12'27.18" east.

Sal's '23' was a yellow buoy with black numbers, squeezed between a racing yacht and an antique cabin cruiser.

Just as my father lifted up the cockpit seat to retrieve the boathook, the engine coughed. It surged for a moment, coughed again, and stopped. Momentum carried us the last 20 yards, scaring two seagulls from the dung-splattered buoy. My father scooped up a seaweed-covered rope, hauled in it, and quickly looped it around the bow cleat. We looked at each other and laughed.

Buildings surrounded Lavender Bay, office towers, apartment buildings, lavish terraced houses, and waterfront mansions. After years of avoiding other people, I thought my father would be upset; however, he settled on the cockpit seat, beer can in hand, taking in the view.

"Now, we wait," he announced.

"Does your brother live in Sydney?"

"He did until things settled down. If you want something to do, get *Squirt* in the water."

While he snoozed, I unstrapped the dinghy and hoisted it over the side. With heat exhaustion a possibility, I sought shade under the sun awning, my back against the cabin, *Lord Jim* in my lap.

My father sat on the cabin roof, billowing his shirt to waft air up his chest as he looked around. A couple of kids fished from a pier; a family barbecued on a terraced garden; the sounds of the amusement park drifted in the still, sultry air.

"I see you found your Conrad."

"My Conrad?"

Lord Jim, like all of his old books, was nothing to look at. It had a dull-green cloth cover with a faded floral motif, the edges browned and battered.

"Did you read the inscription?"

I turned to the first page, 'To Alexander III, from Alexander II. Feb 17, 1992.'

"You're number three." He tried hard not to smile.

"My grandfather gave it to me the day I was born?"

"He paid a thousand pounds for it in Edinburgh."

"You're kidding!"

My father kept an eye on the shore, following a boy hopping from one rock to the next. He stopped to take off his shoes before he crawled under a wharf, re-emerging with mud up to his knees, black smears soiling his pristine white shorts and shirt.

"It's a family tradition. My grandfather gave me Slocum. I used to think it determines who you are."

The boy climbed onto a shell-encrusted concrete wall and waved his shoes over his head. I grinned and waved back. My father looked relieved.

Ben waded out as I rowed to shore. He hopped over the side and plopped down in the bow. He seemed taller than when I'd last seen him, more grown up.

After a hectic three minutes of catching up, he pointed at one of the buildings on the hill. "We're staying in the brown and white."

At least half of the buildings were brown brick; the rest painted white.

We rowed to the far end of the bay. The tide was out, leaving a long trek across gray goo spiked with shells. Mud and green slime splattered all over us.

"Mom's going to scream when she sees my clothes," Ben said as we lugged *Squirt* up the beach. "She's been shopping every day to replace our stuff."

It wasn't the smartest thing he could've said; however, my father didn't seem to care one way or the other. "How are things otherwise?"

"Grandma keeps talking about going home."

"And Sal?"

"He heard Zagarovsky ordered Faro back to New York, so he and Marion left for New York three days ago. Tony's keeping an eye on us."

"Anything else?"

"Tony thinks Faro hired some local punks before he left."

We found the assigned place for the dinghy under a low-hanging tree, a chain and a padlock with a tag. Ben had the key on a string around his neck. He handed it over.

My father locked up *Squirt* and stood up, his hands on his hips. The *Spray* was easily overlooked among all the other boats.

"Sal chose well. Faro's thugs won't find us here."

I wondered how long unnoticed and least expected would last this time.

+ + +

Ben led the way up a steep pathway to a road. Cars lined both sides, so close to the walls we had to walk in the road. The garages opened directly onto the street, plant-filled courtyards, houses, and apartment buildings squashed together. There were few glimpses of the bay.

He stopped at a creamy-sandstone wall. Thorny bushes poked through narrow slots, gray-green leaves sprouting above.

"We're staying here. Sal's friend, Angelo owns it. Sal said he's a green grocer; except he doesn't know broccoli from Brussel sprouts." Ben grinned. "Grandma thinks he's a bookie. Mom gave him ten bucks to put on *Sailor Boy* and got one-hundred-ninety back."

There was a keypad and speaker set into the wall. Instead, Ben reached through a hole, pulled a lever, and pushed back a thick wooden door. Red-brick stairs led past wisteria and ivy cascading over stone walls, spiky shrubs in big terracotta pots, pink blossoms bursting from either side of a forbidding, Aztec-temple doorway.

"Eclecticism was one of the defining features of Art Deco." Now Ben was an authority on architectural style?

Before I could ask, the door opened wide. My sister might have been going to her wedding in an ankle-length white dress. She twirled with the flair of a flamenco dancer and bellowed 'they're here,' before she bolted down the stairs and bear-hugged my father, not letting go even when my mother and grandmother appeared. He carried Jessie up the stairs.

"You're looking rather spiffy compared to the last time I saw you, Sarah," he teased.

My grandmother regarded him, reading glasses perched on her nose, a shimmering silky dress billowing pastel floral patterns, fashion leather sandals, a stylish platinum bracelet and earrings to match.

"You took your time getting here, John."

My father laughed, lowered Jessie to the ground, and hugged her.

"We're together now; that's what's important." There were tears in my mother's eyes, even more after he kissed her.

"Were you followed?" Tony asked when we stepped into the foyer.

"No one I noticed," my father said. "I see you're prepared."

Tony had a black leather holster strapped under his left arm, a pistol butt hanging out.

At first glance, Angelo might have been Sal's cousin with his dark tan and wavy white hair. He was half a head shorter with a red veiny nose. His hand trembled when he reached to shake hands with my father. He grinned at me when we shook. As soon as our eyes met, I knew I could trust him. He was outgoing, and throaty like Sal, his accent more Brooklyn than Australian, though he'd lived there for years. I liked him immediately.

Angelo's apartment covered the entire ground floor, all white walls, floors, and ceilings. Even the rugs, curtains, and couches were white. The paintings were haunting images of ghostly gum trees in fog, foamy waves on a beach, or snowy mountains. The piano was a white concert-Grand Steinway, a behemoth occupying a quarter of the living room.

"Angelo's teaching me to play the piano." Jessie sat on the glossy piano bench as if she owned it. "I can play *Chopsticks*..."

I didn't hear the rest. My grandfather had the same piano, only black. The night of the fire, I'd played *Chopsticks* sitting on his lap. He worked the pedals while I pounded the keys from beginning to end, much to my grandmother's amusement.

"... Sal said I should ask you to play for me," Angelo said from behind me. When I turned around, he held an acoustic guitar, pure white with silver frets. There was a gleam in his eye as he added, "Debussy's *Clair de Lune* perhaps?"

"I've never played it."

"I'm sure you've heard it before," he said, looking past me. He sat down beside Jessie and turned sheets of music until he found what he wanted. "It's for piano, so just the notes."

With a showy gesture for me to follow along, he stretched his fingers, and played the first two lines. When he nodded, I started to play from the beginning. What started with simple, carefully timed notes soon had me fingering the full range of frets. However, it wasn't as difficult as I expected, the slow, melodic notes sounding dreamy like a river in moonlight.

After a curt nod from my father, I tried to put even more expression into it, what he called 'tempo rubato,' stealing time wherever it could be taken. Besides my playing, the only movement in the room was Angelo's finger keeping time.

He waited until I finished before he responded, "You're the musical whiz he said you were." He turned to my father. "He'll be going to Juilliard, of course?"

For a moment, my father seemed as surprised as I was.

Chapter 27

Saturday, two weeks before Christmas, we crowded into our rented minivan to visit the Sydney Opera House. Tony drove, my father beside him with Angelo's directions and scrutinizing a map. Someone had squeezed every street in sprawling Sydney onto a single page, and then folded it into 16 rectangles. At one roundabout, right before a freeway on-ramp, Tony stopped and looked over his shoulder. He paid no attention to the car behind us beeping its horn. He accelerated rapidly, skipping the on-ramp to turn down a side street. After a hundred yards, he screeched to a halt.

"Surely you don't think..." My father turned to look behind us.

"I'm just doing my job." Tony's eyes were fixed on the rear-vision mirror. "It pays to be careful. We've got plenty of time."

"Faro would've made a move by now."

Tony just shrugged; he'd made it clear that going to the Sydney Opera House was not a good idea. He agreed to take us only after he talked with Sal on the phone.

After ten minutes of driving in streets with a tendency to suddenly become one way, or dead-end, or turn into wheel-screeching roundabouts; it was obvious no one was following us. By then, we'd become hopelessly lost in a 19th century maze of more or less identical squeezed-together row houses, all with intricate wrought iron balconies draped with lush flowers and vines.

+++

The Sydney Opera House forecourt teemed with traffic even though we arrived 35 minutes late. Tony braked and swerved into

231

an opening in a long line of taxis. He wouldn't let us get out until half-a-dozen cars went past. He watched every one of them.

"We'll be safe enough here." My father was never so sure of himself.

Tony was just the opposite. "You're crazy. It's too obvious; not worth the risk."

We got out of the minivan as a policeman started our way, his ticket book already out. Tony saw him too and accelerated into the traffic as fast as a minivan could go.

My father took Jessie's hand. "Right oh! Keep together."

He surged into the crowd of tourists and locals sprawled from end to end of the forecourt, enjoying the sunset. No lingering in front of architectural masterpieces for him. My grandmother and Ben stayed close on his heels. My mother tapped my shoulder to get me walking faster.

"We on the five minute tour?"

She added a push. "He's just being careful."

"What did Tony mean by 'it's too obvious'?"

Before she could answer, my father sidestepped a stroller and turned back the way we'd just come. Ben gazed up at shells like sails billowing above a vast terrace of pink granite stairs, likely forming an opinion of the International style.

Trying to be helpful, he grabbed my father's sleeve. "I think we're supposed to go up there, Dad."

"My shoes hurt." Jessie's shoes were polished black leather with silver buckles. They looked uncomfortable, like the lace-ups Ben and I wore.

"It's too exposed!" My father scanned faces on every side.

"You don't think it's safe, John?" my grandmother said.

"Just being careful, Sarah." He was already striding.

We trailed my father under the great pink-granite base and up a small flight of steps to reach the south foyer.

"I need a restroom." Ben itched his neck under his immaculate button-down shirt.

My father searched his pockets for our tickets. "Seats first, restroom later."

"Because the first half is Russian composers," I said under my breath.

"And we wouldn't want to miss that," my grandmother finished. However, he'd turned on his heel, program and tickets in hand, beckoning impatiently. She took Jessie's hand. "You'll wake me if I snore, won't you, my dear?"

Jessie took us all by surprise. "At least Daddy spared us the lecture on tonight's performance."

With laughter barely bottled-up, we trotted behind him up a long flight of stairs. On the right, ushers manned doors carved into wood-paneled walls stretching all the way up to the concrete-ribbed roof. The stairs ended at the north foyer. A glass roof cascaded from the shells overhead, a dazzling view of the bridge and the harbor at sunset. Only a few people remained, waiting until the very last moment to take their seats. A bell rang and the stragglers began to move towards the doors.

My grandmother looked up from perusing the evening's program. "Where on earth did John go?"

"Daddy's over there." Jessie pointed across the foyer at a man with straight brown hair.

"Except Daddy's wearing a blue shirt, same as Josh and Ben." My mother put her hand on Jessie's shoulder, turning her so she could see him talking with an usher.

Suddenly, the other man looked at us, pausing briefly before he turned away. Side on, there was a definite similarity, though his hair was lighter, shaggy like a 70s college student.

My father hurried over, ticket stubs in hand. "We're back down the stairs. Door five."

"Daddy, I saw a man who looks exactly like you," Jessie said.

My grandmother chuckled. "Actually, I thought he was better looking."

He grimaced at my mother. She shrugged, pretending indifference while she tried not to laugh. Not amused, he strode off, his family hurrying to keep up.

"I need to go," Ben announced when we passed a discreetly placed 'men' sign.

My father spun around. "Intermission!"

We found our seats as the lights dimmed. With a crescendo, the concert began: a compilation of Russian composers of the early 20th century—the communist era. 'Avant garde', my father called it, 'a revolution against musical order.' After 45 minutes of torture, it ended as abruptly as it started.

Only then, my mother leaned over me and tapped my father on the shoulder. "Ben really needs to go. I don't want him wandering around by himself."

"They're about to play the Allegro from *Symphony No. 2*. Intermission's in seven minutes. Can't it wait?"

"It can't!" Ben gave me a panicked look.

"Seven minutes won't kill you."

"You want me to pee on the seat?"

"I'll take him." My offer went unheeded.

Ben's knees were jammed together. I still made him wait until the conductor tapped his baton. "Come on baby-bladder."

Borodin's assembly of the Prince's Court followed us down the aisle, Ben whispering 'hurry up,' while I whispered 'excuse me' to people contorting their legs for us to pass. The doors closed behind us, blocking the celli taking up the cause. I looked up and down the long flight of stairs; no one, not even an usher. There were restrooms both ways. Up offered a better view for the distance.

Three women ushers lounged in front of the vast cascading window; a man vacuumed trash from the floor; men in tuxedos prepared the bar for intermission. The restroom was empty, meagerly modern with metal and stone polished to a glassy sheen. Ben pushed past me, rushed into the far toilet, and slammed the door. He locked it and dropped the seat with a loud bang.

"Feel better now?"

"Up yours, mate," Ben shot back, a fair imitation after nearly a month 'Down Under.'

I laughed and went over to the urinal. I'd finished, zipped, and was washing my hands when something made me look over my shoulder. Perhaps he'd been standing there all the time.

"Zagarovsky was sure you'd be here for Borodin," Faro said, quietly bland like his gray business suit and matching walking stick.

He flipped open his cell phone as I edged along the vanity. He stepped closer, his eyes boring right through me, pushing numbers with his thumb.

He lifted his phone to his ear. "I've got him in the men's room. I'll bring him down. Be ready to go." He snapped it shut and smirked at me. I glared back at him. "He's here, isn't he?"

"Who?" It came out a squeak, as if my voice hadn't broken.

"Your father." He pointed his walking stick at me.

I braced myself, set to fling up my arm or duck, glancing at the gap between him and the wall. He turned momentarily and I tried to shove past, knocking his walking stick sideways. It jammed between my thigh and the wall and clattered to the floor. When he reached for it, I kicked it as hard as I could. It spun across the restroom. He went after it and I ran to the door. When I glanced back, Faro was reaching under the far toilet partition. Ben shrieked as I bolted into the lobby.

"There's a pervert in there," I screamed. Everyone rushed over, even the man with the vacuum cleaner. "He molesting my little brother," I added for good measure.

They charged into the men's restroom, the three women ushers in the lead. Through the closed door, I heard Faro shout, "I never touched him."

I turned and sprinted down the stairs. A man now sat on the bench opposite door '5.' He stood up when he saw me. Sunburned face, bristly brown hair, a button-down blue shirt like my father was wearing; he might have been taking a break from the concert except his eyes never left me. I veered away from door '5' and took the next flight of stairs three at a time. I ran all the way to the south entrance foyer before I glanced back. There was no sign of him. Another man in blue jeans and red running shoes guarded the entrance doors. The instant he saw me, he had a cell phone pressed to his ear. I was almost certain he said 'he's here' to his phone.

There was a 'concourse' sign on my right and a long flight of stairs going down. Other than going back the way I'd just come, it was the only way out with him blocking the entry. I started towards the stairs at a brisk walk, resisting the impulse to look back. At the bottom of the stairs was a passenger drop-off area. Five limousines were parked along the far wall. Two drivers in tuxedos stood by one of the limos, both speaking into cell phones. Safe for the moment, I turned and looked up the stairs. I thought the man in the foyer hadn't followed me until jeans and red running shoes appeared.

I backed away, whirling when someone said 'Hey you.' One of the drivers was on a beeline to the far entrance. The other driver, balding with a belly bulging over his pants, still leaned against the limousine, still talking into his cell phone. With a chortle, he stuffed it in his pants pocket and opened the passenger door.

"Faro's got his boxers in a knot. Best get in the car without a fuss, matey."

Behind me, the man was halfway down the stairs. To my left, the other driver was now slowly walking towards me.

"You think?"

My snicker scored a scowl and, "Don't fill your pants. He just wants to chat."

I gave an incredulous look and headed towards the setting sun.

He waddled a few paces behind. "You're being stupid, mate."

When I reached the west entrance, the man who'd been outside door 'five' stepped in front of me. I darted between him and the wall. He grabbed my right arm. I yanked away. His fingers hooked my shirt and ripped off the sleeve at the shoulder. The chubby chauffeur clamped his hand over my mouth, dragging me back with my legs splayed out.

Suddenly, the man let go of my shirt sleeve. He spun around and shouted, "Look out, Chook!"

I bit down on pudgy fingers as hard as I could. He bellowed curses only an Australian could know. I landed on my wrist hard enough to chip concrete. He managed to kick me as I scrambled away. When I got to my feet, there was a third man. I couldn't see his face. He shoved the driver away from me and added a belly punch for good measure.

"Run!" When I didn't move, he shouted, "Now!"

I ran! Weekend tourists flocked to Bennelong Point to watch the sunset, choking the boardwalk, swarming around fountains and restaurant pavilions. My right shoulder ached, my wrist a piercing stab whenever I moved it. I snatched glances behind. I couldn't see anyone following me, yet I didn't slow down until I reached an oasis of palm trees, absurdly exotic in a landscape of concrete and glass. I skirted café tables and chairs cluttering the footpath, patrons like sheep jostling each other in long waiting lines, or posing their bored hungry children for photos in front of Circular Quay.

A day earlier we'd gone to the city to buy clothes for our visit to the Sydney Opera House. We took the ferry from McMahons Point to a wharf on the far side of Circular Quay. I merged into the crowd in front of the terminals, walking as fast as I could without drawing attention. I arrived just as the ferry began to reverse away from the wharf. I waved and shouted 'wait for me' at a crewman who dragged back the gangplank.

"Next ferry mate; nine thirty!" He busied himself coiling thick ropes on bollards.

In the park next to the quay, sidewalk entertainers gathered crowds: an aborigine boy daubed with white droned through a didgeridoo, acrobats with painted faces pretended to be machines, Pterodactyl Man tooted a South American lute, a Cockney clown danced and told jokes. I stopped under the trees, where an old man played haunting tunes on a flute and a nymph-like girl danced with flowing silk. My mother and grandmother would've been enthralled; I watched the road with growing trepidation. A black limousine passed twice while the girl mimicked seagulls. She was mocking the wind, or maybe drowning, when it pulled into the curb and a side window rolled down.

Two men got out, 'Door Five' and 'Red Shoes'. I moved close to a family as the men scanned the darkening park. 'Five' made a beeline for a group of kids watching a purple-caped superhero battle luminous bubbles. He inspected every kid before he glanced at the trees. All of a sudden, he pulled a cell phone from his pocket, held it to his ear, and headed towards me.

I turned and walked quickly towards a man on a bicycle throwing a chainsaw into the air, a hundred awed onlookers urging 'higher.' I thought I was safe until Faro got out of the limousine, raised his walking stick, and pointed it at me. Immediately, someone grabbed my left arm from behind. 'Red Shoes' was breathless, as if he'd run all the way from the foyer of the Sydney Opera House.

"Not one bloody word, mate, or I'll break your arm."

I felt his spit hit my face. "You need breath fresher, mate."

With a savage jerk on my arm, he pushed me through the crowd, down to the harbor, shoving me up against a cast iron railing. I stared down into bilious green water until he spun me around and rammed my spine into a spike. A few paces away, two women admired Sydney Harbour.

"Let me go, asshole!"

His hand went for my neck, choking me. "Nice or nasty; your choice smart-arse." He forced back my head.

One of the women saw my panicked nod. "Oh my God, Maggie!"

"What do you think you're doing?" Maggie was tall, bony thin, her gray hair cut short.

His head snapped around. "Police, mum. This one's a pickpocket."

"He's lying!"

He gripped my shirt at the necktie, lifting up until I gagged. "Shut your mouth, creep." He pulled me from the railing, wrenching my arm again.

I twisted back to face the woman. "Please, could you call the cops?" He slammed me into the fence again.

"Stop it. You'll hurt his back!" the other woman exclaimed.

The man propelled me away from the women. "You'd better check your handbag instead of worrying about him."

Maggie quickly stepped in front of me. "He's hardly a pick pocket with polished shoes and a tie."

He turned to her, nose to nose. "Mind your own bloody business, lady."

She was saying something about seeing his police badge when I yanked away from him, dodging between the two women before he could stop me. He shoved Maggie aside. I bolted down the broad esplanade, weaving through families with strollers, kids playing, and old ladies who always seemed to travel in pairs. A few people shouted after me. When I risked looking over my shoulder, he'd dropped back a hundred yards, his cell phone at his ear.

At the cruise ship terminal, I veered into a narrow lane lined with stone and brick warehouses from the colonial era. Surrounded by busy restaurants and bars, and with no sign of pursuers, I slumped on the curb. Every breath hurt, even with my head between my knees. My right wrist looked like there was a baseball inside it. With my left hand, I pulled off my tie and stuffed it in my pocket.

When I looked up again, a little girl was staring at me. "He's bleeding, Mummy."

There was blood from my elbow to my fingertips.

"Stay back, Fiona." Her father towered over her. "What happened to you?"

I got up slowly. "It's cool."

"You need an ambulance?" He already had his cell phone out.

"It's just a scratch. No big deal." I sounded like a chipmunk.

"Can we take you somewhere?" Fiona's mother clearly wasn't buying it.

"We're staying at McMahons Point." I gave a hopeful smile. Of course, he shook his head. "How can I get there, besides by ferry, I mean?"

"Take the train. Circular Quay to Milson's Point."

She had a 'he's crazy' look, which I thought ironic given her red-beaded headband, hair down to her butt, and long flowing flowery skirt. "North Sydney is closer. If he walks down Blues Point Road he'll be right there."

"Actually, you'll need to catch a train from the Quay to Wynyard first; then, get on the North Shore Line. Just follow the signs."

"Town Hall would be better. It's the next stop," she said. "It's a much nicer station. Lots more shopping. You need fare money?"

Fiona's parents made mine seem quite ordinary.

"I've got plenty." There was no way I was going back to Circular Quay. "Any other way?"

"You could hoof it." He pointed up the street to the massive steel trusses of the Sydney Harbour Bridge.

"How do I get up there?"

"Dunno, mate. I never walked the bridge. Not much point unless you're a tourist."

"You can get there from the Argyle Street stairs," his wife interrupted.

I gave the simple version of my life story as I walked with them to where they'd parked their green, Beatle-era MGB sports car. It was barely big enough for two people. Somehow, Fiona squeezed behind the front seats.

"Go up Cumberland Street. You can't miss the stairs." She held my hand, the one without blood. "You sure you're okay?"

"I'm a tough little critter." I got her to smile.

She called, 'Be safe' as I headed off. Away from Sydney's bright, bustling nightlife, street lights became puddles of yellow glow. A man staggered by, drunk, bloodshot eyes leering at me.

"Going to rain, y'know. Forty days and forty nights," he muttered. He smelled as bad as he looked.

I kept walking, looking for stairs that weren't where they were supposed to be. At Argyle Street, I gazed down on cars racing into a tunnel and under the freeway. On the other side, trees hid most of the road, and another drunk tottering down the footpath, stumbling from one trunk to the next.

"It'll stop if we pray," the man shouted after me.

Cars were parked in the shadows below, among them a black limousine. Its driver loafed on the footpath, blowing smoke signals.

Suddenly, he looked up and shouted, "Hey Faro, it's him!"

Faro walked out of an arched doorway, his walking stick tucked under his arm. We glared at each other until he ducked back into the entrance to the Argyle Stairs. I ran down Gloucester Street, thinking I'd been there before. The Australian Hotel was striking compared to dull little houses like books in a row. Noisy men, and a few women, spilled into the street, all guzzling glasses of beer.

When I stepped from the curb, someone shouted 'Check the pub' behind me. I ducked behind a minivan.

Faro went into the hotel while his men walked down the street, checking every house and car. When they weren't looking, I darted across the street, through a gap in a chain link fence surrounding an archeological site. A week earlier, Ben kept us there for half an hour to watch excavation in progress, a garrulous professor supervising four college students scraping dirt into mounds and carefully placing stones back on walls. More interesting was a sign describing the remnants as brothels that sailors had frequented when their clipper ships docked at Circular Quay.

I climbed over a crumbling waist-high wall, and hid behind it as the men approached. A moment later, they pushed through the gap. One man hugged the fence halfway to the hotel before heading into the ruins. The other man tromped through gravel, straight towards me. I crawled on my hands and knees, wedging myself into a dark corner. It smelled sour, like ammonia.

"Hey, Vinnie?" he called. I could see his head and shoulders when he leaned over the wall. "Smells like a bloody dunny over here."

"Shut the hell up, Chook."

"Faro's probably havin' a beer."

"I told ya, shut up!" Vinnie was pissed.

Chook muttered about hurting his ankle as he crunched across the gravel. I raised my head above the stones. Vinnie heaved himself onto the adjoining wall and stood up. I crept away, following the wall into a tiny room. Spiky vines hung over the stones, the smell even worse.

"Faro always this cranky?" Chook called out.

"He spent a year finding the brat, and you let him get away. What do you think?"

Vinnie placed one red shoe in front of the other, his arms out like an acrobat, kicking loose stones to the ground. I crouched under the vines as stones bounced beside me, hoping he didn't look down.

"Not my fault. Them women got in the way."

"Shut up, Chook!"

"They ought to bloody fix these stones. Ain't safe to walk on." Vinnie kicked at another stone. A mini avalanche tumbled from the wall. "Blimey!"

His arms flailed as he crashed to the ground on the other side of the wall. I scurried from my alcove, keeping low as I clambered over low stone walls. I almost missed a narrow cobbled lane dotted with potholes.

"You're not getting away this time, Alex," Vinnie shouted behind me.

Chook stopped grouching about his ankle. "The only way out, kid, is past me."

"When we're done with you, even your daddy won't recognize you."

It was creepy; blocks of apartments overlooking the ruins, car headlights zooming past on the freeway, a shiny-modern recreation center a ball's throw away, and the two of them chortling in the darkness behind me.

"Sander, over here."

The whispered name swirled in my past. I couldn't remember when or where, yet it was a voice I could trust. He beckoned, only his hand poking out from behind a stack of dirt-covered bricks before he crept away. I followed along a narrow passage, holding my nose against the stench, trying not to think about what might be under my feet. The passage ended in rubble, slipping and sliding as I scrambled up.

"Come on," he whispered over his shoulder.

He paused at an open gate in the fence. Immediately, he ducked back, pressing against the hotel wall. After a moment, he peeked around the corner, down Cumberland Street.

"You're my uncle, aren't you?"

He shushed me. "Not now. The limo's parked on the corner."

"What are you doing here?"

He leaned closer. "Trying to keep you alive. You know who they are?"

"The one with the walking stick is Faro. I've never seen the others before tonight."

"Not that it matters, Faro's not his real name."

I was going to ask his real name when an ear-piercing squawk stopped me. It made even belligerent drivers get out of the way. The police car stopped in the middle of the street, its neon-blue strobe pulsing, reflecting off showroom windows in the metallic building opposite. Inside, people ran on treadmills and rode exercise bikes.

He nudged my shoulder. "Great timing, what." A dozen yards away, Faro got in the limo. "Okay, we're a father and son going to the rec center. We're going to walk across the street like nothing's wrong."

Three cars backed up behind the police car, the last one blocking the limousine. A second police car came down Cumberland Street, no siren, no brilliant blue lights, yet flashing its spotlight on the parked cars.

He grinned. "They're looking for a couple of carjackers." With his hand clamped on my shoulder, we started to walk. He nodded to the police woman after she gestured it was safe for us to cross. "I figure Faro's friends have records as long as your arm," he said in my ear. "They'll be halfway to Melbourne by now."

When we reached the footpath, he guided me under the trees. The stairs to the bridge hid in the shadows. No wonder I'd missed them.

I had a hundred questions. "You followed me from the Opera House?"

"I lost you in the park so I followed them instead." He gave a sheepish smile. "What on earth were you doing there?"

"Waiting for a ferry. If you want to hide something, put it where it belongs..."

"And least expected," he finished.

"It worked for a while."

"You were lucky with those women. Faro had you dead in his sight. Why did you come up here?"

"I was going to walk home, only I couldn't find the stairs."

"Good idea. They'll be watching the ferries, the train too." He looked around. "Stay away from the light. Faro's a good shot."

"He shot my brother."

He nodded as if he already knew. "You need to go before the police leave. It won't be long until they realize it's a false alarm." His voice cracked. "You need to be more careful."

The last thing I wanted was to say goodbye. "I'll see you again, won't I?"

He appraised me from head to toe. "When it's safe. I hope you're not afraid of heights, Sander."

No one called me Sander, not since the fire. Even blond-headed, I was never called 'Sandy.'

"Off you go," he whispered, already backing away. "Keep going, no matter what. Whatever you do, don't look back."

Chapter 28

Immense gray granite pylons staked the ends of the world's fourth longest bridge, a single steel arch from Millers Point to Milsons Point. Near the center, I stopped to test my fear of heights. It was worse at the top of the *Spray's* mast, buffeted by the wind and clinging on for dear life. High above the harbor, Sydney spread out like rippled black satin decorated with a million tiny LEDs, ferry lights like slow-moving fireflies. People strolled past me, admiring the Opera House, its sails lit up at the end of Bennelong Point.

At Milsons Point, I took the stairs down, leaving behind the din of cars and humming girders. I constantly glanced back to make sure no one was following me. Under the freeway, I skulked down mostly deserted streets, staying in the shadows as much as I could until I reached the waterside promenade. I was certain I could see the *Spray's* gaff masts sprouting amongst the yachts on the other side of Lavender Bay, still a long distance away.

According to the schedule at the Milsons Point Wharf, the next ferry arrived in fifteen minutes, McMahons Point the next stop. So much for 'hoofing' it all the back; I was taking the ferry, no matter the cost.

Too tired to do more than lean against the railing and massage my wrist, I watched people stream in and out of Luna Park. Everyone looked happy except a man slouched on an empty park bench overlooking the ramp down to the ferry. He stared at me. I moved closer to the gaping maw of the Luna Park head, where a gang of Goth-kids loitered.

"Get lost, freako." The girl licked blood-red lips. She had greasy black hair drooping over her forehead, silver rings through both eyebrows, dark eyes stoned with desire. Her mute boyfriend had orange-spike hair and octopus DNA—he pawed her doggedly.

Luckily, I spotted Chook before he saw me. He trundled down the same long ramp I'd come down ten minutes earlier. He glared about, his cell phone clamped to his ear, his fat face red and sweaty. I merged into the gang, smelling acrid weed-smoke. I found space between two early-teens who could have been extras in Bram Stoker's *Dracula*, insipid and skinny, and alike enough to be twins.

"Your shirt's DOA, Cuteness." The girl's lace-fronted blouse and ankle-length skirt needed soap and hot water, if not a trash can. She stroked my neck with bony pale fingers, ebony fingernails chewed to the cuticle.

"Fiona doesn't bite unless she's hungry." Like his partner, his clothes were black. His impeccable tightly pressed black pants and a starched-collar shirt separated them.

I glanced at Chook. He was headed my way. "Okay if I join you?"

The ferry was already in sight and slowing down. People were lining up at the head of the ramp. Chook skirted around them.

Fiona stepped closer. "Three's kinky. I'm up for it if you are."

He sidled behind me and held an earplug near my ear, gyrating his pelvis to heavy-metal music. Fiona stayed in front, both of them uncomfortably close, both muttering incantations.

The boy pressed against my side and breathed in my ear. "Cuteness needs a hug?"

I was quite sure I didn't. When I looked around, Chook was just a few yards away, staring at the Luna Park head. If he turned his head even slightly, he'd look right at me. I nodded. They hugged around me, his hands around her neck, pushing me against her. My heart thumped until Chook walked back to the ramp. I squirmed from their embrace.

"You need to relax." The boy pulled a hand-rolled joint from his pocket. He held it out with skeletal fingers, three with silver rings. There was a spiked-leather bracelet on a bird-like wrist.

"Asphyxia's the best." Fiona reached for my neck again.

I eased out of her reach. Suddenly, Chook turned on his heel, scanning back and forth. I edged between them, an instant before his eyes passed me. The boy put the joint between his lips and searched his pocket, pulling out a shiny silver lighter. He flicked the lever while his eyelids flickered at me.

"Adrian loathes his mum, don'cha know?" Her tongue danced on black lips.

"Oh, the angst of it all." He mockingly pawed her front.

"Stop faking, Bondage Boy." Fiona pushed him away.

His belt was for show, wide black leather with sharp metal studs and tie-down hoops, looped silver chains, and a big death's head buckle. It didn't keep his pants from dragging on his hips.

"I'm only tied up on weekends," he scoffed.

He hauled up his pants to show chain bracelets on each skinny ankle. He sidled closer, sucked on the joint, and handed it to me. I brought it to my lips, scarcely touching, thinking viruses, bacteria, and my father's perpetual lectures. I quickly handed it back, not wanting to cough or spit in front of them.

"You're brown." She touched my arm near my shoulder.

Adrian inhaled deeply and held it. "She pretends she's bizarre." He offered the joint again. I shook my head.

Fiona was on it in an instant. "Cuteness got a problem with pot?"

"The guy by the ramp." I jerked my head. "He's been following me for hours."

Adrian's eyes grew. "You're American. My dad was just there on business. He brought me a gangsta hoody." It was tied at his waist, black fleece, superfluous style in Sydney's summer.

I watched Chook watch the ferry disgorge its passengers, tromping single file across the gangway and up the ramp, passing the Goth kids as if they carried the plague.

"The boozer's after you, huh?" Adrian inhaled and blew smoke.

"The fat weirdo, you dingbat." Fiona pinched the joint. "Ooh, how nasty."

"I don't want him seeing me get on the ferry."

When the last passenger got off, Chook glanced around to make sure he hadn't missed me. Adrian blocked his view.

"You live around here?" he asked.

"We're staying with a friend at McMahons Point," I answered.

An attendant opened the gate for people waiting to get on the ferry.

"Adrian lives at Kirribilli." Fiona made it sound exclusive.

"Sucks to be effluent!" Before she realized, Adrian tapped the girl with blood-red lips on the shoulder.

Her eyes bored into me while he explained I didn't want Chook to see me. She was saying 'no way' when Fiona said the magic word, 'weirdo.' In seconds, she'd marshaled her gang and marched them down the ramp with me in the middle, wearing Adrian's hooded sweater. Ten Goths swarmed onto the ferry, much to the dismay of the other passengers. Chook turned away.

When I tried to give back the sweater, Adrian refused. "I'm always at Luna." He clasped my hand, gangsta style.

He stepped off the gangplank before a man dragged it back. From a window, I saw Chook stare at Adrian and his friends as they went up the ramp, back to loitering outside the Luna Park head. As the ferry pulled away from the dock, I hid behind the door in case Chook looked my way.

+ + +

I disembarked with six other people when the ferry arrived at McMahons Point. When I passed the restaurant outside the terminal, Tony got out of the minivan. He crossed eyes with me, nodding once as I walked by.

"Keep walking, straight ahead," he whispered.

With Tony watching my back, I walked all the way to the end of Henry Lawson Drive before he picked me up. He drove into the forecourt of Blues Point Tower, a high-rise apartment building. He stopped outside the front doors, leaving the motor idling as if we were waiting for someone.

I opened the passenger' side door and got in. "Is everyone okay?"

"They were on the ferry before yours." Tony squinted at the mirror and adjusted the angle. "Sarah's a hoot; she bet Angelo a hundred bucks you'd be home by ten."

"What about Ben?"

"He stomped on Faro's fingers before they dragged him from under the partition," Tony laughed. "Ben called him a pervert right to his face. During the fuss, he gave them the slip. I wish I'd been there to see it."

"Me too." I cringed at the thought of what might've happened.

"I expect that's why they let Faro go."

"My uncle was at the Opera House."

Tony cut me off. "We're lucky he showed up. He said Vinnie Krait was there. The guy's a snake."

"I ran into one of Faro's men again at Luna Park. Chook; they called him."

"He's another local rent-a-hood. Not too bright and pit-bull mean."

After I told him what happened at Luna Park, I took off Adrian's sweatshirt.

"Make that very lucky," Tony said when he saw my shirt.

"If I was lucky none of this would have happened."

Tony smiled. "Did he see you get on the ferry?"

"He might have."

"We'd better drive around for a while, just in case."

He put the minivan in gear, and slowly drove up and down the streets lining the harbor's north shore, looking about as if he expected someone was following. It was 9:55 pm when he parked outside Angelo's house. My father opened the door. He beamed when he saw me.

"No one followed us," Tony said quietly.

He stepped aside to let us pass. "Busy night eh?" he said to me. No 'hi', or 'I'm glad you're okay.'

"I met your brother."

He nodded. "You need to be in bed. We're leaving first thing tomorrow."

"You said it'd be a month before we headed off."

"We're not taking the *Spray*. Angelo's lending us his car."

"Because of what happened tonight?"

"Now isn't the time, Victor. Pack your stuff and go to bed."

My father bolted the front door as I turned away. His handgun, the one he kept in the secret compartment under his chart table, lay on the hall table.

+++

We left at 6:00 am, bundling bleary-eyed into Angelo's Ford sedan, my mother and father in the front, the rest of us squeezed in the back. We got lost twice in Sydney's sprawling suburbs of red-roofed houses before reaching a freeway. It joined the Western Motorway and rushed headlong towards a mountain range, hazy like Virginia's Appalachians.

By the time Jessie woke up, we were 20 miles into the Blue Mountains, on a two-lane road demanding concentration. My stomach required food, yet my father drove on oblivious to my suggestions we stop for breakfast. Next to me, Ben read aloud from his growing collection of guides to Australia every time we passed through a town. They had names of explorers and governors from the colonial past. Between the towns, rugged sandstone gorges separated blue-green ridges and endless straggly eucalyptus trees, inciting my grandmother to entertain us with passages from her book on Australia's poets.

He finally stopped at Katoomba, derived from the aboriginal word for 'water tumbling over hill', according to Ben. While he sat in the car and made calls on his cell phone, we hiked through scrub to find the waterfall, the crisp air pungent with eucalyptus, the pulsing drone of cicadas becoming ever louder. Without a map, we turned the wrong way. The trail ended at stairs carved into a spectacular gorge. We climbed down to a rocky outcrop, the first of the 'Three Sisters.'

My father was in a worse mood when we returned to the car. "We left at the right time."

"I've heard it before," my grandmother said under her breath.

"What about Jag?" Jessie had worried about our cat since she woke up.

"Tony rowed out to feed him this morning." My father looked at my mother. "Someone tried to force the lock on the cabin last night."

It was now or never. "Who's for morning tea?" I said brightly.

My grandmother picked up immediately. "I am, and Angelo's paying. He's not much of a bookie."

Once a famous mountain resort, Katoomba still had a dozen small cafes open for business. My grandmother chose one at random and went in by herself. She soon returned with slices of gooey lemon-pastry, coconut-covered chocolate-iced cakes Australians called lamingtons, fresh scones with strawberry jam and cream, paper cups of coffee, and cartons of chocolate milk.

She confronted my parents before they had a chance to complain. "I don't want to hear I'm spoiling them."

+ + +

It took the rest of the day to reach Bathurst. It was only 60 miles, 100 kilometers; however, we stopped at every tourist attraction.

Chapter 29

After two days in Bathurst, we travelled westward on mostly straight highways with shimmering mirage-puddles in front of us, and vast fields of yellowing wheat on either side. From Parkes, the road was endless, three days of ragged scrub and spindly trees, or tinder-dry grass and emaciated sheep. The sun blasted through the windows, turning our air-conditioned car into a microwave oven.

I was thinking nothing had changed since we'd left the café where we'd eaten breakfast in Nyngan, three hours ago, when we reached the outskirts of Bourke, the heart of the Outback.

Bourke, population 2,145, was a tourist magnet with four motels, three hotels, and two caravan parks. My father's decision to rent a cottage for the night was met with dismay. Dahlia House had droopy dahlias in the front garden and a shady verandah with plastic lawn chairs. Inside, the air-conditioning spluttered every five minutes as if gasping for breath. Even worse, the previous tenants were smokers. However, it was cheaper than three motel rooms. He promised to spend the difference on dinner.

The cottage was still being cleaned so we drove to the river and went for a walk, Ben hurrying ahead to study wallabies up close, instead of watching them through the car window. The heat had no effect on him when there was wildlife to see. If there was work to do, like lugging suitcases, he wilted like the dahlias.

"From here on, it's a desert ecosystem," he declared when we caught up.

The algae-green Darling River meandered into the afternoon haze until it disappeared among gray Casuarina trees, raucous with mating cicadas. On the opposite bank, a sparse, red, dry world stretched to the horizon. Except for clumps of spinifex grass, it was as lonely and flat as a windless sea.

My father pushed his hands through his hair before he turned on his heel and headed back to the car. A green cicada followed him.

My grandmother flapped at black flies buzzing her face. "What's got into him?"

Ben shrugged. "Dad's always grumpy when he's too far from the sea." He squatted to inspect a pile of black pebbles, rolling them like marbles.

It was hard not to laugh. "It's emu poop, Nature Boy."

"How can you tell?"

I pointed to tracks in the mud. Among hundreds of tiny paws and bird feet were three giant toes, the center one longer. With emus in the vicinity, my brother went looking. I wandered back to the car. My father had opened all of the doors to get rid of the heat.

"… nice not having to worry. You're probably right." He snapped his cell phone shut and picked up a travel brochure as I approached. "Jessie wants to go for a camel ride." His sudden change in mood surprised me. "There's a place not far from here."

'Not far' was a half-hour's drive on a dusty dirt road to a vast sheep and cattle station. The camels were friendly—mine was called 'Sheila.' She was smelly, bumpy, and attracted hordes of bush flies. Afterwards, despite clothes damp with sweat and smelling like camels, we stopped at a restaurant down the street from the imposing Bourke Courthouse. We stuffed our bellies full of roast lamb, mashed potatoes, boiled peas, and fresh lemonade.

Our cottage was nearly as hot inside as it was outside even after my father turned the air-conditioner to its maximum setting. We lingered on the verandah, watching the last of a fiery-gold sunset, the cicadas settling to an occasional squawk.

"Can we walk to the river?" Ben wanted to see if the emu had returned.

"It'll be more fun than sitting here, and better for us, John." My mother stood up, ready to go. Off the *Spray*, she exercised with a passion.

"I'll be right along," my grandmother said. "I need a drink of water first."

"Me too," Jessie piped in.

My grandmother and Jessie went back inside. The rest of us headed for the river, straggling along Bourke's wide empty streets. Most houses had lights in the rear rooms, almost none in the front. Darkness came quickly to the Outback.

"It's like someone forgot to pay the electricity bill," I said to Ben.

He stared up at the night sky, turning around and around, and walking backwards. "Southern Cross, Sirius, Orion, Canis Major..." He rattled them off.

"Is there anything you don't know?" I kept walking.

A half a block ahead, I could hear my mother teasing my father about the cottage; his response, it was nicer than renting a caravan, his low-cost alternative. I heard the tap-tapping of a cane as someone came down a dark side street.

"Look out, kid!" The man was as surprised as my brother.

Ben ended up on his back with the man's walking stick tangled between his legs. With his hands on his hips and his business suit, the man looked like a grumpy lawyer, or maybe a banker turning down a loan application.

Ben jumped up. "Sorry, Sir. I was looking at stars."

"Watch where you're going!"

Ben handed over the walking stick. The man twirled it twice, and went on his way, his dark suit swallowed up by the night.

By the time Ben and I reached the river, the rest of my family was nowhere in sight. He crouched among tinder-dry tussocks, afternoon heat still radiating from the hard-packed soil. Instead of emu-watching, I walked along the bank, wondering whether snakes were about at night. At least there were no flies, and it was cooler near the water.

I'd reached a footbridge hidden among the trees when my father bellowed, "Victor!"

"Over here," I shouted.

I hurried back to where I'd left Ben. "Any emus?"

"He scared it off." Ben stood up, dusting off his butt.

"Where the hell are you?" my father called in the darkness. "Victor! Ben! Here! Now!"

"We're coming!" I shouted back.

He waited by the road. He turned away as soon as we emerged from the gloom. "Jessie's missing." He jogged up Sturt Street. Ben and I ran after him. "She got separated from your grandmother. Why are there no damned street lights?"

He paused at the first intersection to get back his breath. There was a hotel to the left, spilling amber light into the street. Men gathered out front, cheering for a greyhound race blaring from loudspeakers. To the right were swanky stone houses from an era when paddle steamers carried bales of wool to the sea.

"Go around the block. We'll meet at the Courthouse." He gestured at the next intersection. "Stay together." He turned left, jogging again.

Ben and I went right, running all the way to the next corner before we slowed down. There was a sports field in front of us.

"She might have gone that way." Ben pointed at a hard-to-see path leading towards the river.

259

"You might, not Jessie." I turned left again with Ben right behind me.

The houses on the side streets were smaller and not nearly as grand; little, single-story bungalows with wide verandahs like Dahlia House. At the next intersection was a grocery store, the only shop in Bourke still open for business at 8:55 pm.

"She might've gone in." I led the way across the empty parking lot.

Beyond a squeaky screen-door, was a rack of romance paperback novels and trestle tables with stacks of shiny cucumbers, three for a dollar, $1.19 cans of pork and beans, and five different kinds of breakfast cereal. A gray-haired woman with pink blotchy skin manned the only checkout counter.

She didn't look up from her magazine. "Candy. Aisle four, Dear," she rasped like chalk on a blackboard.

I began. "We're looking for our sister."

She waved at the cucumbers. "She went down aisle four, dear."

There was no one in candy. Farther down the aisle, Jessie peeked from behind a display of six different types of cookies under a sign, 'pick 4 $10.00'.

"He had a walking stick," she whispered the moment we reached her.

I glanced at my star-gazing brother. "Lots of men have walking sticks."

Jessie looked about, mimicking the nervous wallabies we'd seen alongside the highway.

"The boss will be in to close any minute," the woman shouted from the front of the store.

Ben picked up his favorite Tim Tams, chocolate-covered, chocolate cookies with a chocolate cream filling. "She'll get suspicious otherwise."

I grabbed three boxes of Vo-Vos, and pulled Jessie after me. Everyone loved Vo-Vos, delicious pink-iced coconut-flaked cookies with a strip of raspberry jam down the center. I dumped $5 and a handful of change on the counter.

"Don't eat them all at once." The woman had a motherly chuckle as she carefully counted out coins.

As we left the store, a car turned into the parking lot. It was a white box on wheels. Nearly every car we'd seen since leaving Sydney was either a white sedan or a white SUV. Its overhead light came on when the driver opened the door. He stared at me. He might've been the store owner. I didn't wait to find out. Clutching Jessie's hand, I ran down the street.

The center of town wasn't much: closed-up single-story shops, a post office, and the Bourke Courthouse, where I hoped my father would be waiting. We'd just reached the post office when Angelo's sedan pulled up beside us.

My mother leaned across and shouted through the passenger' window. "Get in!"

Ben grabbed the passenger door handle. "I'm riding shotgun."

"In the back!"

I opened the rear door, shoving Jessie and Ben into the car before I got it. I slammed the door shut.

"Faro's here?" I wasn't certain until my mother floored the accelerator.

"Either him or his twin. Everyone down, especially you."

We hurtled down Oxley Street, trying to put on seatbelts with our heads between our knees. The tires howled when she swerved onto Sturt Street. She didn't say a word, or slow down, until she reached our cottage. Then, it was 'damn!' when the car slid sideways on the gravel as she pulled off the road.

"Stay in the car!" She jumped out and rushed up the stairs, the motor still running.

"I got everything out." My grandmother lugged two bags from the pile on the verandah, packed so hastily that a shirt flapped out the side of one of them.

My mother grabbed two more bags. It took three trips before they got everything in the trunk. She slammed her door and leaned down as if trying to find the lever to adjust her seat. When she straightened, she held my father's handgun. She put it in the coffee-cup-holder next to her seat before she turned around.

"Get down! As low you can." She shoved the car into drive and we bumped back onto the road.

"What about John?" My grandmother slouched low in her seat, clutching her handbag.

"He said to leave as soon as I found the kids. He'll meet us at the café in Nyngan tomorrow morning. He wants to make sure it's him before he calls Sal."

"Like you'd mistake him."

"It was dark, Mom. All I saw was a man swinging a cane. I could be wrong."

I had so many questions I didn't know where to start; plus I needed to tell her I might've seen Faro too. After she ran a stop sign, it seemed safer to keep my mouth shut.

A couple of blocks south brought us to the outskirts of town, darkened warehouses, and empty parking lots. My mother went through another stop sign when she reached the Mitchell Highway. After that, her attention spanned between complaining about driving on the wrong side of the road, glancing in the rear vision mirror, and making sure her children stayed out of sight. My grandmother assisted by constantly looking around, as if Faro would leap out of the darkness and attack our car with his cane.

Fifty minutes out of Bourke, my mother slowed down for Byrock, a tiny village on the only bend in the road to Nyngan. Suddenly, she braked, backed up a hundred yards, and turned onto a gravel lane. 'Mulga Creek Pub' was painted on the roof of a low rambling building with a verandah along the front and sides. Spotlights around the parking lot made a bright circle as if they expected customers to arrive by helicopter. Except for a big truck parked alongside the highway and a solitary light glowing inside, the place looked deserted.

My mother drove to the far end of the parking lot and stopped in the shadows. After a minute of uncomfortable silence, she shook her head.

"This is crazy. We'll do it my way this time." She turned to my grandmother. "I'm going back to get him. Get a room if you can. Otherwise, keep out of sight. I'll be back as soon as I can."

We got out of the car. She pulled away, heading back to Bourke.

"I want Mommy." It was the first Jessie had spoken since the grocery store.

"Not to worry, Sweetie. We'll get a room. It'll be fun," my grandmother said.

Jessie wasn't buying it. Her bottom lip trembled. She pawed at her eyes. Suddenly, she hugged my grandmother, sniffling and burrowing into her blouse.

"She'll find him and be back here before we know it." My grandmother stroked Jessie's hair. "There's no need to worry. Faro won't find us here."

Jessie shook her head vigorously. "Yes he will. He's got people working for him. The woman wanted me to get in her car, but I ran."

Before I could ask what woman, my grandmother took Jessie's hand and began a brisk trek towards the hotel verandah. Ben and I straggled behind.

"I can't believe Faro found us way out here," Ben said quietly.

"If anyone asks, our car broke down," my grandmother said over her shoulder.

She walked faster as we passed the truck. It was full of bleating sheep. The smell, even worse than camels in heat, followed us all the way to the verandah. We left a trail of footsteps from the steps to the front door. Red dust covered everything, metal chairs, scorched potted plants, the 'Toohey's beer' sign propped by the door.

My grandmother rapped and waited. Ben pushed past me, pressing his face against a green-glass window and smearing grime on his nose. He moved away quickly when the door jerked open, revealing a gangly red-headed man who scowled at us.

"Youse alright?"

One hand held a towel around his middle, the other a beer can. Freckles covered his pale pink body like splattered paint. My flummoxed grandmother stared back.

"We're shut till next month." The man scratched at his scrawny bare chest.

"Our car broke down," I said. "We need a room for the night."

"There's nothin' in Byrock. Best bet's a taxi to Bourke, mate." He glanced down at Jessie, who looked like she was going to blubber. After a moment, he smiled and stepped back. "One night, eh? No worries, assumin' you don't mind the stink. We're still cleanin' up."

We followed him inside. I smelled smoke right away.

"Had a fire in the kitchen last week." He waved at tarpaulins under a freshly painted wall. "No real damage. Should'a wacked on some paint and been done with it, but the building inspector; well, you know what they're like. Fix this, fix that." He walked behind the bar and dragged a binder from under the counter. "I'll put you in Lawson. Henry was in Byrock, y'know." He grinned at us and assumed a dramatic pose. "'About Byrock we met the bush liar in all his glory. He was dressed like—like a bush larrikin. His name was Jim.'"

My grandmother seemed impressed. "What was Australia's poet doing in Byrock?"

"Following the shearers, I reckon Mum. Twenty thousand bales of wool a year back then. Byrock was a swank place. Five hotels and a rail station. There's just the butcher store left. And the cemetery. It's worth a gander before you leave in the morning. How about fifty, Mum?"

My grandmother opened her handbag, pulled out her purse, and handed over the money. "Is there a chance we could get something to eat?"

"Normally, yeah. Cook's on hols at Surfers. I reckon I can knock up a couple of sandwiches." He snapped shut the binder. "Ham and tomato, and cheese and Vegemite, okay? Maybe some roast beef if it hasn't gone off. I'll bring 'em down in a jiffy. There are drinks in the machine at the end of the hall."

Vegemite was a yeast by-product. It looked like axle grease, slathered on bread with a thin slice of processed cheese in the middle. I hated it—it tasted like very salty beef bouillon. I shared the ham and tomato sandwiches with my grandmother, while Ben

265

and Jessie devoured the rest. With nothing else to do, we watched how to play a didgeridoo on public TV. When it finished, we showered and got into bed. It was nearly 11:00 pm.

+++

It seemed as if I'd only just dozed off when my father woke me by pointing his flashlight in my face.

"Get dressed!" He went to the other side of the bed to shake Ben's shoulder.

"Faro's here?" I found my clothes folded on the armchair.

"Leave the lights off."

He dragged down the sheet to haul Ben out of bed. My bewildered brother stood on wobbly legs. I tossed him his shorts and T-shirt.

My grandmother came out of the bathroom, already dressed, dabbing her face with a towel. "How on earth did they find us way out here, John?"

"No idea, Sarah." He hurried to the window, peering between slatted blinds. "Let's go!"

"Not dressed yet." Ben was tangled inside his shirt.

I jerked it past his head. He scowled, as grumpy as he'd ever been when I woke him for his watch in the middle of the night. My father scooped up Jessie, still sound asleep, and headed for the door. I exchanged a shrug with Ben, grabbed my socks and shoes, and followed. My grandmother closed the doors behind us.

My mother had parked our car beside the truck where it couldn't be seen from the highway. We clambered in as she got out for my father to resume his self-appointed role of driver. Without a word, he examined the map she held out for him. Satisfied he knew where he was going, he started the engine and accelerated onto the Mitchell Highway.

"Back to Bourke, where we're least expected, right?" I suggested.

"Not this time!"

He turned at the next intersection, onto a deserted street, past a one-room school, and a rectangular water tower, until he reached a dead-straight road heading out of Byrock. The bitumen ended abruptly, leaving an even wider road strewn with gravel. The car spewed pebbles and clouds as he put down his foot. From the rear seat, I watched the speedometer climb into triple digits, far too fast for safety. He didn't slow down for seven very long minutes.

He braked hard at a bend. The car slewed, flinging buckets of stones into the scrub. I clung to the armrest with a clammy hand, expecting the car to roll over any second, or slam into one of the gnarly gum trees zooming by.

"John," my grandmother said very calmly.

He risked our lives by turning to glance at her. "Zagarovsky was there. What I want to know is how he frigging found out."

"At least phone Sal and let him know," my mother said.

He didn't answer. Instead, he wound down his window and tossed out his cell phone.

An hour later, we stopped on the side of the road, cramped and dozing in fits and starts to wait for dawn to arrive. A couple of houses and falling-down sheds remained of Gongolgon, a Cobb and Co. stagecoach stop that once had three hotels.

Chapter 30

After our hasty departure from Bourke, we travelled on lonely long roads; day after day of scrub, red rocky earth, sheep pastures, or yellow wheat. We stayed at cheap motels in rambling dusty towns with aboriginal names, eating takeout for dinner and leftovers for breakfast—my father's version of a modest vacation.

We splurged and stayed two nights at the Outback Motor Inn in Coonabarabran. The town's tourist brochure called it 'conveniently located, a rustic, luxurious, colonial farmhouse in a picturesque setting.' It missed on all counts, on the outskirts of town, across the highway from the cattle yards.

"John, we've eaten Chinese five nights in a row!" My mother was exasperated.

"We'll need every penny when we get back to Sydney." He spooned the last of the Kung Pao Pork onto his paper plate. "How about some Chicken Chow Mein?" He passed her a cardboard container, untouched except for a spoonful sitting on his plate.

"I think this is Sweet and Sour Fish, John," my grandmother said sweetly.

"The kids need a change. After tonight, no more Chinese for a week." My mother could be obstinate when it came to her kids.

"It'll be turkey burgers tomorrow," I whispered to Ben, hoping my father would hear me. It would be Christmas Eve the next day.

He stood abruptly, appraised his family sprawled across tawdry bedspreads, the evening meal served in front of the television, tuned to the evening news.

"I'll call Tony on a payphone and see if it's safe to return."

Ten days later, with no sign of Faro or Zagarovsky, we returned to Sydney. In a frantic rush, we readied the *Spray,* blowing his budget for a year in three days. At the top of his list were a new set of sails, which he'd already ordered, two laptop computers to replace what we'd lost, additional charts, and sailing clothes. The rest of us shopped for food for a month and school supplies. With everything stored away and $1,024 of diesel fuel ferried aboard using *Squirt*, we said goodbye to Angelo and Tony. It was January 12th.

After clearing the Heads guarding Sydney Harbour, the *Spray* sprinted up the New South Wales coast, taking advantage of a steady breeze off the port beam and a north-flowing current. It blew off the land at that time of year, parched and dusty like the Outback we'd driven through. During the day, we were in sight of the coast, sometimes so close I could see surfers on long scalloped beaches, gaunt gray trees on undulating hills, or the quilted patchwork of farm fields. At dusk, we headed out to sea and watched the twinkling lights of lonely farmhouses, or the glow from towns offering a safe harbor. The wind faded the next day to a measly eight knots peppered with occasional hot puffs. It made sailing unpleasant, but my father pressed on.

We rotated watches among my mother and Jessie, my father and Ben, and my grandmother and me—four hours on duty followed eight hours off, twice a day. There was plenty of time to relax. When I wasn't on watch or sleeping, I lay in *Squirt* and read, shaded by a beach towel I draped from the mizzen boom, occasionally glancing over the stern at our foamy wake, hoping for a panicked whirl from our fishing rod when a fish took the lure. After eating lamb chops, roast lamb, and lamb stew for most of two weeks, I looked forward to fresh tuna for dinner.

My father leaned against the aft rail and fiddled with the self-steering vane before he took over the next watch. He looked up at the mainsail. "It sets a lot better than the old one."

"It ought to be perfect for $7,000." My mother often teased him, though she'd insisted he buy top of the line. No more eBay bargains for her!

"It included a new jib! Plus I had the staysail re-stitched. Worth every penny!"

Ben poked his head through the companionway. "Like buying me another *Britannica*."

The day before we departed Sydney, my grandmother surprised him with a lightly used, 2001 edition of the *Encyclopedia Britannica*, purchased at a library auction for $75. He brought a volume upstairs for his turn on watch. It had a blue leather cover with gold edges and lettering. It was thicker than its predecessor, inflated with the knowledge of 12 additional years. He deposited it on the cockpit seat and stretched before he sat down.

He glanced back at me, tousled-headed and bleary-eyed. "Any bites?"

"Not yet. There was a bull shark this morning."

He looked around. "No dolphins. It might still be there."

Dolphins often played in the *Spray*'s bow wake or followed astern, waiting for handouts. They left when big sharks appeared.

Her watch over, my mother jotted down our course and position. "Four hours at three-point-five knots, John."

"It'd be less than three knots with the old mainsail. Definitely money well spent." My father was in a good mood despite creeping along.

There wouldn't be a better time. "Does your brother still live in Brisbane?"

"He moved years ago. What lure are you using?"

"Tuna Suicide. Are we going to see him again?"

"What did you think of him?"

"He looks a lot like you," I hedged.

"Your watch, John." My mother headed down to the cabin where dozens of Outback postcards awaited her scrapbook.

He adjusted the self-steering, a few degrees closer to the wind, searching for another quarter of knot to beat her speed. "We're different, though."

"Ben and I are different. We don't even look the same."

He cocked an eye at Ben, kneeling on the cockpit seat, his head buried in his *Britannica*. He was about to say something when the *Spray* slammed into something. It was hard enough to fling my father from the stern rail and onto the dinghy. His shoulder hit my knee. Below, my grandmother screamed.

"Oh my god!" My mother scrambled back up the stairs.

My father grabbed the rail behind him as the *Spray* lurched, veering to starboard, then to port as my mother grabbed the wheel and forced the *Spray* to turn into the wind. He leaped into the cockpit, jerked up the seat and threw out lifejackets.

"Everyone on deck!"

With no answer except my sister's bawling, he bolted down the stairs. I clambered from the dinghy and looked over the side, expecting the worst—a shipping container. Instead, there was a huge gray fish, like a massive Frisbee, unmoving except for a slight flutter of its tail.

"Sunfish," I called out. I'd seen sunfish before, never as big as a beach umbrella.

Ben huddled on the seat, whimpering and holding his head. When he tried to stand, he started to shake. My mother made him lie down and began carefully pressing her fingers through scruffy hair, looking for skull fractures.

271

I pulled on a lifejacket just in case. "Is he okay?"

"He needs a haircut." She was calm. She probably hadn't considered the possibility we might be sinking. "See if anything's broken at the bow."

I ran forward as the *Spray* began to pick up speed, the self-steering already correcting our course as if nothing had happened. I leaned far out over the bowsprit, watching the bow cleave the waves. If there was damage, I couldn't see it.

"There's water in the bilge," my father shouted from the cabin.

"How much?" My mother gave up on Ben's head.

He came to the stairs. "A couple of gallons. I haven't checked it since we left Sydney. We'll keep an eye on it." He nodded at Ben.

She rubbed Ben's shoulder. "He'll have a bad bruise."

"Mom, I have a mild concussion," was Ben's self-diagnosis.

My father decided on the spot. "We'll head for Coffs Harbour."

"Tony said we shouldn't go ashore unless it was an emergency," I reminded him.

We'd seen hundreds of yachts since leaving Sydney; however, the *Spray* had the only gaff-rig. It wouldn't be difficult for Faro to follow our progress with high-powered binoculars from the headlands.

"I know what Tony said!" he said. "I think a mild concussion qualifies, don't you?"

We were midway between Sawtell and Urunga, which made Coffs Harbour a four-hour sail with the sails hauled in tight. Ben had perked up by the time we sighted Mutton Bird Island. It was a prominent windswept, wave-lashed knoll guarding the harbor entrance. My father radioed for a space at the marina as we passed the island. There were a half-dozen meandering sightseers looking at birds, a few more gathered on the viewing platform overlooking the ocean. I climbed onto the cabin roof, ready to lower his new mainsail when he gave the order.

"You steer." He waited until I was back in the cockpit. "Keep an eye out for Faro," he added quietly.

The sun lit up the clouds with red and gold flames, stretching shadows from the mountains, the nearest so close I could see trees on the top. Inside the darkening harbor was a breakwater, sheltering boats from waves rolling past Mutton Bird Island. Basalt and concrete blocks were stacked wide enough to make a road on top. A white SUV was parked on the end, as if marking the entrance to the marina. I motored towards it, noisy seagulls wheeling above as the mainsail and mizzen came down. My parents scurried about, tying down sails, furling the jibs, readying the *Spray* for arrival.

My mother got out the fenders. "Keep your head down, Josh."

"I need to see where I'm going," I replied.

"He ought to be in the cabin." She handed the fenders to my father.

He glanced at Ben, now asleep on the cockpit seat. "As soon as we dock. Not so fast," he said to me.

I eased back the throttle and made a wide turn, lining up the *Spray* with the marina entrance, a pile on one side, the SUV on the other side. There was a man sitting inside it.

"Don't get too close to the wharf." A long wood wharf extended into the center of the harbor. I steered away from it. "Better slow her down more."

I leaned around the steering wheel to put the throttle in idle position. It sounded like a bird hit the side of the cockpit.

"Get the hell down!"

He shoved me away from the wheel, forcing me onto the seat. He slammed the gearbox into reverse and opened the throttle all the way. My mother dragged me along the seat to the companionway, pushing my head below the side of the cockpit when I tried to look out. I scrambled down the stairs, my brother right on my heels. My mother was right behind us. I'd never heard her cuss like that.

"What happened?" Ben rubbed the side of his head.

Before I could answer, splinters exploded from the side of the cabin. There was another loud bang from the forward head as the *Spray* shuddered under full power. Anything loose rattled loudly.

"Everyone on the floor," my father bellowed.

My grandmother thrust Jessie behind the galley cabinets and knelt over her. Ben lay belly down at the bottom of the stairs. My mother squatted next to him. I grabbed the cat and got under the table, where I could see up the companionway. My father was hunched down behind the wheel. The porthole behind Ben's berth exploded, flinging shards of glass like shrapnel into the cabin. Jessie screamed. My grandmother clutched her face. Blood seeped through her fingers. She pulled up her blouse and dabbed at her forehead.

The *Spray* lurched sideways, going full speed ahead. Soon the slap of small waves became further apart and louder, and the bow began to rise and fall with the ocean swell.

"We're clear," my father called. "Is everyone okay?"

My grandmother steadied herself against the bulkhead. Blood trickled down her cheek. There was another gash in her forehead.

"No John, everyone is not okay."

My mother guided her over to the settee and got out the first aid kit. "Ben, take Jessie into our cabin and stay there. Josh, boil some water."

She removed two splinters of glass from my grandmother's cheeks. Using flashlights and tweezers, I picked up hundreds of shiny slivers from the settee, still more from the cabin floor.

+ + +

When I took my father his ham and tomato sandwich-dinner, we were still sailing away from the coast. The wind had faded to reluctant puffs still warm from the land. There were a few faint lights on the horizon, a vast swathe of glimmering sea. Stars filled the sky.

"Three knots, and half of it's current," he remarked.

"I checked the bilge. No more water."

He nodded and gnawed the center out of his sandwich, avoiding the stale crusts. "Should've been toasted. How's Sarah?"

"She's sleeping."

"Which explains dinner." He studied the side of the cockpit where shattered layers of plywood surrounded a hole big enough to put my finger through. The bullet had punched a bigger hole in the opposite side of the cockpit. "I've been thinking about today."

"Something other than I'm lucky?"

He smiled. "I don't think Faro was trying to kill you. Assuming Tony's right about his marksmanship, there's no way he would've missed you from that distance."

"Except I leaned down to adjust the throttle."

"He had a clear shot at your back. He missed by a yard. It doesn't make sense, unless he intended to miss; and then the question is why."

"How about he wanted to scare the crap out of me?"

"Hardly worthwhile."

"He wanted us to keep going; or he wasn't ready to do it?"

"You think like my brother."

He tossed the crusts overboard and looked over his shoulder. If a boat was following us, its navigation lights were turned off. We must've had the same thought; he switched off the *Spray*'s night lights.

"Faro will expect us to run offshore. We'll head back to the coast for tonight."

He sent me below to make sure the curtains were drawn.

Chapter 31

It was our fourth day since the 'episode' at Coffs Harbour, as my father referred to it in the Ship's Log. We sailed north, towards Queensland and the Great Barrier Reef. The coast was never in sight after that first long night, just an endless line of pale clouds to port. Rather than swelter in the cabin, I sought shade on deck with Orwell's *Animal Farm,* my assigned reading for English Lit. A blustery breeze kept the heat at bay, yet the glare was too strong to read more than a few paragraphs at a time. I gave up trying to figure out which of Russian communists Orwell's animals represented, and dozed off. When I woke up, the last thing I expected to see was buildings as far as the eye could see.

"He's expecting us in the middle of February," my father said to my mother.

"Your brother?" I asked.

He glanced at me. "We'll find a marina with a rate that won't break the bank in Brisbane."

"Surely, you don't want to wait around until then?" My mother trimmed pictures from brochures and placed them in interesting arrangements in her scrapbook.

"We can't just turn up on his doorstep. Anyway, we don't have a choice. I don't have his address."

"You came all this way without an address."

I hid my smile in *Animal Farm.*

"It wouldn't be a problem if we'd visited New Zealand as planned."

"He must have a phone number," she insisted.

"There's no way to get in touch with him. He'll contact us the usual way in the middle of February."

"After what we've been through, we have to sit on our butts for three weeks." My mother shook her head.

He thumbed through his guide for marinas. "Here's a marina in Brisbane. The weekly rate is five bucks a foot. All amenities included. Close to the city."

"Five dollars sounds rather cheap." She leaned over to look at the aerial photo. "What's beside the marina?"

"I don't know; some kind of shipping terminal I think."

I took advantage of the calm before the storm. "What's the usual way?"

"Email."

"As in Borrowedin?"

He looked up from his marina guide. "What do you know about Borrowedin?"

"Nothing. I was checking our email and I saw it on your computer."

"What did you see, exactly?" His stare was unrelenting. He expected more than a shrug.

"Some crap about me having problems in school."

"You were back then. Anything else?"

My mother interrupted him. "He lives near here though, doesn't he John?"

"He used to live in Gympie," my father replied. It sounded like gym-pie.

I could see Gympie circled on his chart, a dot so far inland we'd need a car to get there. In a day, it would never be closer.

"When did he move?" I asked.

"What else did you see?"

"Another email was about sending a pen. Nothing important."

He inclined his head as if he didn't believe me. "Four years ago, it was. He sent you your great grandfather's pen, the one he used to write the Second Symphony. I'm keeping it for you."

I went back to Orwell, thinking the interrogation was over.

"What else did you see on my computer?"

"Nothing. I only read the one about me when I was eight."

"Just one?" He was persistent, like a terrier with a terrified rat.

"Where did he move to?" my mother asked, her message clear.

"He never said."

"Bruce used to live in Gympie." I said it the same way Bruce said it: Gim-pee. "He said you looked like a man who helped him in a fight. He was talking about your brother, wasn't he?"

"Probably. What else did he say?"

"Only that the man moved and opened a restaurant about the same time he left. It was near the sea," I added, trying to remember details. They hadn't interested me at the time.

"That's helpful!"

"It was at a tourist resort. Near a national park, I think."

My father pushed the chart and guidebook towards me. "There's nothing but tourist resorts and national parks all the way up the coast."

My mother turned his chart around and gave it a lengthy inspection before she pointed at a long island. "Great Sandy National Park is close to Gympie. It's only a day north of here. We should at least take a look, John."

"Might as well waste three weeks in the middle of nowhere looking for a straw in a haystack."

279

"I'd rather be in the middle of nowhere than a marina next to a shipping terminal."

I choked back a laugh. He leaned over to look at the chart. The park sprawled across the mainland and Fraser Island. It was bigger than some countries.

"There's a marina at Tin Can Bay. It's as good a place to stop as any, I suppose. If it's not too expensive, we could rent a car, and see some more of the country."

+ + +

Pounding surf and perpetual wind eroded the vast sand hills of Cooloola Beach to reveal rainbow layers of red, yellow, and orange, scarred by deep clefts. We steered clear of Double Island Point, the red knob of its lighthouse poking above straggly shrubs. After an hour, we passed houses perched on the last sand hill, another hour before the beach ended at Great Sandy Strait. On the other side was Fraser Island. As islands went, it was dull, flat as far as the eye could see, an endless slab of trees. The only redeeming feature was the surf, long waves rolling onto a pristine beach. It was inviting but dangerous—we saw the dorsal fin of a tiger shark zigzagging among the choppy waves.

With the wind veering west and loosing strength, we dropped the sails and cautiously motored into a tidal estuary dotted with low islands, sandbars, and fishing boats. Without breeze, the water shimmered, so clear I could see silver fish and black seaweed forty feet down.

I put Orwell aside. It was hot enough to shrivel up. "I bet he lives here."

My father sipped water from a flask before he looked up. "Because it's as hot as hell?"

I wiped sweat from my brow and thought it undeserved. "You said he liked to fish."

"I need you in the bow! It'll be cooler up front," he added after I started forward.

He didn't need a lookout. The channel was wide and well-marked, no obstacles he couldn't see from the cockpit. To annoy him, I made a point of leaning out over the bowsprit and waving minor steering corrections to port and starboard sporadically. Once, when the water suddenly became shallower, I signaled which way to go; however he was already turning. When I looked down again, a giant turtle paddled leisurely away.

We passed yachts at anchor, and people fishing from launches, drifting in the tide. A motorboat chugged towards us, its sunburned captain swilling from a can while he pawed his bikini-clad girlfriend. He shouted 'up yours, mate' after my father bellowed 'starboard has right of way' and swerved to avoid collision.

Ben escaped the lecture on 'paying attention' by joining me in the bow. He grinned. "Yet another screw-up because of you."

Through the open hatch behind us, we could hear our grandmother snoring lightly. Every so often she'd grunt, pause, and then resume snoring. The heat didn't seem to bother her.

"It's always my fault. I caused the collision with the sunfish, don't you know?"

Nature Boy grinned. Bit by bit, he was swapping cynical for compliant, morphing into a teenager despite 'Kooky' the kookaburra on the front of his T-shirt.

He sat on the rail. "He's looking for a place to anchor where no one will see us."

So much for staying at a marina and giving my grandmother a break from cooking. An hour earlier, my father had said we'd stock up on food, eat dinner at a restaurant, check email, and look for a place to anchor the next morning.

Ben checked over his shoulder. "He told Mom you weren't ready."

"Ready for what?"

"How should I know?" Ben stopped scanning for fish species as a sea eagle swooped low over the water. "I could live here if it weren't so flamin' hot."

Jessie shuffled past the fuel cans strapped to the rails. "I have to stay here because Daddy's getting mad."

The drone of my parents' voices had become guardedly agitated. They weren't arguing, although it was on the way.

Ben gave the standard explanation. "He's worried about Josh."

"No way will Faro find us here," I said.

Beyond the sand flats, dense thickets of mangrove trees and a maze of tidal creeks provided countless places to anchor the *Spray* where it would be invisible except from the air.

"It's not about Coffs Harbour," Jessie said. "They're talking about the fire."

"Watch out for shallow water," my father called.

Around the next bend was Tin Can Bay.

+ + +

The town of Tin Can Bay sprawled across a low peninsula. After passing the local marina, my father turned the *Spray* around and docked alongside a trawler at a commercial fishing pier, right outside a smelly warehouse. After promising we'd be back by 3:00 pm, we hurried to the town's small shopping area, lifeless in the blistering afternoon sun.

At a small yet well-stocked supermarket, we filled a cart with provisions for a week, and headed to the checkout. Ben and I had almost finished unloading the cart before a young woman stopped stacking cans of pineapple juice and came over.

"G'day Ron! I like your haircut." Her smile matched the 'smiley face' on her 'I'm Chloe' badge. My father stared at her while she started to ring up prices. "Didn't expect to see you today. Brought some friends too, eh?"

He frowned. "You have me confused with someone else."

Chloe frowned back. "Sorry. You look just like him."

My mother put down the fashion magazine she was perusing. "It sounds like you have a double, John."

Chloe kept ringing up items. Nothing was cheap. "Two peas in a pod, Mum."

"Does Ron come in often?" She kept watch on Ben, who was busy inspecting a rack of sunglasses.

"Every Friday, when he goes to the fish market. He's got a restaurant."

"This restaurant, how far away is it?" my father asked.

"Fifty kilometers."

"No distance at all," I said before he could say it was too far.

Behind me, my mother laughed.

"Of course, when my husband and I go, it's by boat. Carlo Point's a hop away then," Chloe added.

"We'll have to visit, won't we John?" She tapped Ben's shoulder. "Any color except purple."

He lingered over neon green frames and bronze lenses. The boring Ben was gone, dorky T-shirt aside.

"You ought to, Mum; especially if you like seafood. 'Sails' is the name. You can't miss it. The roof is covered with sails to keep it cool."

Outside the supermarket, my father took my mother aside.

"It's not a good time," he said quietly.

"There'll never be a good time, John."

Jessie and my grandmother headed towards a small ice-cream store with a herd of happy cows painted across the front windows and door. Ben and I lagged behind, both of us loaded down with plastic bags crammed full of food.

"You really think we should motor across the bay and have dinner at his restaurant unannounced?" He made it sound ridiculous.

"Why not?" my mother replied calmly. "It's not like he isn't expecting us. If you want to call him first, you can probably find a phone number for his restaurant."

He hesitated. "It'll be safer following the plan."

"It's still four weeks away. There's no reason..."

"I know of one reason." My father lowered his voice. "He's not ready."

I wasn't supposed to hear him, and she didn't want to hear him.

"He'll never be ready, and neither will we!" She gave him a few moments to think about it. "I promised Jessie an ice cream."

He watched her cross the street before he handed me his grocery bag. "I'm going to find a telephone. I'll be back as soon as I can. Cold stuff in the fridge. Fill the water tanks while you're waiting.'

"There's no way Faro will find us here," I said, meeting his eye.

"If he can find us at Coffs Harbour, he can find us here."

Twenty minutes later he hurried along the wharf. He untied the *Spray*'s lines before he climbed aboard, started the motor, and backed away.

"I hope we're doing the right thing." He steered into the channel, his mood visibly improved.

"What did your brother say?" I asked brightly.

"I spoke to Erin."

"She's his wife?"

My mother looked up from the chart spread across her knees. "Was I right, John?"

"I'm glad I called."

"There's Bruce's boat." Ben pointed past the Coastguard station.

Down Under was moored on the other side of Snapper Creek. We'd missed it on the way in. It had blue tarps draped over the boom and catamarans flanking either side. The junk in the cockpit gave it away.

"Funny how he keeps turning up." My father handed me the binoculars.

"Not if he lives in Gympie."

"You might be right. Keep your eyes open. Anything suspicious, let me know."

I focused on the shore, going back and forth along the waterfront, not at all certain what 'suspicious' thing I was keeping watch for. Right before we reached Tin Can Inlet, I saw a white SUV parked beside a small beach. It looked like the car I'd seen at

Coffs Harbour. I didn't point it out; the driver was a woman in dark sunglasses. Three children were waist-deep, hand-feeding a dolphin, a warning sign to the contrary.

We crossed a broad expanse of shimmering blue water and turned into an estuary with sand bars lining the sides and crab-pot buoys every few yards. We passed a boat ramp and a small marina with several yachts tied up at jetties, a solitary building resembling a restaurant with big windows looking over the cove. Triangular sails stretched over a terrace at one end of the building, with a two-story blue box at the other.

"Erin said there's a good place to anchor farther on," my father announced. "Everyone look for posts marking the channel. She said some of them are submerged at high tide, but if we wait until the tide goes down, we'll never get over the bar."

Ripples eddied around the tip of the first barnacle-encrusted pole. I pointed it out to my father.

"Already saw it." He gestured forward.

I handed the binoculars to my mother and went to my place in the bow. The *Spray* slowed, chugging past the pole. On either side, sandbars emerged, pockmarked with tiny crab holes. Ahead, the inlet disappeared among mangroves. It looked very shallow.

"I can't see the next post," I yelled. We'd gone about a mile past the restaurant.

"Go where you think best." My father reduced our speed to a crawl.

I waved to starboard, where the water looked deeper. Schools of silver bream swirled through clumps of yellow seaweed. On a nearby sandbar, pelicans sunned their outstretched wings. Ben climbed onto the bowsprit to offer advice.

"Cool sunglasses, Kooky."

"They're polarized," Ben said, as if 'polarized' made up for ugly. He stared ahead. "I think it's getting shallower."

"I think you're right. Slow down," I yelled, waving both arms.

My father took the motor out of gear. We glided closer, drifting across mirrored water. Any shallower and we'd run aground. After three boat lengths, the water became deeper. He still motored cautiously. After the next bend, he stopped the engine. A forest of mangroves surrounded us.

"Safe enough here. We'll tie to the trees for good measure." He slapped at a mosquito.

After the anchor clattered down, Ben and I swam ashore, dragging mooring lines behind us. We tied them to trees, securing the *Spray* so even a cyclone couldn't dislodge her.

"Quick shower and some clean clothes, and we'll head off to dinner," my father said when we climbed back on board.

"More like afternoon tea. It's not even five pm." My grandmother thought dinner should be eaten after 8:00 pm, and never on an empty stomach.

"They'll have an early bird special. Tourist places always do."

She laughed. "John, he's your brother. I'm sure he won't charge you for dinner."

Chapter 32

It was 103 degrees down below. I took a shower, hoping the water would get colder before I turned it off. It didn't. My clothes clung to me as soon as I put them on. Worse than the heat, the smell of tuna greeted me when I opened the door.

"We can't leave until you give Jag his dinner." Jessie held out a mangled can of cat food.

She'd tried to open it, but she'd jammed the can opener. Ever resourceful, she'd used a knife to scoop mush into Jag's bowl. She handed over the half-empty can and the opener, and wiped her hands with a towel. We had a foolproof can opener before Suva. Someone replaced it with a can opener so worn the handle turned without slicing through the lid.

"Daddy says they have a girl my age." Jessie wanted someone her age to play with.

"I might as well kill myself now."

"Do it after you clean up the mess." Apparently, my father was still in a good mood.

She watched me attack the can. "They have a boy the same age as you."

I gave up on the can opener and forced up the lid. "You do the rest." I confronted him. "At Norfolk Island, you said they had one kid you've met."

He flinched. "I wish I had your memory."

"Is that why you forgot to tell me he was my age?"

He was already on his way up the stairs.

+ + +

Pelicans stood at the water's edge, waiting for fish to swim to them, paying no attention to *Squirt* and the six of us crowded in.

"I'm not sure this is such a good idea." My father had sweat beading on his temples.

My mother silenced him with a stony stare. It was a long trip to the restaurant. We tied *Squirt* to a jetty, straightened our clothes, and headed up the ramp.

Ben pulled me back. "What's he like?" he whispered.

"It was dark when I saw him. He looks like Dad, only with longer hair..." I gave a vague shrug. "He's nice, I guess."

"Mom said you're a lot like him."

+ + +

My uncle hurried over as soon as the door closed behind us. Side by side, he definitely looked like my father, not that anyone would confuse them—my father's hair was a boot-camp buzz by comparison, and darker, although he'd stopped dying it six months earlier. My uncle had sunken cheeks and wrinkles. It made him seem years older. They looked back at each other, lost for words.

Suddenly, my mother stepped forward and embraced him. "It's been a long time."

"Twelve years too long." My uncle kissed her on the cheek and whispered something in her ear.

When they parted, his eyes blinked as if he was going to cry, yet he took a deep breath and forced a smile.

My father stuck out his hand. "It's good to see you... Ron."

"Not my choice of names; however, it's worked so far." My uncle grinned and they shook hands. "It's good to see you... John."

289

My father hugged my uncle. "Under better circumstances than when we said goodbye."

"Any problems coming up the coast?"

"Other than someone took a few shots at us at Coffs Harbour?"

My uncle nodded, his gaze fixed on me. For no reason, he smiled. "Lousy shot by the looks of it."

"If it was Faro, I'm told he doesn't waste bullets," my father added.

"I think he wanted to keep us moving," I said.

Uncle Ron looked at me as if undecided. "Very likely."

"We stayed offshore the rest of the way." My father patted my shoulder. It struck me that maybe he didn't blame me after all.

"No sign of Zagarovsky?"

"Not that I saw."

"He'll turn up soon enough." After a moment of awkward silence, my uncle tousled Ben's hair. "The last time I saw you, you were a bulge in your mum's tummy." He grinned at Jessie. "And you, young miss, you weren't even a twinkle in your dad's eye."

Jessie smiled, completely bewildered by the Australian drawl separating our father and uncle.

He turned to my grandmother. "Marjorie, you're as beautiful as ever."

She looked him up and down. "You haven't changed one iota." She hugged him.

Uncle Ron turned to me again. "Sander's become quite the young man, hasn't he?"

"He prefers Josh," my father said dryly. "Anything but Victor."

"He'll always be Sander to me." When he smiled, his eyes crinkled. Up close, his skin was leathery with blotches from too much sun. "No wonder girls are chasing him."

"What did you expect with his family tree?" My grandmother took delight in teasing me.

My uncle shook his head and sighed. "He's so grown up..." He seemed lost for words, yet he kept looking at me as if he wanted to say something. All of a sudden, he turned to my father. "I glad you're here. After all these years, I finally get to say thank you in person."

Other than another family at a table on the terrace, the restaurant was empty. He shepherded us over to a table overlooking the dock. He took a chair from the next table for himself.

"So nothing since Coffs Harbour?" he inquired as soon as he sat down.

"No," my father replied. "Until today we've kept out of sight."

"What about *Down Under*?" my mother reminded him.

"A man we met on the trip; we saw his yacht at Tin Can Bay," my father explained.

My uncle chuckled. "That would be Bruce McKenzie. He wrote me after he met you in the Bahamas, claimed I had a brother I didn't know about."

My father frowned. "We ran into him again in the Marquesas; in Tahiti too. Problems both times. I'm not sure I trust him."

"He saved our butts in Fiji." As if I needed to remind him.

"True; but when Faro turned up at Norfolk Island, it got me thinking again." He turned to my uncle. "I got an email from Sal

Saccoccia. He said Zagarovsky's upped the price; it's $200,000 now."

"I'm not worried about Bruce."

"He's always short of money," my father added.

"Bruce sticks with his mates."

"The $200,000 is just for his whereabouts."

"Assuming you live to collect it."

My father tapped the table, breathed deeply, and shook his head. "It's a lot of money for a phone call."

My uncle chuckled. "Bruce ever tell you how he got *Down Under*? He bought it for a lark after a lightning strike. It sank at the mooring. Only the tip of the mast was sticking up. Ten of his mates hauled it up the next weekend and dried it out. I was one of them. He paid more for the beer than he did for the boat."

"Did you know he's been back for more than a month?" my father persisted.

My uncle shrugged. "Brucie's probably been busy." However, he didn't sound convinced.

He handed out menus and recommended we try the house special, a 'seafood platter' of sautéed grouper, broiled prawns, and local crab rolls with Thai curry. Dessert was another house specialty, a tangy peach sauce and slices of kiwifruit in a meringue bowl, an hour to prepare, and a minute to eat it.

"You're staying at my place," my uncle insisted after we'd demolished dessert.

My mother and father exchanged glances. I hoped they'd agree. After drinking most of two bottles of wine, it would be me who steered the dinghy back to the *Spray* in the dark, fighting off carnivorous mosquitos, and likely running aground in the outgoing tide.

Like me, Ben wasn't looking forward to the return journey. He stirred into action. "Can we?"

"Please Daddy?" Jessie was desperate for a friend, even though it meant leaving Jag.

My father sat back and drained the last of his wine. "You've got room for six people?"

"There's heaps more space than your boat, and air-conditioning."

Air-conditioning cinched it. Not a lot of breeze would reach where we'd anchored the *Spray*.

Nonetheless, my father defended our water-bound home. "A 40-foot boat is bigger than you think."

"Thirty-eight feet, Dad." Ben earned that icy glance.

"Erin has it all organized. You two go in guest room. It has its own bathroom." He directed that at my mother. "Then, there's a bed in my office Marjorie can use after I tidy up in there. Jessie can share Tanner's bed. They'll love it. The boys can sleep on the living room couch."

He was so enthusiastic my father couldn't object.

Chapter 33

"You told Josh that Uncle Ron has two kids?" Ben was pushing his luck asking for the third time; however, with only a few boys his age to play with for two years, loneliness had caught up with him.

"What I said was he wanted two kids." My moody father got up from the couch. "The oldest is a boy."

"Did something happen to him?"

"He's around."

"When are we going to meet him?"

"Soon!"

Before I could tell Ben to drop it, he walked across the tiled hall, heading into the office where Uncle Ron was speedily rearranging furniture into my grandmother's bedroom.

"Where's he going to sleep? There are only two couches," Ben kept on.

"Later," he snapped back.

"Family reunions are fun," I said under my breath.

Ben looked like he'd been slapped. "What's got into Dad?"

"Let it go, doofus."

Tanner and Jessie bounced down the stairs. They giggled as they brushed past Ben and me sitting at the dining room table. They settled in to watch a dance show on TV. Only a few months apart, they were already best friends. Their accents separated them as much as the color of their hair. Tanner was ginger, fitting into her brown-headed family about the same as I did with blond hair.

Uncle Ron lugged three cardboard boxes out his office, on his way to the garage.

Ben nudged me. "You ask Uncle Ron."

He stopped, boxes resting against the wall. "Ask me what?"

"It's not important," I said. Ben looked at me as if my mission in life was to ask about a missing cousin. "He wants to know if you guys have a photo album."

"Bookshelf, middle of the row." He went on his way.

With Ben hanging over my shoulder, I turned pages of their family album, hundreds of photos of Tanner growing up on a farm, her mom and school friends, and a white-headed man who had to be her grandfather. In a separate album, there were a dozen photos of me as a toddler, and four photos of Ben, Jessie, and me together.

Ben waited until no one heard him. "Chicken!"

"I know better." However, I thought it weird too.

Ben viewed the photo album over my shoulder. "You see Tanner's brother in there?"

"He probably has his own album, same as Tanner."

"So where is he right now?"

"Tanner murdered him. She'll probably get you tonight while you're snoring." I got up from table.

Ben scowled and went over to the bookshelves to search for the missing album. "No more photo albums."

"So they lost it, no big deal. Maybe he's at boarding school or something."

"Something?"

"He's in jail. He ran away. Heck, I don't know. Why don't you ask Uncle Ron?"

"Because Dad said not to."

I went into the study to ask why the big mystery. My father sat on the desk, holding a framed photograph. He acknowledged me with a smile, yet kept staring at it. After a moment, he turned the photo so I could see it. I wasn't sure which of the two boys he was.

"You and Uncle Ron played soccer when you lived in England?"

"Actually, the photo is from when we lived in Boston."

On a whim, I pointed at the boy who looked like Ben. " You any good as goalie?"

"Invincible." He was so conceited, I turned away.

One side of the office was a shrine to Fender guitars. Posters of rock guitarists covered the wall, from a time when the Fender Stratocaster was the must-have guitar. There were books on Fender, wide leather belts with Fender buckles, a collection of guitar picks pinned up like butterflies, three Fender guitar cases, two black amplifiers with dozen of knobs and huge speaker boxes, and my uncle's custom-made guitar on a stand.

Like my guitar, you could tell my uncle's Fender was special; its polished curved wood body made you want to hold it. Its long neck was delicately thin and begged to be stroked. Its silver frets were separated by mother-of-pearl diamonds, demanding caresses. I ran my finger across the strings.

"You can play it if you want, Sander."

I turned at his voice. I hadn't heard him return. He plugged it into the amplifier, turned it on, and played a few soulful chords to make sure it was tuned. He held it out to me. My father nodded encouragingly, making me even more nervous.

"I've only played acoustic guitar."

"So play something acoustic."

"He played *Clair de Lune* for one of Sal's friends in Sydney," my father said. "I knew he had talent; however, it was even better than I expected. Quite beautiful for his first time."

Incredulous, I gaped back at him.

"Sounds like he's a candidate for Juilliard. I'm not surprised, not with his DNA."

"It's not my decision."

Resisting the urge to ask 'Who, if not you?', I sat on the couch. The last thing I wanted to do was drop the guitar.

"It won't electrocute you." Uncle Ron grinned and selected a pick from a jar. "Try it out, Sander."

I played a few chords, feeling clumsy, my hands already sweaty. I dried them off on my shirt. The neck was even thinner than it looked, and very smooth. My fingers danced across frets as I plucked at metallic strings. It was nothing like my guitar. Notes reverberated from the speakers; even the air seemed to vibrate around me. No acoustic guitar did that. I played a couple of bars of Beatles and segued into Aerosmith.

"He's hooked," my uncle said when I paused.

I grinned back, experimenting with knobs and levers, making rock music sounds. Before I realized, I was so into the Rolling Stones I couldn't stop. Across the room, my uncle was grinning and beating the rhythm to *Little Red Rooster* with his hand. I was playing from memory, certain my eardrums were about to burst. My heart was pounding when I stopped.

"Not bad for someone who's tone deaf with two left hands," my father laughed.

I knew I wasn't bad. "It takes a while to get used to."

Uncle Ron sat on his desk. "Play *Rooster* again."

My good luck held—I breezed through it the second time. The Stones recorded Willie Dixon's song in '64. It was the blues standard as far as I was concerned. The trick was getting the backbone right, stealthy, yet smug.

Uncle Ron clapped a couple of times. "You ever see the Stones play on stage?"

"Yeah, right."

"Pity. Play it like you control the farm-yard, Sander. You're showing off to the hens, okay."

The third time, I concentrated on getting it perfect, seeing notes line up in my head. It was such an easy guitar to play it might have been made for me.

He clapped a little more enthusiastically. "You know *Satisfaction*?" I nodded. "Pretend you're Keith Richards. Put your heart into it, only make it look easy."

My uncle wanted me to play like the maestro. The first time was okay, the second time was better; I could tell by his smile.

"Sander, you're a natural. The only problem is your style. It sucks, kiddo."

"I'm a bit intense huh?"

"More like a robot. Let's see some strut and swagger next time."

"He means thrust your pelvis like Mick Jagger," my father chuckled.

"I'm too inhibited."

Uncle Ron smiled. "Pity; with your looks you'd drive the girls crazy. How about pretend you're dancing with Dani?"

"Who?"

My father and uncle laughed. I glowered back. I tried to move around more as I played it again. I was a performing klutz, my gangly arms and legs getting in the way if I allowed my concentration to lapse.

When I finished, Uncle Ron took me aside. "Don't get stroppy, Sander. You're as uptight as I was when I was your age, plus you're trying too hard. There's a sexual aspect in rock that *Satisfaction* took to new heights. You know the lyrics, right?"

"Yeah."

"Then, you know it's sexually suggestive. The beat's insistent for a reason."

I blushed bright red.

"Feeling the urge, being sexy, is no big deal. Preening, courting, all of it's natural; it's how we're made. Don't be afraid to let yourself go, beginning with the guitar riff. Focus on the rhythm and move your body anyway it wants go."

I played *Satisfaction* over and over while they cleaned out the office. When it looked like a bedroom, Uncle Ron told me to play it one last time, 'like an oversexed rock star.' When I finished, both my father and uncle applauded. Ben said I was 'gangbusters.'

+ + +

"From the start. On three. One, two,..."

My uncle and I practiced the same set of songs for three hours the next morning, a medley of rock from *Little Red Rooster* to heavy metal, swapping lead and rhythm until I could play either. He was so good on the guitar he could goof-off and it still sounded great.

299

"When you're on stage, playing an instrument isn't enough. You've got to entertain." It was succinct compared to my father's lectures.

He diverted into an improvised solo, dancing with his guitar. I followed him, and we faced off, handing the lead back and forth, his antics, like the music, getting wilder and wilder.

"You're ready," he declared when it ended.

"For what?"

Suddenly, the clock on the wall caught his eye. "Later. Fish cakes can't wait!"

He handed me the Fender to put away and bolted, off to Sails to serve the lunch crowd. My father went with him; he said to feed Jag. My mother said they needed to talk. The rest of us went for a walk, our faces, arms, and anything else not covered with clothes plastered with sun lotion. Jesse and Tanner ran ahead to see the primary school— a collection of commonsense buildings shaded by louvers, verandahs, and overhanging roofs, hidden behind environmentally sensitive landscaping. The biggest building was the library, a creamy box covered with bunting. Next to it, an avenue of tents filled the playground, while caravans, a merry-go-round, and a mini-rocket-ride took over the parking lot.

"The school's 25 years old this month. We're having a fete to buy books for the library." Erin waved to men erecting a stage. "Ron's band is providing the entertainment tomorrow night."

+ + +

There must have been a hundred family sedans, mini vans, and SUVs parked along the road. In the school playground, people gathered around tents turned into gaily decorated food stands, all tasty, yet none of it good for you. Jesse and Tanner gorged on pink cotton candy Australians called "fairy floss,' while Ben made

300

multiple trips to a stand with a machine churning out whipped dairy product. As band groupie, earnest roadie, and fawning nephew, I was too busy to visit the stands. I was lugging my third huge speaker to the stage when my parents came over.

My mother nibbled on a rum-raisin bar from Erin's candy stand. "Are you nervous?"

I heaved the speaker high enough to slide it onto the stage. "Why would I be nervous?"

"You're not?" My father's smirk implied I had reason to be nervous.

She smiled and shook her head. "Ron didn't tell you you're performing with *Closing Time* tonight, did he?"

"I'm what!"

+++

Closing Time was four mid-life-crisis rock fanatics left behind by musical evolution. Uncle Ron was founder, lead guitar, and occasional singer. He could've been Jagger in his black jeans and T-shirt. The rest of the band was a high-school principal's worst nightmare, shoulder-length hair and wacky thrift-shop clothes. They worked through an opening medley of golden oldies for the over-sixty locals, all 13 of them.

I waited behind the stage, feeling profoundly dumb. Erin had a red T-shirt and a flea-market wig for me to wear, a crimson and black Mohawk-style plume. The rooster resemblance was blatant. I put on the wig only when Uncle Ron gave me the 'you're up next' nod. During a short-lived drum solo from Jack, he swapped out his custom Fender for a black Stratocaster, and took over the microphone.

"G'day! On behalf of *Closing Time*, I'm pleased to announce a special guest, fresh from the US of A. By gosh, it's Josh!" He waved me up the stairs. "Let's hear it for the *Little Red Rooster*."

Being on stage didn't faze me. A hundred or so people clapping didn't worry me either. I'd done both when I was called on stage at my school in Norfolk, after coming a close second in the 100-yard freestyle at the YMCA Regional Championship. What bothered me were the lights in my face. I blinked like a barn owl while my uncle manhandled me into position, guitar strap over my shoulder, pick between my fingers, making my hand strum a few chords to check volume. Then, he was playing the lead-in to *Rooster* we'd developed the day before. It was only a couple of bars, yet I missed my entry. I think he expected me to screw it up because he played it again as if nothing was wrong. The band followed along regardless.

Seeing my family gathered in front of the stage didn't boost my self-confidence; Ben had an inane grin to match his lime sunglasses; Jessie jumped up and down with Tanner; and my mother, father, and grandmother had hopeful looks on their faces. Shell-shocked, rooster-wig, blinding lights; I missed my entry again. Uncle Ron stepped in front of me. Up close, he had brown eyes like my father. He mouthed 'Ready,' and started the intro again. After the first few chords, my brain started working. With him taking the lead, I settled down and played without missing a note. He was joking, but I didn't need him calling me a store mannequin. I was well aware I wasn't the haughty rooster I was supposed to be. I started to warm up when it ended. It was the longest three minutes of my life.

"Howzabout Josh, eh? Youse want some more?" Jack shouted while pounding on his drums. It was as loud as thunder. I couldn't hear the applause.

Uncle Ron picked up the audience mood. With a hand on my shoulder, he stopped me from bolting off stage. "Next up, the

302

Stones' number one, *I can't get no Satisfaction.* US-of-A on lead, Ted Morgan on vocals. Let her rip, guys."

Ted played bass guitar, and sang better than Uncle Ron. We faced off around a microphone, banging it out like we'd played together for years. I got everything right and even managed some strut, swagger, and swivel. I was feeling confident when Uncle Ron came over.

"Sing it, Sander!"

My voice started breaking all over again. I got through the chorus, though staying on key was an effort. My extrovert uncle made light of 'sexually suggestive.' The rest of the band clowned around, shouting 'Satisfaction' with each pelvic thrust. Whenever he came close to me, he shouted 'let yourself go.'

At the front of the stage, Jessie and Tanner had coaxed Ben into dancing with them. There were other kids dancing and a handful of adults, even a senior citizen or two, despite the sweltering heat. My borrowed T-shirt clung to my chest, already damp with sweat. Lightning flashed through clouds to the west, thunder booms coming one after the other. It crossed my mind that even the gods were into rock.

The next time Uncle Ron danced by, he pulled off my wig and tossed it into the middle of a dozen shrieking girls. He segued into *A Hard Day's Night*, handing the lead to me so he could play his own interpretation in the background. When he finished, I played my version. We faced off and switched the lead back and forth, getting wilder, bumping hips and singing together. Everyone clapped, my father hardest of all.

To maintain momentum, Uncle Ron pranced around, encouraging kids to come on stage and dance to the band's disco-compilation. I strummed chords that sounded great from the speakers. Jessie and Tanner were the first on stage. They danced around me, bouncing up and down in time to the music. Their energy was never-ending, their pirouettes graceful. Other kids joined them, twirling and hopping around me until the stage vibrated.

When we finished, Uncle Ron punched my shoulder. "You're a chick magnet, mate."

I hadn't noticed the girls until then. There were dozens of them on the stage, some dancing, others hypnotic, from third grade to high school, all of them gazing at me with adoration.

Uncle Ron circled around me, playing his favorite rock interlude, Guns N' Roses' *Sweet Child O' Mine*. "Now you. Play it for them."

I launched into my own on-the-spot variation. The girls applauded instantly. Someone cranked up the volume as the rest of the band came in. Uncle Ron and I started to sing. By then, nearly everyone at the fete had gathered around the stage to watch. Cars passing by in the street pulled up to listen, including a big white SUV. Seven men got out to watch. It would've been amusing if I wasn't trying to remember how to play our other Guns N' Roses song, *Welcome to the Jungle*. Two of them stayed to watch, while the others wandered through the food stands. Twenty minutes later, they left, the first raindrops splattering on the plywood stage.

Chapter 34

Except for a few shrinking puddles, the storm of the previous night had vanished by the following morning. We gathered on a brick-paved terrace beside the swimming pool, surrounded by tropical plants. With a cloudless sky overhead, the temperature was headed to another sweaty day, sunburn guaranteed.

Living onboard the *Spray*, breakfast was cereal with powdered milk, or 'healthy' snacks. Living at my uncle's house, Sunday brunch came on platters spread across the table, pineapple chunks, watermelon slices, banana cake, scrambled eggs, and spicy little sausages my uncle called frankfurters. I loaded a plate and went to sit by the pool.

"Here's our teenage heart throb." Uncle Ron teased me relentlessly.

I looked around. "Where?"

"I'm surprised those girls didn't drag you off the stage last night."

"And beat me for singing off key."

He grinned. "Seriously, you were great, dude."

"Everyone I talked to thought you were incredible." Erin got up to refresh her coffee cup. "And not just girls. One man wanted to know all about you."

"You didn't say anything?" Uncle Ron interrupted.

She gave him an exasperated look. "He's looking for talent for his recording studio. He was very impressed with Josh. He wanted to talk more today. We can't, of course, because we're going to Fraser Island."

I could tell my mother wasn't buying it. Before she could voice her opinion, my father appeared, fresh from the shower. He'd gone for a morning jog along the beach, while Uncle Ron and I swam laps in the pool. I stared at him with the rest of my family, hoping the distraction would keep my recording future under wraps.

He grinned at my mother, his hair lighter than ever before. "Whatcha reckon?" He even sounded like my uncle.

"After twelve years I finally get to see the man I married." She was amused.

We ate and talked, mostly about what we'd done since arriving in Australia. When it was time to leave, we gathered our hats, beach towels, sunscreen, and two coolers of food and drink, and went out to the garage.

Uncle Ron assumed the title of tour leader. "Boys in the *Beastie*, girls in the *Bus*."

The 'Bus' was Aunt Erin's car, a silver SUV with air-conditioning and seating for eight. The 'Beastie' was his car, an early model Jeep Wrangler, hand-painted khaki-green. It had two miniscule doors minus windows, no roof, and a padded roll-bar with a whippy antenna. Ben and I climbed into the back seats and strapped ourselves in as my uncle started the engine. There was a loud irregular gurgle from under the hood, a high pitched whine if he as much as touched the accelerator. It sounded like a dragster before the start of a race.

"Turbocharged, huh?" My father fiddled with the VHF radio.

I thought, 'How would you know?'

Uncle Ron just smiled. He led our little convoy sedately down the main street of town. He gradually increased speed, fast enough for a hot breeze to buffet us. Four cars rushed past us, all SUVs, three white and one like a rainbow. The last SUV pulled alongside the *Beastie,* and stayed there. There were two men behind dark tinted glass, looking right at us.

306

Uncle Ron slowed until it had no choice but to pass. "A couple of drongos doing their IQ test. Pity I can't risk another speeding ticket."

"You're not much of a role model." My father was irony come to life.

Uncle Ron glanced sideways. "Having second thoughts?"

"What do you think?" My father was in a good mood until then.

"Second thoughts about what?" I said.

"Getting in a car with a loony like me." Uncle Ron slowed to a crawl. "I got to tell you, the local yokels reckon I'm the community pillar."

Not amused, my grumpy father stared ahead. I wondered why he bothered to get out of bed. He didn't even look up when a plane roared overhead, its landing gear down. It banked, leveling out again as it neared the tree tops. Its twin engines changed pitch as it dropped steadily lower, wingtips wobbling. It looked like it was going to crash until I spotted a runway through the forest of cypress and casuarina. Three rainbow-painted four-wheel-drive wagons and a white SUV were parked in a row outside a small metal shed.

"It's our international airport," Uncle Ron joked. "Closed Saturdays, Sundays, public holidays, and when there are too many birds on the runway. It's also the head office for Rainbow Rent-a-SUV, crapped-out four-wheelers at exorbitant prices."

Farther down the runway was an even smaller shed. Outside were a little orange single-engine Cessna and a VW bus from the 1960s with a setting sun blazing on the side.

I played along. "That the domestic terminal?"

"Sunset Air Tours." Uncle Ron pointed to a man mowing a tiny patch of lawn. "Bruce's dad; he won the Cessna playing poker at Mt. Isa. He specializes in joy-rides for unsuspecting tourists."

Two minutes later, he turned right, taking the Inskip Point road to a sandy track. It ended at a white-sand beach, deeply furrowed by car tires above the high-tide line. He pulled up beside a 'STOP HERE' sign stuck in the sand, the *Bus* behind us. With the ferry still approaching the other side, Ben climbed out and headed to the shore, eager to explore tidal deposits. I stayed for my father' and uncle's banter.

The car ferry was making a beeline for our beach when a man wandered over, clutching a can and a handful of brochures. His board shirts were frayed, his canvas hat crooked, his T-shirt stained yellow with sweat. It had 'XXXX' plastered across the front, likely his favorite beer given he was drinking it at ten in the morning.

"G'day Ron. Usual rate okay?"

"Dinner for two. This is for the *Bus*." Uncle Ron held out $20. "How's business, Dazzo?"

Dazzo pocketed the $20. "Bloody goldmine, mate. More tourists than cicadas."

Four rainbow-hued SUVs queued behind us, along with a lumbering, army-surplus truck. It was red with 'Rainbow Beach Tourist Tank' painted on the side, a rainbow awning over its passengers. One of the SUVs beeped its horn.

"Dunno what his problem is." Dazzo burped. "After all the rain last night, watch out for Gerowweea Creek. You need a map?"

"I reckon I know where it is, mate. 'Sides, I've got better ways to waste five bucks."

Dazzo gave a demented chuckle, slurped from his can, and staggered off to collect fares.

"The maps are free at the tourist office." Uncle Ron looked over his shoulder. "He'll find some suckers in the bunch behind us."

As soon as the ferry's gates opened, he drove slowly onto the ramp, stopping where the attendant pointed, a car length from the gate. He waved the *Bus* into the other lane, right up to the gate before it stopped. The *Tank* was next, behind us. It left our side of the ferry tilted down.

Uncle Ron watched in the rear-vision mirror. "There's always some moron pushing in."

The car behind the *Bus* was a white SUV. It hadn't been in the queue on the beach. One by one, the rainbow-painted SUVs proceeded up the ramp. The gate banged behind them and the rear ramp rattled out of the water. The ramp in front of us blocked the view and any breeze coming over the bow. Diesel smoke poured into the Jeep, unsettling my stomach enough to make me start thinking what'd I do when I had to throw up.

Ben wandered over and dumped a handful of shells on his seat. "The captain said we might see a dugong."

His lecture on dugongs ended when my father climbed out to gaze into bright blue water with him. I settled for my uncle's wry humor and the sun's morning warmth as the ferry churned towards Fraser Island.

"This place is paradise for nature lovers," Uncle Ron remarked. After a moment, his eyes drifted back to the rear vision mirror. "We have a problem."

"What?" I started to turn around.

"Don't turn!" He used the same tone of voice as my father when he wanted my attention. "Wait a minute and get in the front seat, Sander."

Casually, he opened the door and got out. He stretched and took off his hat, cooling down as he joined my father and brother staring over the side. My father glanced up quickly when he spoke. He nodded and scratched the nape of his neck. He nodded again when I got out, stretched, and took over the passenger seat. My uncle backed away, still talking while my father and brother searched the water for dugongs. I couldn't hear a word over the noise of the ferry.

He walked over to the *Bus* and stuck his head through the driver's window. A minute later, he was back in the driver's seat. The attendant began to lower the front ramp. The shore was closing rapidly. He clicked his belt and reached for the ignition key. He started the engine and put the car in gear. My father was squeezed between the *Bus* and the gate, fiddling with the latch.

"Seatbelt good and tight, Sander." He glanced at my seatbelt to make sure.

He checked the rear vision mirror. I turned and gulped the 'f' conversation-stopper. Faro was standing at the rear of the *Bus*. He looked right at me. Suddenly, he was in front of the *Rainbow Beach Tourist Tank*, his walking stick in hand. He pointed it at me. I ducked, hoping he wouldn't risk it with the *Tank* at his rear.

Uncle Ron slammed the gearbox into reverse. Faro scrambled out of the way, flailing his walking stick and shouting, 'You're dead!'

Uncle Ron revved the engine like the start of a quarter-mile race. The gate wavered an inch and he floored the accelerator. The *Beastie's* tires squealed over the bellowing roar of its engine. It hurtled forward, slammed into the gate, and kept going up the still-lowering ramp. For an awful moment, we were airborne. We crashed into the sea, wheels spinning wildly and throwing out sheets of water before we careened onto the shore.

We were halfway up the beach before the SUV slammed into the back of the *Bus*, shoving it forward. It backed up and smashed into it again. After that, I was too far away to see what happened.

Uncle Ron headed for a track disappearing among the trees. Suddenly, he stomped on the brakes, whipping my head around. The track was blocked a hundred yards ahead, passengers from the ferry's previous trip standing around, gawking at an upmarket Mercedes axle-deep in the sand.

"Bloody tourists can't drive off the bitumen."

He reversed onto the beach and spun the wheel, muttering about letting air out of the tires. A cloud of fine sand billowed up. Even as the Wrangler got traction, the SUV lurched around the *Tank,* down the ramp, and onto the beach. The rainbow-rentals followed it, like ducks in a row. We took off down the beach on a converging course to the water's edge. They were going faster than us.

"The sand's harder below the high tide mark," he shouted. "We'll outrun them when we're on it."

"We ought to head to the police station," I shouted back.

"What police station? There are a few park rangers on the island. It'll take till tonight for the cops to get here from Gympie."

"What about the others?" I shouted over the engine.

"They're on Plan B! Take the ferry back, go to a friend's house, and wait till we get there. Right now, I'm more worried about us."

We picked up speed as we neared the sea, slowly pulling ahead on hard-packed sand.

Uncle Ron glanced in the mirror. "Shit!"

I turned to see what upset him. The nearest car was so close I could see the driver's long hair.

311

"For God's sake, get down Sander."

He swerved from side to side, slewing through the water, sliding into dry loose sand. The other car stayed right behind him. His engine wailed in protest when we bounced into a creek cutting diagonally across the beach. The *Beastie* veered sideways, yet he didn't slow down. When I glanced at the speedometer, the needle hovered at 90, not kilometers, miles per hour.

Ahead, the beach widened, curving right as a broad spit extended into the sea. One of the cars went left, taking a shortcut. The rest followed us down the spit, churning through soft sand.

"Should've let out air!" No wonder Uncle Ron was angry. I didn't say a word.

Our pursuers fanned across the beach, leaving the white SUV like a heat-seeking missile on our tail. A bullet smacked the rear of the Jeep, then another. I sank low in my seat and gripped the armrest. We hurtled around the end of the spit. After that, Fraser Island's entire eastern side was an endless straight beach. The SUV edged closer until it was only an arm length away. It stayed there, a pock-faced man at the wheel driving with one hand, holding a cell phone with the other. He swerved abruptly, and would've crashed into the *Beastie* except my uncle jerked the steering wheel right. We blasted into ankle-deep water. Sheets of water shot out around us. It slowed us down enough for the other vehicles to catch up. A second car drew abreast, slowly pulling ahead, A third car was glued to our rear. They'd boxed us in.

"Bloody stupid not to have gone inland, now I think about it." Uncle Ron exceeded my father for grim humor.

Without warning, he swerved into shallow water again, sending the Jeep sideways and throwing a torrent over our pursuers. I thought he would lose it. Instead, he charged through a gap, panicking the driver of the car beside us. He whacked the rear fender of the Jeep and jammed on his brakes. The rainbow-rental behind him swerved left to avoid a collision.

Back on hard sand, Uncle Ron floored the accelerator. We zoomed past the rainbow-rental. When he glanced at the mirror, I turned to look too. A long way back, the rainbow rental had gone too far into the sea and stopped with waves lapping its doors. We raced up the beach, now hundreds of yards wide. As far as the eye could see, it was uninhabited except for a few vehicles like specks on the horizon.

Mile after mile, the speedometer nudged 105. We pulled ahead slowly.

"Gerowweea Creek coming up!" He veered to the water's edge. "Hold on, Sander."

We bounced over a deep rut where the creek met the sea, flinging out water. A few yards farther up the beach, the creek had carved a waist-deep gully through the sand. It was almost invisible until you were right on top of it. One rainbow-rental slammed to a stop a car-length away. The white SUV followed us into the ocean. The remaining car crashed into the gully, its front out of sight, its rear wheels spinning freely.

He pressed the accelerator to the floor, forcing the speedometer needle to the top of the dial. I gripped the sides of my seat. My father never drove over the speed limit. His brother grinned maniacally; breaking the law didn't bother him. I was surprised when he slowed down.

"Reckon it's time we had some fun, Sander."

He waited until our pursuers closed the gap before he braked hard, working the steering wheel with both hands as the *Beastie* skidded sideways. Two cars roared past us and he swerved behind them, bouncing across the deeply furrowed sand. He charged into silver- gray tussocks, negotiating a narrow twisting path over the sand dunes. At the crest, I glimpsed the two cars turning around. The rainbow-rental was out of the creek and billowing smoke from under the hood.

Banksia and Pandanus gave way to dense scrub and scribbly gum trees. The track weaved among them, up and down sandy crevasses. I clung to a grab-rail bolted to the dashboard. It stopped me from being tossed over the side when the Jeep lurched over fallen logs. If they were too big, he rammed through the scrub to get around them. After a particularly bad section, we slowed to a crawl. The track disappeared in a wall of sand, mud, and vines.

"No way!"

"Probably explains why this trail's not on the map." Uncle Ron changed gear, roaring the engine until the wheels got traction.

We went up sideways, stopping at the top of the hill. Uncle Ron had the same pleased-with-himself smirk as my father when he proved to be right. He switched off the motor and cocked his head to listen. Even the cicadas were quiet; just the wind in the trees and the far-off calls of cockatoos.

"You lost them," I said.

"Not bloody likely. Faro will expect us to head back to the ferry." He rubbed his chin. How often had I seen my father do the very same thing?

"It seems like he's always right behind us ..."

"Just hope he's never ahead!" He gave me a sideways glance. "You figured it out yet, Sander?"

I shrugged, not sure what he meant.

"Am I Nicholai or Peter?"

According to Sal, Nicholai was undercover FBI. Peter was the better musician. Years earlier, he'd conducted a performance of the New York Philharmonic, Tchaikovsky's *First Piano Concerto*.

"You look older," I ventured. Nicholai was the older of the two brothers.

"You'll find out soon enough. The question is, where now?"

"Dad always does something unexpected."

He nodded absently. "Eurong." It sounded like he'd said 'you're wrong.'

"Huh?"

"Eurong Beach Resort. Lots of people so Faro will expect it."

Before I could ask, he started the engine and started slowly down the track into a jungle of lush ferns and towering Brush Box trees.

"No point in making it more dangerous than it needs to be. Sander, you work the VHF while I drive. Channel 73 is the fishing channel. You want Macka, Bruce's old man. He listens to what's biting while he's waiting for customers."

I switched on the VHF and turned the channel to 73. "We're *Beastie*?" I asked. He nodded. "Macka, Macka, Macka; this is *Beastie*, over...."

"Macka 'ere. What can I do yer for, *Beastie*?"

Bruce interrupted him. "Hey Josh!" Before I could answer, he started to laugh. "I heard you docked at Tin Can two days ago, mate. Ronno with you?"

I held out the microphone for my uncle to speak.

"Brucie, I need a favor. Can your dad buzz up to Eurong right away?"

"What's doing at Eurong, mate?"

"I need a bird's eye. Double the joy-ride rate, okay?"

"Wouldn't involve Faro, would it?"

Uncle Ron shot me a suspicious look. "How do you know him, Bruce?"

"I ran into him in Tahiti coupla months back. He was real interested in finding the *Spray*."

"What happened?"

"Promised me two thou' if I let him know when I saw it. He was in Tonga too. Same deal, only the rate was five. The last thing I expected to see was him pulling out of the airport when I arrived this morning."

"Did he see you?"

"Offered me ten grand, mate. After what happened in Suva, I figured they'll turn up here eventually."

"It's a long story, Bruce."

"Josh your nephew?"

"Later, mate. Right now, I need you and Mack in the air. Let me know if you see a couple of rainbows and a white SUV."

"First time I saw him and his dad, I figured youse are related."

"Enough yacker, Bruce. *Beastie* out." Uncle Ron handed back the microphone. "Leave it on 73 for the fishing report, mate."

"I give in. Which one are you? Nick or Pete?" I asked, trying hard not to laugh.

"You're smart; figure it out."

Chapter 35

An endless forest of rusty eucalyptus trees sprouted from a carpet of bright green ferns hiding the sand dunes. The creeks were so clear they appeared to be dry until we splashed across. There were no bridges or properly made roads, just a sandy track with scattered branches for traction, and occasional red plastic triangles warning caution required. One hill was so steep, the *Beastie* skidded sideways. My side lifted off the ground. It was over before I stopped screaming; Uncle Ron had steered with the slope so we didn't roll over. Going down another hill, we slid past tree trunks until he managed to slow down. Any other time it would have been fun; however, whenever the trees thinned out, I could see a rainbow-hued SUV skulking behind us.

"At least it's not catching up," I said.

"No need to. He knows where we're going, and his mates are waiting for us." He took a deep breath. "I'm thinking I ought to let you off up ahead. You could hide till he passes and thumb a lift back to the ferry."

"Running away from a problem doesn't help."

He smiled. "You got that right. Open the glove box will you?"

Stuffed inside were crumbled papers, tatty maps, candy wrappers, leaking bottles of suntan oil, and a snub-nose revolver with a burnished rounded grip.

"It's the same as Dad's."

"Smith and Wesson Model 13, three inch barrel, .357 Magnum. It was the FBI standard in the 70s, before they switched to semi-automatics. I got two for the price of one."

"Nicholai?" I tried to hand it to him.

He chuckled and held onto the wheel. I pointed it at the floor in case a bump set it off.

The trees got larger and blocked out the sky, enormous, majestic trees like we'd seen in Polynesia's rainforests, hanging vines, and regal King ferns, enough birds that Nature Boy would've been flabbergasted.

"Hey Ronno!"

My uncle leaned over to turn up the VHF volume so we could hear Bruce over the roar of the motor.

"There's a whitey hiding in the scrub near the lights..." Bruce kept talking; however, someone else was talking about catching flounder on the flats. "... just flew over another rainbow, mate. It's on the beach, near the first sand blow."

"Head south and look for more rainbows, will ya? Over." Uncle Ron turned down the volume. "The lights are a problem. Lousy traction through there."

He wasn't happy. Before he spoke again, the track had zigzagged up and down two more hills and splashed through a creek, axle-deep, fast-running water sloshing against the doors. We'd just started up the other side, when he suddenly stopped next to a waist-high tree trunk. A yellow and black lace monitor regarded us through creepy eyes. Its tail was so long it swept the ground.

"You can roast 'em, but they're better fried in oil and garlic." He looked at me. I frowned back, knowing what came next. "They're waiting up ahead, Sander. It's time to get out."

I stared back at him, defying him to drag me out of the car.

"He said you were stubborn; a mule-brain like me."

"Zagarovsky wants to kill me because I'm the eldest son; because of something that happened when I was a baby. You're involved too, aren't you?"

"Zagarovsky wants me to watch."

"Why?"

He picked up his handgun, clicking the cylinder with his thumb. "So I never forget, son… Sander."

"I'm not getting out."

He placed the gun in his lap and drove up the hill, glancing about. At the top, he stopped again. I couldn't see the car following us, yet its engine roared erratically, like an irritated dinosaur lurking among the trees.

"They're stuck in the creek. Let's make a run for it." He floored the accelerator. The *Beastie* surged through the sand, wheels spinning in the ruts.

The 'lights' were pieces of wood nailed to trees, painted with red, orange, and green circles. A half-dozen tracks plowed through the sand, imitating a major intersection. It had signs to Eurong, Lake Wabby, and Central Logging Station. There was no sign of a white SUV, or any other car.

"Wrong bloody spot, Bruce," he shouted at the treetops. "God only knows how he sailed around the world and didn't get lost. He meant the crossroads."

It was nearly a mile to the 'crossroads.' The nearer we came, the more the track resembled an obstacle course; trees with gnarled thick trunks, brilliant green Angiopteris ferns, with the biggest fronds in the world, and rotting logs wherever I looked. The night before, Ben kept me awake for an hour, plying his knowledge of the 354 recorded species of birds on Fraser Island. I found grim satisfaction in terrifying hundreds of cockatoos by roaring through their habitat.

319

"You like roaming the world, living on board a boat, Sander?" he asked after a while.

"Mostly it's good." It seemed as if he wanted me not to like it.

"Makes sense, of course. Your mum was a nomad."

I snickered. "It must have been before she had kids."

He smiled. "It's gets a bit crowded at times, I expect?"

"There's always someone to talk to."

"Great fishing though?"

"I caught a Bluefin tuna after we left Fiji. It filled the freezer. It's all we ate for a week."

"Crossroads coming up. Stay down."

He drove faster, and didn't slow down for the intersection. It had homemade 'stop' signs nailed on a couple of trees. Just past the signs, was a propane tank someone had left in the middle of the road. I was about to point it out when Uncle Ron swerved sideways and banged into the side of the white SUV. The *Beastie* bounced through ferns into a pile of sand impaled with broken branches. The SUV stopped opposite. Faro poked his walking stick at me through the passenger window.

"Christ almighty!"

Uncle Ron wrenched the steering wheel and floored the accelerator, back onto the track before he pointed his handgun over his shoulder. He fired at the propane tank. It sounded like a bomb going off. Faro's face screwed up, screaming at the driver.

He stole a glance in the mirror. "Too damned close. We'll divert around them next time."

We lurched right, hurtling along the track, spinning wheels in sand like dry dust until he braked hard. I thought the track had dead-ended. We were almost at a standstill before he followed the track into a dense thicket of gray eucalyptus trees. A cloud swirled behind us, blocking out our pursuers.

"They'll be lucky to stop in time."

Uncle Ron chuckled. "Gets a bit bumpy after this, Sander." He had the same blasé tone as my father. It was 'bumpy' when the waves were so big people got seasick.

Trees determined where the track went. It weaved through the rainforest, skirting rotting logs, splashing through creeks, crisscrossing trails that disappeared into tangled vines and ferns. The next intersection had signs, right to Lake Wabby, left to Central Station. Down the track to the left, two rainbow-rentals headed towards us.

"How the hell did they get here?" Uncle Ron headed the opposite way.

"Maybe they came on the earlier ferry?"

"Get on the radio. Let Bruce know we're going to Wabby." He gunned the motor. "Always plenty of people at Lake Wabby," he shouted.

"That's good, right?"

"What's good is it's a dead-end because of the sand-blow."

It didn't sound like good news to me. The rainbow-rentals followed us, the white SUV too, farther back, yet catching up quickly. It should've taken five minutes to get to Lake Wabby. It took less than a minute at the speed my uncle drove.

People went to Lake Wabby to picnic and swim. They parked their cars at the top of a hill and took the nature trail to a crescent-shaped lake, emerald green like the profusion of palms surrounding it. We rammed the 'NO VEHICLES' sign and roared down the footpath. A man and a woman who were examining two huge eucalyptus trees, bolted into the scrub, both yelling 'no vehicles, mate.' The *Beastie* barely squeezed between the trees. They yelled again at the white SUV, now a few car lengths behind. The SUV was wider. One of the trees ripped Faro's walking stick out of his hands.

The rainbow-rentals veered off the track and forged a shortcut through the brush, smashing down giant fern fronds in the way. They overtook us, and swerved back to cut us off. We smashed into the first SUV so hard my uncle's handgun flew from his hand. The other car leap-frogged a stump hiding under the bracken.

On the opposite side of Lake Wabby, a steep sand hill came down to the water. There were dozens of people sunbathing on the beach, more relaxing in the water, an adventurous handful riding sleds down the sand hill. We raced across the beach, coming dangerously close to a red-headed woman in a bright pink bikini. White sunburn ointment plastered her face. With all four wheels spinning, my uncle headed straight up the sand hill, scattering sled-riders and onlookers. At the top, the sand went on like the Sahara.

Uncle Ron grabbed the microphone from my hand. " Macka, Macka. Hammerstone Blow!"

We hurtled over sand dunes, each ridge blocking the next until blue ocean stretched as far as the eye could see. A little orange airplane was skimming just above the breakers parallel to the beach. It banked, turning away from the surf. Uncle Ron skirted a parched patch of scrub, slowing down until both rainbow-rentals were beside us, racing headlong towards the next ridge. Suddenly, the plane soared over the crest. Bruce leaned out the passenger door, grinning as he tossed out a beer bottle. One rainbow-rental's windscreen exploded. It turned around and headed back the way it had come. My uncle jammed his foot on the brake. The driver of the other rainbow-rental tried to stop before it skidded over the crest, its wheels spinning wildly in the powdery sand on the downhill side. It slid sideways, almost halfway down before it

322

rolled, over and over until it crashed into the stunted gray trees at the bottom.

Uncle Ron got on the VHF radio while I waved at the circling Cessna. "I owe you a beer, Bruce." He turned to look behind us. The white SUV had sought safety behind scrub. Faro got out, staring back. "No walking stick so he's harmless. Unfortunately, so am I."

Chapter 36

'... The Rainbow Beach cops arrested Faro and three of his men when they drove off the ferry. Uncle Ron said they were charged with willful destruction of protected species.'

My father had told me to keep my mouth shut before we talked to the police. 'I would just make things worse,' he said. I didn't write that in my journal.

'Taking them to the Gympie police station was a big mistake. One of the cop cars ran off the road and hit a tree. Faro got away, needless to say.'

I stopped writing. "You think they'll try again?" I asked, doodling 'Dani' amongst fern fronds in the margin.

"It's not over, not by a long shot." Uncle Ron addressed my father with a glance.

My father nodded agreement, seeming more interested in Ben, yawning and rubbing his eyes. Nature Boy had lugged the mother lode from the den, all eight volumes of The Australian Encyclopedia to study up on the flora and fauna of Fraser Island, with special attention to dugongs, dingoes, and the Cicadidae family.

Uncle Ron walked to the sliding doors making up one wall of the living room. "It'll take a few days for Zagarovsky to bring in more men."

"Not if the police find him first." My grandmother headed off to bed. She didn't know that Zagarovsky's name never came up in our interview with the police.

I closed the journal chronicling my life post-Nuku Hiva. Dani's five letters stuck out between the pages. They were bookmarks in my life since meeting her. Suddenly, I wasn't in the mood to write more.

Uncle Ron peered outside. Not a sound—once the sun went down, cicadas stopped mating. He checked the door lock and closed the curtains. My father hoisted Ben to his feet, gave him a hug, and pushed him towards his couch.

"Bedtime for you too." He gave a nod in my direction as he stooped to stack Ben's books.

I rearranged the couch cushions and lay down, not ready to sleep at 10:20 pm, but there wasn't enough light to read after Uncle Ron switched off the table lamp.

Ben waited until the front door closed behind them. "Dad's in a foul mood again."

I stared at the ceiling. "Because of what happened today."

"He was really worried…"

"Me too."

"He was worried about you being with Uncle Ron," he went on regardless. "He told Mom he didn't want you finding out from him."

"Finding out what?"

"Dunno, mate."

"You're delusional. Shut up and go to sleep." I rolled onto my side, staring at the pattern on the couch cushions. Circles and squares spiraled together, getting smaller and smaller.

The front door opened and closed. I could hear my father and uncle whispering in the hall.

"I'll tell him first thing in the morning." My father started down the hall to the guest bedroom.

"There's plenty of time," Uncle Ron said.

"Tomorrow! It's gone on long enough."

+ + +

I woke up coughing.

"You need to get dressed." My father lifted his hand from my mouth, his face just inches from mine.

"Faro's here?"

"Not yet. Tony just called. The accident the cops were in; he looked at the wreck. He's certain someone shot out the rear tire. He's sure Faro will pay us a visit tonight. You're going with Nick."

Before I could stop myself, I said, "I figured Uncle Ron was Nicholai."

"He thinks you'll be safer with him. He's probably right."

I pulled on my 'I love New York' T-shirt as he walked away. It had permanent grease stains on the front and '*Spray*' on the back, courtesy of Jessie and a black marker. He stopped to look down at my brother, who snored the same way he read books; as if nothing else mattered.

"Before you leave there's something I need to say." He took a deep breath. "I'm not your father. Nick is."

I stared at him. That he kept looking at Ben didn't make it any easier. "Is she awake?"

"For God's sake, will you listen for once. After the fire, Zagarovsky tried again. You had to disappear; only you were too badly burned to travel. Nick thought he could distract them by going to Australia. You couldn't go with him."

"Is she awake?"

"She's asleep. I'm done lying to you. There wasn't a choice. We thought it would only be for a few months." He looked right at me. "We love you like you're our son."

"Except I'm not!"

He tried to put his hand on my shoulder. I shrugged him off. I wanted to say I didn't believe him, but I did. Ben went on snoring, unaware he wasn't my brother.

"Victor, you need to understand..." *He* stopped when I glared at him. "We didn't want it to be like this. We were going to tell you when the time was right."

"When would that be?" I sneered, looking around and thinking 'in a million years.' "Where the hell are my shoes?"

"Wherever you left them! I'm sorry, Josh. We don't have much time."

"Suddenly, I'm not Victor?"

"We've been through this. You're Victor because of your mom's nickname. If you want another reason; you remind me of her every time I look at you."

He jerked his head to get me moving. It sounded like he was crying. *He* hurried through the dining room, past the kitchen, into the laundry. I trailed behind, still looking for my shoes, hoping my mother would come down the stairs to see what the fuss was about. I needed to hear it from her.

He waited at the back door with a pair of sandals that weren't mine. After a hasty hug, *he* opened the door and walked out.

I followed him. "It's still friggin' hot."

He shoved the sandals into my hands. "Put them on in the Jeep. He's waiting for you." I stopped in my tracks when I realized *he* was crying. *He* grasped my shoulder. "Be careful, okay? We love you. You might not think so right now, but we really do."

+++

I closed the car door harder than I intended. "He told me," I said, barely able to speak, unable to look back at him. *He* was still watching me.

"I think you already knew. You did, didn't you?"

I kept my head down and tried to squeeze into Ben's sandals. There was no way they were going to fit. I gave up and risked a glance. *He* hadn't moved from the porch.

"I saw one of his emails to you. About me playing the guitar mostly." My head throbbed. "There's some other stuff. It was mostly the emails."

He started the engine and put his banged-up *Beastie* in gear. "You realized why they were only about you?"

"I wasn't sure until later." Now, I wasn't sure about anything. "I'd rather not talk, okay?"

He backed out of the carport. "Get down low, Sander. We want them to see you, not shoot you."

He turned right; driving around the hill rather than taking the shortest way to the main road. I peeked over the door sill. After several darkened houses, we passed a white Ford sedan parked in a driveway. It had a surfboard strapped to the roof.

I recognized the number plate. "It's Angelo's car. He's Sal's friend."

"Sal's been one step ahead all along. I never thought I'd be beholden to him. He had someone keep an eye on you all the way from Sydney. You know I met him right after Zagarovsky murdered his son. It really changed him."

After that, he constantly glanced at his rear vision mirror. If we were followed, it was from a distance. I stayed low, watching spooky gum trees zip by, grim silence until he pulled up outside his restaurant.

"He planned to leave me here all along." My voice cracked like a kid.

"I'm sorry you had to find out like this, Sander. To answer your question, he wanted you to meet me."

"It wasn't a question."

"What happens now is up to you, Sander. I'd like to get to know my son again. I also understand why you wouldn't want me in your life."

"If I call you Dad, everything is hunky-dory?" It came out badly. I saw him wince.

He leaned over and opened my door. "We don't have much time, Sander. Stay close."

"Okay, *Dad*."

"Call me whatever you like. Just do what I say."

I followed him across the parking lot to the outside terrace. He stopped under the sails. The tide was all the way out. Across an inky black inlet, mud flats glistened in moonlight. Beyond the mud flats, a light twinkled on a fishing boat. It looked as peaceful as any port we'd stopped in. The *Spray* was tied up at the dock, dwarfing the for-hire runabouts beside her. The cockpit lights shone brightly. The cabin lights turned portholes into happy round eyes. Even the mast lights were lit up—we never used those except when we changed sails at night.

"Bruce moved it at high tide. I told him to leave on a light so it looks like someone's aboard, and he turns it into a bloody Christmas tree." He started to reach for my arm. I drew back. "Stay here till I call you."

He walked briskly along the verandah in front of the restaurant, disappearing around the far corner of the building. When he reappeared, he beckoned urgently. I hurried to catch up until I tripped over a gas tank. Someone had left it at the top of the ramp leading down to the docks. I shoved the container out of the way. He pushed it back with his foot and walked to the stairs.

"You're in the office, Sander." He pointed up.

He turned and clattered down the steep metal ramp. I went up the stairs, pausing at the landing to see him climb onto the *Spray* and disappear into the companion way. A moment later, all but one of *Spray's* cabin lights went off.

Sal waited at the top of the stairs, petting Jag with his left hand and muttering 'what a good pussy,' all the while holding him securely in the crook of his arm. His other hand held a gun belonging in a *Dirty Harry* movie.

"You'll be sneezing for a week," I said, trying to be cheerful.

"Don't want Jessie getting upset." Sheepishly, he handed over Jag and wiped at his eyes. They were already red. "Let's go inside."

He closed the door behind me, blinking and sniffling. The marina office was full of boxes of boat parts, jars of assorted bolts and screws, and stacks of manila folders and invoices.

"What are you doing here?" I had a hundred other questions.

Sal was supposed to be in New York with Marion until the end of January, a week away.

He stared at the parking lot, breathing heavily. "It's time to end this once and for all." He scratched his neck. "Damn! I'm already itching."

I stared out the window overlooking the marina, imagining shadows were people.

Sal nudged my shoulder. "Won't be long now!" He sounded almost happy.

+++

About ten minutes later, Sal's cell phone chimed once.

"That'll be Bruce. They're in the parking lot."

He crossed the little room, avoiding knee-high stacks of scrappy boating and fishing magazines. He stared at the dark parking lot. When he turned around, his eyes were red and watery, a wonder he could see anything at all.

"Nicholai's my real father," I said.

"Bit of a shock, eh Sharkbait?" Sal tried to focus, blinking repeatedly. "If it was up to me, I would've told you in the Marquesas, if not sooner. John was afraid you'd hate him."

I stared out the front window. In the moonlight, even mud flats were romantic. "You knew all along, didn't you?"

"Since the day you played tag with a Hammerhead. John's goatee had me uncertain for an hour or two. I had to search the Internet to find photos to be sure. The giveaway was you have your mom's hair."

"That night on your boat, when you first called me 'Sharkbait,' was it because Zagarovsky was the shark and I was the bait?"

"I won't lie to you; I wanted to settle the score. Mostly, it suited you at the time. What you did was very brave," he said fondly. "I should've told you the truth the next day; you'd be safer."

"I think Mom wanted to tell me years ago. This is so weird. What am I supposed to call her now?"

"Aunt Virginia."

331

"Right; that'll work."

"You'll think of something. It's a lot to get used to, for both of you."

"They argued about me sometimes. He wouldn't let her tell me anything." It hurt to think about it.

"It's not what you think. Whatever they've done, they did to keep you alive, Josh."

"So it's okay to lie to me?"

"Not much choice with something like this. You've survived 12 years. That takes a lot more than luck."

"You reckon?"

"Don't sell them short, Josh."

"I'm not. It's my real dad who abandoned me and dumped me on them."

"You got it wrong, kid." Sal shook his head repeatedly. "He'll tell you what happened soon enough."

"My dad told me already. Not him! My other…" I choked. "Some crap about him coming here to lead them away from me."

"You think it might be true?" Sal gave up waiting. "While you think about it, be glad you've got two families who love you. Heck, Sarah gave up everything to be with you; she's not even related to you."

I stared at him. It hadn't entered my mind. "Why?"

"You can't figure out the reason for yourself?" I shrugged, which seemed to bother him. "You were three and Zagarovsky wanted you dead. Even Colombian drug lords don't burn kids alive."

He was about to say more when a man stepped from the shadows at the front of the restaurant. At the top of the ramp, he picked up the gas tank. Glancing from side to side, he crept down the ramp, keeping one hand securely on the rail. He paused at the bottom, unscrewed the cap, and edged closer to the *Spray*, careful not to rock the dock. Leaning over, he splashed the deck and cockpit.

Sal watched from behind me, his hand firm on my shoulder. "Standard operating procedure for Zagarovsky's clowns." I jerked away. Sal's hand clamped my mouth. "Quiet."

The man put the tank on the dock to search his pockets. A shudder ran through me as he stooped. He reached out. His lighter flared brightly, lighting up his face before it went out.

"No worries, mate." Sal sounded amused.

Faro tried again, dragging the flame along the *Spray's* deck. When it didn't ignite, he picked up the can and smelled from the spout.

"It's diesel fuel." Sal scratched his forearm. It was puffy and red like his eyes. "John would be pissed if we burned his boat. You too; your guitar's still onboard."

"Where's Tony?"

"Where he's least expected." Sal looked gleeful as he stepped back from the window. He opened the door wide. "Time to earn your nickname." He reached for the light switch. "You ready, Sharkbait?"

A bright fluorescent light lit up the room, and me as well.

Before I could ask 'to do what,' Faro shouted, "Masters, the kid's behind you, up the stairs."

A few heartbeats later, Sal switched off the light and moved behind a drab metal filing cabinet, leaving me in the open doorway. "Talk to me, Sharkbait."

I gripped Jag so tightly he squirmed in my arms. "Someone's on the stairs," I whispered, unable to avoid glancing back.

Sal had heard the creak too—he had his gun pointed at the open door. "Step back when I say, slow and calm."

His hand was shaking as if the gun was too heavy to lift. His face was crimson, veins bulging in his forehead, his neck too. He mumbled something and rubbed at his temples with his other hand. Another stair creaked. Through the open door, a long-haired man looked up at me from the landing, where Sal couldn't see him. He had a sawn-off, pump-action shotgun aimed at me.

"I got him, Faro!" The man stabbed his gun downward. "Get down here, kid!"

Behind me, something thumped on the floor. "Back up now," Sal croaked.

I had to get the man to come up the stairs. "Let me put down the cat." I held out Jag.

The man nodded. I ducked back into the office. Sal was choking, his face dark. His eyes were shut, clenched tight like his teeth. He frantically searched his pockets until he pulled out a small silver cylinder. He dropped it when he grabbed at his chest. The man stepped into the doorway, waving his shotgun from side to side. He saw me squatting beside Sal, now slumped against the filing cabinet.

"Looks like he's havin' a heart attack."

Sal pointed at his mouth. I picked up the cylinder and turned it up, down, and around before I realized one end had to be pushed in before it pulled out. A dozen pills escaped when Sal grasped my shirt.

The man's head jerked around when Faro shouted, "Masters!"

Sal's lips were purple when I popped a tablet into his mouth. It popped back out. I tried again. He coughed until it was under his tongue.

"Gun," he gasped in my ear. His hand scraped across the vinyl-tiled floor.

The gun was under a chair. I steered his hand to it.

"Masters, he's on the boat," Faro yelled from below.

Masters glanced at Sal and me. He pivoted on his heel, strode to the railing, and took aim. Sal shot him in the butt. Masters lurched sideways, dropped his shotgun, and crashed into the railing. He toppled down the stairs. Faro stepped around him. He gave me a dirty look and disappeared inside the restaurant.

My real father jumped from the *Spray* and ran down the dock. He stopped when Faro stepped onto the top of the ramp. They glared at each other.

"You're a hard man to find," Faro said.

"No walking stick this time?"

Faro glanced left. There was someone creeping around on the terrace, a shadow under the sails.

"Dad!"

He heard my scream even as he staggered behind a barnacle-encrusted pile. Bullets thudded into it again and again. Most of them seemed to come from the terrace. Faro pulled a pistol from his pocket, backing down the verandah to get a clear shot at me. I picked up Masters' shotgun and pointed it in his direction. My finger grazed the trigger. It sounded like a car backfiring. Faro spun around, his pistol aimed at me. Before he could fire, Bruce stepped from behind the corner of the building. He punched Faro twice, slammed him into the railing, and tossed him headfirst into mud. By the time I reached the bottom of the stairs, Bruce was halfway to the dock. I ran after him, so panicked I was hardly aware of a gunshot from behind me. I thought it was Masters, firing at me.

+ + +

My dad was shot in the arm a few inches below his shoulder. He wrapped a dinner napkin around his arm and had me tie the ends.

I surveyed my handiwork, certain it was too tight. "You need to go to the hospital."

He gave me an exasperated look. "There's a doctor at the house."

"Hospital!" I was worried. Blood covered his arm before he wiped it off.

"It's not worth spending hours in the waiting room. I heard she saved your life in Patagonia."

"You know about my appendix?"

"He brought me up to date last night. What you did in Suva; very impressive."

I couldn't help but feel proud. He handed another napkin to Tony. There was a gash on his forehead.

Tony used the napkin to sop up blood from his face. "Your diversion worked better than I thought it would, Nick."

"It was too close for comfort. I couldn't get the gun from under the chart table. Damned panel was stuck."

"There was another man on the terrace," I said.

"Not a thing I could do about him, Sander."

"I got him," Tony said. "His buddy was hiding in the bushes. Must've thought he was some kind of ninja. He won't be making babies any time soon."

"Lucky he didn't take out your eye." Sal's voice was still raspy, although he looked much better. He tried to stand. He slumped back in his seat. "Anyone see Zagarovsky?"

"No sign of him. He might've stayed in the parking lot." Tony looked at Bruce for confirmation.

"There was a woman in the car; no one else that I could see."

"He's a skinny little dude, Bruce. Sort of looks like a woman," I said.

Tony was already on his way down the verandah, my dad right behind him.

Sal shook his head. "He's long gone. By the way, Bruce, nice job on Faro. You ever want a job in protection, let me know."

"Dumb-ass pointed a gun at me mate, didn't he?" Bruce drawled with a wink at me. "Reckon I'll take a gander in the kitchen. A cold beer would go down great about now."

Sal waited until he'd gone. "As for you... You..." He pointed at me. "... were awesome."

"Yeah?"

"You faced down a Russian hit-man; one of the best. Most kids would've filled their pants. Not you!"

"You shot Faro?"

Sal sat back. He clicked his teeth, tapped his hands on the table. "I owed him. He killed Dante with that walking-stick gun of his."

I looked down; an eye for an eye was wearying, though I would've done the same thing.

"Your dad came to see me two days after the funeral," Sal went on. "He wanted me to turn on the family. I couldn't, of course."

337

"Once in, you're in till you're dead?" We were in Luperón in the Dominican Republic when Sal had said that.

"My family's like yours. We stick together no matter what." His voice wavered. "There was a contract on Zagarovsky the next day. I should've waited. Instead, I told Nick how to get him, and he did."

I had to sit down. "You started all this?"

"Nick would've caught him eventually. He was good at his job."

"Now what?" I asked.

"We got lucky tonight, just not as lucky as I would've liked. Zagarovsky will run back to New York. He's lost without acolytes. It'll take a few weeks to find Faro's replacement."

"So it isn't over." I felt like *Squirt* when the air leaked out.

"A rabid dog goes crazy when you kick it."

I looked up quickly. "It'll be worse next time, won't it?"

"No telling. The good news is Nick's got time to figure out a way to disappear again."

"Everyone right?" I was relieved when Sal nodded.

"On the other hand, we could take the initiative." He looked past me.

"I'm game." I meant it.

"Why am I not surprised?" I hadn't heard my dad return.

He dropped into the chair across from me, resting his elbows on the table. It was the same table we'd sat at for dinner the day we arrived. He looked exhausted. At two in the morning, I wasn't about to wait any longer.

"What happened to my mom?"

"I don't know, Sander. She disappeared the day of the fire."

+ + +

With a trilogy, a second book can't be **THE END**. Part of me wanted to follow Captain Slocum's route; another part wanted to stay in Australia with my father. I also deserved a lot more than 'she disappeared.'

A Preview of Free Range Chicken

Chapter 36 of *Chicken Too* leaves Alexander (aka Sander and Victor Joshua Walker) and his family in Australia, safe after another attempt on his life. He is reunited with his real father; however, little has changed. Free Range Chicken begins with an explosion the very next morning. One thing is clear, Alex is still very much in danger. They sail up the coast of Australia, the Walker family in the *Spray*, Alex and his father in Bruce's boat.

With a $200,000 reward on Alex' head, each day is a step closer to disaster. After another foiled attempt on his life, he leaves his family and travels to New York to stay with Dani's family while he attends a summer program at a prestigious music college. Except for a missing mother, his problems seem to be over. However, Zagarovsky has a personal interest in his demise. Only Sal can save him.

Chapter 1.

With her mouth full of cereal, Jessie stretched across the breakfast table. She crunched and squinted into my face before she leaned on her elbows, tilted her head, and stared. I rolled my eyes in unhurried circles and pretended everything was the same.

My mother, only she wasn't my mother, intervened from the kitchen before we crossed eyes. "Jessie, elbows off the table and sit down!"

"I am sitting down!"

Sugar and spice and everything nice seldom applied to Jessie. At nine years old, she preferred slugs and snails, though she could be endearing when she wanted. She stared at me through hazel eyes, defying me to blink first. I pretended to waver before rapidly switching my gaze from side to side. On the verge of giggling, she poked out her tongue, her usual response when she was losing.

"Stop annoying Josh!"

"Mom, we're playing a game."

"Who has the worst table manners?"

Outside the sliding glass door, doves fluffed their feathers under a garden spray, making mist over the swimming pool. I used to think I spent half my life in the water. At 12 years old, I went to both morning and afternoon swim-team practice, three hours, six days a week! It might've been more enjoyable if the YMCA pool had a tropical paradise alongside. I turned from 'Sexy Pink' *Heliconia* when Aunt Erin put a platter of toast in front of me. Before I could ask what I should call her, she smiled, not Tanner's mischievous grin, a smile that said we'd get along.

"Erin will do just fine, Josh." At least someone appreciated what I was going through.

"Aunt Erin said my manners are better than Tanner's," Jessie countered, now trying to get my attention by rolling her eyes.

"That's not saying much," Erin laughed.

At 8:30 am, Tanner was in school. It was the first day of the school year, so Jesse walked to the corner with her. She'd been babbling about the advantages of regular school ever since, which didn't include being able to spend most of the day reading Ben's *Encyclopedia Britannica*.

"I'm trying to cheer him up," Jessie said. I was about to say I didn't need cheering up, when out of the blue, she pointed at my nose. "Josh has a mustache!"

There was faint fuzz sprouting on my upper lip. It looked like I hadn't washed my face since the day before.

Overnight, everything changed. Just ten hours earlier, Aunt Erin became my stepmother. Her constantly chattering daughter, Tanner, was now my half-sister. It only got worse. Ben and Jessie were my cousins, not my brother and sister. My mother was Aunt Virginia, though I couldn't say it. My father was now my Uncle John. His real name was Peter. Uncle Ron was my father. His real name was Nicholai, named after the Russian composer, Nikolai Rimsky-Korsakov. And my grandmother? She wasn't even a branch of my family tree. Altogether, it was stab through the heart.

Ben left his spoon in his bowl and looked up. "He's got facial hair?" Our transformed family situation didn't seem to bother him at all. He scrutinized me like a biology specimen. "You need to shave, Dude."

I wasn't in the mood for imperfections, not even a single hair on my chin. It had been invisible until I looked in the mirror that morning while brushing my teeth. "I'll be fifteen in three weeks; it's about time."

"I'll get you a razor for a present," he said jauntily. He jerked back when I flicked at his nose.

"Better fuzz on my face than fur everywhere else."

"Kids have vellus hair." Ben had silvery down on his arms, far more than I did when I was his age. Maybe it was one of those genetic things.

"Body hair changes with puberty. Androgenic hair is thicker and darker." If anyone was born to be a doctor, Jessie was. At nine, she knew more about the human body than I did.

Ben stole a sideways glance at his mom making toast. She hadn't said a word to me besides 'good morning,' both of us happily avoiding the elephant in the room. Ben turned to me, his preteen smirk a sure sign he was about to whisper something he wouldn't dare say in adult company. He stopped just in time as the back door swung open. My father followed Uncle John. They might have been twins; however, a darker tan and sun-bleached hair made it easy to tell them apart.

I could tell from their faces the news wasn't going to be good. My newly acquired father had returned to the restaurant after I was safely back at his house, seven hours ago.

"Everything okay?"

I might have been talking to myself. They crossed to the coffee maker and poured themselves cups.

"Tony cleaned up. There's nothing you'd notice if you weren't looking for it," my real father said between sips.

I expected him to call me 'Sander.' When he didn't, it bothered me.

My uncle leaned against the counter, avoiding my eyes, coffee cup in one hand, the other hand clenched with his thumb pressed on top. Each time he rubbed, it sounded like an anchor rode straining when the wind strengthened. Up in the *Spray's* bow, the creaking rode kept me awake at night. Now, it made me feel like I'd done something wrong, as much as how he looked at me.

Instead of keeping my mouth shut, I asked, "Cleaned up how?"

My father gave an anemic smile. "It wasn't my first choice. Zagarovsky's goons are stuffed in a construction site toilet. It's only a few miles from Gympie. Someone will find them by tonight."

"Nick, the last time Tony cleaned up, they were stuffed in a trawler. It sank on the way to Hawaii." *His* tone was coldly critical, as much as saying even a day in a toilet fell short of his moral standards.

I studied my cereal bowl, wondering if muesli was uniquely Australian. According to Ben, who chose it over little bricks made from wholegrain wheat; muesli was what most Aussie kids ate for breakfast. It came in clumpy sugarless lumps of raw oats, seeds, nuts, dried fruits, and grains, with a handful of extra raisins, slices of banana, and soy milk to make it edible. Muesli looked appetizing on the recycled, biodegradable box.

"They deserved to die." I sounded heartless; I didn't care. Getting rid of Zagarovsky's hired killers was like putting trash in a can. You didn't care what happened to it afterwards.

"Sander?"

I refused to meet my father's eyes. He called me 'Sander' as if he was trying to score points. So what if he'd named me Alexander the day I was born, and called me "Sander' for more than three years?

My uncle stopped creaking. "Josh, we know how difficult this is for you."

"Now I'm Josh?"

He'd made it clear the night before. I wasn't the Victor Joshua Walker that I'd grown up with. More than my name was different; I wasn't *his* son. I filled my spoon with soy milk, no muesli. I'd never tasted soy milk before. It reminded me of coconut water, sweet yet bland. From Ben's expression, he didn't like it either. He separated out raisins and bananas with his spoon. The rest he pushed to the side.

"What we call you is no big deal." Ben's voice squeaked at the end. "You're still who you are, right Mom?"

She exhaled, folded her arms and leaned against the sink. *She* looked at me, blinking. The last time *she* was this unhappy we were in a Tahitian hospital. Ben was unconscious in the emergency room.

"We should've told you when you were seven..." The rest waited until I met *her* gaze. "A boy at school teased you. You came home in tears."

"About being Noah Junior?" My nickname started when word got out that a half-finished boat filled the barn next to our trailer. It made my family sound crazy.

"It was about your scars. You wanted to know how you got them."

"You told me I fell on a heater."

"It was too dangerous to tell you the truth. The accident was all over the news when it happened."

"It wasn't an accident!" *he* interjected.

She went on regardless. "For a couple of years, you always wore a long sleeve shirt so people couldn't see your arms."

"It made me itch something awful."

"There wasn't a choice. If someone remembered and made the connection with you..." *Her* conclusion dangled in silence.

"Forgetting about the fire was the best thing that could happen," *he* said.

"I had nightmares every night."

He interrupted me. "They were never about the fire."

"You didn't forget everything," *she* said, *her* emphasis puzzling. "You were only four, so we weren't sure why you wanted to go to church. You were seven when you asked to join the swim team. It was clear you remembered some things." *She* nodded at my real father to take over.

"When you were little, you used to come to the Y and watch me swim."

I looked at *him*. I wanted to make *him* squirm for years of lies. "Why didn't you tell me about my parents?"

"We wanted to. However, you needed time to get well. We thought if you knew we weren't your real mom and dad, it would be an added complication."

"You were much safer with them, Sander," my father added.

I wanted to ask why that justified abandoning me, yet I kept my eyes in my cereal bowl. Muesli was like trail mix from a health food store, not something you ate for breakfast, or because you liked the taste. The box said it had honey in it. If there was, I couldn't taste any.

"That email about you when you were seven; I was in Melbourne at the time. Someone who I thought was a friend said he saw a woman who looked like your mom," my father said. "It was a risk worth taking."

I didn't know who or what to believe. Months earlier, *he* had said his sister-in-law was dead. Just the night before, my real father said she'd disappeared the night of the fire. One of them was lying.

"It was a trap?"

Ben put down his spoon, giving up on muesli despite what the box said about high fiber and protein. "They were going to use him to find you."

"They were still looking for me after three years?"

"With people like Zagarovsky, when they say they're going to do something, they follow through. Otherwise, they're seen as weak." My father hesitated. "She was supposed to be playing at a church in Fitzroy, not far from where she used to live."

With a glance, *he* stopped me from asking about my real mother. "Remember when we went camping in West Virginia?"

A day after my seventh birthday, *he'd* borrowed a tent and two sleeping bags from the O'Neils, who lived across the road from us. We left the same day and spent a miserable week in the middle of a vast pine forest, hiking, reading, and playing cards. Mid-February was too cold to do anything else.

"What about it?" At the time, I thought going camping was a special birthday present for me. It didn't matter that the tent was tiny and stank of Jessie's dirty diapers.

"We had to leave Norfolk, just in case." *He* glared at my father. It was clear who *he* blamed.

"I told them to leave, Sander. There was a good chance my email was hacked in Melbourne. Going there was a big mistake."

"What happened?" Ben asked.

"I had high hopes; it was the first good lead I'd had. Luckily, I spotted Barkov before he saw me. It still blew up in my face. I didn't stop looking behind me until my car broke down a few miles out of Gympie. I figured a tiny town in the middle of nowhere was the last place they'd look." He smiled and gave Aunt Erin a hug. "Erin's dad needed help on the farm so I stayed."

"That makes it okay to forget about me?"

"Sander, if I returned, I would've led them to you. There was no choice. Anything else would make you less safe. Besides, I had nothing left. Living on the run, it's exhausting."

"Tell me about it, Nick." *He* beat me to it.

My father went on regardless. "I had three jobs until I saved enough to create a new identity, one that Zagarovsky's people couldn't discover. I always planned to go back for you."

"Instead, you opened the restaurant."

He looked as if I'd slapped him. "You don't understand. The next year, you were doing so much better. You'd caught up at school. John sent that email a few days after your eighth birthday so he could tell me you won the 8 and under 100 yard freestyle at the Southeast District Championships."

"Not that big a deal."

She smeared butter on toast. "It was to us."

She'd been at the swimming pool, cheering incessantly for my team. By Sunday, *she* was hoarse, yet I still heard *her* over the roar of applause when my fingers punched the timing pad first.

He perked up. "It was to me too. He videotaped you so I could watch you on YouTube. Not smart, though definitely worth the risk."

I couldn't help myself. "That changes everything."

"It changed things for me, Sander. You were safe. You had friends. Your teachers were planning to move you up a grade. The next year, things got crazy. I could hardly drag you away…"

"You'll always be part of our family, Josh." *She* spoke softly to get my attention.

I looked up at *her*. "I don't even know what to call you."

She came over, and hugged me, one hand massaging my shoulders the same way *she* did on the way home from swim practice. "You'll think of something."

"How about Aunty Mom?" I knew I'd always be able to talk to *her*.

"When you were little, you called me Anti-Sue," *she* laughed. "I think Aunt Vee will do nicely."

He cleared his throat. "I'm sorry I lied to you for so long."

I wasn't ready to call him Uncle John. "Sal said Grandma gave up everything to be with me; and we're not even related."

"Not by blood," she said from behind me. I spun around. "By everything else that counts, you're my grandson."

"But you lost everything because of me. I caused all this."

"Dude, you were three!" Ben interrupted.

"A very cute three, I might add." She picked up the Muesli box to look at the nutrition label. It was in grams, milligrams, and kilo-joules. She caught Ben's eye.

"It's packed full of fiber, vitamins and protein, Grandma."

She winked at him as she sat down next to Jessie. "I thought Sal was coming for breakfast?"

My father hesitated. "Sal left an hour ago."

I hid my disappointment. "With Tony?"

"He is Sal's bodyguard. It's only for a week or two."

Every time I looked at Uncle John, I still saw my father. Like muesli, it would take some getting used to.

"They got confirmation Zagarovsky got on a plane to Los Angeles. Sal's taking advantage of the lull to regroup," my father went on.

"We need to as well," I said under my breath.

He let out a tired sigh, perhaps to show what he thought of that idea.

I repeated what Sal said six hours earlier. "We were lucky last night."

He reacted as the words left my mouth. "It depends on how you look at it."

"We've bought some time!" My father and I seemed to agree on that.

My uncle and father swigged coffee and talked about finding a better hiding place. I chewed cold buttered toast, thinking anything was better than muesli, silently resenting that even though Zagarovsky was on his way back to New York, he was still in control.

"Heading north makes the most sense," *he* declared.

"Doesn't it make more sense to do something they don't expect?" She was 61, outspoken and stubborn like a teenager. She'd clearly had given our situation thought.

"Something like what?" *he* asked.

She peeled and sliced a mango with a sharp paring knife. She divided slices between herself and Jessie before looking up. "You don't have to be Einstein to realize that repeating the past and expecting a different outcome is nonsense, John."

"Not much else we can do at this point."

"We need to change our names. That means new fake IDs. Sal said he'd take care of it, but it'll take a couple of weeks. We'll stay here. It'll be safe until Zagarovsky returns," my father added. With coffee cups in hand, they headed into the dining room to sit down.

Her mouth full of mango, Jessie turned her table manners on me, "Are you going to shave after breakfast?"

"I don't plan to."

"Can I watch if you do?" Jessie twisted in her chair. "Josh's growing a mustache, Grandma." She made it sound as if fuzz on my face was extraordinary.

"All boys do that when they get older, Honey."

"It's because their testicles produce testosterone." Jessie looked to Ben to make sure she'd pronounced it correctly. "They get hairy all over, and make semen."

Was I the only one in the room with a crimson face? Even my open-minded ex-grandmother had her hand over her face, shaking her head. Erin cocked a stunned eye at Jessie. It was all Ben could do not to laugh out loud.

With surprising calm, Aunt Vee said, "If Josh takes after his mom, he'll never be hairy."

Could it get any more embarrassing? I glowered back at her.

"Not my fault she's been reading the *Brit*," Ben hedged. "Grandma said it was okay."

"What Grandma said was 'learning new things is good. Sharing it requires insight.'" With her hand brushing back silver-gray curls, and her eyes bright with mirth, she added, "Josh, I think if you're old enough to call me Sarah, you're old enough to shave. And, I have just the thing to get you started."

She went into her room to get whatever it was. She was gone so long I tried eating muesli. Amongst crunchy nuts and grains, were pumpkin seeds, and flakes of wheat that tasted like honey. It was definitely healthier than American cereal.

She returned with a wooden box. She moved muesli aside, and placed it on the table before me. "When we were on Sal's *Maid*

Marion on the way to Australia; he wasn't sure how things would turn out. He asked me to give this to you when you started shaving."

The box was burled walnut, polished so brightly it mirrored my hands as I opened a tiny gold clasp and lifted back the lid.

"He said it's a family tradition. His father gave him one when he started shaving. He would've given this to his son, but Zagarovsky stopped that."

Ben craned his neck to look inside the box. "No way! He'll cut his head off, like in *Monty Python*."

There were four compartments mosaicked with shiny squares of mother-of-pearl, the same as the iridescent flowers on the fingerboard of my guitar. In one compartment was a straight-blade razor, the old-fashioned kind with a translucent horn handle. Beside it were a badger-hair brush, a tarnished silver bowl with a round bar of soap, and an unlikely cowhide belt.

"Sal said to tell you the bowl is Sicilian from the 1850s. It used to be a salt cellar, so it symbolizes loyalty and friendship, some kind of macho Mafia thing, I expect."

"More like putting salt on the wounds." Despite *his* smile, I wasn't sure if *he* was joking or not.

Sarah lifted the razor from its compartment, the blade honed to dull grey, not shiny like a boat knife. 'Dante' was incised into the handle. "He said there was no one else he would give it to."

"I'm with Ben. I'll cut my throat." My morbid humor drew a discouraging grin from Ben.

Like a scene out *The Godfather*, my grinning father filled the doorway. "Ah leetle blood is all. The tricka is getting the angle just so, Sander." He pinched the air. "Thirty degree. Anda move it perpa-dicular to the blade, never sideways."

"No way am I using it!"

Ben added his support with, "Smart move, Bro. Stick with electric."

"You going to tell Sal you're chicken, Vittorio?" *He* clearly didn't mean it.

"A coupla nicks will man you up, Sander."

They were teasing, of course; yet I rose to the challenge. Everyone trooped into the downstairs bathroom to watch, even Erin. While my father stropped blade and leather, his brother puddled soap and hot water in the silver bowl and worked up a thick creamy lather. As my moment of manhood drew nearer, my feet got colder. The tiles were frigid, virginal white like the marble top on the vanity.

"Let's make this a bloodless sacrifice, and appease the gods some other time," Sarah chuckled.

With lather covering half my face, I gaped at her. As my grandmother, she'd filled my head with stories about of Greek heroes. Not one of them shaved!

"Just go slowly, Sander. You can stop, but don't move the blade sideways." My father pressed the razor into my unwilling hand. "I'll show you how if you want me to?"

"On your face or mine?"

"Yours, of course."

Ben and Jessie thought that was hilarious.

I raised my hand, my eyes switching between the mirror and the blade nearing my foamy nose, expecting blood to appear at any moment.

Behind me, I heard, "It looks awfully sharp."

"Sal will love this photo. Stop looking so serious, Josh."

Ben hopped up for a ring-side seat on the vanity. "He ought to practice with a disposable first."

"Tilt the blade a bit more, Sander."

My hand was trembling as I adjusted the blade angle. I was so shaky that I took hold of the tip of the blade between my thumb and first finger of my other hand. After a deep breath, I touched the blade right under my nose and cautiously lifted my head up until it reached my upper lip.

"He'll cut himself if he's not careful."

"Don't bug him, Daddy. He needs to concentrate."

I tilted my head and looked in the mirror. The razor left a path free of soap, and no blood. It felt tingly. With unwarranted confidence, I turned my head slightly right and repeated the process twice before I breathed out again. If there was any difference, I couldn't see it. Everyone crowded closer. Jessie hopped up onto the vanity to see for herself.

"Do I look different?" I asked no one in particular.

"Still the same." Jessie smirked. "Except you don't have a mustache anymore."

"I didn't have one to begin with."

Ben craning his neck to look at both sides of my face. "You missed a hair, Dude."

"I'll get it next year." I was about to add that I risked my nose for nothing when someone banged on the back door.

"I wonder who that is." Erin stepped past my father and through the doorway.

"No one ever visits this early in the morning," he said to her back.

I inspected my handiwork, not bad at all, a solitary hair left and no blood. In the mirror, gleeful Ben smirked from beside me.

"It looks like you shaved with your eyes closed."

Boldly, I brushed on lather until I bore a marked resemblance to Santa Claus. I had the razor poised under my chin when the kitchen exploded.

The Walker Family's *Spray*

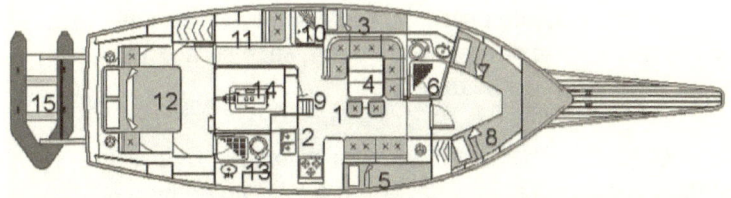

The *Spray*, modeled on Bruce Roberts-Goodson's Centennial Spray 38 ©, which is based on Slocum's *Spray*. Reproduced with permission.

1. Salon

2. Galley

3. Josh's berth

4. Dining table

5. Ben's berth

6. Head

7. Grandma's berth

8. Jessie's berth (*Encyclopedia Britannica* under)

9. Companionway stairs

10. Chart table (secret compartment underneath)

11. Storage/workshop

12. Parents' cabin

13. Parents' head

14. Engine room

15. *Squirt*

Glossary for sailing beginners

Abaft : a seldom used expression for near or towards the stern, often from a given reference point, such as 'abaft the beam', meaning back from the beam.

About : to change direction of the vessel by passing through the oncoming wind (tacking); e.g. to go about.

Adrift : not under sail or engine power, moving at the whim of the wind and sea.

Aft : towards the back or rear of the boat.

Aground : stuck on the ground, a mud bank, sand bar, or worse (rocks or coral).

Ahead : to go forward, or what is ahead of the vessel.

Aloft : anything above the deck and cabin, to go up the mast/into the rigging.

Anchor : a heavy metal 'claw' designed to grab hold of the sea floor and keep a boat from moving.

Anchorage : a place protected from wind and waves, with bottom conditions suitable for anchoring.

Apparent wind : combines both the true wind direction and the boat's speed and direction.

Astern : pass to the rear of a boat, as in to 'go astern', meaning to go behind the boat, or to leave astern.

Autopilot : a computer-controlled mechanical or hydraulic-powered device to steer the vessel. Often connected to a chart plotter.

Avast : To cease and desist. 'Avast there, mates,' if said with a pirate accent, means 'stop screwing around, guys.'

Backstay : the wire cable running from the back of the boat (stern) to the top of the mast.

Batten : a wood or fiberglass strip inserted through the leech of a sail, sometimes extending as far as the luff, to improve sail shape, support the leech, and prevent fluttering.

Beaufort scale: a 0-12 scale of wind strengths (calm through hurricane) and identifying characteristics. For example, Force 6 is a strong breeze, 24-31 mph or 21 to 27 knots. Expect to see long waves with foamy crests and some spray.

Beam : the width of the boat, or a direction, as in 'off the beam' meaning perpendicular to the vessel. Replaces athwart.

Bearing : the direction to something, usually relative to the boat or a chart.

Bear away : to turn away from the current direction usually with respect to the direction of the wind, also 'bear off.'

Beating : to sail as close to the wind as possible.

Becalmed : when the vessel is motionless because of lack of wind.

Below : under the deck, as in 'to go below'.

Berth : a nautical bed, usually narrow, sometimes wet. The expression 'to give a wide berth' is not about a captain's generous berth allocation, but to avoid something (another vessel) by a wide margin. Also, berth refers to where a vessel is normally docked.

Bilge : the part where the side of the boat turns into the bottom of the boat, also the bottom of the boat where smelly water gathers.

Bimini : a sun cover of canvas stretched over the cockpit, and supported by a metal frame.

Binnacle : a stand or support for the ship's compass.

Bitter end : the last part of a line or anchor rode.

Boat hook : a sometimes-extensible pole with a hook in the end to catch things like mooring lines, pets, and hats when they drop in the water.

Bobstay : a wire running from the bow to the end of the bowsprit to relieve the load from the forestay.

Bollard : a hefty short post typically attached to the dock. Used to secure boats.

Boom : the stick attached near the bottom of the mast allowing the sail to pivot with the wind.

Boom vang : a system of ropes and pulleys, or a spring-loaded rod used to stop the boom from lifting up.

Bosun's chair : a canvas seat used to hoist crew up the mast to make repairs.

Bow : the front part of the boat.

Bowline : a temporary knot, easy to tie, and untie after being loaded. See http:// en.wikipedia.org/wiki/Bowline.

Bow line : the rope connecting the bow to the dock.

Bowsprit : the 'stick' extending from the bow, allowing the boat to carry more sail, not to be confused with the anchor roller.

Bridge : the elevated position from which a boat is steered, or an overhead structure requiring care to go under.

Broach : when large waves and/or strong wind cause a vessel to lose control and turn sideways, often heeling dramatically, with a chance of rolling over.

Bulkhead : a vertical partition in the cabin providing stiffening/watertight compartments for the hull.

Buoy : a float used to mark a position or thing.

By and large : a common expression of nautical origin, meaning a vessel performs well going into the wind (by) and with the wind (large), so all possible points of sail.

Capsize : to turn the boat over by 90 degrees, or more. Not recommended!

Cast off : to let go mooring or dock lines so the boat is free to move.

Catamaran :a boat with two hulls side by side.

Chaffing wearing of lines against things causes them to fray and eventual fail. Prevented by chaffing gear, for example, covering the affected part with hose, canvas, or leather.

Chart : a map used on a boat, showing details of the coast and what is under the surface.

Chart plotter : an integrated computer and monitor that presents navigation charts and the vessel's location. Enables courses to be plotted as routes, or tracking of the vessel's movements.

Cleat : a fitting for preventing ropes from moving. For example, a dock cleat.

Clew : the corner of a sail furthest from the bow.

Close-hauled : to sail as close to the wind as possible. Requires hauling the sails in tightly.

Coach house : part of the cabin projecting above the deck, often with larger windows.

Cockpit : a somewhat protected area for sitting and steering, usually lower than the deck.

Come about : to change direction by passing through the wind.

Companionway : the entrance to the cabin, usually as stairs from the cockpit.

Constant bearing-decreasing range (CBDR) occurs when one vessel maintains a constant bearing relative to another vessel, while the distance between them (range) decreases. This is a collision course.

Course : the direction that is a boat is to be steered. Course over ground (COG) is the actual course after including the effect of wind, tide, and current.

Current : a flow of water from one area to another (not a tide, where the water flows back).

Cutter : a single-masted boat with two jibs. Also a fast motor boat often used by the Coastguard.

Davits : a small crane or spar used to lift things, such as a dinghy or outboard motor.

Dead ahead : directly in front.

Dead reckoning : is the process of using estimates of direction and distance traveled, and sightings of landmarks to determine a vessel's position.

Dinghy : a small open boat. Some dinghies can be inflated.

Dock : a place to tie up a boat for a period of time and walk on dry land, also a pier or wharf. To dock means to tie up at a dock.

Dodger : a see-through screen with a hood at the front of the cockpit to deflect wind and waves.

Draft : the minimum depth of water a boat requires in order to float.

Drogue or sea -anchor is a device towed through the water to slow down a vessel. Can be a parachute, a long length of rope, a large cone, or a series of small cones attached to a long line.

Fathom : six feet.

Fender : an inflated cushion between boats, or a boat and the dock to prevent damage to the hull.

Fiberglass :a durable, strong composite of polyester resin and layers of cloth made from glass fibers. Used for the vast majority of boats manufactured since the 1950s.

First rate : an expression derived from the top-of-the-line sailing warships (100 guns) from the 1600s through 1800s.

Flare : a pyrotechnic/firework, either hand-held or fired from a gun to draw attention to a vessel in distress.

Following sea : waves from astern, going in the same direction. Under certain conditions, the vessel can surf the wave, picking up considerable speed and a chance of losing control. Waves that overtake the boat can be especially dangerous if the wave is breaking.

Foot : the bottom of a sail.

Fore : forward or front, as in fore-deck (the deck between mast and bow), and fore-peak (the cabin squashed into the bow).

Forestay : the wire cable from the top of the mast to the front of the boat.

Forward : toward the front of the boat, as in "Go forward and drop the anchor."

Frames : ribs that form the hull's shape, typically used in wooden boats.

Furl : to reduce a sail's area. Jibs and genoas are typically wound around the forestay. In a similar fashion, mainsails may be furled inside/outside the mast, or inside the boom. The alternative is storing the mainsail along the boom by folding the sailcloth.

Gaff : an oblique stick attached near the top of the mast. Used to hold the top side of a four-sided sail, while allowing it to pivot with the wind direction. Also a pole with a sharp hook on the end to assist in bringing fish aboard.

Galley : the kitchen in a boat.

Genoa : a large, powerful jib overlapping the mainsail.

Gooseneck : a fitting connecting the mast and boom, allowing the boom to swivel.

Grounding : an ill-advised contact between the boat's hull or keel and the bottom (ground). Also used in lieu of 'bonding', a process of electrically connecting all metal (engine, thru-hulls, etc.)

and the top of the mast to minimize damage in the event of a lightning strike.

Gunwale : the edge of the side of the boat and the deck.

Gybe : the process of changing course and/or repositioning the sails from one side of the boat to the other with the wind coming over the stern. A dangerous maneuver if the wind is blowing hard. Can occur accidentally if not paying attention.

Halyards : 'ropes' used to hoist and lower sails.

Hank : a metal or plastic hook/device to connect a sail to a mast track or forestay.

Hatch : an opening in the deck or cabin roof to allow light and fresh air to enter.

Head : the top corner of a sail, , to 'head up' is to sail closer to the wind or into the wind also a nautical toilet.

Heading : the direction the boat is going in.

Heave to : to stop the vessel by sheeting the jib to one side and locking the rudder in the opposing direction.

Heel : the vessel leans sideways, induced by the wind's sideways force on the sails.

Helm : the steering wheel, as in the command 'take the helm'.

Jackline : a continuous line running from the bow to the stern for crew to clip on to when moving about on deck. Essential when conditions are dangerous and/or there is a risk of falling overboard.

Jetty : a stone wall projecting from the shore to protect boats in a harbor. Also a quay.

Jib : a triangular sail in front of the mast, with one side usually connected to the forestay.

Jury rig : using whatever is at hand to make a temporary rig in the event of dismasting.

Keel : the very bottom of the boat, usually cast from lead. A sailing boat's keel functions to keep it upright.

Ketch : a vessel with two masts, the tallest one in front and a shorter one behind.

Knot : a speed equal to one nautical mile per hour (1.15 mph or 1.85 kilometers per hour).

Latitude : a geographic coordinate (distance) measured in degrees north or south (up to 90°) of the equator (0 degrees).

Lazy jacks : 'ropes' from the mast to the boom to keep a sail from falling to the side .

Leech : the aft or trailing edge of a sail.

Lee : the side sheltered from the wind, leeward is the direction away from the wind. A lee shore is on the side of the vessel opposite the wind. Being blown on to a lee shore during a storm is a good reason to be safely tied up at dock, or a long way offshore.

Life raft : an inflatable, usually covered raft used as a last resort when the vessel sinks.

Line (s) : there are no 'ropes' used on a boat. They are lines, unless specifically purposed as halyards, sheets, outhauls, downhauls, boom vangs, etc. Also see 'rode.'

Log : a record of a boat's operation with courses and events, also a device to measure speed.

Longitude : a geographic coordinate (distance) measured in degrees east (up to +180 degrees) or west (up to -180 degrees) of the Greenwich meridian (0 degrees).

Luff : the forward edge of a sail, also to head into the wind until the sails invert in shape and flap, sometimes very loudly.

Lying ahull : with sails removed, the vessel rides out a storm at the mercy of the sea while the crew cowers below.

Mainmast : the tallest mast.

Mainsail : the primary sail attached to the mainmast.

Mainsheet : line used to haul in the boom to adjust the sail's shape to wind conditions and direction.

Mizzen : (mast or sail) the mast or sail closest to the stern.

Mooring : attaching a boat to a sunken weight, or a dock.

Nautical mile : approximately one minute of latitude, or 6076 feet, 1.15 land miles, or 1.85 kilometers. Note that definitions of length vary. For example, the *American Practical Navigator* defines a sea mile as an "approximate mean value" of 6,080 feet; the length of a minute of arc along the meridian at latitude 48°."

Navigation : the process of way finding, from the current position to another position, conducting a boat from one place to another.

Oar : a rowing device connected to a dinghy and used to move it (not a paddle, which is used on a canoe).

Outboard : a detachable gasoline-powered motor mounted on the stern.

Painter : a line attached to the bow of a dinghy for tying up or towing.

Pier : a dock extending out from the shore.

Piling : a wood (or concrete/steel) pole driven into the bottom.

Pitch : the bow-to-stern up and down movement of the boat caused by waves.

Plane : when a boat lifts onto the surface of the water, rather than pushing through it. Most sailboats are displacement vessels, meaning they displace their weight in water and do not plane.

Port : the left side, identified with a red light at night. Also a harbor, a nautical destination.

Portlight : a waterproof window in the side of the cabin.

Pulpit : a safety railing at the bow, made of metal pipes.

Reaching : to sail with the wind off the beam, (ranging from 60 degrees to 160 degrees). A close reach has the wind forward of the beam, while a broad reach has the wind aft of the beam.

Reef : to reduce sail area by lowering the sail and tying up what is not used.

Rigging : the various lines, stays, and shrouds needed to support the mast and operate the sails.

Rode : the anchor rope or chain.

Roller reefing : used to reduce the sail area by winding the sail around the boom.

Rudder : the board attached to the steering wheel or tiller which causes the boat to change course.

Run : to allow a line to move freely, also a direction of sail, such as running before the wind.

Running backstay : is an adjustable wire used to hold the mast from the rear, employed during severe wind conditions.

Safety harness : a harness made of webbing (or incorporated into a life jacket) enabling a crew member to be secured to the vessel during hazardous conditions.

Schooner : a sailing boat with two masts, the mainmast behind the first or foremast.

Scupper : a drain from the cockpit, or to enable water to leave the deck through the gunwale.

Sea anchor : see drogue.

Seat locker : a locker under the seats in the cockpit.

Seacock : a shut-off valve below the waterline; sometimes mistakenly called a thru-hull, which refers to a mushroom-shaped fitting penetrating the hull, and attached to a seacock.

Secure : to make fast.

Seasickness : motion sickness caused by the rocking action of the boat going through waves. The primary symptom is nausea, aka puking one's guts out.

Self-steering : a mechanical system of levers , gears, and wind vane to make course corrections via the rudder so that the vessel maintains a constant relationship to wind direction.

Sheets : 'ropes' used to control the angle and fullness of the sail, attached to the jib clew, the bottom corners of a spinnaker, or the end/middle of a boom.

Shroud : a wire connecting the top of the mast with the side of the boat. There may be several shrouds per side.

Slack : the opposite of secure, something not secured, to loosen. Also slack tide, when there is no water movement.

Sloop : a boat with a single mast, one jib, and a mainsail.

Spinnaker : a large, lightweight, usually colorful sail used when the wind is coming from astern to off the beam (perpendicular to the vessel).

Spring line : a line usually from the middle of the boat to a forward or aft dock cleat.

Stay : a supporting wire connecting the mast to the bow (forestay) or stern (backstay).

Staysail : a sail fixed to a stay, for example, a cutter rig has an outer jib and a smaller jib attached to an inner forestay.

Squall : a violent wind that arrives suddenly, often with rain.

SSB Radio : single-side band modulation radio, similar to Ham radio, used for medium to long-range marine communications with fixed channels and frequency selection. Range depends on environmental/atmospheric conditions.

Stanchions : metal pipes secured to the gunwale, holding lifelines to prevent crew from falling overboard.

Starboard : the right side of the boat, associated with green (e.g. navigation lights on the vessel and buoys).

Stern : the rear of the boat.

Stern line : a rope used to tie the rear of the boat to the dock.

Storm sails : very rugged, small sails (aka storm jib and trysail) used to replace larger sails in the event that severe winds make reefing or furling insufficient.

Stow : to put things in their proper place, not to be confused with 'Stow it', a rude expression comparable to 'shut up' or 'get over it.'

Tack : the bottom, forward corner of a sail; also changing direction when going into the wind.

Tide : a periodic rise and fall in water level caused by the gravitational pull of the sun and moon, and the rotation of the earth. Tides vary by location, ranging from a few inches in lakes to many feet.

Tiller : a handle attached to a rudder or outboard motor to enable steering.

Trim : the balance of a boat achieved by distributing the weight fore and aft. Also to adjust the shape of the sails for better performance.

VHF Radio : very high frequency two-way radio (marine application broadcasts in the 156.0 and 162.025 MHz range) with international-standard channels. For example, 16 is the hailing and distress channel. The range is 'line-of-sight' and varies depending on signal strength, antenna, environmental conditions, and obstructions. US Coastguard transmissions exceed 60 miles, while a typical sailboat range is between 10 and 30 miles.

Wake : the disturbance of water caused by a boat's movement.

Winch : a metal cylinder turned by ratcheting gears and a handle to give leverage, used to hoist or pull in the sails.

Windlass : a device for raising the anchor; may be electrically powered.

Windward : generally the direction the wind is coming from. For example, going to windward is to sail close-hauled.

Yawl : a two-masted vessel, the mizzen mast being much smaller and farther aft than that of a ketch.

About the Author

Neil Barry lives aboard his 50-foot sloop, *Imagine,* cruising the East Coast of the U.S., the Bahamas, and points south. Born in Sydney, Australia, he began sailing at 12 years old. While studying architecture in college, he graduated from 12-foot boats to crewing on racing yachts on Sydney Harbour and offshore.

In 1977, he took time off from sailing to attend graduate school, travel the world, raise a family, and build a career as an academic. His next boat arrived 13 years later, a 28-foot cutter that he finished from the bare-hull stage. He sailed with his family on a small man-made lake in Indiana for 17 years before the ocean called again.

Imagine **under sail (a beam reach) in the Abacos, Bahamas, 2015.**
Copyright: Neil Barry

After 30 years as a professor, Neil Barry recognized the need for a new kind of novel, one that stimulates learning, creativity, and critical thinking, while providing entertainment. His *Chicken of the Sea* trilogy combines real places, things, events, and situations with fictional people and an engrossing, believable plot. Readers can use today's digital technology to explore the 'real' world of Victor Joshua Walker, beginning by visiting neilbarrybooks.com.

The author and Sienna, rescued from an animal shelter in June, 2015.
Copyright: Pam Bell, Pam Bell Photography